CHASING PHARAOHS

C.M.T. Stibbe

KINGDOM WRITING
SOLUTIONS
West Sussex, UK

ISBN-10: 0990600424
ISBN-13: 978-0-9906004-2-8

Printed in the United States of America

Library of Congress Cataloging-in-Publication data
Stibbe, C.M.T.

Cover design by www.jwccreative.com
Maps by C.M.T. Stibbe

3rd Edition Published in 2014
Kingdom Writing Solutions
Rustington
West Sussex, UK

www.Kingdomwritingsolutions.org

Praise for

CHASING PHARAOHS

I would recommend this book to anyone who is a fan of ancient Egypt but who also likes their books to be firmly grounded in historical authenticity.
Dee Harrison, Author of Mirrorsmith

Written historically with the knowledge of an archeologist and the passion of a troubadour, readers will be bound by the spell that C.M.T. Stibbe weaves from the very first page.
John Breeden II, Author of Old Number Seven

Apart from being an extremely well told tale, Chasing Pharaohs is full of poetic imagery. The plot is compelling, and so is the historical background.
J.G. Harlond, Author of The Empress Emerald

This writer knows how to capture a reader and keep them there. I was easily transported into the heart of Egypt and felt like I was right there sharing the magical journey.
Julie Shaw, Author of Our Vinnie

This is quite stunning - no other word for it. It's exciting, intriguing, sensuous, characters to care about, and what can only be described as visual artistry in the narrative.
Kay Christine Fenton, Author of The Fortune of Annacara.

ACKNOWLEDGMENTS

Firstly, my love and gratitude to my husband, Jeff. Without him, none of this would have been possible. To my parents for adopting me. Mum and Dad, thank you for giving me a chance. You're the best!

I cannot express enough thanks to the copy editors at the Script Doctor and to the proofreaders at Kingdom Writing Solutions. To Ann and John for their encouragement and to Terri for her friendship.

I could not have completed this project without the support of my brothers and to my son, Jamie for staying young at heart and never taking life too seriously. God bless all of you.

www.thescriptdoctor.org.uk

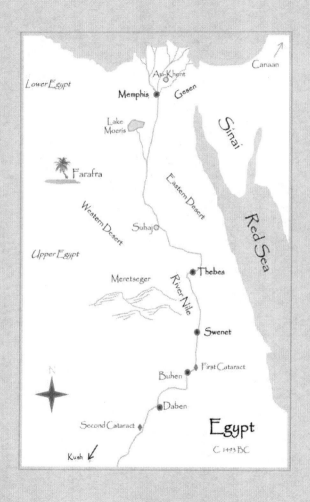

Canaan

Lower Egypt

Asi-Khent

Memphis   Gesen

Sinai

Lake
Moeris

Farafra

Eastern Desert

Red Sea

Western Desert

Suhaj

Upper Egypt

Thebes

Meretseger

River Nile

Swenet

N

First Cataract

Buhen

Daben

Second Cataract

Egypt

C 1493 BC

Kush

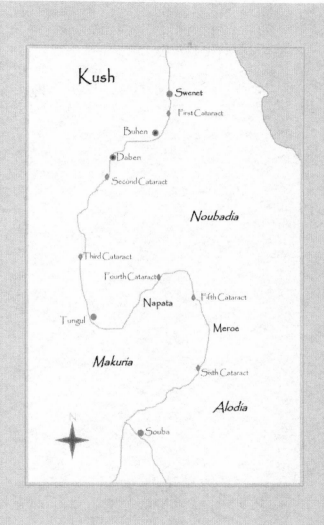

Kush

Swenet

First Cataract

Buhen

Daben

Second Cataract

Noubadia

Third Cataract

Fourth Cataract

Fifth Cataract

Napata

Tungul

Meroe

Makuria

Sixth Cataract

Alodia

N

Souba

CHARACTERS

Ahmose, Vizier and cousin of the Pharaoh.

Aset, secondary wife to Pharaoh Kheper-Re and mother of Prince Menkheperre.

Bunefer, Court singer

Hapuseneb, High Priest of Amun.

Harran, Pharaoh's scribe and interpreter of dreams.

Hatshepsut, sister and Great Royal Wife of Pharaoh Kheper-Re. Queen of Egypt.

Jabari, Lieutenant to Commander Shenq.

Ka-Nekhet, Pharaoh of Egypt and father of Pharaoh Kheper-Re and Queen Hatshepsut.

Khemwese, Bodyguard to Pharaoh Kheper-Re.

Kheper-Re, son of Pharaoh Ka-Nekhet and Pharaoh of Egypt.

Menkheperre, son of Pharaoh Kheper-Re and Lady Aset.

Meru-Itseni, Armor-bearer to Commander Shenq.

Meryt, Attendant to the Queen, beloved of Commander Shenq.

Mkasa, Lieutenant to Commander Osorkon.

Nebsemi, Bunefer's daughter

Neferure, daughter of Queen Hatshepsut and Pharaoh Kheper-Re.

Neshi, Chancellor to Pharaoh Ka-Nekhet and Pharaoh Kheper-Re.

Nurse Inet, wet nurse to Queen Hatshepsut.

Osorkon, Commander of the Division of Ptah, overseer of the southern Migdols (fortresses).

Osumare, wife of Pabasa.

Pabasa, bowman.

Pen-Nekhbet, wearer of the royal seal, Chief Treasurer and overseer of Thebes, General of the Divisions of Amun and Ra.

Puyem-re, Chief of Prophets.

Shenq, formerly armor-bearer to Pharaoh Ka-Nekhet and latterly Commander of the Divisions of Amun & Ra.

Tau, an Alodian outcast.

Tehute, Captain of the Pharaoh's guard.

SHENQ

A young jackal ran from the battlefield, nose stained with blood. She had come to root amongst the dead before the soldiers came, before the offal was loaded into carts and taken away. A wedge of geese honked overhead and the creature ran after them, snout tilted to a purple sky. She never saw the river as she ran wildly into the spray and she never saw the crocodile floating in the reeds.

Bowman Shenq almost winced at the high-pitched howl and his mouth twisted into a grin. He curbed the horses with a tight rein, feeling the footplate of the Pharaoh's chariot straining beneath him. The divisions of Ra and Amun waited in the trees at the water's edge, watching the rearguard of the enemy for any signs of retreat.

It was here the Alodians came after a long journey upriver, five hundred of them flooding towards the garrison post at Swenet. Their armies were bigger this time and smarter too, and how they managed to breach the border fortresses further south, Shenq never knew. But on they came with their spears and shields, barking and shrieking. They were nothing but ignorant field hands with weapons they hardly knew.

"Do you see their faces, Shenq?" Pharaoh Ka-Nekhet said. "Do you know why they paint themselves?"

"For battle, lord?" Shenq counted the prisoners in his head, staring at the red paint on their jaws.

"They paint themselves to cover their ugliness. They're no better than dogs." Ka-Nekhet spat in the sand and chuckled. "They come because they think I'm dying. Nothing will kill me, Shenq. I'm invincible. Like a god."

Shenq looked at the old man, lips spraying spittle and wine. *He's no god. He's flesh and bone like all the others.*

"How many do you see, boy?"

"Fifty, lord," Shenq said, flicking his eyes towards the prisoners.

"*Fifty,*" Pharaoh grunted. "This is all that's left of Alodia. They should be ashamed of themselves."

"King Kibwe-Shabaqo has a younger brother in Alodia, my lord," Shenq corrected. "Prince Ibada."

Ka-Nekhet raised his chin and sniffed. "He's not old enough to lift a sword."

"Boys turn into men. And there's always next year."

Ka-Nekhet cackled. "You're not afraid of anything are you Shenq?"

Shenq was afraid of mourning. That terrible sound the women made when the bodies were carried home, a sound that chilled bone and soul. If he had his way there would be rejoicing, especially now that the divisions of Ra had restored order and brought the rebels to heel. They had killed nearly five hundred in the night.

"See your father?" Pharaoh Ka-Nekhet said, pointing to Commander Cambyses through a mist of sand. "Watch him, boy. He'll make a man of you yet."

Yes, one day he could be like him, Shenq thought. Long black hair and eyes the color of the rising sun, and a bronze breastplate to blind the enemy. Shenq was fourteen and tall for his age—like father, like son—only he would be mightier if he could manage it.

"I should make you a prince," Pharaoh said, adjusting

his striped headdress and wiping the sweat from his brow. "You're all I have left."

Shenq felt his stomach curdle as he looked at a boy, cringing on the footplate of his tutor's chariot. "Prince Kheper-Re is strong and—"

"And what, Shenq? He's a coward. He's nothing like his brothers."

No, he's nothing like them, thought Shenq, remembering his childhood friends. The dead princes had once fired arrows from these very chariots, glittering, advancing. The very sight of them was just as terrifying as the grief Shenq felt.

Pharaoh Ka-Nekhet snatched the reins and slapped them against the front guard. He gave the command to advance, slowly at first to clear the trees. Shenq watched the Alodians as they reeled and stooped under a rain of bronze-tipped arrows, and he heard the rattle of spears and the dull ring of metal.

"Draw!" Pharaoh raised a hand, veins rippling on sun-baked arms.

Shenq felt the tingling in his chest as he drew his bow. He barely heard the command to *loose* and it was only a few moments before arrows thrummed towards the enemy. Warriors sank to the ground, staring with an unfocused gaze and some let out a primal howl as the chariots rammed them, sending their bodies beneath the wheels and the kicking hooves.

Shenq looked back and saw several of their own men toppling headlong over the front guards, bodies shot through with spears. But the chariots tore on towards two rocky spurs, penning the Alodians in like cattle.

"Stand fast!" Pharaoh Ka-Nekhet shouted, reining in his team.

Shenq studied the prisoners as they waited in a huddle, eyes rolling and bodies a shine of sweat. One dragged a dagger across his own throat and smiled as he did it.

"They're killing themselves," Shenq said.

"They're welcome to it," Pharaoh Ka-Nekhet muttered as he jumped from the chariot.

Nine was hardly a number to celebrate but the rest were dead or groaning in the dirt, all except one. A boy with a crooked smile crawled out from behind a dead horse, khopesh sword flashing in his hand. Shenq knew he would never make it to the river even before his father's axe spun through the air, cutting him down in a flurry of sand. Commander Cambyses threw off his bronze-scaled breastplate and ran after him, chest dripping with sweat. He wrenched the axe free and there was hardly a pause as he drew the blade down through bone and brain.

Mercy-killings. Shenq hated them worse than the stink of blood and he hated the pleading eyes. His father once told him, *sometimes we must hasten death with a friendly axe, son. It's better that way.*

"Tell your father to kill the princes," Pharaoh grunted as he peeled off his leather bracer. "I'll take the King."

Shenq hitched his bow over his right shoulder and jumped off the footplate. He ran through a small group of archers scavenging amongst the dead, faces oiled and shrouded against disease. His father was too far off to concern him, advancing on the prisoners with a raised hand. But when Shenq glimpsed a warrior, rising from behind a mound of bodies some twenty feet away, he stopped and nocked an arrow, pulling the goose feather back to his ear. The shriek was worse than anything he had ever heard as the warrior ran towards his father with a spear in his hand. Shenq hurried the first shot and missed, and as he drew again he saw the enemy spear ripping through the sky, sturdy like a weavers beam. It sheared right through his father's chest and burst through his back.

"No," Shenq said in a thick voice as all other words stuck in his throat. "*No!*"

The blood-red shaft pinned the great Commander to the earth, quivering as it held. Somewhere in the distance a war horn blew and Shenq rushed to his father's side, wailing and cursing the enemy. He heard the snapping of wood before someone covered his face.

"Don't look," the Captain cried, forcing Shenq around.

Shenq looked up and studied Captain Tehute's face, mind screaming with dread. *Why is he staring at me? Why doesn't he say something?* "I want to see my father—"

"He took off his breastplate. He knew the risks."

"Please."

"He's dead." The Captain's lips seem to tremble as he said it.

A wake of vultures circled idly in the sky, *dung-eaters* the tribesmen called them. Shenq wanted to stay on the battlefield and pretend his father was still alive. But there was a throbbing pain in his heart that made him light-headed and he could barely stand. There were no tears as the soldiers carried his father away, only dry sobs. All he saw were slivers of sunlight as they flooded through the trees and a flame-red shadow hurrying through the tall grass, swift and feral like the dog it was.

Tehute pulled back and drew his bow. The odds should have been in his favor but his target twisted through the undergrowth like a sidewinder and the arrow plunged into a tree limb.

"Go after him, Shenq!" Tehute shouted.

The command rang in Shenq's ears for a moment before he bounded towards a belt of palm trees, grass slapping against his calves. It was likely a looter, skittish at the sound of the Pharaoh's wails. When he broke through a cluster of papyrus stems he saw a man crouched in the river mist, slaking his thirst. He was an Alodian shadow-hunter by the look of him, all feathers and bones and dressed in a red shúkà.

Aim for his brow. That should kill him.

Shenq hid behind a palm tree, bracing himself with the most effective weapon he had. He studied the warrior's bow, how it was strung, how it was made and, creeping forward, he placed a pebble in the cradle of his sling. The Alodian must have heard the rotations over the sound of splashing water and he turned too late to save his eye. Blood trickled from the hole in his face and the other eye stared at Shenq as if committing him to memory. He cursed before bolting into the mist only Shenq had no idea what he said.

Mouth open, he took chase, arms flailing through the long grass as if swimming for the furthest shore. On and on he ran hearing the sound of his ragged breath, smelling the foul stench of offal stronger than a plume of steam from an antelope's stomach. When he reached the fringes of the battlefield, the Alodian had disappeared.

"Did you find him?" Captain Tehute shouted as he rounded on him.

"No, sir." Shenq hung his head, feeling a thickness in his throat.

"Walk with me."

Shenq tore his eyes from a group of bowmen as they led his father's horse from the battlefield. Cambyses, Commander of the Division of Thoth, had protected the Pharaoh with bronze and fire. Now Egypt would mourn for seventy days and then they would forget him just like the rest.

The whinnying call of a kite brought Shenq back to the present and he saw the speckled underbelly as it flew overhead, wings stretched out like fingers in the bountiful blue. It was an omen, good and bad.

"Tell me, why didn't you kill him?" Captain Tehute wiped a hand over his forehead.

Shenq wondered how he knew. "I took out his eye."

"Remind me what makes a good fighter, boy?"

"One that removes all risk," Shenq said, reciting every profanity in his head.

"I trust you had a good reason to keep him alive."

Shenq swallowed hard, looking at eyes blacker than a beetle's shell. "He was a demon, sir."

There was something unearthly about the Alodian, the sheen on his powerful limbs, a look perhaps. *No mortal moves that fast,* Shenq thought.

"But this *demon* has lost an eye. He'll be back for one of yours."

"He'll never find me."

"He got a good look at you."

Shenq felt the heat flushing through his body and he blew out a series of short breaths. The man-creature had etched his face in his mind and there was no escaping, not from a shadow-hunter if that's what he was. *Shadow-hunters* belonged nowhere so his father said. They were outcasts living in tombs, skin rotting from their bones.

Tehute took Shenq to the dead boy with a crooked smile. His back glimmered red where the axe had sheared through his spine and the khopesh lay nearby, basking in the earth like a curl of liquid metal.

"Look at him. Even *he* tried to run," Tehute said, nudging the sword with his foot. "But he wasn't fast enough, was he?"

"No, sir." Shenq felt the sting of shame. Only none of it mattered now that his father was dead.

"Take it," Tehute said. "It's an officer's weapon."

Shenq crouched, listening intently as if he could still hear the boy breathe. Tears came only he had no free hand to brush them away and when he sobbed the Captain's arm was there to steady him.

"How many gods do you pray to?" Tehute asked.

"Only one," Shenq whispered.

"Then you pray to your *one*," Tehute muttered, giving Shenq his water skin. "And I'll pray to my six."

Shenq turned away from the carnage, hearing his father's voice. *Master it. Always make your weapon count.* There was an embossed lion on the fuller and a string of letters etched below the crossguard, letters he didn't understand. "What does it say?" he said.

Tehute took the khopesh and tilted the blade. "*Faithful*

and True," he muttered. "Can't say it's as curved as many. You'll need a sheath for it."

Shenq nodded, distracted suddenly by a small group of prisoners stripped of their tribal headdresses and collars. They formed a tight ring around the King of Alodia, a giant of a man with a gentle face. Gold disks hung from stretched earlobes and a red *shenti* kilt fluttered against his thighs. The soldiers had already killed the princes and all those that resembled him. But there was a boy by his side with a hungry stare, chest pale against a sun-baked body.

He wore a prince's collar once, thought Shenq, resisting a smile. "What will happen to them, sir?"

"They'll make good soldiers," Tehute said.

Captain Tehute was as blind as the rest of them. But it was there, a tilt of the chin, a curve of the cheek. Shenq should have hated the boy but he couldn't, so he studied the round face that twitched into a smile, a hesitant smile he would never forget. The boy was unlike his father except for a humble spirit that lurked behind the eyes, a spirit that if kept hidden would keep him alive.

"Blindfold them," Pharaoh Ka-Nekhet shouted, turning to Shenq with a grin. "Come boy and bring me that sword. We have a royal throat to cut."

KHEPER-RE

It was the season of low water during the first month of Shemu and a crimson sun basked for a moment on the horizon before spreading its limbs across the desert. A creature howled from the hollow of a fallen tree, a frenzied sound that rose and fell in the river mist.

Pharaoh Kheper-Re listened as he tried to pray, turning his ear towards the grasslands. *What are you?* he murmured, seeing visions of a slathering dog crushing limbs to fragments.

There was something out there playing with his mind, something evil that wouldn't let go. It had howled on the eve of his father's death twelve years ago, only now it howled every day. Pharaoh Ka-Nekhet had passed to the Great Fields, *no one seeing, no one hearing* and no one had the faintest idea what had killed him.

Poison, Kheper-Re almost murmured, missing him all the more. The idea was ridiculous. He would need to forget it, and immediately.

He watched old Djoser's fingers as they lightly rubbed moringa oil on his legs, dressing the sores with perfumed bandages. The prickling in his muscles had begun again and he rocked back and forth to ease the pain. He took one sniff at his breakfast and waved it away. "Gods, man, can't you find me a cup of wine?"

"You must *eat*, Nisu," Djoser said, reaching for a cup. He tasted it gingerly before offering it. "Wine is god's blood and better taken with food."

Kheper-Re began to sweat, mind racing for answers. *I am alive for one more day and I shall drink away the rest of it*, he thought. "Thieves broke into father's tomb and you expect me to eat! They took all his books, his weapons."

"Greed makes them do it, Nisu."

"It's the jackal. He's been roaming the marshes for weeks now and nothing will drive him out."

"Jackal?" Djoser removed a fresh *shenti* from a wicker basket and hooked it over one arm.

"Long ears and a pointy snout. And that bark, that long-howled bark that never stops. I can't leave the palace. I'll be killed if I do."

"Why not use the tunnel, Nisu."

Yes . . . the tunnel. Kheper-Re's father had built it many years ago, a tunnel to save his family during times of war. It ran from the kitchens to the river, only now it was alive with snakes. And who's to say the jackal hadn't taken up residence in a nest of roots, waiting with open jaws.

"You need young soldiers, Nisu," Djoser said. "Your general is too old. He's taken at least one arrow in the arm. What good's an arm with an arrow in it?"

What good indeed, Kheper-Re thought, longing for his private hours. He wanted to sit in the sycamore groves, admiring the sheen on the tranquil pools and the dragonflies amongst the lotus. His glorious palace stood in the curve of the great river, backed by cliffs redder than a pomegranate. Only today there would be no private hours. The Chancellor would likely bring up the level of the granaries and the terrible looting in the hills. There was chaos now, not order.

"Your new Commander arrives soon, Nisu. He'll bring lusty men and they'll kill that jackal."

"Shenq?" Kheper-Re said, slipping his feet into a pair of gold braided sandals. "He'll kill it with that sharp tongue of his."

He was already feeling like the underdog especially after looking at a mural of his likeness hurling a throwstick in the marshes. There was a tower of dead giraffe at his feet and he wondered if the artist had mistakenly added the creatures in place of duck.

"I'm a weak garrison the priests have taken by storm."

"Then it's time you stood up to them. Priests are lower than gods, Nisu. And you are a god."

Kheper-Re made a face. Priests were a tricky lot with all their spells and false prophecies. They said he would be well before the Festival of the New Moon but his legs were like two hot stones covered with itching flesh. He felt oddly alone and he wondered if it was going to be a black and hopeless summer much like the last. There was a quickening rhythm in his head, mostly the sound of buzzing from the fear he felt. That was why he built the palace on the west side of the river, close to the mountains, close to his father's tomb. He felt safer that way.

But he wasn't safe was he?

"Nisu, you haven't eaten for two days," Djoser reminded, placing a broad collar over Kheper-Re's head decorated with a winged scarab and inlayed with gold beads. "Wine will only make you sick."

"Sick? I'm already sick!" Kheper-Re said. He had been heaving like a cat with a hairball since dawn.

"There's no poison in the wine, Nisu. I have tasted it myself."

"What about the stew?"

"Stew?" Djoser echoed as if trying to recall the very meal. "It was duck stew, I think."

Kheper-Re cared little for the type of meat and looked around his chamber with a critical eye. The guards were docile nobodies, inclined to let a thief past with a smile.

The only person they had let in was the Chief of Prophets with a tray of food. "Did you taste it?"

"I did. I like stew."

Kheper-Re was glad at that. Djoser tasted all his food and it was a wonder he was still standing. Poison was a horrible death, all that frothing at the mouth and clawing at the belly. Devoted tasters were hard to come by.

Puyem-re . . . Kheper-Re murmured the name of the Chief of Prophets from the corner of a smile. The priest brought his stew daily, offering Djoser the first sip. But it was only a *sip*, hardly enough to make a man cough.

Kheper-Re struggled to stand, hobbling at first on unsteady legs. But he would walk all the way to the Southern Palace if he had to, through a bevy of curtsying ladies unable to lower their eyes. There the lady Aset languished in a garden of persea trees watered by a groaning *shaduf* and the sound of a nearby fountain likely lulled her to sleep. He prayed she dreamed of him.

"I want sons, old father," Kheper-Re whispered. "Many sons."

Ten of his children had died since the New Year and there was a curse on his house. Queen Hatshepsut had born nothing but stillborns and he wondered if rutting her was worth the effort. When he looked in the mirror, he saw roguish black eyes and a chiseled jaw. He was handsome so his father said.

"The lady Aset has given you a son, Nisu. A fine boy."

"Yes . . . yes. But Aset is a lesser wife." Lesser in status, Kheper-Re thought, but so much more in his heart. She was beautiful with her raven curls and heart-shaped face, and a passion that made him tremble. He couldn't see her now she was with child. It was safer that way so the midwives said. But if he could only see her one more time . . . "What must a man do to get *sons*!"

Djoser sucked on a lone front tooth and stared at the ceiling. "Dung, my lord."

"Dung?"

"A salve of dung will keep a member hard for hours," Djoser reminded, tying the fastenings of Kheper-Re's broad collar. "Take your father, for instance. He had a fruitful reign. It was the dung that did it."

Kheper-Re longed for a cartload of it to free him from this endless misery. Enough to ensure his member was no longer a spec on the horizon but hard like a ship's prow. Priests collected dung from the sacred crocodiles that basked in the pool on the north side of the palace. Big brown mushy piles of it as he recalled.

A rattle on the door brought him out of his reverie and he flinched as he saw the plump-lipped beauty on the threshold. Queen Hatshepsut, *she-who-is-foremost-of-women*.

"Sister," Kheper-Re said, wishing he was somewhere else.

"Sun of my heart," she said, bowing her head. A circlet of cloisonné shimmered at her forehead and the beaded terminals chimed as she moved. "I have news. I am with child."

"May the gods bless you a thousand times," Kheper-Re said, rattled with the memory of their last coupling. She had seduced him with kind words and cups of sweet-scented god's blood. Rather urgently he recalled.

"And the Chief of Prophets had a dream about rats," she said with an eager hitch to her voice.

"Rats?" There was never anything good about rats.

"Rats shrink from a rising tide, my lord. It means the flood will be higher this year. It *means* you'll have sons."

Of course it did. The flood was equal to his virility. And the last time they'd coupled, hadn't he crowed for her like a barnyard cock?

"Amun has favored me," Kheper-Re murmured, saying a wordless prayer to the god. The storehouses would be full, the farmers' tithes generous and bards would sing of his greatness.

"You are highly favored. Lady Aset is also with child."

Kheper-Re thought of the lady Aset as briefly as he

dared. If loving him didn't kill her, birthing a son surely would.

He watched his sister and her eyes of topaz, glaring with a cruel hunger. She despised his indifference, his inability to love her. And what was *love* anyway? A series of hot, sweaty hours in a blaze of drunkenness, all arms and legs and a name he had forgotten. The thought made him thirsty and he shouted for more wine.

He remembered a girl he had taken to bed once, breasts small and succulent, and a waist he could span with both hands. When he awoke the next morning the same girl had somehow aged in the night and her dugs were larger than his head. How did that happen? he wondered, peering over the rim of an empty goblet.

"In Thebes, a Queen must never go into her husband without invitation." Hatshepsut smiled a little wider this time. Her breasts strained against green linen, hugging tighter than snakeskin. "So she waits with her ladies for days and months, and all the while her womb is aging, and all the while she wonders if she is loved. When her children are born dead, the Pharaoh chooses a new Queen and the old Queen is put away."

"Remind me never to become Queen of Thebes." Kheper-Re felt a sudden ache behind the eyes.

"When crops fail and wars are lost, who do the people blame?"

Kheper-Re peered at her breasts and it was hard to keep his mind on the matter. "The gods?" he said, shrugging.

"*You.* And if you fail to bring the floods, the people will starve."

Kheper-Re allowed her words to hang in the air for a time. If the people starved they might ask for another Pharaoh and looking at his sister, he wondered if she had the best of that bargain. It was fortunate she wasn't a man.

"They won't starve," he said. "Amun cares for every one of them."

It was a lie, of course, the best he could offer. Amun was a hollow statue with a door in his divine behind and his voice was so familiar it sounded like a priest he knew.

"You haven't asked for me in days," Hatshepsut said with the same dark smile.

"Three hundred wives, so little time. My seed must be sown in as many pastures as the gods deem fit. In your case, it has already taken root—"

"To council you, to hear your secrets," Hatshepsut reminded, baring her teeth. "I am the Queen, your own blood."

Kheper-Re wanted to ask why she was so against being a bed-slave only he knew he would rue the question. "It is, as you say, all about blood and there's plenty of that on the battlefield."

"All kings have secrets. What are yours, brother?"

Secrets? He wouldn't trust her with a secret even if his life depended on it. "Here's one," he said, rising from his chair, longing for the safety of the gardens. "I'm to have a new set of eyes in my court. A fresh set of ears."

"Whose?"

Kheper-Re saw the smirk as he sauntered towards the door. "Ah," he said, spinning on his heel to face her again. "Commander Shenq. He's coming home."

"Shenq?"

He heard the gasp as he lunged for the corridor. The Queen had a fondness for Commander Shenq. A rather unnatural one, he hated to admit.

He almost ran through the great hall, a large room lit with torches and painted with scenes of hunting. Priests stood around a large brazier, recessed into the floor and surrounded by four pillars. They were at it again, all that chanting and wailing. He couldn't stand the noise.

Bird song filled the open-air courts and a large sycamore stood like a sentinel over a pond. There were fish in the murky depths, fatter than a man's leg.

"Bring me a rod and some bait," Kheper-Re shouted

to a passing attendant, huddled over a walking stick. "I would like to fish after breakfast."

Horns blasted on the pylons announcing the rising sun and he saw a thickset shadow hovering at the entrance to the garden, dazzling in blue and gold. Only it was not the thickset shadow he had hoped. Osorkon, Commander of the household garrison, had seen fit to waste his time.

"Great Bull, may you live forever," Commander Osorkon said, bowing over stocky legs.

"Oh, I will," Kheper-Re said, sinking back on a chair that had followed him out of his apartments.

"I thought I might find you here, my lord. It has been too long since I saw your glorious face."

And it might just be the last, Kheper-Re thought, staring at shrewd brown eyes. The man was sturdy, charged to lead the divisions of Ptah and Set, and there was too much gold beneath that thick neck. "We have no appointment, Commander."

"Great Bull," Osorkon began with a loud intake of breath, "I must speak to you. The Chief of Prophets predicted I would be the next Viceroy of Kush—"

"Then the Chief of Prophets will lose his head."

"You would regret cutting off mine, my lord. It will never lie to you."

"I'm lied-to a hundred times a day," Kheper-Re said wondering why Osorkon wanted Kush.

Great commanders never begged only this one had a motive in his outstretched hand. He was beginning to hate the name *Osorkon* and he had no use for a snake unless it floated in a bowl of soup. The wretch had asked for Kush, no *begged,* because he was the color of Nile silt and part-Kushite himself. And the Chief of Prophets had no business handing out promotions as freely as a bag of nuts.

"I have ideas further west," Kheper-Re announced. "My father's tomb had been ransacked because the Medjai are undermanned. There is no one to lead them."

"But, my lord, the Medjai—"

16

"Are tomb guards, yes. My beloved father deserves only the best." Kheper-Re ignored the look of defeat and smiled. "You should be flattered."

"I am flattered," Commander Osorkon said, head dropping over a great barrel chest.

"Surely, you welcome being closer to home in your old age. And you are *old*," Kheper-Re reminded, seeing the frown, the puckered lip. Osorkon's head was smoother than a naked skull and grey stubble peeked out above his temples where he had omitted to shave.

"My lord, I took a vow to protect you unto death."

"And so you shall. You must be tired of clutching that sword, tired of screaming curses and threats. Why not rest awhile in the hills." After a respectful pause, Kheper-Re flapped a hand. "Ah, here comes the Chancellor."

A single trumpet revealed a portly man at the garden gate whose jeweled collar almost reached his naval. He was more richly attired than the High Priest and both dined on the best of Amun's offering table.

"Chancellor Neshi," Kheper-Re said, sharing a wink. "I hope you have exciting news."

"Very exciting news, my lord." Neshi stood with a wide stance, face beaming like a wheel of cheese. He greeted Osorkon with a slight tilt of the head and eyed Kheper-Re with a tight grin. "Commander Shenq arrives tomorrow."

"Amun be praised!" Kheper-Re dismissed Osorkon with a wave. He saw the scowl and the dragging feet. The old Commander would hesitate just long enough to hear what he needed to hear.

"Has Shenq been apprised of his new post?"

"He has, my lord. He is honored to serve your house."

"He will be required to play Bao and Senet."

"He plays both games well. As you know he's part *Shasu*."

Kheper-Re was afraid of the *Shasu* if he was honest. They were a bunch of nomadic shepherds that bred like

17

rabbits. Commander Shenq was a strong-boned man with eyes richer than tree sap and Kheper-Re had a burning desire to be like him; an obsession born out of admiration.

"Do you remember Shenq's father?" he murmured.

"Of course. Commander Cambyses was the greatest commander Thebes has ever had."

Kheper-Re frowned, recalling the memory as fast as a rush of blood. He had not seen Shenq for many years and he wondered how much Neshi knew, how much Neshi remembered. Commander Cambyses had died by a demon's hand and it was likely the same demon that howled below his window.

"The southern tribesmen call him *Kemnebi*, the Black Leopard," Neshi continued. "He's skilled with the khopesh and has retained the title of Swordsman of the South since your father grudgingly surrendered it. He's self-taught. There are no instructors in the art."

"That same sword killed the king of Alodia. Blood poured from his open throat like the innards of gutted fish."

"Most poetic, my lord," Neshi said, bowing from the neck. His eyes sparkled like two raisins in a lump of dough. "The prince is eager to meet Commander Shenq."

"My boy would like a friend," Kheper-Re said, warming to thoughts of his son. "Is the Commander married?"

"He *was* Your Majesty, to the eldest daughter of Vizier Ahmose." Neshi lowered his voice. "Miserable girl and unfaithful so they say."

"She was battered to death, a terrible matter." Kheper-Re recalled the incident with a wave of disgust. The girl had taken a lover whose attentions had become violent.

"And his mother?"

"Also dead, my lord."

"So much grief, it's a wonder he's sane. I want my own men, Neshi, my own household. Shenq will bring good soldiers and I'll be safe. Tell him to bring me a bodyguard and a scribe."

"A scribe, my lord? You already have twelve."

"There was a *Shasu* boy that served my father. What was his name?" Kheper-Re thought it began with an *H* but he couldn't sure. He had an unconquerable spirit that appealed to him.

Neshi bit his lip, eyes floating to the sky. "Another *Shasu*, my lord? The palace will soon be overrun with them."

"Find him, Chancellor, and get rid of the others."

Neshi raised his chin, attempting to suck in a generous belly. "Strong Bull, I must remind you that many of your attendants served under your late father."

"They're all rotting and should be buried with him." Kheper-Re waved his hand and watched the Chancellor leave.

His eyes were briefly lost in the glint of a dragonfly's wing and he remembered his father's voice. *You must stay ahead of your enemy, boy. It's foolish to think you have friends.*

Kheper-Re felt no sorrow. Trusted servants, the last vestiges of his father's reign should have been a comfort. But these had betrayed him, whispering his secrets to the outside world. He would seal them in his father's tomb. It was the safest thing to do.

KHEMWESE

The Migdol, known as the Sand Rabbit, was a three-tiered *mastaba* built on a rocky slope. Long spur walls followed the natural contours of the knoll, each carved with the emblem of the city. Two tower gates rose above the inner and outer enclosures flanked by guardrooms and teeming with watchmen . Since it was part of the desert territories, it fell under the dominion of Commander Shenq.

Daylight seeped through a loophole in the fortress wall and a young bowman sat at its footing. His skin was the color of ebony and from his ears hung two small tusks set in silver rings. Khemwese was Alodian by birth, brought to Thebes as a child. He hardly remembered his father, a man richer in spirit than the city he came to plunder. But he remembered his last words more.

Before God, I declare my son . . .

Then the soldiers slit his throat and hung him upside down from the prow of the Pharaoh's flagship. They said he was a raider, a common thief.

"I have my mother's face," Khemwese murmured. It had saved him.

Old Ka-Nekhet was dead now and his wine-sop of a

son was hardly to blame. Long years in the quarries enhanced Khemwese's build and he was sold for two deben and one kite of silver to the Captain of the Pharaoh's elite. And here he was sitting on the parapet with a *Shasu* boy, Harran from Canaan, a prophet with child-like eyes.

"Commander's back," Khemwese said, pitching his chin towards the desert.

Harran gave an expression somewhere between a smile and a smirk and ran a hand over a closely cropped beard. "We'll get a flogging and a few sharp words. The dead should have been buried by now."

Khemwese didn't mind the sharp words since he rarely understood them. It was the dead that bothered him, red painted faces and collars of human teeth. They attacked the Migdol during the fourth watch and their carcasses lay beyond the outer wall. Vultures had already made a meal of them, swooping overhead and etching their shadows across the dunes.

Harran shook his shaggy head and swatted a fly with one hand. "The sycamores are turning yellow. I saw it in a dream."

"The land's cursed then," Khemwese muttered. A dozen ideas came to mind, each more imaginative than the last until the silence was shattered by a shout.

"Stand!" a voice bellowed from the guardhouse.

Commander Shenq walked into the courtyard with seven men, each wearing the black and gold regalia of the *Kenyt-Nisu*, the Pharaoh's courageous ones. A wealth of black hair hung to his waist and his tall rangy body glowed with sweat.

"We lost twenty men last night," Commander Shenq cried. "But the Alodians lost seven hundred of theirs."

Cheers surged through the courtyard, silenced by a raised hand. The Commander turned a full circle, eyes bouncing from man to man. "I have good news. The middle lands are safe and the forty-day route is well guarded. Pharaoh says we are champions. You will all be rewarded with a belly-full of wine and as much food as you can eat. I say we feast."

The soldiers pounded the flagstones with the butts of their spears, cheering and whooping.

"Khemwese!" Commander Shenq shouted. "Come down and bring the prophet with you."

Khemwese felt a churning in his gut as if he could already hear the thrum of the bow. By the fire in the Commander's eye they were in for a flogging and the stripes on his back were still raw from the last one he had.

"The dead need burying," Commander Shenq said, restating a martial rule. "Your watch, your job."

Khemwese never spoke as he dug the trench, dragging the bodies in one by one. He glanced over at the Commander, arms bare and bronzed, scoring the ground with his axe. It was a rare man that took a punishment with his men and it was a rare spirit that went on through the afternoon without tiring.

"Heart like iron," Khemwese muttered to Harran. The Commander had a presence, an uncanny bravery if he could give it a name. "Do you trust him?"

Harran gave a grin that conveyed a secret. "Oh, yes."

Khemwese dragged the last corpse by its arms and flung it sideways into the pit. "Look at them. They were already dead before they came here."

"The dead don't walk."

"These did."

Khemwese heard the grinding of the wooden gate and he saw a young lieutenant loping towards them. Jabari was his name, lean and bald, with a ring through his nose. He was from Noubadia if Khemwese could guess, earlobes dripping with ten rings each. He carried a basket of roast meat and a jug of beer.

"Eat," Commander Shenq said, offering the rations. He was almost as tall as Khemwese with a mind sharper than a surgeon's knife. "The Pharaoh needs a bodyguard and a prophet. So here I am. And here you are."

"Me?" Khemwese said with a watery mouth. He had no idea why the Pharaoh wanted him, brainless as he was.

Shenq turned to face Harran first, studying him with a wide grin. "They say you're a prophet. They say you interpret dreams. Do you?"

"HaShem interprets dreams, sir," Harran said.

"Be careful of the priests. There are so many of them."

"I'm not afraid of the priests, sir."

Shenq narrowed his eyes. "You don't believe in the gods of Thebes?"

"No, sir. There is only one God. If we have more than one master, surely we will love one and despise the other."

"You're a wise man." Shenq turned and stared at Khemwese. "And you? You've served Captain Tehute for some years now. Where is your loyalty?"

"I go by your voice, Maaz," Khemwese said, hoping the Commander wouldn't mind the tusks in his ears. He had more than a spot of color on him with the beads at his throat.

"Call me, *sir*. You're a bowman not a bond servant."

"I'll call you Maaz if it's all the same." Khemwese eyed his superior with awe. *Maaz* was a form of respect in Alodia.

Shenq merely nodded. "Our Pharaoh needs good men to shore him up. Brave men. He believes there's a storm coming and hot winds always blow in from the south."

Khemwese imagined a horde of Alodians ten thousand strong and one thousand deep, and he could almost hear the snap of their demon wings. "There's something out there isn't there, Maaz?"

Khemwese had seen animal tracks in the sand and a frame of skins amongst the trees. It was a regular haunt for young women searching for love and there was a man willing to give it. Only this one had a jackal's heart.

Shenq patted the ground and urged them to sit. "King

Ibada took the throne after Kibwe-Shabaqo died. Only he wasn't as fortunate. There was a traitor amongst his nobles, a headman called Tau. He wore a red shúkà like the warriors we buried, and he had a house and four wives. Ibada was generous, boasting he could take control of the Two Lands with a brother at his side. Only Tau got too greedy. So with a few powerful words, he stripped King Ibada of a new bride and an army of ten thousand men. All because he thought he could have whatever he wanted. Ibada caught up with him in the desert and tied him to a tree. He left him there for the *dung-eaters*."

Khemwese was conscious of a strained silence. He had heard of King Ibada, the sacker of cities. But he had never heard of Tau. "Where is he now?"

"If you shut your eyes," Commander Shenq said, "you can almost feel his breath on the back of your neck."

TAU

Tau watched the woman as she stirred a pot of stew, thin shoulders huddled over the fire. He had only known her for a week or two and she wasn't a virgin like the others. There was a baby in a basket beside her and sleeping babies never worried Tau. Screaming ones were another matter.

He stared up through the branches at the Migdol, remembering better times. He had once been headman to King Ibada, sharing his palace, his horses, his women. Betrayal had eroded any trust between them when he stole the king's favorite wife. They tied him to a tree when they found him and they made him watch her burn. All the while he yelled to the snake god, snot streaming down his painted face. He was in love then, but not now.

The squeak of the metal frame made him wince. "I'm hungry, woman," he whispered. "How much stirring does a pot need?"

"The meat is barely cooked," she said, lifting eyes the color of mud.

"A king never waits for his supper." Tau took a deep breath, feeling a surge of anger. "On your knees!"

The woman knelt and held up a steaming bowl. He would have dashed it on the ground if he wasn't so hungry.

That was the thing about Umaya. She was humble when she put her mind to it.

I'm tired of wandering the earth and sleeping in holes, he thought, chewing stringy meat. And he was tired of dusting his body with sand so the soldiers would never find him.

For a few heartbeats he imagined he was king. He replayed the memory in his mind, changing it sometimes to suit his mood. It had been twelve years since he joined the Pharaoh's army and stole the horse. He thought he could fly like the sacred falcon when he sat on its back, only he was as earthbound as a donkey and just as stupid. The horse belonged to Commander Cambyses, a man with no mercy, and he flogged Tau until the world went black. That was the day before the battle of Swenet.

He watched from the foothills all those years ago, standing in the heat until his legs ached. The dull ring of swords was louder than a blacksmith's anvil and he could still see the chariots and the Commander in front of them. His target was only thirty running paces into the thick of it and Tau walked onto the blood-soaked field until he saw the spear on the ground next to the prisoners. He crouched to pick it up and turned sideways to take aim.

"Why do you paint your face?"

The voice crashed through his thoughts and he looked down at the woman. She was still kneeling and her eyes were heavy with sleep. They were pretty eyes, brown with specs of yellow. "To conjure spirits," he said. "Do you like spirits?"

She shook her head at that. "They frighten me."

"If I take enough of this," he said, rubbing a small vial between his fingers, "I'm never afraid."

The opiate was calming but it caused dreams, vivid ones. He let her chew on the idea for a moment.

"I would like to see them," she said, moistening her lips.

She looked like she was willing to do much more than share a vial. *She's nervous, fascinated but nervous.*

"Where's your husband?" Tau said, enjoying the moment, enjoying the power. "You do have a husband?"

The woman raised her chin—too quickly, he noted.

"Husband?" she repeated.

"The captain," Tau said. Captain Tehute would be searching for her soon amidst the palm trees, thick with fruit at the desert's edge. "I know all the women, Umaya, especially you."

"I live alone," Umaya stuttered.

Liar . . . Tau thought, feeling the tingling in his limbs. The baby was proof enough. Her husband would be back at dawn to light a lamp in the household niche, going down on his face to worship Khepri, the god of the rising sun.

"Rise," he said, watching her struggle on stiff legs. She was old, too old perhaps.

Many women came from the villages to seek pleasure from a one-eyed warrior with the appetite of a stag. They all knew each other yet none were friends.

Tau saw the hunger in her eyes as he pushed her back against a tree and his mind separated from the pleasure of her body and the excitement it caused. Through the leaves, he saw a narrow loophole in the fortress wall and he imagined the boy with the sling. He was closer now than he had ever been.

Commander Shenq, he mused, was a dead man. Well . . . almost, if killing was better than hunting, and he'd hunted for long enough. There were two others that had drawn for the watch, eyes gloating over the parapets at dawn. One was a giant with tusks in his ears and the other had a prophet's gaze. Tau had seen both of them burying Alodians in the late afternoon and he had raged at the loss of friends. There was nothing left of his army now, nothing but bones and teeth.

Bones and teeth . . . He needed a new collar and he needed a bed. The Captain's bed would do for now. The worn-out old soldier never returned at night. He would never know.

The sun scored a gash along the gullies and palm fronds pulsed in the breeze. White streamers fluttered from towering poles, emblazoned with gold falcons and blushed by the rising sun. There was a wake of *dung-eaters* in a shallow pool, hackles stained with blood and feathers outstretched. Tau could hear them hissing as they squabbled over a carcass.

The woman's groans mimicked those of a dying man, brazen and pointless. All he could think about was the agony he would inflict on the boy with a sling. He had already killed the boy's father . . . and then his mother.

He groaned suddenly in a rictus of bliss. It had given him a thirst for revenge.

SHENQ

A breeze blew in from the east, throwing ripples across a lean stretch of water below the east wall of the Migdol. Commander Shenq sat under the shade of a palm tree, listening to a chorus of water birds. Women filled their jugs from the *shaduf*, chattering and laughing in the cool of the dawn and some jostled stiffly with one another, vying for rank and favor.

Shenq surrendered his thoughts to memories. Widowed young, he sought never to bind himself to another woman. But a waiting maid to the Queen had caught his eye, beautiful she was with a childlike face and grey-green eyes.

"What are you grinning at?" Captain Tehute asked as he settled beside him. He pulled the khat from his bald head, revealing deep-set eyes and rugged features.

Shenq tried to shake off the memory and he paused to think of the right words. "It has been four years since my wife died. It's lonely in the tent."

"You? Lonely? You've refused every girl in Thebes."

"Not all."

In truth, Shenq enjoyed the hunt. He had last seen the maid at the Feast of the New Moon, a brief interlude when he was last on leave. The Queen's entourage took to the river to pay homage at the Sanctuary of Hapi and Shenq watched from the riverbank as the boat glided by. A young girl sat at the beam, trailing her fingers in the water, a girl so pure Shenq thought he had seen a ghost.

"You're a commander. Breach her."

"She's a *child* not a harlot."

"I was married to a child once," Tehute said. "Only I'm lonelier now than I was before."

Shenq felt sorry for Tehute. His wife was a drifter, seeking love wherever she could find it and it was worse now she had birthed her first child. "When did you last see her?"

"Day before yesterday. My sister keeps the baby. It's better this way." Tehute stared at Shenq for a moment and then shook his head. "I hope you find happiness with this girl of yours. You've changed from a terrified boy into a vicious fighter. For twelve years that sword has been your only friend. Your honorary title is now a real one— Swordsman of the South. And women? They come after you in droves. Yet you fend them off with bitter arrows. Now you're in love. I wonder if you know what it means."

"Hunters hunt. Killers kill," Shenq said, feeling the pulse in his throat.

"You're merciful when it suits you. You wept when your father died. But it was your mother's death that changed you." Tehute patted Shenq's shoulder as he had all those years ago, a hand of comfort to stem his quiet sobbing.

"It was *how* she died," Shenq reminded. Wild dogs had ripped the skin off her back.

He watched an archer by the name of Pabasa, brought to the region at the time of the previous Pharaoh. The same ship, the same wretched Alodians. There were ten of them as he recalled. Pabasa was willful, back latticed with stripes and shoulders sagging now that he had lost his pride.

"Did Pabasa cry out when you flogged him?" Shenq

said, eying Pabasa's scars like ridges in the shallows.

"Alodians never cry out." Tehute removed the stopper from his water skin, taking several gulps. "He's a deserter. I won't go searching for him a second time."

"Does he still have a wife?" Shenq asked, studying the women at the well with their black-hooded eyes. There was no sign of Osumare.

"He's got a punching bag if that's what you mean."

"She could leave him, you know."

"She can't run far enough."

Shenq knew Pabasa would desert again. It was only a matter of time. "These bowmen," he said pointing at Khemwese and Harran, "how would you rate them?"

"Harran knows his target before he shoots. He's not fast, just accurate. Khemwese can shoot up to twelve arrows at the count of twenty."

Shenq raised his brows. Khemwese likely held all his arrows in his bow hand rather than pulling them from his quiver. He was a Kamau, *silent warrior*, notorious for stamina and stealth, and he had the instinct and nature of the animals he hunted. Shenq remembered the young boy on the deck of a narrow ship, watching his father's blood as it pooled towards him.

"Khemwese's impressive then," Shenq murmured.

"They'll both find themselves at the forefront of the *Kenyt-Nisu*."

Shenq savored the tribesmen. They had a quiet strength he admired. Khemwese would learn the Theban customs and if he survived, he would return to Kush as a client ruler under the management of the Viceroy.

"Does he remind you of anyone?" Shenq asked.

"Khemwese? He's more developed than most, a denser chest and a longer arm. He can perform at high intensity with a faster recovery than my northern warriors. Take yourself for instance. You have higher endurance, yet he has faster bursts of energy—"

"If you recall, those that bore a likeness to Kibwe-

Shabaqo were put to death, violently so my agents tell me. Our late Pharaoh must have been blind."

"Your words are bitter and badly chosen, sir." Tehute murmured, keeping his voice low. "Kibwe-Shabaqo had to die. He wouldn't stop attacking us."

"And his sons?"

"They were all killed. We couldn't risk war with Alodia."

Shenq sighed with relief. If Khemwese wore the finery of an Alodian nobleman, Tehute might have remembered. The boy that had once stood on the Pharaoh's flagship was now almost ten hands tall with muscles thicker than a bullock. He was twenty-four years old, two years younger than Shenq.

"And Harran?"

"A *Shasu* tribe settled in the north near the eighth Nome of Pi-Atum. Pharaoh Ka-Nekhet decided to cull the vine since their numbers almost exceeded ours. Harran was one of the many brought to him as a captive. He was favored because he could read and write."

Shenq stared at the ground, a deceptive maneuver that placed all warriors in the periphery of his vision. "Do you ever think of the man that killed my father?"

Tehute nodded. "All the time."

"You said he was familiar."

"There was a young man in the Pharaoh's guard," Tehute began, eyes distant. "The Pharaoh found him in the desert half-starved and brought him back to Thebes. He was sturdy and good with a knife. Only he was a thief. He was flogged for stealing your father's horse."

"Pity, I should like to have known his name."

"Too long ago, my friend." Tehute turned to Shenq, eyes rooted on him with paternal compassion.

Shenq heard the rustle of the reeds by the river, umbels sweeping in the wind, and he saw the girl carrying two urns. She was brittle as if a gust would blow her over in a moment and she froze when she saw him.

"Greetings Osumare," he said, jumping to his feet. He meant it kindly but the look she gave him was far from happy. He ambled towards the well, examining a rigid body swathed in dark veils. "I'll work the long arm and you sit here on the wall."

Osumare set the urns on the mud-brick surround and sat down. She tugged at her veil, covering the lower half of her face.

"Tell me about Pabasa," Shenq said, taking the urns and setting them down on the wall.

Osumare looked down, unable to meet his eyes. "My husband likes to hunt. He goes to the wadi to catch birds. He has a friend there."

Shenq lowered the wooden arm of the *shaduf*, watching the water as it spilled into the skin bag. "What does this *friend* look like?"

"He has scars." Osumare's nose puckered and she trembled slightly. "He's not from around here. The women say he's a healer."

The women were liars, fornicators, and yet none of them would allow a girl with a few bruises to draw water at the same well.

"Pabasa doesn't come home at night does he?" A twitching mouth and glistening eyes told Shenq she was crying and as soon as he saw it, she turned away. "Do you have enough food?" he asked, filling her urns to the brim. The garrison paid the soldiers in meat and grain at the end of each week and Pabasa was no exception.

"I eat what I can," she said, still looking away.

Scraps perhaps but she looked half-starved to him. Here was a girl who had never seen a full plate of food. "I'll send Khemwese with meat and bread."

He would have sent Harran but the boy would only crumble at the sight of her. He loved her once until he became a priest. "May God bless you," Shenq said, giving her the urns.

Here was a woman shuttered behind closed doors

without a friend. The very sight of her caused a well of grief to gurgle to the surface and Shenq wondered if she ever smiled. As the wind whipped a coil of sand along the dusty road, he could no longer see her small figure beneath a cloud of veils.

There's a devil out there, taking my men, he thought. And if he wasn't quick enough, the same devil would take the women.

KHEPER-RE

"Greetings O divine one," High Priest Hapuseneb said, leaning over the royal cheetah and offering a thinly bound scroll. "It is always a pleasure."

"Is it?" Kheper-Re said, snatching the scroll and patting the cheetah's head with it. It did little to wake the beast. "What news?"

"There is pestilence, Great Bull. Some say it's the work of the devil. Some say he roams the desert. Some say he's outside these very walls. The order of Ma'at is at risk."

Kheper-Re leaned back in his chair, tapping the scroll against his knee. The audience chamber was thick with perfume and half his noblemen were heavy-eyed and tired. He glanced at the Queen beside him, raising his chin a little higher. She hadn't spoken yet. But he'd silence her if she did.

"The scroll, my lord," Hapuseneb prompted.

Kheper-Re unfurled it and stared at an inventory of cows. Nicely drawn, he thought, only what it had to do with him he couldn't imagine. "Cows?"

"Yes, my lord. Our cows have yellow eyes dripping with mucus and oxen are rarely seen. Calves have been torn from their enclosures, half-eaten and left to die . . ."

Kheper-Re hardly heard. He was tired of the endless whittering, tired of others arguing his version of events. The cows were under a spell, for Horus sake, controlled by a demonic finger. Even the High Priest was too much of an ass to see it. He glanced again at the Queen, dressed in a sheath of yellow. The cobra at her brow flickered and the parietal feathers of the vulture shuddered as if it swallowed.

Gods, I'm drunk, he thought.

". . . and the farmers are hiding grain," Hapuseneb said.

"Throw them in the dungeons!" Kheper-Re snapped, squeezing the scroll in his hand. The cheetah growled beneath him and rolled on its side.

The outburst had caused several heads to jerk and Kheper-Re almost laughed. It was late afternoon and he was in a gloomy state. The doctor had lanced three unsightly boils from one buttock and he could hardly sit.

"My lord," Hapuseneb said, face gaunt. "There is the issue of tithes. Cows are puny and diseased and goats are scarce. It's an abomination. The farmers should be thrashed."

"They're hiding goats in the tombs of the artisans, Great Bull," interrupted Puyem-re, Chief of Prophets.

Kheper-Re hated Puyem-re just a little more. He was a pasty little man with an odd smell and there was something gnarly about him he couldn't put his finger on. He sucked down his eighth cup of wine, flinching more at the bitter taste than the desecration to the tombs. "And how would you know, Prophet?"

"I make it my business to know, your gracious majesty," Puyem-re said, voice childlike and soothing. "We do not want a curse on this land."

"If these tombs are full of good meat, seize it. If diseased cows are being offered for tithes, burn them. What do you care about Thebes if you have not already done this?"

"My lord," Puyem-re stuttered, bowing from the waist,

36

"we cannot break into the tombs of the artisans. It's sacrilege!"

"The farmers did," Kheper-Re reminded. "And so did you."

The council responded with a charade of open mouths, hands clasped in prayer. Kheper-Re wanted to laugh as he stared at a parade of bellies. The priests were richer than the crown.

"Your gracious majesty," Puyem-re said, wincing. "Forgive me. In Amun's name, forgive me. I can't bear to think of this great Egypt wasted by disease."

"Egypt is the academy of the world, the envy of foreign princes, and yet you believe it's already a dried up cesspit. Come now, do you not see the flood will be excellent this year?" Kheper-Re imagined the gleaming strip of water suddenly swollen like a fat snake.

"Indeed, Great Bull, but our storehouses cannot take the strain," Hapuseneb intervened, waving a flaccid hand at Puyem-re. "We have seven months of grain, maybe eight. Even the sacred sycamores no longer light the eastern gates. Has Hathor abandoned us?"

The sycamores were grey and scaly now, leaves sallow. Kheper-Re tried to sort through his tangled thoughts, wondering what had caused it. He heard the howling then, a sorrowful strain. The very sound of it would curdle all the breast-milk in the harem unless someone put a stop to it. "Arrest that dog!"

"*Dog*, your majesty?"

"Yes, you fool!" Kheper-Re said, jabbing a finger at Hapuseneb's face. "All you can think about are cows when there's a dog outside ready to rip out our throats. Have you no shame? Out, all of you. *Out!*"

Kheper-Re wiped a hand lightly across his brow as he tried to catch the faint chant of the fountain in the gardens. He was quickly relieved of the council, listening instead to slapping sandals as they departed.

Cows, who cares about cows? He stared between the flames

of a lighted brazier, soothed for a time by the popping embers. He was the Great Bull, son of Ra. *Bull*, yes, that's what he was. He had astonished the harem master by taking seventy women in a week. That was ten couplings a day.

He glanced at his sister, skin smoother than quartzite and cheeks dusted with gold ore. She was as sure-footed as a horse and twice as shrewd. "You promised me a son," he said, hips bucking in his chair like a stag in rut.

"We will have many sons just like father did." Hatshepsut made a face.

"Only they're all dead now. Amenmose, Wadjmose, Ramose . . . Having sons is not as easy as holding a draw and letting an arrow fly."

Kheper-Re imagined the arrow sailing through the sky and he knew it would likely miss the target by ten long feet. The doctors made him concoctions to improve his virility but none of them worked. In a way, his torment had only just begun.

"And I'm tired of doctors," he whispered, swallowing excessively. "They've made me sit on more anal poultices than I've sat on chairs."

Hatshepsut cupped her mouth with one hand and giggled. There was a young girl at her feet with wide enquiring eyes and a horse's tail for a braid. Kheper-Re leaned forward for a better look. She was strangely beautiful in a simple way and he wanted to touch her.

"What is your name?" he asked.

"Meryt, my lord," she stammered. A collar of gold and pink quartz rested against a small bosom which seemed to heave with nervousness.

Kheper-Re grinned as he gripped her hand. A pulsating desire spread through his body, raw and unrestrained. Wetting his lips, a lurid scenario played in his mind causing his legs to cross in order to harness the beast. *I shall bring her pearls and silks from the furthest reaches of the world,* he thought, wondering if he could toy with her in the late afternoons.

"You have a delightful maidservant, sister. Perhaps I will make her a wife."

"She's only a child."

"I have rooms full of them."

"She's *Shasu*."

Kheper-Re was surprised and dropped the girl's hand. She didn't look *Shasu* to him. He would have a son off anything if he had to, even a haunch of mutton-spawn.

"Swear, sister, on the tenets of Thoth," he said, pointing at a pile of papyri on a nearby table. "Swear you'll give me a son."

"I swear," Hatshepsut said.

It was good enough for him. Despite her swearing to tell the truth on a pile of papyri she believed to be sacred, she had never convinced him of her fidelity. He imagined several adulterous males hidden behind a curtain in her bedroom, bodies smeared with animal fat.

"Let us see what the gods bring," Kheper-Re said, listening to the sound of approaching footsteps. "Go to your bed and rest."

Hatshepsut removed an oil lamp from the dais and kissed him on the cheek. He offered his hand to Meryt, studying her slim, reedy body as it shivered with fear. Why were the untouchable so beautiful?

Vizier Ahmose entered, a gold seal bouncing against his breastplate. On its face was an engraving of the sacred Nile perch, an odd talisman for a noble.

"Cousin, I apologize for the delay. I have the last of the signatures," he said, walking forward with wide steps. "This sworn statement declares Prince Menkheperre, son of Lady Aset, as rightful heir. It also includes an addendum for Queen Hatshepsut. If she produces a son, hers will naturally inherit."

Kheper-Re studied Ahmose, a spirited man with a body made perfect by years of archery and heavy weapons—a body unlike his. "Then the lady Aset has earned the title of Great Royal Wife."

Ahmose wetted his lips and gave a jerky nod. "Cousin, your passion for the lady is blind to all reason—"

"Marriage is between two hearts, cousin."

"Marriage is a contract, my lord."

"I am supreme in all matters and I enact laws after Amun. I am the breath of Ra, his voice, his body."

"I do not deny that you enact laws, but I must deny the title of Great Royal Wife. It belongs to Queen Hatshepsut."

"The law does not prohibit two Great Royal Wives and nor do the gods. I know because I have asked them."

Kheper-Re watched Ahmose closely, determining anger in a reddening face. He wondered what juicy little secrets floated around that bald head of his, hidden so well beneath a striped headdress.

Ahmose lifted his chin, flaunting a playful smile. "If Queen Hatshepsut can have a healthy daughter, she can have a healthy son."

"Yes . . . yes, of course," Kheper-Re said, biting his lip. *She can have a healthy son off any man except me.*

"And the Queen is such a beauty and far surpasses any other lady of your household in intellect. What a son she would make."

"And the lady Aset?"

Ahmose shrugged, eyes sparkling. "She has no manners or morals. If she were mine, I would beat it out of her. You are too doting, like a boy in love."

"What has *love* got to do with the getting of a son?"

"Apparently, it has taken precedence. I understand you hardly seen the Queen."

"She was here a moment ago."

"You know what I mean."

"The moon was in its first quarter when I last lay with her." Kheper-Re refused to admit he hadn't touched her since. "It's an unlucky omen as well you know. I shall be lucky if she gives birth to a squirrel."

"We are ruled by superstition. I have never looked to the sky for permission to touch my wife. I have four sons, cousin. *Four*!"

Kheper-Re swallowed, pressing his lips tightly together. He did not wish to remind the Vizier he had five before one died in battle. "I'm encouraged. But the Queen is cold. Perhaps she has a lover if only I could prove it."

"*Invent* it, you mean."

Kheper-Re refused to quail under such scrutiny. He knew Ahmose had never met a challenge he could not conquer. "There is one she favors."

"Who?"

"Commander Shenq."

Ahmose snorted with laughter. "He's my finest soldier and no fool."

Kheper-Re pulled in his stomach and struggled to speak. Shenq was his champion—braver than Set. But it crossed his inebriated mind that he wasn't about to trust his sister around such a splendid stud. "If I find his cloak under her bed—"

"Your soldiers are more loyal than your harem maids," Ahmose said, throwing his head back in another bray of laughter.

"What of it?" Kheper-Re felt his forehead tighten. "Perhaps we should look closer, cousin, to the schoolroom."

"Senenmut? He's a clever man," said Ahmose. "Not well liked, I fear."

Kheper-Re recoiled even as he said the name. *Senenmut* . . . He was tutor to the princess, born of farming stock and little better than a goat. "Rumor has it my sister likes him very much. They say he has his ways of coming and going. I say only the Queen is privy to his coming."

Ahmose flapped a hand and sneered at the jibe. "It is in poor taste, my lord. They are merely jealous. She values his wisdom. That's all."

Kheper-Re hoped it was all. Only he couldn't help

feeling a bite of jealousy no matter which way he looked. *Jealousy.* He tried to drown the feeling in a cup of wine. Even his nobles were vying for his throne. "Tell me, why do you think Commander Osorkon asked for Kush?"

"He *asked* because he has family south of the first cataract if it pleases you, my lord."

"It doesn't please me. Nothing pleases me!" Something screamed inside Kheper-Re's head—the part of him that was unwilling to accept the truth. His nobles wanted power and they wanted him dead.

"It's all a game to him, isn't it?" Kheper-Re said, heat rising to his cheeks. "And he plays it for all its worth."

"It's worth a great deal," Ahmose said, nodding.

Kheper-Re stared enviously at the cheetah curled up beside him, head resting on its paws. There were no worries in his wooly head. "How long have you been Grand Vizier of Thebes?"

"Eleven years, my lord." Ahmose bowed low. "And I am truly honored."

Kheper-Re felt the prickle of tears in his eyes. In truth, he found it hard to deny Ahmose anything. "Don't thank me. I'm tired of your lectures. They are as contentious as they are long. Has Commander Shenq arrived?"

"He has indeed. He will be a great asset to your house, my lord."

Kheper-Re half-regretted his own inadequacy. He hated war and the posturing of high-ranking soldiers. It was far better to hide in his chambers, cowering under a blanket. He froze when he saw the beetle, scuttling along his forearm. With a flick of a finger, he tossed it into the brazier and watched it curl and hiss amidst the coals.

More omens, he thought, amazed at how many there were. "Will Shenq rid me of the barking jackal and the nightmares in my head? *Will* he?"

"He has a king's sword and he knows how to use it," Ahmose said, nodding. "And he'll avenge your broken soul."

TAU

Tau stood at the stern of a small boat, propelling the craft forward with the haft of his spear. He studied the villa in the river mist, walls burnished by the sinking sun. There was a leopard on the lintel and a familiar name beneath it, a name he often whispered in his darkest dreams.

Some years ago, a bier had once passed through those main gates with a trickle of mourners by its side. It had been a sad day for Commander Shenq. His wife had gone missing three days earlier and they found her body by the river, skull crushed by a mace. Tau chuckled as he remembered it but not half as much as when she screamed. Grief had no part in his world. He was immortal like the *shakāl*, the guardians of the dead, and if he wasn't immortal, he was certainly invisible.

A black heron probed among the shallows spreading its wings like a canopy to catch prey. It hardly moved as Tau leapt over the bow of the boat with a bundle under one arm. The boughs of a nearby sycamore groaned in the wind offering sanctuary to a nest of twigs.

He could have sworn he could smell pork and when he saw the carcass in the roasting pit, he smiled. The

43

Commander's houseboy had been eating forbidden meat and it wouldn't hurt to take a bone or two. For evidence.

Tau ran north along the river path, a well-trodden route the nobles used to access their villas by the river's edge. The gentle drone of a dragonfly alerted him to food and his tongue snatched the insect, crushing it on the roof of his mouth. He could smell eggs in the undergrowth and, parting a curtain of papyrus, he found the shallow burrows of storm petrels and the eggs they had left behind. He'd last seen the birds lifting into the sky like a flock of demons. They had seen him coming.

On this warm night in the first month of Pa-Shons, the raucous sounds of frogs stopped suddenly and a menacing whisper floated on the wind. Tau made the sign of the evil eye as his teeth crushed through the eggshell and he swallowed the yoke whole.

He crouched in the long grass beside the avenue of sphinx watching the new warriors of the Pharaoh's guard as they trudged towards the palace gates. Commander Shenq was at its rearguard, bow in hand, turning now and then as if he sensed something. They had arrived from the Migdol of the Sand Rabbit and here they would stay, protected by high walls unless they chose to wander outside.

Tau had waited too long of course, hunger getting the better of him, and he watched the doors slam shut knowing there would be other times. He nocked an arrow. It was worth getting to the heart of things. The broadhead struck the center of the lintel; a blood-red circle flanked by two cobra's heads and a pair of outstretched wings.

There, that will give them something to think about. It was sacrilege to defile the solar disk of Ra, especially as it was a symbol of protection.

Loneliness forced the beast to emerge, a vile creature that preyed on the most vulnerable. Tau's nostrils were splayed to the scent of his own filth and he longed for scrubs and sweet oils. Shaking out a woolen cloak, the body of a small cat tumbled into the mud. He stooped and grabbed the meal, biting into its abdomen and picking the hairs from his teeth. Thirst drove him to a nearby pool where he brushed the surface of the water with an outstretched hand. A face with a hollow eye socket reflected between the ripples and he flinched as he saw it. He had become the night, walking as a man at dawn and as a dog at dusk, a shadow that outwitted all shadows, a thief in the night to cast down kings.

Tau had learned to be left-eyed and to hold a bowstring in his left hand. But his sight was as fickle as a giggling whore in the darkness and he cursed the day he was blinded. The hollow in his head was packed with a ball of black faience fired with manganese, reflecting the vista it currently surveyed. Looking north along a narrow spit of land, he could see the palace pier and a line of flickering torches. There was no way in except under ground.

Horns announced a priestly procession to the sanctuary of Amun as the sun began to set and Tau wanted to see the Pharaoh, the frail-hearted monarch who had no use for his legs. There were statues of his likeness all over Thebes portraying limbs the size of tree-trunks. It was an entertaining substitute.

Mimicking the croaking sound of the sacred ibis—the call of a king to his subject—Tau attracted the attention of one priest. The man fell silently out of the ceremonial ranks and ran into the trees towards him.

"What news?" Tau said, imagining a Pharaoh's body on the embalmer's bench.

Puyem-re was dark-skinned beneath a smear of white paste, an obligation all priests had to honor the gods. He was a boyhood friend, abandoned in the same Bedouin camp as a child, and one whose heart was not as white as the linens he wore.

"Many things, great lord," Puyem-re said, pale eyes floating over Tau's body. "Oh gods, your face is a delight to me."

"Where's the Pharaoh?"

"He only visits the shrine at sunrise, master. Surely, you know that."

Tau had seen a tight formation of warriors that surrounded the Pharaoh's litter at dawn. The outermost rank twisted and turned like the wheels of a cart, bows drawn, eyes restless. All dressed in black and gold, these were the *Kenyt-Nisu*, an impenetrable body of men.

Puyem-re shuffled closer. "He has the sweats so the High Priest tells me. They say he can hardly walk."

"A little smoke is good for a fever." Tau narrowed his eyes to the gatehouse, wondering how well the tunnel would serve, how far it ran under the palace. The nobles would be good and warm if only he could stuff it with kindling and light a fire. "And how is our Queen?"

"She's the stronger of the two. She has a warrior heart."

"Is she beautiful?"

"She's like Isis, master. Only there's a dull-eyed tutor in her bed at night. She must have a son so they say."

Tau saw the humor in it and shrugged. "You'll convince her to dabble in magic. Tell her the spells will bring sons."

"I've given her potions. She dreams almost as much as her brother."

"Tell her the potions will make her immortal," Tau said. "And so will a dagger."

Puyem-re chuckled. "Poison is the way in, master."

Tau nodded. He was half-way in already. "Priests burn adulterous Queens, isn't that so?"

"Oh yes, master. They wrap the bodies in goatskin and drop them in shallow graves. They have no name."

Tau began to sweat. He would build a burning pyre of women on *dung-eaters'* island just to welcome his ships. There was so much to do. "Where are my armies?"

"All in good time, master. They'll be here before the feast of the New Moon."

"You promised they would be here before the Festival of Min."

"A great hawk told me they are eight miles south of the first cataract. The same great hawk told me your *Murrani* are already here."

The pride Alodian army had been camped seven miles south of the first cataract for more years than Tau cared to count, breeding with the local women and getting fat on the land. Now they were close and lead by the same great hawk they called the Panahasi.

"Where is my gold?"

"Your gold is in the north valley, master, where only you can find it."

"And my weapons?"

"You'll find plenty in the foothills. Look for a small tomb with the name *Sanakht* on the lintel. He was a doctor so they say. When you see a bow hooked to his statue, you will know your armies have arrived."

Tau was glad to hear it. Pharaoh Ka-Nekhet had gone to the Great Fields, his body laid to rest in a magnificent tomb—no one seeing, no one hearing. Only Tau *saw* and *heard* from a lofty roost all those years ago and killed eleven guards, smashing the outer door with his axe. But there were four more doors to access and two were false, and Tau had no time to smash them all before the Medjai came. He took what he could to the north valley where he found an abandoned tomb dedicated to a royal prince. It was the perfect place to hide it.

He watched crimson pennants fluttering at the palace gates, halyards slapping against the dowels. The noise disturbed a small kingfisher perched on a leafy node amongst the sycamores at the water's edge. It darted between the evergreens leaving behind an aroma of citrus and cypress.

"Tell me about the *Shasu* prophet?" Tau said, senses heightened by the scent.

"He's a mystery. Even I cannot pray him out. So we

play a little game. I bring the Pharaoh poisoned wine. And *Shasu* chases it away. Those are special eyes, master."

"Bring them to me."

Puyem-re bowed his head. "Your beloved warrior will bring them to you."

Tau pointed in the direction of a large villa in precinct of Khonsu, surrounded by a high wall and the object of his earlier scrutiny. "The Commander should beware the long-bolt. One day, it will be drawn by magic."

"You are a genius—"

"I saw these near the front gate," Tau said, holding out a pig's thigh and trotter. "Pork has never pleased the Pharaoh."

Puyem-re looked long and hard at Tau. "I'll be sure to tell him."

"And tell him there's a demon by the river, a spirit blacker than night. Go and tell him what you have seen."

Puyem-re inclined his head, eyes flicking towards the shrine. "Stay out of sight, master" he advised.

Tau nodded. Daytime was filled with the deep twang of bows and he wasn't about to be decorated with black-feathered shafts. He caressed a collar of bones and teeth, conjuring magic of the deepest kind. Ten thousand Alodians would march on Thebes soon, burning the city gates to the ground.

He ran through the underground until he found the canal and he crouched to catch his reflection in one of the pools. It was there he saw the child some way off, brown as a nut, collecting pebbles in the shallows. The waters were greener than the leaves in the glow of sunset and the heat of the day still rose from the earth. The child watched the *dung-eaters*, counting them with a finger, and loading a sling, she struck one in the chest with a pebble. The bird went down with a growl, blood pouring from an open wound. It was a male thankfully and not the large female Tau had nurtured.

He flexed hard muscles honed from carrying the

heaviest of weapons and, grinding his teeth, he approaching like a wolf on the prowl. The child looked up at the sound of snapping twigs and her honey-colored eyes darted back and forth until she saw him.

Tau's knuckles strained against a tight fist and he held back, savoring the moment when she would see the knife and run. She was unable to stand, unable to scream and the atmosphere was as thick as the sludge he stood in. But she had seen the knife in his fist and she knew how close he would need to get.

There she was, owl-eyed and twitching, and there wasn't a bump of womanhood on her bony chest. Tau hoped she wouldn't cry like a peacock when he plunged the blade into her little belly. His heart raced as he crouched slightly and then he lunged. It was too soon, he knew, but it was worth the pleasure of a chase because she would run and he would catch her. That's how it was with children. They were quick when threatened.

She jumped backwards and turned rapidly, winding between the grass stems into a thicket, light as an impala on her feet. He was enjoying the chase until a branch snapped back and caught him in the face, grazing the only eye he had. All he could see between the grasses was a tiny shape as it sped onwards, disappearing into the trees. She often met Khemwese at the end of his watch, taking him home to her mother for a bowl of broth.

That's where she'll go, he thought, thundering through the undergrowth and along the river path.

There she was running ahead, a little brown slip of a girl with a mass of dark curls. She was close enough to have stopped at some point, turning no doubt to see if he was following. She wasn't afraid, not like the women he'd killed before.

I'll give you afraid, he thought, charging like a bull with a crazed longing.

There was only one person he killed each time he saw a woman and that was the one that left him with the

Bedouins, the one that nursed him as a babe.

The little girl ran down off the path to a lane that led to the village, and Tau took off after her, crashing through a veil of leaves and stopping suddenly as he burst into a clearing. He hesitated, seeing only shadows and the last rays of sunlight before the Atum slipped beneath the horizon.

"Dog-man!"

He heard the yell, the distorted voice as if the words were too hard to pronounce. *She's deaf,* he thought. *This tiny child is deaf.* But she must have heard something. A snapping twig, a high-pitched whistle unless her senses went beyond his.

He never saw the pebble as it careened through the branches, smacking him hard in the mouth.

HATSHEPSUT

Sixty calcite bowls provided the only light on this hot summer night, oil lamps flickering in their yellow-veined bellies. Queen Hatshepsut sat on her terrace, listening to the deep tones of the drums and a single pipe carrying the sad strain of summers past. Handmaids swayed to the steady beat and all the while, a breeze spilled into the chamber bringing with it the fresh scents of the garden.

Hatshepsut studied the court singer, shorthaired and sturdy and skin darker than ash. Bunefer was the daughter of a royal scullery maid though what was *royal* about a scullery maid, Hatshepsut couldn't fathom. A little girl twirled at her feet, plump arms outstretched. *Such a precious child*, Hatshepsut thought, marveling at cheeks dimpled with a smile. She had brought a basket of star-berries as a gift.

What is it that makes the berries flicker like lanterns? A full moon was what her mother said. They were bright yellow in color, dripping amongst the glossy leaves of the *Nebes* tree. Some were cloudy and bitter, and too many turned the belly inside out. There was such beauty in poison.

Hatshepsut toyed with a mirror in her lap, occasionally holding it up to examine her reflection and sometimes to study the maid behind her. There was no art in Meryt's appearance, no kohl about the eyes and no wig for hair. Most maids enjoyed court banter, most tried to return it. But here she was, hands clasped in front and stiff with terror.

Hatshepsut's eyes snapped to the door when she saw Inet, red-face and stumbling with a cup in one hand. She was late of course.

"Where have you been?" Hatshepsut said, dismissing the women all except Meryt.

Nurse Inet drained the goblet slowly and wiped her mouth with a finger. She waited until the last of musicians departed. "With your glorious brother," she said.

Inet's eyes were lost in the sparkling fabric of a hanging drape before she shuffled towards Hatshepsut's bed, a wooden frame that resembled a flagship in all but a mast. She fell amongst the cushions and chuckled for a time, rubbing her fat ankles with a free hand.

"He's well, I hope?" Hatshepsut said, betrayal rocking her mind to the core.

"A little sickly but the fever will pass."

"He has a fever?"

"It will pass," Inet repeated, swinging her feet over the side of the bed and never once letting go of her cup. "He's a little pale though."

"He's been pale all his life," Hatshepsut muttered, wondering if a ride in his chariot would bring the blood to his cheeks. She nodded at the cupbearer and pointed at Inet's outstretched cup. "Did he have any news?"

"News? Oh, I forget. There was something."

Hatshepsut inclined her head, hoping to hear what that *something* was. She pretended to look at the reflection of the moon, glossy and full, on the surface of the river and she thought she saw a perch knifing through the swell. There was a man dressed in a black wool cloak crouching in the shadows beyond the alchemist's garden. It was the guard, she thought, so diligent in his duties. She wanted to shout a greeting only she had forgotten his name.

"Now I remember," Inet said, all perky Hatshepsut could spit. "Commander Shenq is home."

Shenq . . . Hatshepsut swung her head round. She savored a vision of copper thighs corded with muscle and arms so thick they could wield a sword for hours. "When did he arrive?"

"Three days ago."

Three days ago? "Why didn't you tell me?" Hatshepsut glimpsed a secret smile over Inet's shrug.

"I wanted to spare you any shame."

Hatshepsut remembered Shenq's rejection like a punch in the gut. She knew she wasn't beautiful, not like Aset. When she looked in the mirror she saw brown eyes flecked with gold and a chin pointed like the butt of an almond. Senenmut once told her brains were the way to a man's heart not beauty. She wondered if it were true.

"Are you pleased?" Inet said.

"Pleased?" Hatshepsut was ecstatic. She couldn't stop thinking of amber eyes beneath a sweep of lashes. They were kind eyes.

"He won't like you now, not with a child in your belly. You'll have to learn some tricks." Inet grinned, flicking her tongue from side to side and snapping it on the roof of her mouth.

"He's never liked me. Not like that."

"You're the *Queen*. Of course he likes you." Inet chucked her chin at Hatshepsut's belly. "This child is further along than I thought. It's not the Pharaoh's, is it?"

"Swear you won't tell. Swear on all the gods."

Inet spared her a sidelong look, eyes wider than before. "I swear."

Hatshepsut loved the light in Inet's eyes, the hennaed hair that peeked out from behind a yellow scarf. Her face had never changed since taking Hatshepsut to her breast. Oily skin, that's what it was. Women never aged when they had oily skin.

"I had to do it." Hatshepsut glowered, eyes circling the room. An oil lamp sputtered in the breeze and the sound made her jumpy. "Pharaoh can't . . . ."

Hatshepsut wouldn't say what the Pharaoh couldn't do. How the desire had gone, how boredom spreading across his face every time she touched him.

"Girl, this child will not save you," Inet said. "Nothing will save you."

"I need *sons*. Can't you see? Aset has his heart—"

"And you have his mind since he's released himself of it."

Pharaoh disliked the priests and their omens, hiding instead in his apartments and bowing to a frenzy of fornication. Egypt needed a warrior for a king. She was that *warrior* so Puyem-re said.

"Don't you think Kheper-Re looks thinner? It's his legs," Hatshepsut said, attempting a compassionate wince. "He can hardly walk."

"He's the Pharaoh. He doesn't have to walk."

"He looks so . . . so weak like he's dying." He had grass for legs and a belly full of wine. It was a wonder he could speak.

"He's not dying," Inet said. "He drinks too much that's all."

"He might die before the New Year. If he does, I'll become regent for Prince Menkheperre." Hatshepsut leaned forward and lowered her voice. "And if the prince dies, I shall be Pharaoh."

Inet snorted her disdain. "Careful, child. You'll rouse the gods."

"My brother is the runt of a maidservant. *I* am true-blood. The priests know it and so do the people."

Hatshepsut thought of Puyem-re through a haze of excitement. He had given her enough poison to put a cow to sleep, only her brother merely vomited as if purging from a fever. She had given smaller doses in the beginning not enough for him to taste and now his food was so sweet he couldn't taste anything at all. It was a slow death mimicking river sickness in all but sweats.

The faint murmur of a fountain in the gardens trickled her name, even the priests said she would be the first of all living creatures, rising up as the Pharaoh of the Two Lands as Amun ordained. It was partly true if she could make them all believe it.

"Keep your voice down, girl," Inet said, hand flying to her chest. "You can fool the people but not me. There'll be talk."

"Talk? What kind of talk?"

"A woman can never be Pharaoh. Who's heard of such a thing?"

Hatshepsut was too agitated to think. She let a smile slip from her face but she thought twice before sharing a wink. "Women have ruled before," she murmured.

"As regents," Inet reminded.

"Then I shall be the first woman-king. Let's see if I'm right."

Hatshepsut caressed the narrow stem of her cup, decorated with a snake. It curled around the base like a boa crushing its prey, like long fingers around the Pharaoh's neck. The stain of blood on her hands would last for eternity unless she could find a scapegoat. Poison had been the only alternative and she had found the means. She lifted both shoulders as if conscious of a chill.

"What is it, child?" The nurse narrowed her eyes, legs still swinging over the edge of the bed.

"Nothing. . . It's nothing."

Hatshepsut felt her face pucker, throat pulsing with a rush of bile. She understood the intricacies of emotion, casting hers aside so it never stood in the way of what she wanted. And she *wanted* the throne.

"Undress me," she said to Meryt.

She felt delicate fingers around her waist as Meryt untied her gown and swept it over a chair. The girl was huge-eyed with innocence, too beautiful to stand beside her. No doubt she wanted her freedom. What slave girl didn't?

"Have you seen my emerald ring?"

"Emerald ring, my lady?" Meryt asked.

"Greener than your eyes, girl, and the size of my thumbnail." There was no emerald ring much as Hatshepsut desired one.

"I have never seen it, my lady."

"It was here this morning," Hatshepsut said, exchanging scowls with Inet. "Find it and I will give you a house of your own."

The girl's eyes began to shine and her body flinched. "Yes, my lady," she said, bowing her head and rushing for a large cedar chest in the corner of the room. The sound of clinking necklaces made Hatshepsut smile and she ignored the shaking of Inet's head.

"Not there?" Hatshepsut asked.

"No, my lady," Meryt stammered. "I don't see it."

"Go, give me some peace. Look again tomorrow."

Hatshepsut slept hard that night in her wood-carved bed with Inet on the floor beside her. Senenmut's arms were warm against her shoulders and when she heard the knock on the door, the sky was already the color of pomegranate.

"Dress me, quickly!" she whispered, tapping Inet with her foot.

The nurse merely snored and Hatshepsut helped herself to a fresh tunic from an open chest. Still heady with spite from the night before, she saw Meryt amongst the women, placing a bowl of goat's cheese on a short-legged table. "Open the door, girl!"

Puyem-re rushed in, cloak sweeping the floor. "Greetings, my Queen," he said, bowing low.

Hatshepsut could tell nothing from his face when he lifted it, tight-lipped and pale as if he may have brought bad news. "What is it?"

"Amun has spoken. I have dreamed."

"What have you dreamed?"

"The sword is drawn, your majesty. The ancients have consented."

Hatshepsut dismissed her attendants with a wave. Her brow was tight with a frown. "What are you saying, priest."

"Amun has confirmed the succession, my sweet lady. The throne does not belong to your brother or your stepson. It belongs to you."

Hatshepsut slapped both hands against her mouth and gasped. Only Amun knew her deepest secrets and he had sent a priest to sanction them. "I've prayed for this day. We've prayed, haven't we Senenmut?"

Senenmut sat bolt upright in the bed and yawned. He dragged a hand through an unruly mass of brown hair. "Will the Counsel of Thoth agree?"

"They will agree if I have dreamed," Puyem-re said, flinching at the sight of him. "You are a farm-boy, what would you know?"

Senenmut raised his chin and eyed the priest with daring. "At least I bathe and dress as befits my status." He was naked.

"Look at him," Puyem-re said, pointing. "Can't you see he's climbing your ladder, my lady? He's almost reached the top."

Hatshepsut chuckled. They were all so jealous of him. "Tell me about this dream?"

Puyem-re bowed low, "Many years ago during the month of Panipt, Amun-Ra found Queen Ahmose asleep in her bed. She was like a goddess and as beautiful as a lotus. He anointed her with perfumes and you were conceived."

"Very original," interrupted Senenmut, stony face brightening. "But will they buy it."

"Of course they'll buy it. The Oracle of Amun has confirmed the succession." Puyem-re held up a gnarled finger, blackened with ink. "Queen Hatshepsut will be

Pharaoh of Egypt before the year is out. It's her father's will and the will of Amun-Ra."

"Yes!" Hatshepsut hissed, pressing her hands together.

"Aren't we forgetting something," Senenmut said, lower lip protruded, giving him the appearance of a glowering schoolboy. "Pharaoh Kheper-Re still lives."

"What about the tonics?" Hatshepsut said.

"I'm puzzled." Puyem-re shrugged, eyes drifting downwards. "A paste of dung is deadly when mixed with wine. But when rubbed on the body—"

"He was supposed to drink it," Hatshepsut said, feeling a knot in her stomach. For years, her brother was a helpless target and now Commander Shenq had reinforced his armor.

"Animal dung does not belong in wine or beer, my lady." Senenmut shook his head and smiled in that mischievous way of his. "It should be mixed with food."

"And what if it doesn't work?" Hatshepsut sighed wearily.

"She has a point," Senenmut said, lips curling in vague bemusement. "A rather big one. What if his taster dies? Won't it be obvious?"

"I shall say it's a plague, a contagion. Who can disagree?" Puyem-re said. "I'm confident he'll be dead before the New Year and our glorious Queen will be Pharaoh."

Hatshepsut pursed her lips and tried to think. "What about Commander Shenq?" The question was fair even though it was met with two pairs of staring eyes. "Well, what about him?"

Puyem-re offered a condescending smile. "We must distract him, my Queen. We must bring him into *our* camp. I think he'll be most obliging."

Hatshepsut realized they were losing the thread. This was a warrior capable of elaborate battle plans and executing them with great style. "He won't do it."

"He will, my lady. We've got him by the throat."

Hatshepsut began to circle Puyem-re like a cat, eyes narrowing with every step. She wanted to grab his tunic and hold him within an inch of her face. He should have been more afraid of her. "Your life is so easy, priest. You carry a torch for the god every morning, wash Amun's statue and seal the shrine at dusk. You eat a side of ox almost every day and all you have to do is see into the future. If you could truly *see* you would know Shenq is not a camp-follower."

Puyem-re glanced down the bridge of his nose and sniffed. "He cannot refuse a message of love. No man can."

"What are you saying?" said Senenmut, sidling closer to Hatshepsut.

"I'm saying, the Queen must seduce him. I'm saying, she must destroy him."

SHENQ

Shenq was exhausted by a sleepless night. Pharaoh had tossed and turned in his canopied bed, sobbing like the child he was. An arrow had found its way to the front gate, peeling off a large chunk of paint from the symbol of the sun. It was a sacrilegious act that would cost a few heads.

It was evening, a feast day in honor of the princess and a celebration of her first blood. Attendants carried baskets of roasting meat and exotic fruit and there was a dead peacock in the center of the Pharaoh's table still dressed in its feathers.

Shenq sat with Commander Osorkon in the first court, glancing at the colossal statues of the gods with their red skin and mysterious smiles. "Four of my men have deserted, sir," he said, long legs straddling a bench.

"They're nomads, Shenq. They survive the harshest climates and have the grit of a camel." Commander Osorkon drained a cup of wine, fleshy fingers wrapped around a goblet. "They'll simply return to their homelands, or what's left of them."

"What makes you so sure?" Shenq asked, studying the bronze breastplate of his companion. Wrought in fish-scale armor, it barely covered his portly frame.

"They are what they are. Wanderers. Free spirits." Osorkon licked a greasy bone and grinned.

Shenq swallowed back a cup of wine. His throat was suddenly dry. "If I were to desert, the fortress at Daben would be my choice. The garrison oversees northbound ships and they have the monopoly on all trade goods. It would make the perfect hideout for a deserter, a deserter with a cause."

"They're *nomads*, Shenq, drifting on the wind. They have no cause."

"Then I pray they don't find their way back to Thebes. They'll bring armies with them if they do.

"They're heading south where they belong." Osorkon lifted his chin, sporting a smile that danced about fat lips. He was suddenly distracted by a girlish squeal and his eyes shot to the Pharaoh's table.

Kheper-Re sat on a high dais, mouth twisted in laugher. He toasted the lady Aset on his left and patted her thigh. There was no hiding their love even as Kheper-Re handed the lady a necklace of Ombos gold and kissed her neck as he tied it.

Shenq could feel the heat of Hatshepsut's eyes and his heart rate increased to a steady hammer. Turning his head to elude her, he nodded at Osorkon's lieutenant, hoping for an opportunity to talk privately.

The warrior was dressed in the blue shúkàs of the moon-warriors and his head was a drape of braids. Mkasa was a full-blooded Makurae orphaned by the time he was seven years old. The Alodians plundered his village some fifteen years ago and he was forced to watch his mother and sister burn until the Egyptians came to free what was left of them. Vizier Ahmose adopted him and brought him home, and Shenq loved him as his own brother.

"I gather Pharaoh has employed General Pen-Nekhbet to watch the precincts," Commander Osorkon said. "I doubt any rebels will get through. It should be a quiet year."

"Not necessarily, sir," Shenq said. "My Captain found an arrow in the sun disk last night. Dead center it was. Must have been a good archer."

"Irritated farmer more like. Their tithes are higher this year than last." Osorkon gave a rough cackle as if his lungs were filled with water. "I asked for Kush, Shenq. I shouldn't have bothered."

Shenq grinned at that. There was a miles-worth of difference between *bold* and *stupid.* A noble never asked the Pharaoh for a promotion no matter how obvious it was.

"The southern tribes are not asking me to be Viceroy," Osorkon said, lowering his voice. "They're begging. They need a man to lead them, one that knows their culture. I have an order with over a thousand signatures. Will you sign it?"

"An order? On whose authority?"

"Think, Shenq, *think* of what we could do. You and I, Commanders of Thebes, going out against Kush. These are exciting times."

"You forget, I'm relegated to a balcony, sir. How exciting can that be?"

"Do it for form's sake." Osorkon stood and handed Shenq the petition. "I'll return to central command at Buhen and hand in the city keys. Put in a good word for me."

"I will, sir," Shenq said.

Osorkon glanced at the Pharaoh with a tired eye. "The Pharaoh has a new scribe and a bodyguard by his side. He must be re-writing the Book of the Dead."

Shenq sniggered and watched his old commander as he strode off towards the door. A younger man would have torn out a throat for that promotion only this one labored over useless petitions, hoping for a few signatures more. He snapped his fingers at Mkasa, drawing him to a secluded corner. "What news?"

"The Alodians want war," Mkasa said, crossing his arms. There was a small gap in his front teeth that forced a gentle lisp. "If we don't fight now, it will be too late. The arrow is proof enough."

Shenq gazed at smoke-darkened eyes. Mkasa was a seal-bearer, wearing the talisman of a Nile perch. It deterred the tribesman from touching him and it glinted against his breastplate like a winking eye. "Some of my men have gone missing. Where do you think they are?"

"A military allowance doesn't make up for much, sir," Mkasa said. "Their allegiance is to Tau."

Shenq watched the skyline where broad strips of pale blue hung over the horizon. "Where is he?"

"My agents tell me he's living in the marshes. He's a whoremonger by the smell of him and spends a great deal of time watching. He's very interested in you."

"Me?"

"He's a man with one eye, sir. And there aren't many of those." Mkasa lifted a hand to turn the disc of lapis in his earlobe. "He's a stinking lecher and the boy with him."

Shenq knew the warrior would find him one day especially with the help of a few spearmen in his company. "The boy?"

"Jabari's younger brother. You can't blame him for seeking better pastures."

Shenq wouldn't blame him at all. "He's broken his oath. He's forfeited an honest promotion. Tau's bought him with traitor's gold."

"Honest promotions don't bring much, sir. My captain earned a goat last month and a small quail. There wasn't much flesh on either."

Shenq agreed only he didn't say so. "I should have killed Tau when I had the chance."

"You were a boy then. And a lousy shot."

Mkasa's tongue was sharper than a kudu horn and Shenq colored with shame. "There'll be no mercy for him a second time."

KHEMWESE

Khemwese stood at the gatehouse of the palace watching the sunrise and a full moon, big and round like a hollow eye socket in the sky. In Alodia, they likened the sun to a great dog that chased the moon-ball around the earth and sometimes on good days, they shared the same sky.

A woman passed through the gate with a small child. The court-singer they called her and a widow he knew. She was tall and sturdy with a proud expression and he liked her as soon as he saw her. Only he had no idea where she lived. He had a feeling he would be sure to find out.

He munched on bread and bowls of stew with Harran at his side. The boy had a scar above one eye, stitched with animal gut. He had been bathing in a canal and saying his prayers when Pabasa attacked him, full of bluster and wine, and muttering something about a good set of eyes. The Alodian spent the night in a cell after a good flogging and fed scraps from the Commander's table. They weren't much, just scratchings and the like. And now he was out again, only it wasn't right in Khemwese's opinion. The warrior was dangerous and up to no good.

"Receive the sun and take up your spears!" Captain

Tehute shouted as he inspected the men.

It was the same drill each day. When the horns sounded, the palace gates opened and Jabari escorted the warriors to their stations. Only today had the smell of crypts and dead things, and for a moment Khemwese wasn't sure if he wanted to go inside.

He sensed Pabasa beside him, muscles tense and breathing through a half-closed mouth. Ribbons of steam rose from his chest and he stared at a water buffalo struggling against the river current, chin resting on the surface of the water.

"Do you think he'll make it," Khemwese whispered, staring at the beast.

"Too many crocodiles," Pabasa muttered.

Khemwese gripped his spear and watched the Captain with a careful eye. "I saw you talking to the Chief of Prophets yesterday," he whispered. "What did he want?"

"It wasn't the Chief of Prophets."

Khemwese was sure it was. There was a man outside Pabasa's door at night smeared in white paint with a hood over his head. "I saw him through the door."

"You can't see in the dark."

"I never said it was dark." Khemwese wanted to laugh at that, only he remembered hearing Pabasa arguing with his wife shortly afterwards. He only lived next door. "How is Osumare?"

"She has no heart for me. It's the shepherd she loves."

"Harran," Khemwese corrected. "His name is *Harran*."

"I should have taken his eyes out when I had the chance," Pabasa snarled, leaning heavily on his spear "He had no right to look at her."

Had? Khemwese had an admission at last. "You had no right to attack him."

"I'll kill every stinking *Shasu* and every woman I can get my hands on," he said, loud enough for Harran to hear. "And I'll kill you too."

"Why me?" It was a fair question. Khemwese had done nothing to deserve a killing.

"I know who you are. Don't think I didn't hear our king's words, *before God, I declare my son*. If the Pharaoh knew, he'd boil your head in oil."

"But he doesn't know, does he?"

Pabasa stabbed his temple with a finger. "You don't remember how he died do you?"

Khemwese felt a deep restlessness and saw only black. All dishonorable things were done in the darkness . . . "We were blindfolded," he murmured. He remembered that much.

"We were blindfolded so we wouldn't see our king die. So we would never know who killed him."

Khemwese refused to be bitter. War meant death and that's what they had come for. He could still smell the blood under his feet all those years ago even before they took the blindfolds off. When he tried to remember all he saw was a blank face. In a way he was glad.

Captain Tehute advanced and looked them both in the eye before passing down the ranks. Khemwese sighed loudly, smelling the lentil broth and fat-soaked bread from where he stood. They had eaten goose stuffed with figs the night before. There was no end to the Pharaoh's generosity and all he had to do was wait inside Ra's chamber at daytime and go home at dusk. *No man must look on the face of the Pharaoh whilst he sleeps. He becomes Ra in the darkness.*

Khemwese felt something in the hollow of his gut, a warning sign. Pabasa's threat played in his mind like a bad song. *I'll kill every stinking Shasu and every woman I can get my hands on. And I'll kill you too.*

Without hesitating he broke through the lines and sprinted along the avenue of sphinx to the river path, ignoring the Captain's shouts behind him. He scanned the swaying sedge for landed perch amongst the stems. Sometimes he found one snagged by the water's edge and fat enough to eat.

He stopped outside Osumare's house, pressing his forehead against the lintel. He had no gift to offer her but he shouted her name all the same. It was quiet inside, too quiet for his liking.

Girls like her don't go to the well with the other women. No, they're shunned and must cover their faces.

He pushed the door open and stood for a moment adjusting to the darkness of a single room. There was a flickering lamp in the household niche light enough to see a three-legged stool in the corner and a small hard bed to sleep on. Taking the lamp, he stooped under the frail ribs of the ceiling inhaling the musty stench of mud brick and he shouted up the stairs to the roof above. But there was no one there.

He padded to the storage room at the back of the house where two full-bellied jars stood to attention. Between them a woman lay face-down on the floor. His head jerked back when he saw her, eyes pale and staring as if they didn't recognize him. He whispered her name in short hard breaths, waiting for a voice in the darkness.

"Osumare," he murmured, touching her hair.

It was then he saw the coil of rope around her neck, a matted garrote. She couldn't have done this herself. She had been spurned enough to try.

Khemwese looked up at the beams and saw a claw of metal. It was too meager for her weight and not high enough to hang a hog. He was afraid at what he had found, afraid at what the villagers might do if they caught him there. It couldn't have been Pabasa. She had been dead too long for that.

By the look of torn fingernails, she had fought her attacker and there was blood on her thighs—the grotesque marks of rape.

Khemwese sobbed as he broke through the open door, gasping for fresh air and he ran along the river path towards the palace, stopping beneath a palm tree to catch his breath

A black kite perched on the fulcrum of two branches, white flecks looped across its back like a stately collar. As the sun's rays seeped through the trees, a movement in the undergrowth disturbed the bird and it lifted from the roost, coasting between the pinnate leaves and whinnying in rapid sequence.

Khemwese heard a war cry, thick and threatening, like the dry crack of thunder. And that's when he saw the man, chest raked with fresh scars and skin blacker than the midnight sky.

Tau . . . stinking rotting, Tau.

Khemwese unsheathed his dagger and hurled himself at Tau. All he could see was a lopsided grin as they collided, air filled with grunts and shouts. Khemwese poured all his strength into the attack, blade biting thin air as he twisted and turned.

That's all he remembered until he collapsed, struck in the leg from behind. Mud and grit sprayed into his face and he tried to roll sideways as the silhouette of a knife slashed his forearm. The wound burned like a spider bite as he was pushed beneath the shallows straddled by a weight that made his lungs burn for air.

With an angled thrust, he forced his dagger into hard muscle and the load on his back shifted unexpectedly. Tau was fast, Khemwese would give him that. And he was even faster as he lurched for the trees running to who knows where.

Khemwese caught his breath and staggered to his feet. His back was soaked in blood but there was no pain except in his arm. He couldn't fathom how far he ran along the avenue of sphinx or how long it was until he heard the sound of hooves behind him. Vizier Ahmose had returned from a hunt with Commander Shenq, arms stained with blood to the elbow and carrying a frame of dead oryx.

Shenq patted the dun horse he rode, fingers caressing the dorsal stripe which ran along its back. He was clothed in the textiles of the gods, a bolt of color in a drab desert. He dismounted and shouted to an attendant to bring water for his horse and he saluted to the Vizier who went on ahead with the small group, grimy and bursting with laughter.

"Rinse the cavity," Shenq said to an attendant, pointing at the field-dressed carcass. "Pharaoh will eat the tongue and thigh for supper."

Khemwese dared not look at the Commander's eyes, magnificent in their way, but he felt them burning at the slash on his forearm.

"You should behind the Pharaoh's door," Shenq shouted. "Are you a deserter or are you just late?"

Khemwese felt himself swallow, mind coated with fear. "She's dead," he panted, trying to fight back tears. "Osumare . . . She's dead."

SHENQ

The hunt at dawn was unsuccessful. Shenq's horse had bolted twice, tearing off into the desert with rolling eyes and the deeper they had pressed into the trees, the less oryx they could find. Something had spooked them away from at their favorite watering hole and Shenq wanted to know what it was.

The audience chamber was thick with incense and a group of priests stood beside the Pharaoh's throne, incisors spewing out more with each wave. Shenq couldn't help feeling like a prisoner held against his will. Osumare was dead and Khemwese had narrowly escaped a flogging. He hadn't done it, of course, and neither had Pabasa. It was the demon in the woods, the *man-dog* as the villagers called him.

"A woman is dead you say?" Kheper-Re said to the Vizier. There was terror in his dark eyes as they flashed around the room, bouncing from man to man.

"Yes, my lord," Vizier Ahmose said. "She was violated."

"You say my bodyguard found the woman?"

"He did, my lord."

Shenq knew Khemwese hadn't been himself since

finding Osumare. But there was good news. Tau wouldn't be too hard to find, especially now he was wounded. He had used two good legs to run from Khemwese's dagger which suggested he was gored in the belly or higher.

Shenq hoped the Pharaoh would send him out to find the *man-dog* instead of having to spend long weeks in the palace shooting nothing but rabbits from the balcony. By the look of it, the fishermen on the river had more fun than he did.

Kheper-Re clasped his hands and cleared his throat. "Have they caught the man?"

"It wasn't a man, my lord."

"Then what was it?"

"A dog."

Shenq stifled a smile. He knew what was coming next. The Pharaoh had the imagination of a twelve-year-old and the jumpiness that went with it.

"Can a dog do that?" Kheper-Re looked around the room for confirmation. "Throttle a woman."

"You say your dreams are littered with wild animals and hordes of angry men, cousin. Yet our commanders have sighted no unlawful armies." Vizier Ahmose sent the Pharaoh a glare that promised a reckoning. "There's a dog out there, you said so yourself. It would be advisable to send your best man before it's too late."

Pharaoh sat with the same bewildered look on his face, reaching for the Queen's hand. His eyes seemed to search the room as if the whole world had passed him by. "There are hundreds of soldiers posted along the river. Are they blind?"

"They don't know what to look for," Ahmose said, rather ominously Shenq thought. "There is one I recommend."

Kheper-Re's eyes brushed over the gathering and settled on Shenq. "You don't think—"

"I most certainly do. Commander Shenq knows exactly what to look for. He's the only one to have seen him. This dog wants someone."

"Of course he wants something! You don't think he's just chewing bones and lying about in the sun. He's a god slayer!"

"My lord," Ahmose said, raising a hand. "He wants *someone.*"

"He won't get me," Kheper-Re said, snatching a fig from an attendant's tray and chewing rather loudly.

"Not *you*, Great Bull."

Kheper-Re looked relieved and insulted at the same time. "Then who?"

Ahmose seemed to flex the fingers on his sword hand. "Commander Shenq."

Shenq almost felt the ground rumble beneath his feet before the outburst came. Any mention of his name was worse than blasphemy now.

"I won't part with him, do you hear! If my armies are incompetent, replace them. If my walls are not high enough, raise them. Burn the marshes if you have to. Find him!"

Tau had gone to ground and Shenq wondered if they needed shovels not spears. The soldiers searched the marshes every day, finding little more than fish heads and half-eaten rabbits, and a stewpot likely left by a traveler. There was nothing to suggest an army gathering amongst the trees.

"There's a knot in my belly," Kheper-Re said, sucking in breath. "It's bigger now than before. I asked Harran to read the stars, to pray, to meditate, anything to relieve me of the burden. He's a prophet of HaShem. Surely the Great God knows something. Only he keeps talking about the sacred sycamores. They're dying, cousin. I'm dying."

"You can't be dying, my lord. You're immortal."

Kheper-Re dabbed his eyes with a napkin. "If they die, I shall die."

"Those are some old trees," Ahmose said, voice low. "They won't die."

The High Priest took over for a time, talking of the history of the first sapling and all talk of trees made Shenq yawn. He allowed his eyes to feast on the girl kneeling at the Queen's feet. Wrapped in a green sheath and draped in seed pearls, her breasts were no bigger than a man's fist. He would like to fondle those breasts if he could, only she was a child and he began to muse over his chances.

"Her name's Meryt," whispered Vizier Ahmose, shoulder pressed against Shenq's. "Beautiful, isn't she?"

"She's a ward of the Queen."

"She has a good heart. She has good hips. Don't let the Pharaoh see you looking. He'd cut his way through a tangle of roots to get to her first."

"She's from Geshen. He won't touch her."

"*Shasu*? He'd rut a goat if he could."

Shenq raised an eyebrow and absorbed that in silence. He was ashamed to let his guard down even for a moment but he was unable to conceal a bubbling joy. "I could meet her in the women's gardens."

Ahmose shifted on sore feet. "They're not exactly open to the public, Shenq. It's a harem. Not an aviary."

"What if I paid a eunuch?"

"Since a eunuch has lost more than his pride, a deben of silver should do it." Ahmose scratched a hooked nose and stared at the ceiling.

"Gone are the days when any of us won several hundred hands and a bowl of foreskins," Shenq said, keeping his voice low. "Queen Ati of Punt sent fifty gold shields last week. Pity we can't use them."

"Our glorious Pharaoh has no time for war. He says our borders are wide enough."

"Look at him. No wonder he thinks he's dying. He's being poisoned."

"Of course he is. It's those priests. They're hiding all kinds of things in clods of manure."

A horn sounded and Kheper-Re clapped his hands. "Call the prophet!" he yelled.

Harran appeared dressed in a tunic and striped *tallit*. The stiff bow he gave the Pharaoh caused a modest murmur and Shenq saw the Chief of Prophets stiffen.

"Stand and prostrate yourself before Ra," Puyem-re commanded through clenched teeth. Shenq noticed mud spatters on the hem of his long shenti and his white painted skin seemed to ooze with sweat.

Harran merely bowed his head. He took no notice of the priest's clucking tongue. "Tell me your dream, my lord,"

Kheper-Re dropped his head, letting it sag over his chest. His passing of gas was so loud, Shenq was convinced he could go out in the desert and call antelope.

"Night after night," Kheper-Re said, "I dream of blood, waves of it surging over the dunes towards the palace. What does it mean?"

Too many eggs, Shenq thought. It was no wonder Pharaoh felt light-headed and weak. He ate raw eggs to thicken his semen and according to the doctors it was now the color of yoke.

"Alodians, my lord," Harran confirmed.

"Alodians?" interrupted Puyem-re. "Here's a man that doesn't prostrate himself before the Great Bull of Thebes and the best he can say is, *Alodians*?"

Shenq studied Harran wondering what was going on between those thick eyebrows. The boy was a marvel. He was honest too.

Kheper-Re held up a hand. "Let him speak."

"My lord," Harran said, "there have been sightings of men wearing red shúkàs, shaking spears and rawhide shields. They are a warring group, hard not to notice in the desert."

"How many?" Kheper-Re asked.

"Four hundred perhaps."

"Do you hear, priest?" Pharaoh bellowed. "Four hundred duskies trampling a path towards Thebes. My men will chew them up and spit them out."

Puyem-re seemed rankled by the comment and rubbed the wide dome of his forehead. "My lord—"

"It is a shame you didn't bring word from Amun," Kheper-Re said, chin tilted. "Surely, Amun speaks to you?"

"He speaks to me all the time, my lord," Puyem-re said, inclining his head. It was a half-bow and Pharaoh wasn't much fond of *half* anything.

"And you," Pharaoh said, pointing at Harran. "Does Amun speak to you?"

"It is HaShem I hear," Harran replied with a chill in his voice. "He is the God that sees."

"Ah, a contest of gods." Kheper-Re smiled. "And what does your God see?"

"Trees, my lord. Dying trees. There are demons in the darkness. They shake the ground with their very whispers."

"Great Bull, this man's a fake!" Puyem-re gave the sign of the evil eye. "Can't you see it?"

Kheper-Re looked more amused than angry. "Why would he lie? He knows as well as you a prophet's life is not without peril."

"My lord, I have been Amun's voice for sixteen years."

"What good has it done?" Kheper-Re pointed at Harran. "*This* prophet can see through walls. Do you know what he told me? He told me he saw poison vials secreted under a man's armpit and star-berries floating in a cup of wine. My, my, the *Nebes* tree has been busy. There are three pairs of eyes in my service. My Lord Commander has a sword he's itching to use and Khemwese is a dab-hand with a whip. It would be so dangerous to rouse all three. I am well protected, Chief Prophet. My sister, on the other hand, is not."

Shenq wondered if the comment was an invitation or a jibe. After all, the skinny beggar had been seen leaving the Queen's apartments on many a night with an armful of scrolls. It was likely he was changing an age-old edict with the help of a royal seal. And he wasn't the only one watching the Queen's door.

"You have been in the bosom of this family for some years, priest," Kheper-Re said. "Yet today you smell like sweat and your clothes are covered in mud."

"There was barely enough time to bathe before you summoned me, my lord."

"Were you digging a trench?"

Puyem-re ran a hand through a wispy stubble of hair. He was unable to win at this sparring of words. "Your majesty—"

"Go!" Kheper-Re dismissed the priests with a nod and turned to the Queen. He seemed to study her jewel-draped sheath and far-away stare, grimacing to show how little he liked it. "My lady, do you have anything to confess?"

"No, my lord," Hatshepsut said, painted eyes peeking out from beneath a beaded wig. "I have nothing to confess."

"It falls on me to govern this realm, my love. It is an urgent task and I intend to do it with, or without, your help," Kheper-Re said, holding out a vial. "Do you know what this is?"

"I have never seen it," Hatshepsut said, hands clenched on the arms of her chair.

"Look again."

"As Amun is my witness, I've never seen it."

Kheper-Re gave a shrug. "Hemp seed and dung, so my Commander tells me."

"Brother, you insult me."

"Sister, you're killing me." Kheper-Re half laughed. "Vizier Ahmose will escort you to your room. The Commander and I have much to discuss."

Kheper-Re rubbed his temples and sat back in his chair. He watched the Queen leave with a hot-headed scowl. "I won't let her beggar my realm, Shenq. She's a hazard we can't afford."

"I fear her majesty does not always listen to wise counsel, my lord," Shenq said, nodding.

"Measure that sweet piece of bronze at your hip Shenq. It will be an honor-killing if I have proof."

"It cuts both ways, my king," Shenq said. "The oath I swore said nothing of killing Queens, or any women for that matter."

"Then you're a bigger fool than I thought. There's some dark art in her head, I swear it. Its not like her to be this way."

Kheper-Re shook his empty cup at the cupbearer and eased himself out of his chair. There was a moment or two when he wobbled back and forth before an attendant offered him a cane.

"And what's this I hear about pork? The Chief of Prophets claims there's a pig-pit outside your gate."

"Pork, my lord?"

"You heard."

Shenq stared at the Pharaoh for a moment, casually he hoped. "Hogs tend to wander onto my land. They're burned if I catch them."

"Ah." Kheper-Re seemed to like that well enough, stretching those two scrawny legs of his. He paced in front of his throne for a time, staring intently at the floor. "Be careful not to burn the sacred sycamores, Shenq. I would hate to think it was you all along." He lifted a finger at the sound of a dog howling and raised his voice. "There, Anubis. He comes for the dead."

"It's just a dog," Shenq comforted. The beast was probably lifting his filthy leg against a tree. No wonder the leaves were turning yellow. "I've seen their tracks in the mud. It is a mating call."

Shenq hated dogs. One tried to take his arm off once even after he'd filled it with a tree-load of squirrels.

"Nothing *mates* at this time of year," Kheper-Re insisted.

Shenq pushed up his bottom lip and inclined his head. *Sounds like a common dog.* The Chancellor had several sighthounds, one of which found its way into Shenq's villa.

Tired of unwrapping an affectionate dog from his leg, he popped it with an arrow. It made for a rich and chewy broth.

"I am nearing the sunset of this world," Kheper-Re said, swaying slightly on a cane intended for a cripple. "It is known that he who makes peace with the priests has nothing to fear. But a real soldier is like a falcon among sparrows. It is my father they will remember, a mighty conqueror and founder of a great dynasty. I am just a sparrow, and when I pass to the Great Fields, Egypt will be ruled by a bunch of women."

"You are young and you have a son, Pharaoh," Shenq reminded. He liked prince Menkheperre already plump with the muscles of a soldier in training. The boy was his ward, a keen learner and friend.

"Yes, a meager boy whose existence is threatened by disease. My seed is spent. He is the last. "

By all accounts the Pharaoh was spending his seed abundantly and Shenq had seen a few girls waddling in the gardens, bellies bigger than wine jars.

"I shall die soon, Shenq. And when I do, it will be from natural causes. If the doctors find any poison in my body, I shall tie you between two horses. I hear it's a painful death. First the arms are dislocated and torn free. And then the mind goes."

Shenq sniffed. "I'll look forward to it then."

Kheper-Re brought a shaky hand to his forehead, body sagging. "Do you remember the battle of Swenet?"

Shenq nodded. How could he forget?

"My father saw a spirit that day. It came out of the mist, slick as the wind. I heard the clashing of swords, the screams. Then all was quiet. A great man died on the battlefield, an honorable death. Your father was golden like the midday sun. But he was mistaken for mine."

Shenq shook his head. "Pharaoh Ka-Nekhet wore the blue war crown at the battle of Swenet, my lord. There was no mistake."

"You went to my father's tent that day. I heard what he said." Kheper-Re had a glassy stare that seemed to focus on the floor. "He said I was his biggest disappointment and you were his biggest triumph. I wanted to wail with the slaves. I wanted to strangle the jackal that followed us to Thebes. It was all his doing. Father told us it was the spirit of the prince of Alodia. But he knew what it was. The creature is older than time. It lives in the marshes hunting for souls. It will never give up."

"Would you like a seat?" Shenq offered, wondering if the Pharaoh was near to swooning. "Perhaps on the chair?"

Kheper-Re sat down hard, cane clattering to the floor. "Go and find that dog," he slurred, waving a hand at Harran and Khemwese. "You, go with him."

Shenq was overjoyed. He was about to run out of the audience chamber with three of his best men when the Pharaoh called him back with a shout. "If you're not back before dawn—"

"You'll burn my house and all that's in it," Shenq finished.

They jogged to the first court, seizing weapons from the armor-bearer before lunging through the open gates. Torches sputtered along the avenue, casting a mellow glaze over the path and sending up thick vapors that made Shenq's eyes water. He listened to the croaking frogs and Harran's happy voice, willing to engage any enemy with a simple prayer.

As they reached the river path, a cacophony of birdcalls interrupted the peace and Shenq held up a hand and paused. Something had disturbed them and it wasn't a child this time.

"We're being watched," he whispered, unsheathing his sword.

Harran pulled the tallit and tunic over his head, setting his outer clothes down beneath a tree. There was something moving on the river, near a sandy spit of land. Somewhere between the water's edge and a belt of trees, Shenq could hear a ripple of water and he saw the heads then, bobbing above a silvery sheen and drifting towards the shallows camouflaged in the darkness.

He lifted six fingers and hunkered to the ground, smelling the stench of human excrement. These men were brave to swim the river and if they were unafraid of the water-horses and the crocodiles, they were not afraid of anything.

Shenq felt his muscles twitch and he wanted to stretch out his limbs as darkness closed in. Inching forward, his sword brushed over the long grass, eyes following the line of the river. Something broke through the water, and he jutted his chin towards it, calculating seven running strides from their position.

These men were close, almost a breath away.

The first of the rebels thundered through the thicket, knife poised in a downward lunge. His right breast was exposed to the tip of Khemwese's spear and he wailed in agony as it broke through his skin.

Snapping twigs exposed a second and Shenq's sword slashed through a wall of slime, shoulders slamming into muscle as a spray of warm blood hit him in the face. He grabbed a long braid, wrenching it downwards as Harran flew in, knife slashing at the warrior's throat.

The woods rang with screams and shouts, and the darkness was no help at all. Somehow Shenq's sword raked across flesh and bone and somehow the rebels would not wear down. He was aware of one chilling feature these night-men had. They could see in the dark like rats.

He saw the flash of weapons, nose twitching at the smell of blood, and he sensed a presence behind him. Throwing down his sword, he unsheathed his knife just as an arm squeezed his throat, robbing him of breath. He struggled against a slippery body and the heavy weight across his back. Down he fell like a stone, twisting in the mud until he rolled face up. The point of his knife glanced off the rebel's parry and he heard a deep, throaty laugh. The rebel caught Shenq's wrist, slamming his hand against a tree. The knife sung as it grazed a stone, lost somewhere in the darkness around them.

Strong hands slapped his face and instead of cutting his throat, the rebel lunged for a lock of his hair. Shenq squirmed beneath those powerful thighs until the load above him stiffened and fell over his right shoulder with a thud.

For a moment Shenq's gaze met Khemwese's as he was pulled to his feet. A silent word of thanks passed between them and it was then Shenq realized he could trust the man with more than his life. Khemwese could have left him to die without a single tear of remorse.

Harran was breathless, hand wrapped around his knife. The desert had not honed his skills to fighting in the dark and his eyesight was not as acute as Shenq's.

"More time in the training arena for all of us, my friend," Shenq encouraged, wondering if the scribe had a heart for ink rather than war. "Fetch a torch."

Harran ran towards the avenue of sphinx and wrenched an upright torch from its bracket. The light fell on six rebels bleeding in the dirt. A torrent of braids and cowry shells hung down each back and red shúkàs clung to lifeless bodies. The lower half of their faces were painted red and there was a mystery to them Shenq did not like. Only one still breathed; a young boy Khemwese had elected to keep alive. There was a fatal wound in his neck and blood pumped onto the path in a thick pool.

"Who are you?" There was no response and Shenq didn't expect one.

Alodians made blood-oaths never to speak when captured and this boy expected to die. If he was afraid he gave no hint of it and his eyes flicked towards the river before they rolled back into his head. There was meaning in that final gaze, a subtle message only Khemwese would know.

"Who are they?" Shenq said.

"*Murrani*," Khemwese said. "Prophets and conjurers. They are greatly feared amongst their own kind."

"Then they saw us before we saw them," Shenq said, thinking of the boy and his shifting eyes. "I say we take a look along the river."

Khemwese went back to the gatehouse in search of a cart for the dead and Shenq took Harran along a path that appeared to cut through the reeds near the river's edge. The torch shed light on broken papyrus stems, freshly cut by the look of it and they found a cavern of braided grass and a floor of rushes. Pharaoh was right. They would need to burn the reeds as far as the bend in the river, closing sinkholes and tunnels from this crazed thief.

The tunnel Shenq did find stretched east as far as the river and to the west, was a pile of rocks where a door had once been. There were weapons and a stash of jewelry, and cartouches that reopened an old wound breaching a dam of grief Shenq had stubbornly walled shut.

Prince Wadjmose, it said. *Amun's most beloved.*

Shenq felt his skin bubble with unease as he scrabbled through the goods all stamped with the prince's name. It wasn't until he found a small box decorated with the eye of Horus that his lips streaked into a grin.

Payment for blood and bruises, he thought, just as the wind began to rise.

TAU

Tau watched the southern curve of the river for ships and all he could see was a flock of whiskered terns following the fishing boats home. He thought he could smell *Murrani* sweat at the river's edge and the sweet incense they liked to burn, and he yearned for sight of the Panahasi, the man who led them. Perhaps he was on *dung-eaters'* island. Tau mimicked a falcon's screech just to make sure.

Silence.

The wound at his waist bled each time he ran and his swollen lip throbbed each time he smiled. *Curse that child*, he thought, wondering how she could have heard him.

Something had changed and there was a stronger force battling with his. Thoughts became a churn of memories and he wondered what was real and what was fancy. He relived the murder of his most recent victim; a spearman's wife who's pleading nearly brought him to his knees. She told him he was ugly.

She lied, the voices said. He was magnificent. The flaw lay in her.

Osumare was beautiful and he had no wish to shame her. But the voices were insistent, imploring over her tears.

He wiped his hand on his chest, blood still oozing from the scratches. Women were an anomaly. Their scheming minds persuaded and flattered yet they diminished a man's strength, robbing them of their pride. His warriors must have no wives—no chattels—no opinion. Pabasa would obey him now.

A full moon threw a lurid beam on the river and a breeze came from the south, fanning the reeds and sending ripples across the river. He called again for the *Murrani* but there was no response and he began to doubt Puyem-re and his lying tongue. The *zrip. . .zrip* of a reed bunting alerted him to food and he threw his knife, spitting the tiny morsel on the end of it.

Tripping over a gnarled tree root, he swore loudly, hearing a trickle of laughter. He lifted his head and nearly dropped his supper. The little girl stood on the river path illuminated by the moon, elbows wide from the body and baring her teeth.

"Man-dog!" she shouted. "You stupid."

Tau was enraged. He skewered the bunting off the end of his knife and looked up to take aim. Only she was gone, tumbling through an orchard of *Nebes* trees whose berries flickered in the darkness. He blinked and frowned. He wanted to run after her but he knew it was folly. She would be as far as the market place by now, running on hardened feet and screaming for help.

He crouched above his underground den, sniffing the air. Something had disturbed a pile of twigs at the entrance and there was a bittersweet scent that reminded him of citrus. It was more than a tunnel now. A wall of rocks separated his burrow from a corridor that ran almost as far as the avenue of sphinx. The priest had brought him food and tools, and if it wasn't for a cluster of sycamore roots, he would have breached the palace gates by now.

He was about to crawl into the darkness when a female *dung-eater* waddled nearby, growling for tidbits and giving him the eye. She was accustomed to the sound of his whistle, killing small birds and bringing him gifts. Sometimes she nestled her head against his thigh as if she demanded comfort and sometimes she groomed him.

I'm worth more than a king now, he thought, marveling at how large she was. The size of a ten-year old boy, he imagined.

She took flight suddenly at the sound of a war cry and snapping branches. Soldiers came with their six-tailed whips and torches, crashing through the undergrowth like a bloat of hippo.

Tau dived into his underground den, nostrils quivering to an array of human scents. His hands searched instinctively for his weapons and the sacred box but there was no sign of them. He could hear the pulse in his chest and he could smell smoke. The soldiers had set fire to the marshlands, flames crackling and curling through the reeds.

Anger drove him away from that place and he ran through the papyrus beds towards the river, cursing with every step. Gripping his knife between his teeth and reserving a second in his belt, he waded through the smoky water away from the shouts and the thundering feet. The soldiers would never find him, not unless they had a nose like his. He looked from left to right and made up his mind.

There was a villa almost a bowshot away and on the lintel was a name, *Vizier Ahmose, beloved of the Pharaoh.* The ramp stretched down to the river and the open gates surprised him. They led to a garden filled with fig trees and date palms, and there was an open terrace where lights flickered through gossamer drapes. A low throaty growl brought him face-to-face with a large dog whose teeth were sharper than the ones round Tau's neck. Its high pointy ears and black coat were softer than a newborn's scalp and there was a tremor in the bushy tail.

Shakāl, he thought, a breed prized amongst the Imazi Bedouin and thought to be the spirits of the ancestors.

Tau pulled out a second knife from his belt, keeping his arms tucked close to his sides. The beast approached with a snarl, yellow teeth visible behind a raised lip. The sound was no louder than the drag of a gardener's rake, and there were veins in the creamy eyes like marbling on a stone.

The dog leaped forward and Tau rushed in, head down, daggers up. He warded off the leap with his left hand, thrusting his knife upwards into a muscular belly. Warm blood rained down on his arm as the dog sprung back on all fours increasing the gap between them. He was confident it had suffered a serious injury until it leapt forward again, only this time sharp teeth clamped around Tau's calf, ripping and dragging.

Tau was conscious of a spark of excitement as he plunged both knives into the back of the dog's neck. There was no pain in his leg, not even when the teeth give way and the animal slumped to the ground. When he looked into the dog's eyes it was his mother's face he saw. Gods, he hated her for leaving him. He had been five years old then. Or was it six? He re-sheathed his knives and stroked the *shakāl* as it died, honored to be so close to such a sacred animal.

There was a large pool near the terrace covered with lily pads and Tau let his feet drag in the cool water for a while, thankful there were enough torches in the garden to see by. He dropped on all fours when he saw the guard, slinking through the shadows and calling the dog's name.

Tau lifted his shoulders above the water and hurled the knife by its tip, hearing only a faint whir as it spun through the air. The guard stooped as the knife struck and he tumbled to the ground, blood pooling on the tiles.

Tau bolted through the terrace into a large room, feet slipping on a glazed floor. Water and blood dripped from his *shenti* and he didn't like being dirty in such luxurious surroundings. When he was a child, the Bedouins threw him in a defecating pit for talking back and he could still remember the panic, the heart-skipping stench of filth.

He moved along the walls, aware of the scent of roses. He always enjoyed this part, like the time he took the milking maid by surprise in the lower precincts. Two voices grew louder now, increasing the urges in his head. He had no real way of satisfying them and all he could think about was the power at his fingertips. He backed into the shadows when he heard a sound, a maid striding towards him with a pretty singing voice.

She won't be singing for long, he thought, streaking along the wall behind her in two long strides. Clamping one hand around her mouth, he drove his dagger into the soft flesh of her back. She hardly groaned as she fell, head lolling on his knee. Her staring eyes fixed on a wood-beamed ceiling tied with papyrus rope. It was the last thing she saw before she died.

He heard another sound then, the soft rustle of a woman's gown and he turned in time to see a young girl with reddish-black hair. She dropped a bowl of incense pellets when she saw him and screamed at the top of her lungs.

Tau grabbed her as she swung away, holding fast to her tiny wrist. "What's your name?" he whispered, staring at eyes so wide they almost burst from her pale face.

"Iutha," the girl stammered, hand covering her breasts.

Tau covered her lips with a finger and shook his head. "No screaming, my love."

Mystery always fascinated him. It should have fascinated her. He hardly had time to notice wide hips and skin like goat's milk as he slammed her up against the wall. Grasping a slim neck, he saw the fear in eyes and he felt the tiny vibration of a scream as she struggled. But a prickle along his spine warned him of another presence and he twisted around still keeping a tight grip on the girl.

"Put her down!" a voice said.

Why not, thought Tau, taking his hand away from her

neck. She slid to the floor like a sack of rags.

A warrior stood behind him, nostrils flaring and chest thrust out. Tau knew him by the blue woolen threads in his braids and the lapis disks in his ears.

Mkasa of the moon.

Tau lunged forward aiming for a muscular gut. The blade of his knife glanced off a silver studded belt as Mkasa jumped back. Tau swung in again, making a series of short arcs. On the outward swing his heel struck a scatter of incense pellets and he began to slide.

Mkasa sprang forward and grabbed his wrist, twisting with such strength, Tau wondered if it would snap. The knife flew to the floor, brushed aside by an agile foot. Mkasa was behind him now, one arm cutting off the air in his windpipe and the other wrapped around a Makurae dagger, curved and wrought of silver. Tau could feel the twist of cold metal as it plunged slowly into the wound at his waist. Ripping, slicing.

He didn't cry out. Mkasa's dagger was in the wrong place to kill him.

"Who are you?" Mkasa said, voice raspy with anger.

Tau knew what to do. He bent his knee and struck Mkasa in the shin with his heel. He heard a yelp and took flight, stumbling over the dead guard in the gardens and streaking down the ramp to the river. He knew the warrior was behind him, closing in, breath warm against his neck.

Tau jumped in the river and sank beneath the waves, hidden in a swirl of sand. He held his breath and when the ripples disappeared, he kicked against the current and headed south as Mkasa ran north. A dull burn in his side threatened to squeeze the strength out of him and when he found a sandbank, he lay in the soft mud to catch his breath.

When it was safe, he pitched and tripped through the reeds towards the village, every step more painful than the last. He was thankful for a light in the window of a small house and bursting through the door, he saw Umaya, mouth open as if to scream.

Something popped inside his wound, something like a burst water skin. He barely heard the howl from his own lips before he collapsed at her feet.

KHEPER-RE

"He killed my dog," Vizier Ahmose said ruefully, head resting against the back of his chair. "*He killed my dog!*"

"I heard you the first time," Kheper-Re said. He remembered the cantering beast, tail outstretched like a rudder and taller than a goat. The wretched dog terrorized the ships on the river and likely barked all the fish to Memphis. "You know it's illegal to own a *shakāl*. You owe me your foreskin."

Ahmose tore off a piece of bread and dipped it in oil. "Best guard-dog I ever had."

Kheper-Re didn't think so if it was dead. "Did Mkasa get a good look at this intruder?"

"He was a shadow-hunter, covered in scars and stank like a whore. Mkasa stabbed him good and hard. It usually makes them talk."

"It should have killed him," Kheper-Re said.

"He vaulted over the ramp and into the river with that deep wound of his. He's crocodile fodder now."

Nothing survived the river, least of all a man leaking a jug of blood. Kheper-Re was hopeful they had seen the last of him. "Have some wine, cousin. Or beer, if you prefer. It's crane today. It's always crane on the sixth day of the month."

"He cut my dog wide open," Ahmose said, eyes glazed and staring. "Imagine that."

Kheper-Re jerked away a plate of food, imagining instead a steaming pile of dog guts.

"The embalmer put seventy-five stitches in his belly," Ahmose continued, lowering his voice to a sob.

"Cousin, this talk of killing is putting me off my supper—".

"Killing has never been your realm! Nor will it ever be. That's why you have Shenq. Only what good is he confined to your bedroom?"

"That's hardly fair. He's here to guard *Ra*," Kheper-Re said, glancing at Shenq. He stood on the balcony, stiffer than a spear. "He caught a few of these *shadow-hunters* last night if you must know. Isn't that so, Shenq?"

Shenq closed his mouth to a yawn. "Yes, my lord."

"See, I'm the midday sun cousin," Kheper-Re said. "The god of the people."

"Then you must give your people what they want. And what they *want* is to be free of this blood-sucking tyrant."

"I thought you said he was dead."

"Wounded. I never said he was dead. Why not let Shenq have your new weapons, the ones that lie rusting in your tomb. He has more need of them than you."

"How dare you."

"You're nothing but a pretty man sitting on a golden chair. The bards will have nothing to sing about when you're gone."

They'll sing until they're hoarse, Kheper-Re thought, until he had a vision of jeering crowds and a spray of rotten fruit. "I want them to sing, Ahmose," he said, clawing at his cheeks. "Make them sing!"

"The gods give us one life and in that life we must serve our people. Have you served yours?" Ahmose spat on the floor and looked Kheper-Re in the eye. "Look at your hands. Are they calloused like a soldier's? Do you even know which side of your bow is the *back*? You think dreams are more important than the exercise yard. You think it matters how wide your collars are, how many cups of wine you drink, how many girls say they love you and mean it. I won't sit meekly by and watch Thebes go to the dogs. Keep your weapons then for the afterlife. They'll be plenty of wars there."

"I'll take my Commander with me. I shall take him whether he is dead or not!"

"Oh, I think you can do better than that. You'll leave him behind for your son, the true Pharaoh of Egypt."

"Am I so unloved?" Kheper-Re let out a primal whimper, berating himself for not wearing his crown. "Do my people hate me?"

"If they get so much as a whiff of your cowardice, they'll hate you."

"I'm so alone, Ahmose."

"You have your sweet sister, my lord, and several hundred courtiers," Ahmose said, spittle flying from his mouth. "Get some sleep, your majesty. I only think of your comfort."

"I'm quite comfortable here," Kheper-Re whispered, gripping his chair. He was more despondent than he had been in days.

"God be with you, cousin," Ahmose said, standing. "I have business with Commander Shenq."

Kheper-Re heard Ahmose and Shenq whispering in the corner as he undressed for bed. *Soldierly things and mad dogs*, he thought. It was the last thing he remembered as he lay amongst a nest of pillows, waking in the night to a horrifying scream. Since there was no one bending over him with an enquiring expression he must have dreamed it.

Blasted dreams, he murmured, reaching for his cup.

The wicks had been kept burning and the translucent bowls shuddered as if they breathed. The smell of tallow made his stomach turn and he was irritated at the lack of unguents. Djoser was disinclined to refill the oils especially if no one noticed.

It was midnight. Ra was awake. And he had noticed.

Kheper-Re sipped the wine beside his bed, noting a bitter aftertaste on his tongue. It was thick like blood and warm against his lips.

Making his way to the balcony, he saw grey mountains against a black sky. His father's footsteps were ingrained in the gullies and paths, and the miserable man likely wandered the corridors of his new palace wondering where all his treasures had gone.

"Bastards," Kheper-Re murmured, wanting the thieves all the more. Even his brother's treasures had been snatched by a hand blacker than Set.

He could still see Prince Wadjmose and Shenq thundering across the plains in their chariots, swords aloft, screeching wordless battle-cries. Gods, he missed them. If only he could take back the years.

"Family," he whispered, "my family."

"My lord?" Shenq grunted, struggling to stand.

Kheper-Re jumped at the voice and the drawn bow in Shenq's hand. He had been shooting rabbits again. "I was just thinking of my father. I expect he's enjoying a bit of celestial totty. You haven't seen my piss-pot have you?"

"No, my lord." Shenq shook his head. "It's never on the balcony."

"I thought I heard a dog barking, only you would have woken me if there was," Kheper-Re said, edging back to his bed.

"Whilst we're on the subject of dogs, my lord," Shenq said. "I wonder, is this dog after kitchen scraps or is he part of a singing troop? He's been at it all night."

Kheper-Re spun on his heel. "You heard him? Why didn't you wake me?"

"No point shooting at shadows at least not from the balcony."

"Is that all it is to you, Shenq. Shadows?"

Shenq pointed at the river. "I would have a better chance of finding him down there."

"Keep watch," Kheper-Re hissed. He wasn't about to fall for that trick. "And don't look at my face."

"Wild horses couldn't drag me to your bedside after midnight, my lord."

"I'm glad to hear it. When the moon is high, you may leave."

Kheper-Re lay in his bed thinking of his dead brothers. Only their names were fading and sometimes he felt as if his heart had turned cold. The world was not as safe as it once was. He had been safe in the arms of his mother. He had been safe in the arms of his tutor, only he wasn't safe now he was a man. He couldn't find it in his heart to weep for them and when he thought of his father, he heard a rasping voice that did little more than chip away at his pride.

You're a disappointment, Kheper-Re. You lost again to your brother. Can't hold a sword, can't hold your own . . .

Kheper-Re pushed his thoughts away and thought of his sister. She was the pride in his father's eye, a gallant child sitting astride a horse and bolting into the unknown. She had more fire in her gut than he did, clothed in gold with a cloak rippling behind her. She even carried a spear wrought in bronze and her smoky voice shouted, *I am Hatshepsut, Pharaoh of the Two Lands*. She shouted it as if she honestly believed it and what was more, she was wearing her father's false beard.

Girls . . . nothing but dress-up and pretend.

Two nights ago, he dreamed of the gardens at the old palace in Memphis where he grew up. There were columns of polished granite and bubbling fountains, lily ponds and the drag of a peacock's tail. Torches burned through the night and so did the bitter scent of frankincense. There were good diviners then; real diviners, not the ones of today that only pretended to interpret dreams.

Harran was different. There was something unusual

about the boy, an undefined strength. He dazzled like a beacon on a hill, challenging the divinity of the pharaohs. A month ago, he suggested that if Kheper-Re was Ra and woke during the night, the passage of the divine barque beneath the earth would be interrupted and the sun would not rise at its usual time.

For three nights the High Priest watched the sun, especially on the occasion of a sleepless night and since Kheper-Re never slept, it was a test worth executing. The following morning, the High Priest assured him there was no change in the sun's rising.

"Am I not Ra?" Kheper-Re had asked Harran, hoping for encouragement.

The boy looked straight at him and not at the floor as others would have done. "Ra doesn't sleep in a bed or eat food. Ra doesn't hear. Ra doesn't see," was the quiet reply. "You believe in many gods, many of which you cannot name. Why have so many when you can have One?"

Kheper-Re remembered being startled. It occurred to him then that his forefathers were playing a very dangerous game of make-believe. All his life he had believed in Osiris, Horus, Ra. In fact, he named Montu, the god of war, as one of his favorites. A contradiction in his current circumstances perhaps but it was vital to appear threatening even if he hated the idea of wearing a sword or anything vaguely dangerous. He didn't for one moment expect to win a place in the Field of Dreams unless he *believed* and he refused to gamble a kite of silver on the very existence of the afterlife. In truth, he trusted Harran more than his father because the boy's interpretations had been right every time.

If tongues of fire burst through the floor of his throne room and destroyed his treasures, Ra would not save him. He would be deserted and left to die and Anubis would do little more than bark.

Kheper-Re gazed at a calcite lamp bearing the inscription; *A lamp will be lit for the offspring of Ra in the night until the sun shines again upon his face.* The god was an immortal champion and visible on every wall.

Kheper-Re decided to begin a long road of testing the priests, to face up to the chilling fact that the gods might be nothing more than chiseled stone. Far from running from the unknown, he had become obsessed with it and he had just the men to rouse him. Commander Shenq was his breastplate, Harran his helmet and Khemwese his shield. He was finally safe from the thing that barked at his door even though it was as grasping as bindweed, suffocating everything in its path.

Dead in the river? He hardly thought so. It was likely doing backstroke in the moonlight.

But he was safe behind high walls because he had a full-bodied army and he was *safe* because he had a prophet that believed in a God far greater than the gods he knew. One thing was certain, if Amun-Ra was who he said he was then Kheper-Re would have heard his voice.

A wick on the far side of the room sputtered and finally died and he heard scuffling from the side of his bed. He pulled the sheets up to his chin and began to count the stars on his ceiling, wondering if his attendants were ever tempted to look at Ra when he slept. He'd cut a few limbs off if they did.

Djoser rose from his pallet, naked and pasty in the glow of the lamps. But the sound of clanking suggested he had somersaulted over a piss-pot, voice hoarse with blasphemy.

Kheper-Re suppressed laughter, filling his nostrils with the scent of beeswax. And then it suddenly occurred to him.

He couldn't possibly be Ra if he was tucked up in bed.

SHENQ

Shenq walked through the first court with a bowl of moon-fish and goat's cheese. He watched the sparrows as they chattered in the dawn, faintly at first as if groggy from sleep. The ensign of Thoth, the god of wisdom, snapped back and forth in the wind and the clanking sistra sent musical pulses through the courtyards. It had been weeks of the same dull view and he swore a solemn vow he would escape it somehow.

A large black cloud cast a shadow over the gardens and a wind gusted through the flowers, ripping petals from their stalks. Shenq walked past a long procession of priests carrying bowls of beaten metal filled with incense and precious oils. Their eyes seemed to follow him from gate to gate and once he was beyond the great hall, the procession disappeared altogether. A whiff of mullet and eel pie wafted from the kitchens and by the time he arrived at the Pharaoh's door, his belly grumbled like an iron rasp.

"Hungry?" he said, giving Khemwese the bowl of fish. He caught a whiff of urine nearby and wondered if the warrior had been peeing in the incense ewer again.

"I could eat a side of ox, Maaz," Khemwese said, tipping the bowl to his lips.

Shenq didn't doubt he could, judging by the size of him. The wound on his arm had healed nicely, skin sewn together in a straight line. Tau's wound was likely to putrefy and crawl with maggots, and he wouldn't be hard to find with a stink like that.

"The Captain will be here shortly with beer and stew," Shenq said. "Pharaoh will be in the temple for the entire morning. It takes that long to divvy up the High Priest's tithes."

Khemwese and Harran usually slept on the floor when Pharaoh forgot to send them home. Sleep was precious, if it ever came at all. "If you feel inclined to play a round of Senet at the Pharaoh's table, be sure to put the pieces back exactly as you found them."

"Yes, Maaz."

Shenq sidled closer to Khemwese and lowered his voice. "Jabari's younger brother has been seen by the river whispering to a friend. Seems he got a raw back for it."

Khemwese shrugged. "Issa's defiant so Captain says."

Shenq was as curious as he was suspicious. "He should be keeping the Pharaoh's table loaded with meat."

"Lazy, Maaz, that's what it is. Says his arrows are poorly made."

"And you would know?"

"I would, Maaz. They dip all over the place when he shoots them. Something's wrong with the fletchings."

Shenq smiled. "Something's wrong with everything, isn't that so?"

"Something's wrong with Bunefer. She refused me again. Says I have an ass for a brain."

"May be you do." Shenq frowned. The woman Khemwese loved was gutsy and prone to slamming doors. "Ever seen anything strange by the river?"

Khemwese lowered his head as if dredging through his thoughts. "One night, I saw two men wading through the long grass. One had a bow on his back and a rabbit in his belt. Must have good night-eyes, I thought."

"Pabasa and Issa," Shenq murmured, as if he didn't know. Pabasa was the one with an ass for brains. "Did you follow them?"

"I did, Maaz, as far as I could. I could have sworn they were right in front of me. They should be locked up for good this time."

"I have a better plan." Shenq knew where they had gone. It was to an underground hideout to make friends with a stranger. He nodded at a guard. "Bring Pabasa and Issa to me."

He turned back to Khemwese. "General Pen-Nekhbet's men are scouring the upper precincts and the river. Seems they found a pile of rabbit coats in a tree not far from here and some jewelry. Pabasa's a dead man if he had anything to do with it."

"He's a dead man if he didn't, Maaz," Khemwese said, grinning.

"Pabasa's from Alodia, same as you."

"Not every man from Alodia is a brother. Not every man from Thebes is a threat. I stand on my own, Maaz. I go by your voice."

The swiftness of the answer pleased Shenq. Khemwese was no threat to the Pharaoh. If he was, he would have already lopped off the royal head in one swipe and no one would have been in the least bit sorry. At least no one Shenq could name.

"So you're a prince. I was there. I heard his voice." Shenq whispered, throwing out the bait. He had never forgotten Kibwe-Shabaqo's words. So much so, he tried to have them translated by a scribe when he got back to Thebes. Only the tongue was too ancient.

Khemwese tugged at the small tusk in his right ear. "I was all he had, Maaz."

"It's more than that. You're a prince amongst thieves," said Shenq, hand resting on the pommel of his sword. It must have been familiar to Khemwese, a sword that was his by rights. "When it's over, Pharaoh will send you back to Alodia to rebuild the villages."

"Pharaoh will never send me back, Maaz."

Shenq bit his lip and almost winced. Pharaoh was a tight-fisted beggar when it suited him. "He won't live long. You'll be home before you know it."

"Do you remember my father?"

Shenq did and he often spared a thought for him. "He was a Kamau. He wasn't afraid of anything."

"They say the warrior that killed my father was the son of a leopard. He just had more fire in him, that's all." Khemwese looked hard at Shenq. "Do I look like my father?"

"There's something in the eyes," Shenq said, studying a dreamy quality, an elsewhere look he had grown to admire. "The south wall of the palace is dedicated to the King of Alodia. It says, *Year one, seventh of Mesore, under the majesty of Pharaoh Ka-Nekhet who is given life. His majesty triumphed over the wretched Kush and brought home its chieftain.*"

Shenq had never spoken to Khemwese about his father until now. The memory was nothing but a sore he prayed would heal. *We are all fatherless*, he thought, hoping Khemwese bore no grudges. The giant would do well to learn the protocols of kingship, provided he didn't kill the Pharaoh first.

"What do you know of Tau the Alodian?" Shenq said, brushing aside the memory.

"He was raised from cattle stock and savage like a hog. He'd kill oryx, hauling the carcass and leaving a trail of guts."

Shenq waited for Khemwese to continue and when he didn't, he said, "That's hardly odd. I always leave the guts."

"Alodians prize the guts, they eat them raw."

Shenq felt a faint smile playing at the corners of his mouth. Tau was leaving a trail all the way to Thebes. And how many rebels would have followed it? A hundred . . . a thousand?

"Pabasa would go out into the dunes to hunt fox,

Maaz. Sometimes he wouldn't come back for days. He thought Tau was a hero. He thought Tau would be Pharaoh of Egypt."

"A cattle driver has no right to call himself Pharaoh," Shenq said with a wolfish grin. He was beginning to wonder if Tau was a half-wit, guts and all. "What would you do if you found him?"

"I would skin him. It's the Alodian way. There are many ways to skin a rabbit, Maaz, but only one way to skin this one."

Shenq tasted a bitter tang in his mouth. They said his mother's body had no skin and no eyes. It was her necklace that identified her. "How would you find him?"

"A jackal doesn't have to bother himself about his next meal. All he has to do is wait by the waterhole at dusk. That's when the frogs are hopping and the gazelle feeds. He'll wait all night if he has to. But that's where you'll find him."

Shenq chuckled at that. Tau had been a regular visitor of the river since they arrived. Trouble was, he had more than one burrow. "Call me when Pharaoh's ready," he said nodding at the closed door.

If he could persuade the Pharaoh to take the prince hunting, dusk would be a good time to go. In the meantime, he made a small detour to the women's gardens. Poppies were delectable at this time of year and the *poppy* he had in mind was likely to be on display. He doubted Meryt was easily tempted by a man slick with oil and since she never so much as gave him a nod, he wondered what chance he had.

He found the gateway of Isis barred by a eunuch bulging with the weight of his ornaments. What was Shenq thinking? A scrawny stable boy?

"Have you seen a dog?" Shenq said, trying to make conversation. It was highly unlikely one would scurry past on a sunny day.

The bodyguard frowned and looked about. "A ranger

was it, sir?"

Shenq had no idea what a ranger was. "Pointy ears about the size of a calf and a bit snarly?" The dog trick never failed. No matter how large a man was, most were terrified of dogs. And this man was sweating.

"That spearhead looks like it needs sharpening," Shenq advised. "Go to the armory and I'll watch the gate."

The man shot off without looking back and a deben of silver remained snug inside Shenq's belt.

The peristyle court was cool, sparrows flitting from highly painted columns to nests on the horizontal members. Blue lily and delphinium surrounded a pool and fruit trees rustled in a light breeze. A framework of vines surrounded two pillars at the north end of the court and Shenq found a place to hide.

He peered between the branches, studying a group of young women reclining beneath a canopy. It had been some years since he had considered taking another wife. His first had died in his arms and the memory still haunted him, sometimes in his dreams, sometimes in his thoughts.

Three ladies stood in the shade, painted in kohl and draped in the finest linen. A fourth stood by the pool, dark hair woven with precious stones and dressed in a sheath of cream and gold.

Beauty too rich, he thought. *This poppy won't fade. And if I don't snatch it soon, it will be gone in a day.*

A woman's voice called from the doorway of the Queen's apartments over the sound of a lyre. "Meryt! Where are you, girl?"

"I'm here, nurse."

Inet waddled to the pool, hitching her skirts above the knee. She pressed Meryt's hand to her ruddy cheek and smiled. "I told you to fetch flowers for the Queen not gossip with these neighing horses."

"I need air, nurse."

"We all need air, child. Where's my wine?"

Meryt took Inet's arm and walked her away from the

women. "Won't you stay with me?"

Inet wiped a tendril of hennaed hair from her forehead. "The Queen has asked for you. You know what she wants, girl."

Shenq could almost see through the gown Meryt wore and the frothing veil at her shoulder. So delicious was this ripening seed, he wanted her with an urgency that startled him. The relationship between the women intrigued him and he wondered if the nurse would serve as a courier.

"I've looked everywhere, nurse," Meryt said, giving a modest smile, "in the bed, under the bed. I can't find it."

"Of course you can't find it," Inet broke in. "There is no emerald ring. She made it up."

"I don't understand."

"She won't part with you, child," Inet said, snatching a grape from the bower and popping it in her mouth. Her face puckered from the sour taste. "Not unless her brother asks for you. And he may ask for you. I've seen him looking."

Meryt smoothed down her sheath and sat on a stone bench. "I don't want to be married, nurse. Not to him."

"Our Great Bull is handsome and generous. He can be merciful too when he puts his mind to it."

"You don't mean it."

"Oh, I do. He asked for a virgin once only she went missing. The soldiers found her hiding in a laundry basket. Pharaoh said he would be merciful. So he cut out her tongue and said that was mercy."

"He's a monster!" Meryt slapped a hand in front of her mouth.

"Calm yourself, child." Inet pressed her hands to her hips like a full-bellied wine jar. "Hiding won't help you."

"Please," Meryt blurted, "don't make me marry him."

"I see no reason to give Pharaoh any more choices. He has over two hundred after all. We must see you wed, the sooner the better. Ah, here comes my wine." Inet grabbed the arm of a passing attendant. "Go child, and say nothing of this to anyone."

All this talk of marriage gave Shenq a queasy feeling in his stomach. And as for rings, he had plenty of those. He watched Meryt run through the courtyard, cheeks white with fear and he could only imagine what nightmares she had.

Whistling quietly, he caught Inet's attention and she crept towards the vine armed with a smile. "I thought I saw a cock-bird," she whispered, loud enough to be heard.

"Will you take a message," Shenq whispered.

"I will, sir" Inet replied, fingers flapping with impatience.

Shenq placed the kite of silver in her outstretched hand. "Tell the lady Meryt you have found her a husband. Tell her he has an emerald ring."

"She belongs in the House of Women," Inet said, breath sour with wine. "You've no right to ask for her."

"I have more rights than you know. Tell her I mean to make her happy."

"You're a sweet boy and a foolish one," Inet said, pressing a hand to his cheek. "You had better pray your emerald ring is large enough to free her."

Inet bounced off in the direction of the Queen's apartments, looking back once and that was to smile.

Shenq was conscious of a light tapping on his shoulder. The eunuch had returned, only this time with a sharper spear. He pointed to the rising sun and urged Shenq from the gardens with a forceful nudge.

Kheper-Re hardly lifted his eyes from a game of Senet with the prince as Shenq entered. "Is my guardhouse satisfactory?" he said, nudging Harran on the floor with his foot.

"It is," Shenq replied sourly, suddenly yearning for it.

"How are my safflowers?"

"Exquisite, Pharaoh." Shenq was amused at the matronly query and began to pace.

"Or perhaps you prefer red poppy over our native

lotus?" Kheper-Re pouted and his nose twitched. "You have more oil on your back than duck. It's a woman, isn't it?"

Shenq often used citrus oil after a bath. The scent was exotic, a characteristic by which he was well known. "It's the lady Aset," he offered. The Pharaoh would take it as a compliment.

"You're a brave man," Kheper-Re said, lowering his eyes to the floor. "Is she swayed by your rugged charm?"

"Not at all, my lord, her sights are set much higher." *As mine are*, Shenq thought, knowing how the game was played.

The memory of Aset gobbling mullet in salt brine was not one he relished. She sat beside him during a feast, lips puckered against his cheek and playfully squeezing what she thought was his thigh.

"All women belong to me," reminded Kheper-Re who would rather argue than be ignored.

"Girls aren't as exciting as my collection of snakes." Prince Menkheperre interrupted, tapping his feet against the struts of his chair.

"But they will be," Shenq encouraged with a wink.

"Father pumps them all day long so I can have brothers. But now his staff hangs like a horse's tail," Menkheperre said, measuring a small distance between his thumb and forefinger.

"Life has returned." Kheper-Re waved Shenq over to the table. "My staff is now higher than the tide."

"Would the prince like to go hunting?" Shenq said. "A large herd of oryx has been sited on the west bank."

"Oh please, father," Menkheperre said. "I should like to go."

"I would go too only my chariot is ruined," Kheper-Re said. "There is a malfunction to the chassis."

"You have a thousand," Shenq reminded, wondering if the Pharaoh would be generous enough to let them go alone.

"There's never anything to shoot at."

"What about lions?"

"They are scarce and only come out at night. Besides, the course is rutted and spoils my aim. I came home a year ago with an empty quiver and not a single kill."

Shenq rued the hunt as he remembered it. Hundreds of people lined the streets that day waiting for the Pharaoh's return. Four empty packhorses brought a wail to their throats but it was the fifth that sent up a round of wild laughter. One miserable rabbit hung on a wooden frame with over thirty arrows in its sorry back.

"We'll be back before you know it," Shenq encouraged, hoping they could go as close to dusk as possible.

"See you bring me a belly full of meat." Kheper-Re said, taking a sip of wine and flinching at its bitterness. "And if you should see this *dog*, give him my regards."

An arrow in his windpipe, Shenq wanted to offer but they were hunting oryx not dogs. Any whiff of Shenq's true intentions and the hunt would be off.

"My doctor has asked me to give up meat," Kheper-Re continued. "He says it will bring sons to my wives. I'll wager you had a fat cow for your breakfast."

"I had a whiff of moon-fish, my lord," Shenq corrected, desperate to leave.

Kheper-Re seemed dogged with hunger as if he would snatch any cast-off morsel. "I could kill for some meat."

"There is a salted carcass in my kitchen," Shenq offered, picking a thread of chewed pork from his teeth. Quartered and smothered in tasty sauces, a piglet would be well disguised.

"Give it to me. You shall have anything, up to half my kingdom."

Shenq longed for a posting in the north. Brain tumbling with ideas, one thought did come to mind. "I should like to marry."

"He should," Prince Menkheperre confirmed. "He

needs an heir, father. And a wife would remove all threats to our harem."

Shenq was impressed. Menkheperre's request was artful coming on the heels of the Pharaoh's earlier accusation.

"Women? Who wants *women*? They hold us to terrible account," Kheper-Re chortled as a spray of wine exited through his nose. "My old diviner said, *a palace without women is like a crown without jewels*. It's all nonsense naturally. I had a dream about a man with a red face and he couldn't interpret *that* to save his life."

"The man in your dream is an Alodian headman, Father Per'o," Harran spoke up, using a much-favored title. It would win him a few of his own if he used it more often. "Their faces are often painted and marked with tattoos. Only this one plunders the tombs of the kings to raise an army."

"How do you know this?" Kheper-Re said, growing very still.

"I *know* because it is the part of the dream you left out."

Kheper-Re sniffed and then he was silent for a time. "I must praise your HaShem for such wisdom."

"It's time to assemble your armies," Harran said.

"But you could be wrong." Kheper-Re stared up at the ceiling, eyes swimming amongst the painted stars.

"He's never wrong," said Shenq, swallowing a groan. Talk of armies frequently made the Pharaoh's blood boil. "He should be Chief of Prophets."

"Then he'll give me a pledge," Kheper-Re said, eyes round with anger though it was hard to tell. "One finger from his drawing hand."

Shenq wondered briefly if the stump of what was left of Harran's finger could still wrap around the drawstring. The boy was persistent and a good archer when he put his mind to it. "And if he's right?" Shenq asked.

"Then he shall have up to half my kingdom." Kheper-

Re seemed to search Harran's face for any flicker of terror.

There wasn't much of the kingdom left, thought Shenq, apart from the Northern provinces and no one wanted those.

"I think it's time to pay this demon off," Kheper-Re said in a bubbly tone.

"What with, my lord?" Shenq said, hurrying his words.

"With *you*, my precious friend."

TAU

Tau wandered through the tall grass wearing a belt-full of knives. He caressed his head, feeling the grooves of a fresh tattoo whilst scanning the river for any sign of his kill. But the oryx had bolted from an arrow in its leg and he wouldn't find it again until dusk.

The wound at his side had almost healed except for a trail of slime that dripped from a stitching of horsehair. Umaya was good with a needle. *A little too good*, he thought, wincing from a sharp pain each time he unhooked his bow.

Two to kill, he thought, breathing life into their names. *Khemwese, Mkasa . . . who's next I wonder?*

It was early evening when he saw three warriors gathering speed along a game trail in the grasslands. They were noblemen dressed in black and gold, horses caparisoned in the colors of the Pharaoh's guard. Their quivers were full of hunting arrows with fletchings whiter than goose down, fletchings just like his.

Habit made him follow them until the sun began to set and he could smell the sweat on them, thick and stale. They tracked a large herd of oryx for several miles and, by the blood on their arms, they had already taken one down.

A boy with scale armor inlaid with precious stones pointed to a buck some way off but the horses were lathering and failing. The warriors dismounted beneath a stand of sycamores and led the horses to a canal.

As they refilled their water skins at the lip, Tau studied eight quivers on a packhorse and three ornate wooden bows, tips curved and strengthened with horn. The arrows flew at twice the distance of his own and he would need thick armor to take all three warriors at once. One man at a time was good enough for him, one at a time to torture them good and long.

He kept behind the margin of trees and crept towards the dun horse. Snatching a dozen bronze-tipped arrows from a quiver, he replaced them a handful of small-game arrows with blunt heads. He could see the black horns and the red-brown chest in the haze of the underbrush and he knew the buck would emerge for a moment before disappearing altogether.

The boy with a gold breastplate took aim, bow-arm solid. The first shot struck behind the shoulder and the second pierced the flank, and the animal limped out of range. Tau couldn't be sure but there was part of an arrow peeking out from behind the hock.

My kill, he thought, wincing. He crept back beneath the trees and watched.

"Don't threaten him, my prince," Shenq said, hand out to warn the boy. "Let him find a place."

"Good eye, my lord," a second warrior murmured with the symbol of Thoth engraved on the wide leather bands at his chest. "He's your kill."

My lord? My prince? Tau couldn't believe his luck. This was the royal son of Pharaoh Kheper-Re, a young hawk in the nest.

"How long before I can take this boy to war, Ituri?" Shenq said as the prince mounted his horse and took off at a slow trot.

The voice was rich, deeper than Tau had ever

imagined and his eyes were rooted to the one he hated the most.

"Two more years, Commander, though he would rather go now. He talks of you all the time. Wishes he could be like you."

"He's an excellent shot. Only the buck he took was another man's kill."

Tau began to feel tense. He wasn't usually this nervous, only Shenq had spotted the arrowhead in the animal's leg and he would see how roughly hewn it was when he pulled it out. Sand-warriors and shadow-hunters used arrows with flintheads but not a noble. No, theirs would be Theban forged and decorated with the colors of their divisions.

Shenq held up a hand. "Can you hear anything?"

Ituri looked about and scowled. "Just the buck panting."

"No, *that*," Shenq said, pointing up between the trees.

"It's a vulture, sir. Three, I think."

There was a hissing croak in the sky and Tau looked up to see the large shadow, floating on a thermal. That's my girl, he thought, seeing the *dung-eater* in her dirty plumage. She was almost as old as he was.

The sound of hoof-beats took Tau by surprise. The Commander and the royal tutor had already mounted their horses, tearing through a knot of trees and out of range. Tau cursed himself for watching the bird, and he followed them west for a time and then south, and then they were off again down a narrow path, shaded by a vault of *Nebes* trees.

They can't have seen me then, Tau thought, pausing to catch his breath. Not him perhaps but Shenq knew something was out there and it wasn't just the buck.

Tau kept as close as he could, sprinting along the shaded paths and keeping Shenq in his sights. *Something will jump out at you if you don't slow down*, said the voices in his head, all prickly and insistent.

That might be true, Tau thought, but it didn't change the fact that Shenq was only fifty yards ahead with a royal prince and a tutor. So close. So *very* close. And rather than ducking and dodging through the undergrowth like a frightened sparrow, why not sprint like the jackal he was.

The path veered sharply to the right before straightening again and, pulling up before the bend, he waited just to be sure. He took a breath and, quicker than a cobra, he darted around it with a dagger in his hand.

A female hippo crashed through the undergrowth towards the river, mouth a churn of grass. She was only ten feet from where he stood, running on stumpy legs. Tau moved out of her way and ran for the open fields, branches whipping at his face. It was foolish he knew, but he couldn't stop running through the waist-high grass and there was nowhere else to go.

Glancing back, he saw the narrow trail his body left behind, fool's tracks so easy to follow and he lunged for a culvert without breaking stride. Soaked in the cool waters of the canals, he bounded up a gentle slope, crouching as he reached the top.

What a view, he thought.

He grasped his side and saw a bloody trail of slime oozing through his fingers. The stitches were now a row of tiny yawning mouths and the stench was sickening. He took a deep breath and watched the thicket ahead of him where a majestic set of horns curved under a canopy of trees. The buck lay with its head lowered, steam pluming from its nostrils.

Be patient, boy, thought Tau, studying the prince as he crouched in the long grass, twenty feet from the buck. *It will be some time before he gives out and that's only if he doesn't leap up and trample you first.*

Menkheperre stopped suddenly, cowering under Shenq's wagging finger and they whispered for a time, drinking from their water skins.

Just out of range, Tau thought, crawling forward on his

belly until he found a troop of barley stalks and a tall palm tree. He could see the prince clearly now, dark-eyed and handsome, cheeks flushed from the heat. And he could hear his voice.

"Where's your sword?" Menkheperre whispered, staring at Shenq's bare hip.

"I rarely take it on a hunt, my lord," Shenq muttered.

"Grandfather gave it to you, didn't he?"

"He thought it would make a man of me."

"It did little for the King of Alodia," Menkheperre said, dropping his head. "Imagine being killed by your own sword?"

"Better than foreign metal any day," Shenq said, eyes flicking here and there.

"Khemwese's royalty isn't he? It's something in the eyes."

Shenq seemed to grin at that. "You've been listening at doors."

"I'm right though, aren't I?"

"He is as noble as he is humble," Shenq said quietly. "You can trust him with your life."

"And Alodia will finally be on good terms with Egypt when our friend is on the throne."

Shenq patted his lips with a finger. "Not a word, my prince."

So that's who he was. Khemwese was the son of King Kibwe-Shabaqo. Only he would never rule. Not now that Ibada was on the throne with four sons of his own.

Tau raised his body slowly behind a screen of leaves, sighting on the boy with an arrow notched. He enjoyed the thrum of the bow as the arrow flew above a sea of grass. There was a loud grunt as one man went down, arms flailing as he tried to steady himself.

"My lord!" Ituri yelled.

Shenq pulled the prince behind a screen of trees and there was silence for a time before the arrows came. Tau saw them cambering towards him from a dusky sky, tearing through papery leaves and fibrous trunks. He saw a blur of movement and took aim. The arrow crested to one side in a sudden breeze and he heard the crunching of detritus and smiled. He couldn't be sure, but the prince was on the run, leaving Shenq to brave it out with a few blunt arrows of his own.

I'm hardly small game, thought Tau, wondering if he could evade a rain of them.

Dung-eaters mewed in the sky, attracted to the smell of blood. The female was with them and Tau whistled two high notes and one long one, tempting her to fight. A shaft of light was all he had to see by and he held his breath to listen. She plummeted to earth and there was a scuffle of wings before the snap of thin dry bones.

Tau could hardly see through the silent trees, thin rays of light fading with the sinking sun. Shadows pressed close and he could see dancing lights from the berries of the *Nebes* tree and a man beneath them, long hair streaming behind him in a gust of wind. He had a bow in his hand, arrow nocked.

And the others? No, I mustn't think of the others. One is dead and the other is half-way to the palace. Tau walked on with a knife in his hand. His example of daring would knock Shenq off his stroke.

The first arrow slammed into his chest and a second bounced off his thighs. Tau fell heavily to one knee, nearly biting his tongue. Shenq reloaded a third, studying the blunt tip through narrowed eyes. They were no use to him now, not unless he had a dagger.

"Where's my bird!" Tau yelled.

Shenq dropped his bow and unsheathed a knife. Tau had never seen it before. Enemies rarely matched their weapons in the field and this man was far enough away to draw the small axe at his hip.

"Dead, my friend," Shenq said, eyes full of secrets.

Tau saw the *dung-eater* lying on the ground in a thin shaft of sunlight, neck skewed at an unnatural angle. A patch of skull peeked out through the down on her head, sloughed off by a sharp knife.

"You'll pay for this." Tau hurled his knife through a parting of leaves.

It missed as Shenq twisted to one side, evading the strike. *He can see in the dark, you fool,* the voices reminded. *Better be quick before the light fades.*

Tau unsheathed a second knife in his right hand, flicking the fingers of his left. Shenq rushed forward at the invitation, long-legged and fast. But Tau never lost sight of him, anticipating a blow to the head, knowing the simple tactic worked every time. He spun sharply on his heel and raced to one side, still feeling the sting of a knife on his back. Running was the best line of defense against a bull like this, only Tau wasn't running anywhere.

It could have been worse, he thought, feeling the burn between his shoulder blades. Shenq was fast enough to kill him. But this was a scratch. Only a scratch.

The next one will go deeper, the voices said.

Tau faced Shenq, waving his knife from side to side trying to stop his next attack. Sparks flew off the blades as they scraped together, metal singing against metal. The dusk was throwing shadows between the trees and Tau knew he was running out of time.

Rushing forward, he brought his dagger up in an arc and down again with deadly precision. Shenq's eyes were wider than walnuts as the blade went in, weaving through the flesh at his shoulder like a bodkin.

Tau pulled the knife free with a rapid tug, but it fell from his hand and melted into the grass. He leapt backwards to gain space and unsheathed a third, thrusting as fast as he could, finding nothing but empty space.

He circled in the shadows, slashing, whirling, whatever it took to drive Shenq down and gut him like a fish. He never lost a beat, he never lost a stroke but somehow he couldn't see the man with a hundred lives. He turned a full circle, seeing nothing but trees blackened by a sullen sun.

He felt the sting as something raked at his side, tugging away at the stitches. He would bleed out if his heart continued to pound.

Because the faster it beats, the more you bleed.

The knife had come out of nowhere as if a disembodied hand circled in midair, and Tau knew he would need to counter fast if he wanted to live.

I might trade a cut for a kill, he thought, jumping back suddenly, hearing a whoosh by his left ear.

He bent to the ground and tacked to one side. There was a spirit in Shenq that evaded even the darkest of demons and Tau tried repeatedly to sidestep him with a few thrusts of his knife.

The pain . . . This is madness, he thought, pressing his offhand against his gut and finding a bloody slit.

He was tiring, swinging lower, slower, and all he could see of Shenq was white teeth and a mouth twisted in a moue of anger.

You're down and done for.

A hollow opened up suddenly beneath Tau's heel and he staggered, legs kicking out from under him. A warm body straddled his as he hit the ground and his arms were pinned above his head. The point of a dagger caressed his throat and he waited for the deadly strike.

That was too easy now, wasn't it?

Shenq's ragged breaths hit Tau in the face, cursing and spitting. But none of it mattered to Tau. He had skinned Shenq's mother and gutted his father, and beaten a bloat of a wife. He was already victorious, wasn't he?

Tau turned his face away and there, pegged between two stems of wormwood was a sliver of silver, a knife sharp enough to pluck out an eye. He knew one of his hands was slick with blood and twisting it sharply, he heard it pop from Shenq's grip.

Grabbing the weapon, he drove it sideways into a wall of muscle and Shenq fell sideways as Tau punched out.

KHEMWESE

Khemwese stood guard on the inside of the Pharaoh's door, leaning heavily against the frame. It was midnight and he was tired on his feet. Pharaoh and Vizier Ahmose played another round of Senet, waiting for Commander Shenq to come home. By the sound of a smashing fist, Pharaoh had lost again.

"Gods, where are they?" Kheper-Re said, fingers tapping the tabletop.

"They'll be here soon enough, cousin," Ahmose soothed, spreading bare toes through the leopard skin rug. "Shenq's never let you down before."

"He's dead."

"He's not dead. How can he be dead?"

"I can see things in the flames. Light things. Dark things. Things with snapping teeth. I wish I could sleep."

Ahmose squinted at a brazier with lion's feet for legs. "Can you really see things with snapping teeth?"

"Sometimes, when I'm alone."

"What does your prophet say?"

"He's been whittering on about trees all evening," Kheper-Re said, propping his head up with a fist. "I sent him down to the kitchens to get some food."

"What good is a man when he's hungry? Send him home. Sleep sharpens the mind and I doubt he's had much of that."

There was a smell of frankincense in that room, heavy and bitter, and it reminded Khemwese of his childhood where there was another palace, another king. He rubbed his sword arm, still stiff from the training arena. The royal throat was a few strides away and he could cut it if he wanted to. Only he was no longer a young boy with a mind full of hate. He was no longer a grieving son with a restless dagger in his belt. He was wiser now in the ways of HaShem, only what this God looked like, he couldn't imagine. Sometimes he dreamed of a tall man with black skin and a head of grey hair like the storytellers he once knew. And sometimes he just felt Him brushing against his skin like a fresh breeze. Yes, that was HaShem. Everywhere. Always.

Somewhere in the great hall, Khemwese could hear hissing coals. The Chief of Prophets was refilling the braziers and afterwards his ear would be pressed to the Pharaoh's door.

"I married a young girl last night," Kheper-Re whispered. "Well, not *married*. Rutted. Too many of the royal wives still have their maidenheads. And what's worse, half the palace seems to know about it."

"Half the palace is taken up with fools, cousin, and the other half doesn't care a whit.

"Except Senenmut. He seems to have deer meat to offer at every occasion. I'm sick of deer meat."

"It's very thoughtful of him to bring you meat."

"He's a tuft-hunter. And it's probably poisoned."

"You have tasters."

"I *had* seven."

"Bring your sword and train in the arena, cousin. That's where the action is."

"The action is in my sister's bedchamber. I've heard some troubling tales. There's a cobra amongst the flowers with poison on his tongue."

Ahmose laughed. "All monsters are poisonous, my lord. Never feed one. You'll only have to kill it afterwards."

"Someone's been goring the Queen and not with a royal poker. The world is a dark grey place." Kheper-Re sniffed. "Where is Shenq? He's a shining beacon on my terrace with his gold breastplate and cufflets. The very sight of him will frighten our demon away."

"It may also give him something to shoot at."

Laughter took the place of suspicion and very soon the Pharaoh had regained his spirits. He gave Khemwese a long hard look. "Go home now, Kamau."

Khemwese longed for an empty ewer and found one in the great hall just as the last echoes of priestly chants died away in the open courts. The metal sides almost sang from the gush of urine and he sighed loudly in relief.

He thought of Bunefer whenever he could, wondering if gifts of eel and beer were enough to win her heart. She had a seven-year-old daughter who waited for him on the river path at night. Nebsemi was deaf and her senses were sharpest at night.

He walked to the terrace and saw dark clouds curdling in the sky and the moon brighter than a lantern. Pabasa and Issa were in chains again, enjoying the darkness of a tiny cell and a bowl of broth every other day. They were weak but not yet ready to talk.

The gardens were bright with torches and nurse Inet bobbed in the Pharaoh's t-shaped pool, floating like a piece of mutton in tallow. Water held memories of another time and sometimes Khemwese imagined a dead man hanging from the prow of a ship leaving behind a wake of blood.

"Father," he murmured.

He heard Pharaoh's tight-lipped murmur from the adjacent terrace, voice louder now as if he cupped two hands to his mouth. Khemwese glanced over his shoulder at the great hall, seeing only soft shadows the oil lamps cast. The palace was a cluster of passageways and richly colored swathes, hiding places for wicked men. If Puyem-re was hiding, Khemwese would sniff him out and snap that bony little neck.

"He's guilty," Vizier Ahmose said with an angry hitch to his voice. "Why hesitate? Let me kill him and be done with it."

Khemwese swallowed hard and put a hand out on the baluster to steady himself. The two balconies were only feet apart and he could hear every word.

"Yes, yes, I know," Kheper-Re said. "There someone behind him. There has to be. I want to understand—".

"Understand? There's nothing to understand. He wants the throne, cousin. He's been plotting for years."

There was silence for a while as Khemwese waited over the sound of a creaking chair. *Give me a name,* he thought, longing for it, praying for it.

"So you'll plan his murder?" Kheper-Re asked.

"Let him live for a while. *And* those little whipping boys of his," Ahmose grunted. "You never know where they might lead us."

"I loved him once," Kheper-Re said with a sob in his voice. "My father loved him."

Thunder rumbled in the distance and Khemwese could hear the faint concussion of rain on the roof. But it was short-lived. It hardly ever rained in Egypt. He filled his lungs with the scent of wet mud, straining his eyes in the darkness. There was something out there beyond the gardens, a long-eared jackal perhaps, he couldn't be sure.

Kheper-Re snapped his fingers. "Send in the singer!"

Khemwese swung on his heel and saw Bunefer ushered in by the priests. She had been waiting all evening to sing for the Pharaoh, waiting just as he had. One hand covered her belly as if it was the time of the red moon and there was a veil on her head embroidered with silver thread. Slow strides brought her to where he stood and he stretched out a hand to steady her.

"You're beautiful," Khemwese summoned from deep inside his throat. "So beautiful."

"I'm tired," she said, hugging a harp to her chest.

"Where's the little one?"

Bunefer turned and hesitated. "Went after a rabbit, she said."

Khemwese saw the frown that sprang into two raised eyebrows. The child was good with a sling but she rarely wandered off at night.

"I'll look for her on the way home," he offered.

Bunefer gave a ghost of a smile and nodded. She wasn't used to suitors, at least not one with a gold buckle for a belt and an embroidered sash.

I want her to share my blanket, he prayed. *She's my joy.* "You've been crying," Khemwese said, noticing a trail of tears against those black cheeks of hers.

"The Queen is with child," Bunefer whispered. "These first months have made her foul-tempered and suspicious."

"She has no right—"

"She's the *Queen* and I am a handmaid. I know my place."

"My proud Bunefer," Khemwese murmured, watching the tilt of the chin and the ambling walk as she turned. He could have watched her all day.

The Pharaoh's garden was rich in reds and blues, and when Khemwese looked up he saw winking stars like precious stones in a handmaid's hair. Water spilled from the lip of an urn, pattering against painted tiles and all the while vapors swirled from the braziers, thick with sweet-smelling incense.

He felt a light tap on his shoulder and almost jumped. There he was the traitorous priest, dried paint peeling from his body and spatters of blood on his shenti. He looked like a crocodile Khemwese once killed, teeth crooked and a bitter smile.

"I have news, Kushite. Would you like to hear it?"

Khemwese felt the dread coil inside him like all things poisonous and he barely nodded.

"The prince is back," Puyem-re said, pausing for a while. "He's wounded of course. Said he saw a man with a silver eye and skin darker than mud. What demon would that be?"

Khemwese shook his head. If he could guess it would be Puyem-re. The sour old goat was wearing a scowl like a worried dog and there was more than a sparkle in those little black eyes.

"He said the Commander's still out there, stabbed perhaps by a demon's spike. You do believe in demons?"

Khemwese nodded. "I've seen a few by the river, shaking out their crusty wings and snapping in the wind."

Not seen, perhaps. *Imagined.* There was a lot in his muddled head right now that made no sense and he wanted to run from the worst demon of them all.

"The Commander's missing, boy. Deserted. Now go and tell the Pharaoh."

SHENQ

Shenq awoke to the sound of dripping water and he groaned loudly from the wound in his thigh. His shoulder wasn't much better and he gritted his teeth remembering how the knife went in, ripping and twisting as it came out.

His hands were tied above his head and he could feel water beneath his feet. There was a steady sigh of wind like the draft though an open door and a mote of light danced in the distance, revealing a tunnel and a cage of roots. But under the smell of mould and decay, there lurked another odor.

Incense.

Shenq felt his skin crawl and his throat clench. There was something in there with him, only he couldn't see it and he craved light, any light. Even the steady patter of his heart was better than silence and *silence* was death to him. He longed for the river where mist loitered for a time and then disappeared into the quiet pools. Anything was better than this.

He heard the footsteps, wet squelching sounds through a welter of water. Someone was walking down the tunnel towards him, carrying an oil lamp. It was then he saw two naked women opposite hanging by the arms and tied to a twist of branches. One was a miller's daughter and the other a milking maid, sheaths wadded up beneath their feet. He whispered in the hope of waking them but he knew they were already dead, and he imagined their faces had they lived, vibrant faces, screaming faces, his mother's face.

He closed his eyes, listening to the *swish* of water. He was still alive and that was the part that bothered him. If Tau wanted his eyes, he could have taken them. Instead, he chose to tie Shenq up so he could torture him all he wanted.

"Did you sleep well," a voice said with a boyish lilt.

Shenq could smell the incense now and the choking smell of food. Puyem-re left a basket of meat at Shenq's feet and pressed a cup of wine to his lips.

"I'd almost given up on you," Puyem-re soothed. "Tell me, did you kill anything?"

If I had it would be on a spit in the kitchens, Shenq thought, knowing Puyem-re sought to humiliate him. He drank the wine. He was thirsty enough. And he was tense, wanting to dart out with a knife in his hand and split the beggar from cheek to cheek. Only someone had trussed him up like a roasting hen and pinned him to a tree. It was a sycamore if he could bet on it, and a big one at that.

"I stitched you up and cauterized the wounds. Master wants you alive for now." Puyem-re studied Shenq through squinty eyes, waving a hand in front of his nose. "Where's that stink coming from?"

Stink? What stink? What man ever smelled good after a hard tussle with the devil? There was a chill about the place that made Shenq uneasy and he clenched both hands to keep from shivering. Through the corner of his eye, he could see a pile of glistening rocks used to plug a wide hole, *glistening* because water was seeping through every tiny crack. They were the same rocks he had seen in Tau's burrow.

Drip, drip, drip.

"I saw General Pen-Nekhbet two days ago," Puyem-re said, lowering his voice. "Seems he wanted to send a few hundred men to the hills."

I hope he leaves a few down here . . . Shenq felt something crawl along one finger and crushed the insect in his hand. He could hardly breathe and wondered how long before he suffocated altogether.

"I told him not to bother. It's a graveyard not a battle-yard. And we don't want Pen-Nekhbet's men crossing swords with the Medjai now do we?"

Why not? A good clashing of swords never hurt anyone. Shenq was puzzled. The Medjai were guardians, defenders of sacred turf. Not enemies of the Pharaoh's elite.

"We have an interest in the Medjai. They are so close to our hearts. I expect you're wondering why we let you live. Eyes like yours see in the dark, yes, but there are others that can see into the future. Master's gone to find that *Shasu* boy. Those are *unusual* eyes."

"It can't be done," Shenq said, surprised at the roughness of his own voice.

"If my master can raise the dead, he can do anything."

"Then he can breathe life into these two women," Shenq said, jutting a chin at the dead maids. He wanted to see *that* while he still had eyes.

Puyem-re gave him a sharp look. "Magic is for kings, my sour and suspicious friend. Talking of kings, you will write a letter to the Pharaoh. You will tell him Tau-Nefer, King of the Greater Lands, demands an audience. Oh, and you'll tell your Pharaoh there are ten thousand men outside the gates."

"I'll do no such thing," Shenq said, seething. He knew Tau wasn't a king and there was no army. He would have heard the stamping of ten thousand feet if there were.

"You would do well to keep your thoughts to yourself, Commander, or you'll end up like these poor girls. Sleep while you can. Master hopes to be back before the wall gives way."

Shenq wanted to ask where *master* was but it would likely come off as facetious. In his own way he knew. Tau was waiting for Harran along the river path and Shenq hoped the boy had enough insight to shin up a tree.

"Don't try anything. I can hear every rustle from my couch." Puyem-re seemed to be holding the oil lamp rather tightly, Shenq thought.

The priest shuffled off into the darkness, drenched in a nimbus of light. The odor of blood seemed to have faded and so too did the cold. It occurred to Shenq that the passageways were too close to the river and it was only a matter of time before they collapsed altogether.

Drip, drip, drip.

He regretted not telling the Pharaoh how bitter Tau was. How he wanted to blind the whole world. How he coveted the Pharaoh's three most trusted guards because he was afraid of them and how he wanted to equip himself with their unique skills. Only Harran could save Thebes now with those earnest prayers of his.

Shenq strained against the ropes but they wouldn't budge and the world seemed to spin around shame. He was a prisoner, wet and hungry, belly longing for that basket of meat he couldn't reach.

Don't hate your master even if you are the first to recognize all his weaknesses. He is the anointed one, chosen by God. He deserves all these things no matter what he's done.

The memory of Harran's voice kept him alert even as he rested his head against a knot of fibrous roots. He knew the boy wasn't there. It was all in his mind, his dim, hazy mind.

He had no idea how long he had slept before someone called his name over the stirring of dry leaves. A child waded through the tunnel towards him and from her hand fell a lacing of beads, twinkling on a black ocean. It occurred to Shenq he was dreaming, drugged by the wine Puyem-re gave him. The little girl must have blown in with a drift of incense and she would waft out again if he blinked.

"Uncle . . ."

Shenq opened his eyes again and there she was, standing on an upturned basket and sawing at the ropes. There was a long-bladed knife in her hands, too big for a little girl.

Nebsemi. He could barely see her over a rush of water caused by the severed root. "How did you find me?"

Nebsemi watched his mouth and nodded. "I saw you fighting," she whispered in that hollow voice of hers, eyes tracking the shadows in the tunnel. "They carried you here."

The thought of Tau's hands on his body drew another shaft of fear and Shenq heard his teeth chatter. A cold sweat seemed to settle on his skin and there were voices rattling around in his head.

"Are they sleeping?" Nebsemi said, pointing at the maids.

Shenq blew on her face to stop her from looking. And when she turned back he mouthed, "Cut me loose."

Shenq could feel the knife sawing through the bonds on his right hand and it was some time before it swung free. He half-collapsed in the water, soaking the child from the waist down. She cut him loose on the other side with a single slash.

"Dog-man's gone hunting," Nebsemi said, making the gesture of a bow. "He's gone to get some eyes."

There was a stony roar in the distance and Shenq's eyes melded with the water swirling like a slick black snake. *The dam's about to burst,* he wanted to say only the words stuck in his throat. Meat floated between his toes, rancid meat, crocodile meat and he licked his lips, desperate for water.

"Don't drink it, uncle," Nebsemi said, watching his face and slipping the knife into her belt. "The trees did and now they're dying."

So that's it, Shenq thought. No wonder there was a trail of yellow sycamores leading from the river to the palace gates. Their roots had been hacked away to restore the old tunnels.

Nebsemi reached into the water and pulled out a rock slimy with mud. "For my sling," she said, nodding.

Shenq felt her arm as it crept around his back. He was not about to lean against a frail child but the truth was, he could hardly walk. They waded through the tunnel, following a float of star-berries each twinkling like a silver chain. Nebsemi had dropped them in the water so she could find her way out.

Shenq's leg was throbbing now and every step brought on a biting pain. He could hardly manage a meager slope that brought them face to face with a stairway and a faint flicker of firelight. The tunnel widened out into a large circular chamber with two narrow slots for doorways and a brazier burning in the center. A blaze of lamplight revealed a wall of snakes carved in stone and goddesses painted on the walls with arms raised to the sky. On the floor were cushions and rugs, and short-legged tables laden with persea and figs.

Shenq paused, taking time to collect himself. A stitching awl lay on a bench, blood caked on the point. *My blood,* he thought, struggling to keep a grip on his mind. There were puddles of it between the slabs on the floor.

The brazier spat and crackled, throwing out a cloud of scented smoke. Shenq could see a priest through a lazy tail of vapors, head thrown back as languid as a flower on its stalk. He was sleeping and there was a rhythm to his deep breaths.

"Puyem-re," he murmured.

The child took the sling from her belt. If she knocked the priest senseless from here, Shenq thought, it would be a marvel. He could hardly move, thigh screaming with pain every time he stood on it and blood trickled from the wound, reminding him of a bloat of meat redder than a

Kushite's tongue. He wanted to rush forward and strangle the man with his bare hands but it was the pebble that struck first, cracking bone.

"Good shot," Shenq whispered, patting her on the arm.

Nebsemi inclined her head to study him, offering the knife. Shenq hobbled towards the groaning priest and slit his throat. Puyem-re never made a sound, toppling forward into a nest of cushions

He'll bleed out slowly, Shenq thought as he wiped the knife on his *shenti*.

Laying the knife-hilt on his wrist, he bowed graciously to Nebsemi. "Yours, my lady."

He saw a flicker of a smile before her head snapped round, eyes bigger than barley loaves, and hands flapping in the air. Somehow she sensed a presence just as Shenq heard voices.

He looked for his bow and quiver, and found them on the floor by the bench. There was no sign of his knife or the small axe he kept in his belt, and hooking the bow over his back, he motioned to a door. If he was lucky, the tunnel ran west towards the offices and storerooms of the Pharaoh's private courts.

They ran uphill in the darkness, seeing only a shard of light ahead and when they burst from the trunk of a large sycamore, Shenq could see the palace pier between the trees. The tunnel had collapsed somewhere in the middle and there was no way in to the palace now.

"Go to the guardhouse, child," Shenq mouthed, unable to walk. He heard a savage howl rising from the quiet of the earth alert to the scent of blood. "Bring the captain to me."

Nebsemi ran on ahead, faster, bolder, with the sling in her hand. The wind drowned the sound of her feet as they pattered against the stone slabs, branches groaning overhead. On and on she ran towards the palace gates, waving her arms and forcing a scream.

TAU

Tau awoke to the sound of groaning. He thought it was a bad dream until he remembered where he was. The house was dark and stank of death, and he slapped Umaya on the shoulder to shut her up. His mind was full of roots and gushing water. The tunnel was gone and there was no one to light the beacons now the priest was dead.

And Shenq? He would have drowned if it hadn't been for the child. The very thought of it made Tau's flesh stir and he stood very still just thinking about it. After years of searching, he finally found the eyes he craved. Honey-glazed eyes like the ones in his dreams.

But a man can't see through another man's eyes! The voices said.

"Oh, yes he can," said Tau aloud. He can change them like clothes.

You should never have gone after the prophet, the voices said.

No, he should never have gone after the prophet. He should have stayed and guarded the tunnel himself.

A second groan revived his anger and he leapt out of bed. Umaya whimpered and sobbed, and after a time her eyes rolled back in her head and she slept some more. Tau fed her some broth and sweet herbs, only she had missed

130

her moon-time and there was a pool of vomit on the floor.

"Umaya," he said, tipping her face towards him with both hands. "Go to the hills. You can't stay here."

Tau knew the thing in her womb would grow too big and one day she would die bearing it. He no longer desired her. He no longer needed her except to keep the lamp lit in the hillside tomb. It was where Puyem-re had secreted the weapons.

He tucked a duck-bill axe in his back and slipped through the door, hoping to glimpse a sail on the river embossed with the flint-headed serpent. But there were no long ships, galloping through the swell in time to the rowers drum. It was the demons of Apepi that spoke through the leaves, tiny mouths in every vein.

You could have been a soldier, they said. *But you weren't good enough were you?*

He ignored the voices in his head as he sped along the river path and his pulse quickened when he thought he saw a shiny breastplate rising up through the silent earth and dashing into the river mist. *Ghosts,* that's what it was.

Mesmerized by the yellow streamers of dawn, Tau heard the jangle of weapons on a westerly breeze. For a while, he waited until he was sure, each step covered by the rustle of the sycamores overhead. He whistled two shrill notes, one long, one short, like the signal of the Pharaoh's guard. It had to be him. It was that time of day.

"Who's there?" the voice called out, gracious and unafraid.

"Do you remember me?" Tau said, seeing dark spangled eyes beneath well-formed brows.

The Vizier tilted his head to one side. "Should I?"

"I am the spirit of the land," Tau reminded, studying the heavy bronze breastplate. "I took the Commander's horse, don't you remember?"

"You're no spirit then," Ahmose said, knife held in a competent grip. He chuckled, voice rich like a fine wine. "Should I know you?"

"You're Ahmose, Vizier to the Pharaoh."

Ahmose raised a hand as if warding off the sound of his name. "Look, whoever you are—"

"I think you know who I am. And why I'm here."

"You're a shadow-hunter," Ahmose said with a new edge in his voice. "And you are far from home."

Tau knew Ahmose inspected every crease on his face and the teeth on his collar. *Oh, yes, I wear human and animal teeth,* Tau wanted to say, cheeks sore from grinning. He studied Ahmose closely with a measure of caution. *He's not afraid. Not even a twitch.*

"You're a deserter," Vizier Ahmose said, "Deserters are hanged in Thebes. You would do well to keep away from the palace or your feet will never touch the ground."

Tau stopped grinning, anticipating the taste of blood. "You think I'm evil down to the very bones."

"What do you want?"

"There's a Pharaoh on the throne, a man with no right to rule. Born of a secondary wife and a commander, he's hardly king's-blood now is he?"

"Some would say he's god's-blood. He has more rights than you."

"Me?" Tau said. "We're not so different you and I. We both want a sanctuary, a place to call our own."

"You don't know me."

"I know everything about you." Tau knew no weapon would penetrate the bronze scales at Ahmose's chest. He would need an axe if he wanted to kill him. "How your wife took to her bed because she had been violated by the Pharaoh. How you pretend it never happened and how you struggle whenever you see him. Oh, I know how you struggle, Ahmose. I see it in your eyes."

"You're nothing but hell's hound." Ahmose flared, lifting his dagger. "A peeper, isn't that what they call them? I should drive this through your black heart."

Tau could not pretend to be staggered at the words. He wasn't much more than a *peeper*, dirty and stinking in his current state. He was giddy with anger and he could smell the rot in his teeth.

Ahmose came on with his knife like it was part of his arm, and Tau jumped to one side to evade the strike. *Now's your chance*, Tau thought, as he saw the great man take two more strides before he turned, too far, too slow. Tau unhooked the axe from his back and hurled it through the air. The glossy blade split the Vizier's face in two and he staggered first before crashing to the ground.

"Now you remember," Tau whispered, crouching over a recoiling body with a mouthful of bloody teeth. "You drove me out with a cattle prod, all for riding the Commander's horse."

Tau searched the glazed eyes but there was no more life in them. *They were beautiful eyes*, he thought, warm and ripe.

Then he pushed the axe in further, leaning heavily on the grip.

HATSHEPSUT

Hatshepsut sat at her table, caressing a bronze mirror. She had been praying to Hathor since midnight and now it was sunrise, and there was still no news of Puyem-re. Meryt read a story of a sailor washed up on an island but Hatshepsut had no mind to listen. Instead, she reached for a third bowl of stew.

"You are very accomplished," Hatshepsut interrupted, chewing. "Where did you learn to read?"

"My mother taught me, my lady," Meryt sat on the floor and closed the scroll on her knee. Her hair sparkled with blue stones and her eyes were pale in the sunlight.

"And both our mothers are dead."

"Yes, my lady."

"Mine was a queen," Hatshepsut said irritated by Inet's snoring. The nurse lay on a bed of cushions hugging a jug of wine. "What was yours?"

"She was a seamstress, my lady. She made dresses for the lady Asenath."

Hatshepsut knew lady Asenath, wife of the late Nomarch of Am-Khent. She was an honored guest at the Feast of Opet and quite a looker according to her brother.

Handmaids brought in bowls of barley and venison

stew, and Hatshepsut was already stuffed. She was wondering if she might manage a fig when she heard her brother shouting across the great hall. It sounded as if he had executed another diviner.

"Do you miss your homeland?"

"I can still see the eastern mountains, my lady. At night the sea is as green as the sky. Sometimes the clouds are so dark they seem to wrap around the earth and in the morning there's a yellow haze on the horizon."

"What are the houses like?"

"We live in tents, my lady."

"How primitive." Hatshepsut dabbed perfume on her jaw. She knew they lived in hovels wrapped in goat-hide and the men stank of sheep. "Do you have a lover?"

"Oh, no, my lady," Meryt said half-laughing. "I'm too young."

"Fourteen is hardly young. Do you bleed?"

"Yes, my lady."

"Then you're a woman." Hatshepsut tried to remain gentle, though her heart was sour.

She gripped the hand-mirror and stared at the painted reflection. Hazel eyes languished beneath arched eyebrows and a long braided wig covered with a vulture cap should have brought all men to submission. Only it had done nothing for Commander Shenq.

"I believe all my ladies should have husbands. There is one they all pine for. Commander Shenq. But you must understand the Commander is notorious for his roving eye. He's from Susa." She said the last word as if it were the most licentious of all cultures. "He touched me, right here," Hatshepsut said, cupping her breast. "Soldiers, they're nothing but thugs."

"Not this one," interrupted Inet, struggling to stand. She had woken at last. "He's gracious and kind."

Hatshepsut silenced the nurse with a cold look. "He's *bitter* because his wife left him for a Kushite. He watched me bathe once. But you mustn't tell. My brother would kill him if he knew. There's so much betrayal in the palace. I can hardly keep up. Did you find my ring?" Hatshepsut dared to ask.

"I have looked everywhere, my lady."

"It must be found. Do you hear?" Hatshepsut said.

Meryt bobbed her head, chin trembling. "Yes, my lady."

An attendant knocked on the door and stood nervously on the threshold. "The High Steward," he stammered, "the Chief Overseer wishes to see you, Your Majesty."

Hatshepsut began to wonder if Senenmut deserved so many titles, especially if the attendants had such a hard time remembering them. "Send him in"

Senenmut rushed in and prostrated himself on the floor. It was a shrewd move, and one that always made her feel special. *Yes, he deserved those titles.* He loved hard for them.

"Rise" she said, eyeing his muscular thighs and rugged face. "What news."

"It is always a pleasure to look upon the divinity of a daughter of Ra." Senenmut sent Meryt a dismissive nod and waited until she had left the room. He held his arms out wide. "Come to me if you love me."

Hatshepsut did and rushed on him, gazing up at kind eyes. She could feel her nails digging into her palms, trying to stop a surge of lust. And backing away she felt her head nod, eyeing him with equal curiosity. He was attractive in a disgusting way. That's why she slept with him. Every night.

"The Chief of Prophets is dead." Senenmut took a deep breath, placing one hand over the ornate buckle at his waist. "The priests found his body in one of the river tunnels."

"Dead . . ." How many other secret passages were there in the palace? She had visions of Senenmut crawling out of a hidden door in her brother's bedchamber, dagger in hand. "How fitting he should die in the darkness. No one will ever know our secret. Not now."

"No one will ever know how much I love you, my Queen. I am your champion, your only champion."

She looked down at her hands just to make sure they weren't trembling. "What now? What about our plans, our—"

"Thoth has heard our findings, my love," Senenmut smiled, flicking a loving gaze. Only there was bleakness in that look that made her shudder.

"And . . ." she said impatiently, sensing some hesitation.

"Though the great god is in agreement with your claim to the succession, he cannot oust our beloved Pharaoh unless he dies of natural causes. And he seems quite well."

"*Well?* How can he be well?" Hatshepsut was incensed. Kheper-Re had eaten a large bowl of roasted beef for breakfast laced with some type of fecal matter.

"Beloved, your divine father chose his only surviving son as heir on his death bed," Senenmut said. He hesitated as if he didn't know what else to say. "When the statutes were drawn up by the High Priest, the Council of Thoth witnessed his royal seal. The documents are not in our favor. But the dream most certainly is."

What about a knife? Hatshepsut thought, wondering if she could hurry it up a bit.

"You will be Pharaoh, my love, *after* your brother dies. Of natural causes."

"And I will help him as I always have," Hatshepsut said.

She stood abruptly, fingers rubbing her throbbing temples. Without stuffing a vast quantity of poison down her brother's throat there was only one option left. She took a knife from a wooden box and stared at the pointy tip, pondering what it would be like to stab a man. Surely, it would be the same as stabbing a plucked goose, only harder because it wasn't a goose. It was her brother, a living, breathing relative. The only one she had.

"Don't follow me," she said with a frown, scurrying towards the door. "You will regret it if you do."

Hatshepsut barely glanced at the wall hangings in the corridors, promoting the divine order of kings. She listened for footsteps behind her but the halls were silent just as she knew they would be. Her mind conceived a plan so terrible; she delighted in it as if it were a brief sexual errand. Removing her sandals, she tiptoed barefoot towards the great hall, hiding her knife behind the sash at her waist.

A large Kushite stood at the Pharaoh's door, eyes close-set by a frown. His enlarged pectorals reminded her of a pet baboon she had once seen in the Temple of Swenet. The High Priest, Pi-Bak-Amana, kept such beasts behind the high syenite walls and she wondered if there was a troop of them behind the Pharaoh's door.

"Open it," she demanded.

She could feel the heat from his body as he reached for the door. His striped headdress likely concealed a bald head oiled with balanos and she wondered what it would feel like to the touch. The man was attractive, almost princely, and she felt the familiar stab of lust as she almost danced across the threshold.

Let's get this over with, she said to herself.

A breeze blew through two open terraces in her brother's apartments and she delighted in the cool of the late afternoon. Three calcite lamps glowed and flickered, and the drapes of the canopied bed trembled just as she did. Kheper-Re sat in a chair with a large medicinal poultice on his forehead. His back to her as she tiptoed across the room and by the sound of a few throaty snorts, he was sound asleep.

She clasped the dagger in her hand and twisted slightly on her heel. So intense was the temptation she gasped for air. *Sweet Hathor, let it be quick. If I place the blade on the center of his chest and thrust upwards . . .*

"Don't," a soft voice said, breaking through her

thoughts. "Drop it."

She nearly gagged as her brother stood, only it wasn't her brother. It was Harran, a darkly charismatic man with large staring eyes. He took the dagger from her gently, twirling it in one hand before slamming it on the Pharaoh's gaming table. The same hand touched his lips in a gesture of confidentiality before he drew out a chair.

"My Queen," he said, urging her to sit. "Killing a person is like killing the world. Life is too valuable."

"I never meant to . . ." Hatshepsut said, feeling a chill down the ridge of her spine. She wondered what he was doing sleeping in the Pharaoh's chair. And where was her brother? Bucking and groaning in the harem?

"Surely, our Pharaoh deserves a life same as you."

"I wouldn't have killed him," she sobbed, eyes fixed to the ground. "I couldn't. He's my brother, my family."

"But you have a knife." A current of air played with the hair at his temples, eyes sensual and brown. He couldn't have been more than eighteen.

"No. . . I meant to frighten him, that's all."

"There are three punishments for murder, my lady, decapitation, drowning and burning. They even extend to Queens."

"Don't tell anyone. Pharaoh is a hard, cruel man . . . a slave to his own passions. I have suffered so much. Have I ever had a choice?"

Harran inclined his head. "Your eyes plead but your voice is harsh. I wonder if you're honest."

"Of course I'm honest. I'm the *Queen*," Hatshepsut bristled as a new idea invaded the first. "Besides, I knew you weren't the Pharaoh."

"Then who did you think I was?" Harran said, eyes tapering into slits.

"The intruder, the *man-dog* everyone's been talking about. He's like the guardian of the dead. I've seen him myself."

Oh gods, he is quite beautiful, she thought, studying waves of dark hair that fell to his shoulders. *Shasu* men were not worth looking at in her opinion but this one was exceptional.

"You're afraid of something," Harran said.

It wasn't true. She wasn't afraid of anything. "It's the food, the wine—" Large tears fell from her eyes. She could feel them streaming down her cheeks. He would see them too and feel sorry.

"That's not what I mean," Harran paused and seemed to watch her for a time, eyes dropping suddenly to her belly. "Your son, he won't live."

Hatshepsut was lost in his jet-black curls and hardly cared what he said. "My diviners say he will."

"Your diviners lie." His voice carried authority unusual in one so young. He was puzzling and mesmerizing at the same time.

"You won't tell will you?"

"It's for the Commander to decide," Harran said.

Hatshepsut couldn't help thinking if Senenmut had made her do it. Raising him to Chief Steward was a mistake and bedding him was an even bigger one. He almost controlled her.

"Let me go." She inclined her head, hoping he would hook his arm around her waist and stop her. Surely he found her appealing. All men did. But there was no passion, not even a shudder behind his sash. "Don't you see? My brother won't believe you. You and that bodyguard there."

She saw a sudden flicker of disgust in Harran's eyes as if a walking stick had been kicked from an old man's grasp.

"Please let me go," she repeated, tongue wetting her lips.

He waved his hand and stood back to allow her to pass. He was a remarkable man, one she would like to see again.

She slipped out of the open door and turned to face the bodyguard. He fixed his eyes on some distant object pretending she was not there.

I'll make you see me, she thought, looking up at a bland face, eyes black and unyielding. "It appears you will answer for me, guard. I trust you know what to say."

Khemwese hinted at a smile. "I shall say the prophet plucked out the wart of Isis. And I shall say Egypt will no longer be cursed.

SHENQ

Shenq walked stiffly towards the southern terraces, favoring his left leg. He gripped a small pouch in one hand, feeling the contours of a large ring, greener than a sycamore leaf.

"An intruder has been reported in the alchemist's garden, sir," Jabari interrupted, meeting Shenq at the gate of the women's quarters. "We took chase and found a rack of dead rabbits. And we found this," he said, holding up a dogs' tooth collar.

Shenq hesitated beside a pillar where a delicate curtain swayed back and forth, jewels twinkling amongst the pleats. "Have a word with your brother. He might know who's been eating them. And while you're at it, let him out to resume his duties. Pabasa too."

"Sir?"

"They're more useful *out* than *in*."

Jabari gave a slow, disbelieving shake of his head. "Sir, they'll kill us all."

"They will serve in the guardhouse and you will lend an ear to their whispers. Wherever they wander, you wander. Do you hear?" Shenq dismissed Jabari with a nod.

Shenq's throat tightened as he saw the Queen,

wrapped in a red sheath and leaning against the balustrade. Her arms stretched downwards as if she greeted a friend and she sighed deeply. A counterpoise of beaten gold lay against her back and a beaded headdress peeled musically in the breeze. She lifted her head to the sky, almond painted eyes watching the clouds as they floated before the setting sun. There was nothing Shenq could see that incited her curiosity and he naturally assumed she was praying.

Behind a stand of sycamores and beyond the palace wall, he saw a figure loping by the traps, careful not to set them off.

Ah—self-doubting creature, you have made your announcement. You aim to take others down with vile words and trickery. Even the deceiver is better bred and he's no match for HaShem. You forget, I'm His champion and my sword will cut you down.

Shenq unhooked his bow and sighted on the target. He knew who it was and aimed for the waist. The arrow flew straight, and by the way Tau staggered, it reopened a rotting wound. A howl in the papyrus thickets made him shiver and there was a strained silence that followed it.

"Go after him," Shenq muttered to a guard.

"Did you see it?" The Queen pointed to the trees. The question was limp as if all the strength had been wrung out of her. "This spirit knows all my secrets, all my pain."

"They'll get him, my lady," Shenq said, troubled by her reference to *it*. Within a forest of wetland sedge they had found another dead girl. It was not a report he wished to share, ladies being terrified of such things.

"You are truly wounded," Hatshepsut said, eyes fixed on the stitches at his shoulder.

"A graze," he said, feelings his muscles tense.

"It's the beast that has changed me," she murmured. "I'm not as I was."

Shenq sighed loudly. It was as if the notion had boldly jumped into her head and rolled off her tongue. He hoped with all his heart, she had not invited the fiend. "The guards will search the gardens and the wasteland beyond. I must go—"

"I must talk with you . . . There's no one else I trust." Her voice fell away as she looked at the bandage at his thigh. "You could have died," she murmured.

"But I didn't."

"Dear Shenq, tell me what to do. My brother won't speak to me . . . He won't even see me."

The comment droned out Shenq's thoughts and he was shocked to see the Queen's face, a smear of tears. The Pharaoh's lack of interest did not mean he was impotent. The love-struck fornicator couldn't have been further from it. "He has not been well, my lady, and you are with child."

"He's well enough to see lady Aset." Hatshepsut made a claw with one hand, mouth sagging into a frown. "He's well enough to lie with her."

But is she well enough to lie with him? Shenq mused. He wanted no part of girlish rumors and he saw no point in adding to them.

"He loves her," Hatshepsut persisted, gaze tumbling into his, "and he abandons me. So I wait for opportunities. I wait for a man worthy to father my child."

Shenq couldn't believe the words he had just heard. He felt the light caress of her breath on his arm and moved a step backwards. "That is your husband's privilege, my lady."

"I won't pursue him."

"Pursuing is never the woman's realm." Shenq knew Hatshepsut couldn't help herself. Restraint did not come easily.

"The gods favor you, Shenq. *I* favor you. I dream of you. I dream of making sons with you."

Shenq's legs went numb and he felt as if he had plunged into a lagoon of lust. "My lady, I am the Pharaoh's confidant, his Commander. I will not turn against him."

"Then you do not love me."

"I love you as a subject to his Queen. But I love the Pharaoh more." With the truth laid bare, he took several steps backwards and bowed.

Hatshepsut glowered, hand reaching to her throat. "I've had lovers before," she said, patting her belly. "But you must never tell. You must burn it from your mind."

Shenq could almost feel the lick of the flames against his cheeks, knowing she would never give up. The jackal howled again, only this time it was somewhere behind the high stone walls likely sniffing the air for a way in.

"Come," she said, leading him to her apartments. "We must talk privately."

She took two fresh cups of wine from a bearer's tray, eyes flicking over Shenq's body like a teasing flail. "How many summers has it been since we were alone?"

Shenq raised one eyebrow, staring at the canopied bed. "One?"

"Three," she confirmed. "That's how long it's been."

"You have a good memory, my lady."

"Oh, I do, Shenq. And that's not all I have." Her eyes explored his mouth as she walked towards him. "I have called you here in secret. There's something you should know."

Shenq took the cup she offered. He had more feeling in the fingers that grasped the golden stem than the rest of his body and he was certain he would lose his mind if he drank the wine.

"My brother wants to replace me," she said. "He has no further use for me."

"But you're with child," Shenq said. He heard the terseness in his voice and he tried to disguise it with a smile.

"He says I'm cold." One finger twisted a curl at her forehead, lips set in a pout. "Do you think I'm cold?"

Shenq felt like a goat dragged down a mountain, hooves slipping on smooth rock. "Pharaoh has never loved anyone more than his own sister."

"He makes me drink potions in the bedroom. He's so ... so . . ."

"So?"

"So reckless."

Shenq knew the potions had to be exact. More of one ingredient intensified pleasure and more of another caused unconsciousness. And Pharaoh would likely find the latter dull.

"He threatened me." Hatshepsut faltered as if she needed time to conjure enough drama. "He says I cause his nightmares. He says I'm the reason for his stillborns."

Kheper-Re had planted his share of seeds in dried-up troughs and it was no wonder they grew little more than weeds. Every once in a while when the moon changed, he would bully his wives and there was always a lingering of fear amongst them. "It's a bluster of words, my lady. It'll blow over in a day or two."

"Drink," she said, peering up at him under a fringe of gold beads.

There was a sharp aroma around the rim and, if his senses were correct, the cup was laced with coriander and radish. He had tried over seven different varieties of love potions in a harlot's hovel in his younger years and he knew most of them when he smelled them. But this would make him numb and wistful, and he had no desire to be either.

"You would have made a great king," Hatshepsut said.

"I make a better Commander." Shenq sensed a gnarl of irritation. He knew with certainty that father Ka-Nekhet would only have considered such a proposal if all his children had died.

"If you serve me," she crooned, "I will give you Thebes."

Shenq almost believed her but he was a man of sense and without the reaction of a housefly, he would be dead in a week. "The Pharaoh is very much alive, my lady."

"He is sickly and unlikely to last the month," she said,

placing her cup on a table.

"He is served by the best doctors in the world. He expects to live far longer than his enemies."

Hatshepsut looked pained. "Enemies?"

Wives, Shenq wanted to say only his voice would be curt and hard. He wanted to find a chair and rest that wounded leg of his, only he would never get up again.

Suddenly her arms were around him and she began to sob against his chest. "I'm afraid of him," she confided. "I'm afraid he'll kill me. There's no one to protect me. *No one.*"

"These are hard times," Shenq said with a smile, placing a protective hand around her back. The other hung by his side, cup tilted and wine trickling on the floor.

"I can be strong," she said. "You'll see."

Shenq could almost smell the cruel blood that flowed through her heart. She fought a war with herself that she could never win. "I swore an oath, my lady."

"And now you will swear another," she said.

Shenq felt her hands on his back and he took a sturdy breath aware of a tender pulse in his groin. The sensation was so unexpected; he tuned out all other emotions, smelling nothing but the wine on her breath. The leopard pelt fell from his shoulder, plucked by earnest hands and he was conscious of a slight intake of breath.

"You will swear to love me, on Amun's breath. You will swear to serve me."

"My lady," he said. "Nowhere is safe from your brother's spies. Even your cupbearers are at risk. The last one hadn't finished speaking before a sword found its way into his neck."

"You are my king," she said, pulling his head towards hers, mouth grazing his.

Shenq felt nothing like a king and lifted his head. The kiss wrenched at his heart. He had no love to give her. "My lady," he said, dropping the cup and grabbing both her hands. "Think of the cupbearer. Do you want me to die?"

"The cupbearer died?" she said at last.

Of course he died. You don't think the Pharaoh would have given him another slice of pie and a cup of wine? "His body was hung upside down in the training yard, my lady. There was a terrible stench to it as I recall and host of flies."

"You loved me once," Hatshepsut said, giving a half-shrug.

Sheer drapes caressed Shenq's shoulders and vapors rose from the braziers thicker than broth. It was suffocating if he was honest. His thoughts were muddied with visions of a cracking flail, and all he needed was the Pharaoh to burst in through the door and his day would be complete.

"I love you, Hatsu, like a brother. But not like this."

"I hate you!" She was angrier than a bull, he thought, reading the signs of a pounding fist against his chest.

He felt oddly touched she found him pleasant enough to bed. But she was a fool. It wouldn't be long before she felt the shudder of metal in her guts or the strangling rope, whichever came first.

He let out a loud sight of relief. One full cup of that mysterious brew and his rod would have been higher than a king's standard. *They skewer rats for less*, he thought, turning suddenly as he sensed another presence. A young girl stood behind him, skin as smooth as alabaster and eyes of green.

Meryt, his mind tossed up and down like a shipwreck. *How much had she heard? How much had she seen?*

He wondered if it was the heady perfumes that had caused him to become aroused. He tried to look away but the girl was pure; something a common soldier could never grasp. A collar of green malachite rested against firm breasts, breasts he could see clearly through a slender sheath. He tried to guess the texture of them, soft against his chest.

"Go and fetch the nurse, child," the Queen said,

stepping backwards, eyes darting suddenly to Shenq. "She usually swims at this time of day."

Meryt hardly gave him a second look, spinning on her heel with the grace of a dancer. Shenq hoped she had not witnessed the Queen's infatuation, believing he was an eager participant. A hundred fabrications came to mind and no matter how he arranged them they would be hollow, futile.

She would be in the gardens soon, he thought. "My lady," he said quietly, trying to measure the Queen's expression. "I must go after the intruder."

"No. You are the Pharaoh's protector. And mine too."

The order took him unawares and he noted an edge of impatience in her voice. A commander was required to go with his men, not cower like a grandmother over a spindle. In truth, his warriors had the patience of a sea bird for the outgoing tide, and with the steely determination they were famous for they would bring the intruder back, hobbled and covered with blood.

"I will send Lieutenant Jabari to you when he returns." Shenq bowed and ran from the room.

He kept to the shadows of the peristyle court, making his way to a t-shaped pool surrounded by a trellis of trailing vines. It was there he hid himself to watch the women until he heard the rush of footsteps behind him.

"What are you doing here?" Inet said, holding out her arms like a felucca in the wind. She was wet, gown clinging to generous thighs.

"Looking for a prowler. You?"

Inet slapped a hand in front of her mouth and giggled. "You surly boy."

"I have the ring," Shenq whispered, unfastening a pouch at his waist.

"Thank Horus. You have saved her from the Pharaoh," Inet said, nodding as she spoke. "He likes to dress up in a boiled leather mask and harness."

Shenq rolled his eyes and took a deep breath. He had

seen the tack draped over the Pharaoh's chair and wondered what it was for. "When can I see her?"

"They say a poppy fades after dark and is best seen in the morning."

"It's evening," Shenq reminded. He had a mind to wait all night.

His eyes wandered to a pair of shapely buttocks and the sight of Meryt bent over a flowerpot eclipsed any innocent pictures painted by the nurse. It was a small wonder he didn't sleep at night. He hoped the nurse had the wit to keep her mouth shut. The last thing he needed was the Queen's wagging finger and a few sour words.

"You are a wretch to make me go back and forth," Inet said, pouting. "I am a rabbit between two dogs."

"Woman, I promise you are not the rabbit."

Shenq looked over at a brightly colored canopy where women gathered, some reclining on couches and some sitting on a thick layer of cushions. Meryt stood with her back to him, talking it seemed to a matron. Her hair was a torrent down her back, as sleek as a moorhen's wing.

"Bring her closer, nurse, so I can hear her voice."

Inet waddled off in search of the girl and brought her back to the pool. They sat on the blue-tiled edge, trailing their feet in the water.

"I heard you dreaming last night," Inet said, wiping her face with a square of blue linen.

Meryt gave the pond a longing gaze. A tiny jewel winked at her throat and her skin reminded Shenq of a pearl oyster. "It was nothing," she said.

"You need a man to keep you warm."

"I have a blanket."

"You have beauty. Why waste it?" Inet prodded Meryt in the ribs.

"I don't want to marry," Meryt said, flinching from the poke. She smiled a little, familiar it seemed with the nurse's jibes.

"There are worse men in the palace. They'll make you

buck and whinny like a horse and pay less than a ferry ride."

"I don't understand."

"It's best you don't, child." Inet's eyes became drowsy at the drone of a bee. "There is one that can save you. I saw his face in the flames."

Meryt scanned the braziers, eyes flicking from left to right. "There's nothing in the flames, nurse."

Shenq drew a deep breath, savoring the sight of a cringing girl. He could allow himself that much pleasure, surely.

"I saw him a moment ago," Inet said, "a handsome man with a gift. What if I said it was an emerald ring?"

Meryt wrapped her shawl tightly around her shoulders with the uncanny look of a horse being lead to the knackers. "Who is he?"

"The one that brings you letters," Inet whispered.

"Commander Shenq?"

"Of course Commander Shenq. Who else? He loves you, child."

"He's the Queen's champion."

"He is yours now. He wants you for a wife."

Meryt almost recoiled. "If it pleases her majesty."

"Her majesty is rarely pleased these days."

Shenq did not relish the idea of so much fat being cast into the fire and he knew Meryt would never marry him if the Queen did not approve. He rushed forward with a fixed grin and bowed. "Ladies."

Inet turned to Meryt and said, "Pull up your veil and hide your face."

"I apologize for the intrusion," Shenq said, heart thumping against his ribs. "It's the practice of senior officers to patrol the grounds in order to protect the Pharaoh."

There was much giggling and pointing from the canopy and one girl pulled up her sheath exposing a fat pair of buttocks.

"There has been an intruder," Shenq said, tearing his face from the buttocks. "The Pharaoh will pay a handsome reward to the man that finds him."

"A Kushite is it?" Inet said, pushing Meryt behind her.

"There are a lot of them winging north to Thebes and this one has an appetite for blood."

"Is he handsome?" Inet tipped Shenq a wink.

"If you like your meat dark, then yes."

Shenq wondered why the nurse cared. Tau had a smell on him worse than the embalmer's drains.

"You wouldn't murder a man in front of the ladies now would you?" Inet said with her nose in the air.

"To tell you the truth, I wouldn't go so far as saying I would murder at all. Trouble is, thieves take better to an arrow than a kind word."

Inet gave Shenq a sideways smile before retreating to a sundial. Meryt tried to follow but Shenq blocked her path. She teetered on her heels, recovering quickly with a backward step.

"Lady Meryt," Shenq said, hoping she saw him as an honest man. "Did my message offend you?"

"No, sir," Meryt said, cheeks losing a portion of their healthy fire.

"But you didn't reply?"

Meryt hesitated and looked away. "No, sir."

"Perhaps I've overstepped my bounds. Forgive me." Shenq tried to swallow but there was no spittle in his mouth. To his horror, she said nothing, looking at him as if she had stumbled on a nest of vipers.

"I've never thought of myself as a husband again until this day." Shenq knew the choler in his voice belied the smile on his face. He was moving too fast. "I offer my hand as a husband and my sword to protect you."

"But you're not my kinsman," Meryt said.

The voice cut him to the quick. But there was a part of him she did not know, a part that might redeem him. "My mother was from Canaan."

"Canaan?"

"Yes."

"Now I see it," she murmured with an upturned, pale face.

He wondered what she did see and hoped it wasn't the absurdity of his actions. His heart was already bound to hers with the certainty of a three-stranded chord. "Take this to the Queen," he said, offering her the pouch. "It's the emerald ring she craves."

Meryt slapped a hand in front of her mouth, tears of relief clouding her eyes. "Oh, thank you, sir."

"Can you love me?" he said, hoping the jewel would persuade her.

"If it pleases you, my lord," Meryt returned, offering a smile.

It pleased him enormously only he lamented her sense of duty. "I will wait as long as it takes," he said with a murmur. "You have my word, I will not force you nor will I touch you. Not until you're ready to be a wife."

If there was ever a time he needed a woman more, it was now. When he came home with only the twang of a bow in his head and the thundering of horses' hooves, the hearth was a lonely place.

Shenq took her hand and pressed it against his cheek. He had never been so sure about anything in his life. Only there was one thing that bothered him.

Had Pharaoh seen her first?

HARRAN

It was nearly the dawn when Harran walked along the river. He felt like a bent-backed man with legs stiffer than a chair. The Pharaoh had kept him later than usual, lamenting over his sister's murderous intentions. It took two jugs of wine to pry a coil of rope from his hands and now he was sleeping like a baby.

Harran sauntered homeward with an empty belly and he wondered if it was still worth knocking on the Commander's gate even at this time of night. It would be breakfast in an hour.

A mournful bark echoed across the wetlands, disturbing a boy and a girl without a stitch of clothing between them. They picked up a basket of linens and ran through the reeds towards the footpath.

"Greetings," Harran shouted, amused.

They turned to wave but a second howl drove them harder and they scampered along a drover's path to the village. They were hardly doing laundry if they were naked.

Harran breathed slow breaths and listened to a rustling in the long grass, trusting the jackal, or whatever it was, would show itself and be caught. Only this enemy would give him more than scratches, needle-sharp mind and faster than the blink of an eye. Frogs chattered at the water's edge and a red-throated loon moaned in the crown of a tamarisk tree. It launched into the sky, beating a path for the opposite shore, and there was a stench in the air as sour as curdled milk.

Beyond a cluster of date palms to his left, Harran saw movement so slight he could have missed it. Giving his eyes a moment to adjust, he targeted on a shape that hunkered to the ground. Anyone he met at this time of night was likely to be a deserter and his mind raced with possibilities. Behind a curtain of shrubs, a man stood gazing at him, dagger in hand. His skin was as gnarly as old leather and his head glistened with sweat.

Tau.

Harran forced his mind to center on the threat and he unsheathed his knife. *He'll spring out like a wounded antelope. They always do.* The action was swift but Harran was ready.

Tau launched forward, head lowered like a spooked horse. He broke through a flurry of leaves as Harran threw his knife. It hit the trunk of a palm tree, sinking an inch or more into the wood. Harran groaned with disappointment. Even with practice he couldn't always hit a running rabbit and he twisted on his heel, baffled.

"Prophet!"

The sound came from all around, first behind him and then in front. Harran's voice caught in his throat and he froze, one hand hovering over his belt. The knife was all he had.

He listened to snapping twigs and dry leaves, and he heard Tau breathing before he saw him.

"Unarmed is unmanned," a voice said to his left.

Harran had never seen a man uglier or smelled a stench more nauseating, and he stifled the impulse to vomit. There was a wound in Tau's side, stitched with horsehair and puckered like a drawstring purse.

Tau was drawing in lungfuls of air in a way that suggested he was laughing. He reversed his dagger and offered it handle first. "What's this now? You won't take it?"

Harran tried to swallow the bitter tang in his mouth. He wouldn't touch the bone handle, greasy with blood and spells. Instead, he watched a rolling black eye as it played his, knowing there was a trick behind it.

If I stay calm, he'll stay calm. If I move . . .

Harran dropped and rolled towards the river, listening for the crashing pursuit. He kept on straight and found himself stumbling down the embankment, heel clipping against rocks and branches scratching his cheeks. Twigs snapped behind him as he bowled into a thicket, hearing a shout over the pounding of his heart.

Coward, it cried. And he was.

He crept into a hollow near the water's edge and lay on his back looking up at a thatch of roots. It was a living den, he thought, feeling the cold touch of crocodile eggs at his shoulder.

He turned slightly to look at them, shattered and lying in pieces, the leftovers of a once thriving nest. The young were long gone but the rustling of leaves nearby alerted him to a large green eye. He saw the scaly hide and he held his breath as the trunk lifted off the ground for a moment and then settled back on four splayed feet.

Whether the crocodile had spotted him he had no idea but it waited under the beam of the moon, listening to his beating heart.

Barukh atah Adonai . . .

He had forgotten the words and he clenched every muscle in his body, begging to be let go.

The creature blocked the only way out and there was nothing he could do but wait. He counted to over a hundred before the creature moved, slowly at first to a foul-smelling pool, spilling into the black waters leaving nothing left but a thick grey tail.

Harran crawled out and wriggled through a tangle of branches. He streaked up the slope and along the river path towards the Commander's villa and he was out of breath by the time he reached the gatekeeper's lodge. From the roof of the barrel-vaulted entrance was a cluster of metal chimes and he brushed one with his hand.

"I'm a coward," he whispered, glancing up and down the path.

He was alone in the dark, seeing ragged shadows and bloody teeth. Tau was out there watching him, laughing perhaps in the quiet of his den. When Harran looked south to the edge of a barley field, he saw spikes surging like breakers towards the curve of the great river and when he looked left he saw the river path, swathed in darkness and winding towards the palace.

He lifted a hand to the heavy iron ring on the front gate. It swung open faster than he could cough and there was Khamudi, Shenq's houseman, wearing nothing but a friendly smile.

"I was swimming," Khamudi said, wiping the water from his bald head.

Harran bowed, keeping one hand pressed against his chest. "Is the Commander awake?"

"He's up and bathed," Khamudi said, pointing along the garden path bordered by shrubs and small plants.

Harran berated himself. It was later than he thought.

Torches still flickering in their sconces and lilies bobbed on the surface of a rippling pool. Khamudi had the good grace not to ask questions even though a critical eye studied Harran's torn tunic.

"What happened," said Shenq, taking Harran through a doorway with yellow painted jams and inscribed with the word *Kemnebi*.

Harran sighed loudly as he studied the entry walls, painted with scenes of hunting. There were four columns in the room carved with palm-shaped capitals and drapes hung from the ceiling, wafting back and forth in a breeze. The sight of it made him drowsy, only the smell of rich food kept him awake.

"I tried to kill Tau. And what's worse, I made a pig's farce of it."

Shenq had fresh bandages on his thigh and shoulder and he was walking better than he had in days. He led Harran through an ante-room into the main hall and pointed to a table of food.

"Where did you find him?" Shenq gave Harran's belt a cursory look, no doubt seeing the empty sheath.

"East of the river path, hiding in the trees."

"He's well, then?"

"It's not funny, sir."

"He's just one man with an eye for vengeance. Maybe he can't see further than a bowshot in the dark." Shenq offered Harran a seat and sat down himself.

"He can see alright. He chased after me."

"He's been waiting like a begging dog for weeks," Shenq said, passing a bowl of goose liver dipped in lemon oil. "And now he's not man enough to kill a prophet."

"This spirit knows all things. sir. It hides in tents, behind walls, in minds."

"Nothing hides in tents except the Pharaoh." Shenq rested his head against the back of his chair. "Ask yourself why Tau can't fight it out like a man? Why he waits on the river path at night watching the city gates and the river."

Harran stuffed the meat in his mouth and chewed on it for a while, savoring the flavors of garlic and marjoram. "He's waiting for ships."

"There are no ships."

"If he wins Egypt, he'd have the whole world."

"He doesn't have enough men." Shenq snorted. "Looks like a game for two players."

"It's not as simple as that. He's not alone. Not entirely."

"Puyem-re was a temple rat-catcher with a few crooked men. The question is, am I to follow the scent of blood or the scent of gold?"

"Both," said Harran, feeling suddenly pleased with

himself. "I had a dream and it was no ordinary dream."

"Go on."

"I saw a tomb in the mountains," Harran said, remembering the flat-topped cliffs beneath a starry sky and a large door in the eastern face. "There were paintings on the walls, gods in their chariots and horses with hogged manes and headstalls. It was a king's tomb. I'm certain."

Shenq leaned forward, clutching a goblet in both hands. "Prince Wadjmose built a tomb in one of the northern valleys only no one knows where it is. Except High Priest Hori perhaps."

"Hori?"

"He oversees the temple of Mentuhotep II. He was a tutor to prince Wadjmose."

Harran knew the prince's name stirred happy memories for Shenq and some sad ones too. "I saw a man sitting outside warming his hands beside a fire. He was dressed in a head-cloth of gold and he carried a mace. There was something familiar about him."

"Tall, short?"

The vision was a blur of precious stones and wide-buckle belts. The man could have been any of those for all Harran knew. "I can't say."

"Do you think this is where Tau keeps his gold?"

"I do, sir. And this is the man that watches over it."

"You have something else on your mind." Shenq smiled.

Harran was beginning to fear that smile. Shenq's arrows were always too close to the mark. "After Pharaoh went to inspect the harem last night, Khemwese and I played Senet for a few hours. Only I—"

"Fell asleep," Shenq finished Harran's thought.

"When I woke up the Queen was standing over me with a knife. She thought I was Pharaoh."

"And?" said Shenq, waiting.

Harran gazed into oval eyes, sparkling with a hint of humor. "Sir, I took the weapon from her and then . . . And then she tried to seduce me. She tried to seduce Khemwese too. On my life, I don't know what caused it."

Only he did know what had caused it. It was the magic in the woods, the creature that called himself Tau.

"Then you and I have much in common."

"But, sir," Harran begged. "If she doesn't overcome this she will be drowned, burned . . . taken away from all she holds dear. "

Shenq gave a nasty laugh. "Then she's cut off her own foot, my friend."

SHENQ

Dawn had not yet trickled over the horizon and the nimbus of the full moon still cast a glaze on the river. Shenq stood outside the front gate of the palace, warming himself by a brazier. He could see a light flickering amongst the trees, a fishing boat perhaps setting sail before sunup.

Tau was out there somewhere cutting throats and sleeping off the effects of poppy milk, and here he was confined to the palace precincts and growing less and less comfortable with the arrangement.

Grinding shanks and the drone of the locking bar brought him back to the present and there was Harran in the first court dressed in a white tunic and hair a tumble of freshly washed curls.

"What is it?" Shenq said, yawning.

"It's the Vizier's seal, sir. We found it hanging from a tree. There's blood on it."

Shenq snatched the pendant from Harran's outstretched hand and tilted it towards a lighted torch, studying the tell-tale signs of a struggle. "He was on his way to the Northern provinces. He should be in Neb by now."

There were too many deep dens in the woods and Shenq knew how easy it was to drag a man down any one of them. "Call Jabari and do it quietly. Tell him to take a few men to scour the river and tell him to send a rider to Neb."

The sound of Harran's swallowing was hard and loud. "The Captain's wife has gone missing too, sir."

Shenq had lost interest in Umaya, even though he hated to admit it. "In her case, I doubt it was kidnap."

"I told Pharaoh there was a curse on his land," Harran whispered as he kept up with Shenq as far as the royal apartments. "I told him to turn from his idols or he would lose his soul."

"He's faced worst odds. He's already lost his mind."

"Oh, no, sir. There is nothing *lost* about his mind. He knows he will sink in a pool of burning sulphur when the time comes. I tried to tell him I would not be there to bandage his feet."

Shenq marveled at Harran's tenacity. The Pharaoh was not just a drunkard. He was willfully eccentric. They found him with the prince inspecting a troop of *shabtis*. The funerary statuettes were made of faience, some carrying mattocks and hoes, and some holding whips.

"*I* shan't fish in the river," Kheper-Re said, munching on a duck's leg. He was brooding over the legend of Osiris whose phallus had been swallowed by a catfish. "It would be sacrilege to hook the same one."

"Father, it's a myth," Menkheperre said, spooning a mouthful of stew from the hollowed-out back of a roasted swan. "We could hunt hippo. There's a pod of them near the first cataract and a pool to catch them in."

"Hippo? I hope you're not suggesting a trip upriver. You know how choppy it can be at this time of year."

"The fresh air will do you good, father. I would like to go."

"Then you're a fool. There's a demon on the river in case you had forgotten. You don't want your glorious father sliced up before your very eyes." Kheper-Re flapped a hand at Shenq. "See how the boy taunts me, Shenq. He's bored, that's what it is. *Bored* of playing soldiers with his little wooden men."

"They're not soldiers, father," Menkheperre said with a scowl.

"I had a virgin this afternoon, Shenq. It's good to get back between the shafts."

"Glad to hear it, my lord." Shenq considered it reluctantly and nodded all the same. He hoped the *virgin* was not Meryt otherwise the Pharaoh would find the parched desert a nice change.

"She was the size of a hippo," Menkheperre affirmed, lips covered in feathers. "I saw her puking in the gardens."

Shenq heard himself exhale, too loudly it seemed. If she was the size of a hippo and prone to morning sickness, she was not the lady he feared.

"I can't seem to hold a woman for long," Kheper-Re complained, eyes searching the inside of his cup. "The maids bore me to death with their incessant chatter. I want someone to read to me, Shenq, someone clever. Bedding is such dreary work. I wouldn't share a cage with any of them. There is a child I desire, a shepherdess. I could make an exception in her case, Shenq. Small bones, small breasts . . . quite exquisite if you like them young. And rumor says she can read. I have a mind to make her a queen."

Shenq bit his lip and took a deep breath. "I wouldn't trust a rumor, my lord. Girls don't read not unless they're already queens. Did your lord father teach you nothing?"

"He taught me never to trust them," Kheper-Re said, nodding. The cords in his neck shuddered with each swallow. "Tell me; did *you* kill the Chief of Prophets?"

"He tied me up and left me to drown. Sounds like an enemy to me." Shenq wasn't about to offer up Nebsemi's contribution. It was the pebble that had likely killed him.

"It had to be done though you weren't the one to do it. We need information, Shenq, not a bloody corpse. You should have heard the High Priest. He was bellowing obscenities from the east bank."

"He's annoyed then," Shenq said, yawning in the heat of the afternoon.

"He was spitting poison, my friend. And that's not all. He swears someone will hang for it."

Shenq sat down at the table and pressed his elbows into the arms of his chair. "*Who* will hang?" he felt inclined to ask.

"Puyem-re was a holy man. His rank demanded a trial by the ordinances of Amun-Ra," Kheper-Re said with a deep sigh. "He was Chief of Prophets. We can't carve him up like common meat."

"He spent an idle life inventing prophecies people were stupid enough to believe. He was a traitor."

Kheper-Re held up a warning finger. "The Chief of Prophets had a tame falcon, Shenq. Only *holy* men can tame falcons."

"He kept mice up his sleeve, my lord."

"Mice?"

"He was a *fraud*," Shenq said, saying the last word like a curse. "I delayed too long. I should have killed him months ago."

Kheper-Re studied Shenq's face for a moment before he answered. "Did he say anything before he died?"

"A few grunts, my lord."

"Was it quick?"

"It's never quick."

Kheper-Re clutched his belly and swallowed. "If I had just eaten lunch now would be a good time to lose it."

"My lord, the Chief of Prophets was a thief. He stole from the royal coffers."

"You can't prove it."

"I'll wager my best horse I can find it."

"You know how it goes," Kheper-Re said, lowering his voice and stretching his legs beneath the table. "The priests will re-open father's tomb, take what's left of his gold and refill my treasury. I'm far from poor."

"You'll be begging in the streets by harvest."

"Now, Shenq, I insist you forget we ever had this conversation." Kheper-Re pursed his lips, looking on with a supercilious glance. "And don't give me that sour look. You can trot around the courtyards if you want, but the outside world is not available to you."

Shenq swallowed a glob of bile. He was exhausted and he wondered if he could even stand. He would take his case to the Queen. After all, she had his silence to pay for. "I'm no more than a spit-turner, my lord, a custodian. I wonder if you really need me."

"Of course I need you," Kheper-Re said, gleaming. He threw back a cup of beer, expressing a loud belch behind a fisted hand. "There is no one better. Not even Osorkon, though I pray the gods shut his ears if he should hear it. Perhaps it's a curse rather than a blessing."

Shenq couldn't help feeling like a quail recently plucked by a scullion, naked and sore. "Are you familiar with the guardians of the dead?"

A cloud crossed Kheper-Re's face, signaling that he had. "*Shakāl.* They're man-eaters."

Shenq jutted his chin towards the mountains. "There's a man in the hills that likens himself to such a beast. No one has studied him as I have. I can find him."

"This man is like a runaway horse. He'll come back when he's hungry. And then you can trap him with that mouth of yours."

"Ask yourself this, if the High Priest didn't break open your father's tomb, then who did?"

"It is a question I have often asked myself," Kheper-Re said, tempering a smile that slithered across his face. He beckoned to Harran. "Let's ask the prophet."

Harran stepped forward and bowed. "My lord, this spirit wants possession of your strongholds, your stores—even your house. He could break down these walls at any moment. Who would protect you then? Complacency is the enemy."

"Send Shenq," Menkheperre interrupted, brows drawn tightly together. "He's a commander, father, not a nursemaid."

"He's *mine*!" Kheper-Re said, choking on his rage. "After I'm done with this enemy, I'll have his liver for dinner."

"I'd like to see the enemy," Menkheperre said, voice steeped in frustration. "I'd like to stick him too."

"You couldn't stick a pig," Kheper-Re snapped.

"He could, my lord," Shenq intervened. "He's a better shot than me."

"He's a child!" Kheper-Re slammed his cup on the table, sending round loaves of honey bread flying. "Look at him. He's too small to lead an army."

Shenq watched Menkheperre carefully. The boy didn't flinch. He merely chomped on his food, looking at his father with embarrassment.

"I have guards posted at the city gates, the borders. We are well protected." Kheper-Re sucked down another cup of wine, rage cooling as it always did.

"This fiend has found his way through the borders and the city gates," Shenq cautioned. "It's only a matter of time before he bleeds through these very walls."

"You seem to have so much news, Shenq."

"I have more news if you care to hear it, though I fear the godsblood will make you deaf." Shenq walked forward and eased the cup from Kheper-Re's hand. If he drank any more he would purge more than his lunch.

"Ra is never drunk, my friend," Kheper-Re slurred. "It is sacrilege to say so. I forgive you because you are a friend, whatever that is."

Shenq put the rim of the goblet under his nose, smelling a rare mixture of spices and bitter sap. There was enough pulp in the dregs to make a book.

"Her majesty has taken stock of some interesting weaponry," Shenq said at last. "The ceremonial dagger your father bequeathed has a sharper blade than mine. I just thought I'd mention it."

Kheper-Re grasped the arms of his chair. "What does she need a dagger for?"

"To protect herself? Your prophet found her in your apartments during the night." Shenq saw a muscle flicker on Kheper-Re's neck. "On your orders, I'm sure."

The sound of a fist slashing through wood gave even Shenq a start. The table flew across the room and landed in pile of splinters against the wall.

"I'll destroy her," Kheper-Re cried. "I'll tie her to a stake and watch her burn!"

HATSHEPSUT

"Where did she find it?" Hatshepsut said, gazing at the green stone that languished on her middle finger.

"You'll be kind to her for several years if you know what's good for you," Inet said, smoothing the knots from Hatshepsut's hair. "She's a sweet thing."

"Meryt has no class, no breeding. What future is there for such a girl?"

"She can read. She told me the litany of Ra is full of heresy."

"She said *what?*"

"The litany of Ra—"

"I heard what you said and I don't give three straws what she thinks. A maid is hardly an authority on the sacred texts. I should cut out her tongue."

"I wouldn't do that if I were you. The Pharaoh was looking for a maid to warm his bed. He asked for the shepherdess. I pretended I had no idea who he meant."

"He's a fool."

"A dear fool. But I would keep the girl out of sight if I were you." Inet inclined her head towards a shout in the gardens.

Hatshepsut lurched to her feet and ran to the balcony,

crouching to stare between the balusters. The palace gardens were bright with safflower and poppy, and a gardener watered the trees that lined the pathways. A warrior stood with his back towards her apartments; a slender man with smooth amber skin.

Shenq, she murmured, sensing a quiver of desire.

He stood still like a man listening to the sounds of nature, fiery eyes trained on every facet of the garden. She imagined a soft, doting look on his face, a look she had promised herself often enough. There was elegance in such a man, dashing across the desert, homing in on his prey with a killing bite. She longed to take the risk, to touch him just to see what would happen.

I will tell him my troubles and he will make all things right. And with a little shake of my head and a wide eye, he will be tempted.

She tiptoed back to her bed, hands trembling against the damask drapes. "Go, Senenmut," she persuaded, fingers latching onto his shoulders.

Senenmut lifted his head and opened one eye. "Your brother knows what we do," he scowled, eyes heavy with afternoon sleep. "Every time I read the stars he asks me how you are."

Amun forbid, Hatshepsut thought, wavering on her feet. She prayed her brother never asked after her. Not like that. "For Horus sake, Senenmut, *go!*"

Senenmut grabbed a cloak from under the bed and slipped through the open door.

Hatshepsut pressed a hand against her belly, wincing with a shortness of breath. The babe was restless inside her and she wondered if it would come early by the time of the full moon. She stared at pots of kohl and perfume on a cedar chest, and a collection of wig boxes stacked against the wall.

What to wear . . .

She tiptoed into her audience chamber and sat on a gilded chair. A maid followed her with a brush dipped in kohl, pressing her to sit still. Closing her eyes Hatshepsut saw a gown of purple with a collar of amethyst and quartz, feeling a fresh breeze from an ostrich fan. Yes, purple was the color of kings.

"My lady," the voice startled her. And there was Meryt, graceful as a heron with a face full of smiles.

Hatshepsut shifted in her seat and a wave of dizziness washed over her. "Tell me, girl. Who gave you this ring?"

"It was Commander Shenq, my lady."

Hatshepsut felt oddly queasy at the sound of his name. She dismissed thoughts of him loving Meryt enough to free her. No, Meryt must have begged for the ring, begging in ways Hatshepsut dared not think. Nothing would do not even Meryt's soft voice as she hennaed her breasts and rubbed the aches from her calves. There was something between the nurse and Meryt, a nod here, a wink there. And when Inet took Meryt to choose a wig, Hatshepsut heard the Commander's name whispered more than once. It wouldn't be hard to prize gossip out of Inet with a jug of wine. It was cruel of course, but then all things she did were cruel.

"Where is my gown," Hatshepsut said with a slit for a smile.

Meryt found a pale green gown. Onyx beads and blue pearls dripped from each pleat and there was a wide stitching of lotus on the sash.

"I ordered it from a Siwan merchant, if it pleases your majesty."

Clever girl, Hatshepsut gasped, knowing the determination of the vendors at the palace gates. The cloth was unlike anything she had ever seen, transparent as a dragonfly's wing. She raised her arms and felt the caress of gossamer on her naked stomach and the tickle of a sash around her waist.

"You will need a shawl, my lady," Meryt said, eyes flashing prettily in the lamplight.

Hatshepsut almost laughed. A shawl would ruin the

dress and it would cover the sensuous lines of her body. And they were sensual, weren't they? "Nonsense, girl. *You* need a shawl to cover that silly head of yours. Inet will escort me. I like her better than you."

Hatshepsut stared at Meryt with a fresh loathing, breasts covered as if her sheath had a second layer. Only a hint of skin showed between the folds, giving a man no cause to look at her. The poor girl even bowed hesitantly as if tortured by the comment, hand over bosom in that annoying way of hers.

I expect she wants me to thank her for the ring, Hatshepsut thought, feeling the drag of a wig over her head. She never thanked her for the gown. "You are a marvel, Inet. I am truly a goddess now. Come, we need air."

Hatshepsut shaded her eyes with a flat hand as they walked into the gardens. The canopy provided the only shade only it was too far away from the men. "I won't sit under it. He'll never see me there."

"It's too hot," Inet complained, "and your cheeks are pinker than a pomegranate."

Hatshepsut saw the soldiers on the far side of the garden where the great sycamore almost leaned into her brother's apartments. The second in command whose name she had forgotten straddled the wall and gestured to the desert beyond, and the Commander crouched amongst the blooms re-setting the traps.

"Sit down, my lady," Inet encouraged, pointing to a stone bench.

"Can he see me here?" Hatshepsut whispered, thankful to have a hag for a companion.

"Perhaps you should cough, my child. Or faint."

"I won't faint in this dress. You will leave when he comes?"

Inet gave her a strange look and waved a fan in front of her nose.

O gods, why won't he turn? Surely, he sees me. "I want him to come to me tonight. I want him to love me, Inet."

"You talk as if he has no choice. He's a busy man. And there are spies everywhere, child."

"He's not too busy to see his Queen."

"Commander Shenq won't look at you," Inet said, wiping a glob of sweat from her forehead.

"Don't be so heartless."

"*Heartless*? Oh, child, you don't know what it means."

Hatshepsut began to fidget. "Why isn't he looking? What must I do?"

"Perhaps he prefers boys."

Hatshepsut had never thought of it before. Shenq had been married once but there were no children. He must have lain with his wife. What kind of man wouldn't lie with a wife?

Inet chuckled. "He's pretty in a rugged way. I've seen men look at him."

But does he look at them? Hatshepsut narrowed her eyes. "He's not looking at anything except those traps." Hatshepsut didn't much care about traps and wondered why Inet had not offered her the fan. "Am I flushed, Inet? I feel hot and flushed."

Inet shrugged. "Looks like you're about to burst a vein."

Hatshepsut snatched Inet's fan and waved it in front of her face. "It's too much he doesn't see me," she said, smelling a myriad of scents and a tickle inside her nose. The sneeze was out before she could stop it and the soldiers turned suddenly to look at her. Hatshepsut giggled and dismissed the nurse with a flick of a hand.

"Your Majesty," Shenq bowed, separating himself from his soldiers. His eyes floated downward as if they followed a falling leaf.

"My, it's hotter than I thought," Hatshepsut said, giving him a sideways smile.

"I'm surprised to see you here," Shenq said, signaling for the cupbearer and shouting for his men to leave. "I thought you would have slept longer in the afternoon since you sleep so badly at night."

If he dared to bring up the incident with the knife, she would flog him just enough to break his skin. "How is our beloved Pharaoh?" she said, tipping the cupbearer a wink.

"Alive," Shenq said quietly.

Hatshepsut was disgusted and amazed at the same time. She downed the wine in less than three gulps replacing the cup on the bearer's tray. She caught Shenq's eye in a choke-hold and decided to change the subject. "Does Pharaoh read the secret texts of Ra?"

"He does, my lady. Though what good it does, I can't imagine."

"You are a scholar of course," she said, noticing how his eyes avoided her hennaed breasts as if they were unsightly.

"I have a mind."

"A mind to ignore our gods."

"A mind to doubt them, my lady."

Hatshepsut stood, beckoning him to follow her. "Has he seen the lady Aset?"

"She comes and goes. I hardly notice."

"She comes when you are going, isn't that so?" Hatshepsut said, measuring a pair of sharp eyes with caution.

"What the Pharaoh does at night, my lady, is his business." Shenq looked about, allowing only the flicker of a smile. "Though she does bear children almost yearly."

"Girls," Hatshepsut reminded.

"And one son," he confirmed.

Hatshepsut felt her knees tremble, feeling the rise in her own desires. She stared at a bed of irises taunted by a dragonfly and purple-headed cattails that swayed in the breeze. "I hear he will take one of my ladies to wife." And when he said nothing, she said, "Meryt of Geshen."

She heard Shenq clear his throat before answering. It was good enough for her. "Pharaoh's choices are his business, my lady."

"Of course they are. Why are you here, Shenq?"

"We have been re-setting the traps, my lady. We don't want any more intruders."

She pondered over the word *intruder*. The man she had seen in the trees was a one-eyed warrior scarred from battle with a voice that oozed the sweetness of the gods. She felt heady with lust. "Will you walk the corridors this evening?"

"No, madam. As you know, the women's quarters are assigned to my second-in-command."

She cursed under her breath, heart sinking. *I am a goddess. How can he not notice the sun in my hair, the curve of my thighs, the glint of gold everywhere?* She shook her head, listening to the chime of her headdress. "Do you rest in the afternoons?"

"Rarely." Shenq smiled.

The afternoon rest period was available to all the Pharaoh's nobles, many attendants alike. Hatshepsut knew she was appealing in a way that made men stare, but his eyes were cold and without desire. "We could play Senet."

"I doubt that's what you have in mind."

Hatshepsut could hardly see through a veil of shock. His seriousness was galling. "If you won't enjoy a mild flirtation, you're no better than a eunuch."

"A eunuch is not without joy, my lady."

"Your duty is to your Queen."

"My duty is to the Pharaoh, my lady. I will protect him with my life."

"He's a lucky man. But I have no champion. Does no one love me?" Hatshepsut felt queasy again but she forced herself to try a smile for politeness sake.

"Your people love you."

"But do *you* love me? Perhaps you love someone else. Would you tell me if you did?"

"Your majesty, I am charged to protect your family from a threat beyond that wall. I hardly think this is the time to talk of love." Shenq offered a restrained smile. His golden eyes slipped down to her belly, a suspicious gaze that seemed to tear through the wall of her womb. "Our gracious Pharaoh is overjoyed. I pray the child resembles him in all but temper."

"You have no right to talk to me like that." Hatshepsut knew her voice thundered with a rage she had no control over. A wave of guilt bubbled to the surface like a man a killer tried to drown.

"I have more rights than you know, madam. Touch my men and I will tell Pharaoh you tried to kill him."

"You're jealous then?"

Shenq burst out into horrible laughter and the sound made her shiver. "Wives are burned for infidelity and any children they carry are sent away inheriting little more than a tent in Canaan. If that child is Senenmut's, Pharaoh will have all the proof he needs to light a fire."

"You are merciless," Hatshepsut said, pouting.

"*Honest* is the word, madam."

"I have never lied."

"Never?"

"Never!"

"Then you had better hope Anubis doesn't come for you in the night," Shenq said. "Poison is a silent threat, my lady. Far worse than the one outside these walls."

KHEPER-RE

Kheper-Re felt the movement beside him, warm against his flesh. He lifted his head from the pillows just to look at her. It was on days like this, he never felt more alive.

"Aset," he murmured, lost once more in a pair of black eyes. "My Queen."

"How can I be Queen when you already have one?" Aset asked, blinking away a tear.

Kheper-Re wanted to sob then. The wine had misted his wits and he clutched the memory of when they first met. She had been young then, twelve or so, with the sparkle of innocence in her eyes. That's how he thought of her. That's how he saw her. "No one will tell me what to do. *No one.*"

"Your father never intended for you to share the throne with a murderer. With a Queen, yes, but not a murderer. All she does is sit with that star-gazer looking for dead things in the cinders and smoke."

"Senenmut?"

Aset nodded with a look that suggested Senenmut was not a friend a wise man would want. "She sharpens a dagger on a whetstone and rides chariots in the desert with the princess. Their arms are thicker than the soldiers they ride with."

"Ride, you say?"

"Neferure rides," Aset said, her dark eyes drinking in the sights around her. "She rides very well."

Oh yes, I know about riding, Kheper-Re thought, seeing a girl's thighs wrapped around a lanky soldier. Neferure had stalked Jabari with that smile of hers, imprisoning him with a few well-chosen words. "Shenq will flog him. Twenty strikes should do it."

"We mustn't lie together again," Aset murmured, clutching her belly. "The babe—"

"The babe is no more than a date pip, my love." Kheper-Re refused to quail under the orders of a harried midwife. "The doctor will examine you. My prophet as well."

"No, not the prophet," she whispered.

Kheper-Re put a finger to her lips. But she was as restless as a baby bird, teetering on the edge of a nest.

"I don't like him," Aset said, keeping her voice low. "Those huge eyes see things."

"He's a prophet. He's supposed to see things."

"He even knows what I think," Aset complained.

Kheper-Re looked beyond the terrace to a wall of reed blinds, squinting as if he could see through right them. He wondered if Harran was man or spirit, whether he left footprints in the sand.

"He doesn't cower like other priests," she said, "and he won't bend the knee. You are firstborn of Ra. Why don't you make him?"

"Yes, I am Ra," Kheper-Re whispered, knowing a curse when he saw one. He was the mortal chosen to masquerade as Ra and he was a failure at both. The smell of food alerted him to Djoser, carrying a plate of roasted sparrows.

"They're poisoning all of us," Aset said, knees drawn up under her chin.

"You're hungry, that's all," Kheper-Re said, waving Djoser to the bed. He was suddenly hungrier than he had been in days.

"Its air I need," Aset said, gasping.

"It's a doctor she needs," Djoser grunted.

Kheper-Re snatched an oily sparrow and devoured it with a few hungry snaps. He threw his legs over the side of the bed, teeth still crunching through bones and crispy flesh. "I must go, my love."

"Go?" Aset said, fighting for breath. "Go where?"

Anywhere, Kheper-Re thought not wanting to engage in a suspicious stare. There were always bitter tears after a lying down. "To the harem."

"Who is it? Who has caught your eye, my royal bull?"

He heard her bitter laugh and recoiled. "A pharaoh must have many sons."

"You swore you wouldn't take another wife." Aset colored as if he had struck her face. "A slave girl, yes, but not a *wife.*"

Kheper-Re gave a broken smile, enjoying the power he had. "I will lift up any girl that gives me a prince."

"Who is it?"

"Never mind who," he soothed, knowing Aset's loathing for shepherd's spawn. "I must honor Ra, my love. And he has spoken."

There, that should do it, he thought, meeting her eyes briefly. Ra only talks to divine kings. Not women with hollow eyes, misted from an afternoon of love.

Aset clutched her belly, thighs sticky with blood. "Say you won't leave me. Say you won't send me away."

Kheper-Re forced himself to stand, looking away from the bloodstained sheets. "Give me a son, woman. Then I'll promise."

"O sweet Hathor, look at me," she said, looking down at her knees and waving to an attendant.

"Open the blinds," Kheper-Re barked at Khemwese. The gorge began to rise in his throat and he tried to swallow it down. "I need air."

Khemwese rushed in and raised the reed mats on the terrace. A shaft of afternoon sun added some cheer to the gloomy chamber and Kheper-Re sucked in a perfumed breeze. *Praise Horus for the lotus,* he thought, taking three deep breaths.

The attendant scooped Aset in his arms and almost ran from the chamber, trailing a tangle of bed sheets.

"Is lady Aset on the bricks," Khemwese said.

"The *birthing chair,*" Kheper-Re corrected, grimacing at the plebeian comment. A smarter man would ask for forgiveness.

He covered his nose with a hand and sauntered to his new gaming table. "I beat the Commander at Senet last night. He was a little irritated, I think. Of course it was selfish of me to cheat . . . but why not."

Khemwese stared at him as if someone had put a needle through his eye. "Nisu, we must leave—"

"A few sticks and he was done for," Kheper-Re continued, hoping Shenq would no longer think of him as an incompetent cripple. "Ah, here he is. Tell me Shenq, where do you hide in the afternoons?"

Shenq pressed a fist to his chest and bowed. "Hide, my lord? I hunt with the prince."

Kheper-Re knew several hours were frequently devoted to his son but several hours were also devoted to a garden trellis. "The women's gardens are a treat at this time of year, iris and lotus in particular. Let's walk," he said, taking Shenq's arm. "How is the Queen?"

"A little anxious, my lord."

"Sounds like a war going on."

"Just a small situation," Shenq said with a pained catch in his voice. "Seems her majesty is being fitted for a war crown."

Kheper-Re felt he was in a blaze of arrow fire and his fists went rigid. Last he saw, his sister was reclining on her couch looking like an old cat going to sleep. "Is she out of her mind?" The belching of the cupbearer distracted Kheper-Re for a moment and he looked over his shoulder, feeling the burning gaze of several nobles like a dagger in his back.

"Walk on and smile," Shenq encouraged. "They must believe you are immortal like the stars."

"She'll swallow my sword, Shenq, you'll see." Kheper-Re was tempted to wrench an antler tine from the oryx head on his wall. They were good for stabbing, sharp enough to inflict a mortal injury but blunt enough to cause suffering. He saw his sister's pleading eyes then, crawling with maggots in an open grave. "The throne is *mine* not hers."

"She might need reminding."

"I wanted to take a longer nap this afternoon but naps aren't as safe as they used to be. I might be bludgeoned in my bed."

"No throat is safe," Shenq said, offering Kheper-Re a seat under a blue canopy. He sat in the chair beside him.

"This demon whispers in corners," Kheper-Re said. "He sees what I see. He knows all my secrets."

Shenq shrugged as if it were no great concern. His eyes seemed to follow a butterfly in a clump of cattails "You only have to give the word."

"I am Ra," Kheper-Re said smugly, reminding Shenq of his divineness, his strength to overcome all adversity and that he was still in the world. There was no reply and he didn't expect one. "My sister has tried to seduce you hasn't she?"

"She has, my lord. And I have refused her."

"She came to my tent during the first month of planting," Kheper-Re said, recalling the festival of the Sailing of Sekhmet with some pleasure. "We played a game of Bao and she let me win. I should have known then. And after I had bedded her, I realized it was to cover the seeds already in her womb."

Kheper-Re wiped a cool sheen of sweat from his

forehead and leaned towards Shenq. "I would lace my sister's wine with wolf's bane if I knew it would kill her. I'm sick of her threats."

"Let her make all the threats she wants, my lord. She may be without a tongue before supper."

Kheper-Re laughed at that. He looked up at the doorway to the southern palace and the standing statues of his beloved father. They were vibrant in colors of red ochre, eyes of obsidian gazing out over the earth and revealing a hint of amusement. There were other images of him painted in the stone blocks roping elephants in Niy, a kingdom in northern Syria. It was some time before he could speak.

"Do you remember him, Shenq? He was a great man. My son will be just as mighty."

"Prince Menkheperre knows how to cipher and shoot, and he's brave," Shenq said with a softened tone.

"Not *that* son, you fool. *This* son."

"And if it's a girl?"

Kheper-Re hid his displeasure behind a pinched expression. "Girls? Who wants girls?"

He remembered the birth of princess Neferure with some regret. When the child grew up she took to chariots and warfare as if her head merited a crown. She was a flash of white with the Commander's second at her side and not only was he at her side, he was behind and on top by all accounts.

The memory became more distant like a hawk in the sky until a scream pierced though his thoughts. Lady Aset was in harness now and pushing forth a healthy boy with a face like the sun. Only in his mind, the child's face turned pale and winked out suddenly like an oil lamp. He got to wondering how difficult it would be to make a swap with a babe in the village if Aset's son died. It was a vile thought unless he could get away with it. Visions of a bucket lowered from the palace wall in the dead of night excited him, depending on what they put in it.

"I shall call him Djehutymes, *born of Thoth*," he said at last. "He will be a boy commander like my father."

"A mighty name," Shenq agreed. "Your father would be proud."

"You should have sons, Shenq. I want you to have sons. Take a woman, any woman from the Queen's house. I order it."

"I would be honored, my lord."

Two women rushed towards them, a red-faced nurse and a girl with pale green eyes. Shenq jumped to his feet, eyes snapping to the wall.

"My lord," Inet said. "Lady Aset has given birth to a son."

Kheper-Re hardly heard. He studied the nurse's companion as if she were a rare breed of horse, hair silken and black like a mare he once had.

The shepherdess. "What is your name?" he asked, offering his hand. Her fingers felt warm in his.

"Meryt," said a young voice.

"It is a pretty name. It means *beloved*. How old are you?"

"Fourteen, Your Majesty."

"A woman then. Our women breed as soon as they bleed. Walk with me," he said, offering his arm. He felt a tremor of desire, washed down with spite. She was afraid of him. "Perhaps you would like to see my new birds."

"I should like that, my lord."

"I have ostriches, loons, pelicans . . . It is always better to have more than less. Some die, you see. They're like wives. Perhaps I should take another wife. What do you say?"

"You already have a wife, my lord."

"I have several." His eyes ran down the curve of her forehead to her belly, flat like a virgin. "The master of my harem advised I should take a *Shasu* woman. Only they're a lower cast. Perhaps he was suggesting a little more variety. But that wouldn't make much sense now would it? It would be degrading for a Son of Ra to wrap his tongue around a haunch of pork. But I could bend the rule, just this once."

Kheper-Re smelled the rich scent from Meryt's hair, nose twitching at the assortment of flavors. As they approached the birthing chamber, he turned to face her, eyes following the curve of her sheath. Her breasts were no more than a mouthful and legs lean like a shell-duck. She was a scrawny slip of a girl.

"You will come to me," he whispered, lips almost touching her ear. "You will have no peace if you refuse."

"My lord," Meryt said, eyes glistening with tears. "I beg you—"

"Begging is for dogs, my lady." Kheper-Re brushed a cheek with his finger. She was lovely, so very lovely. "Tonight you will eat food from solid gold plates and taste the wine of the gods."

In truth, the plates were made of wood with a thin coating of gold but this simple wench would never know the difference. He winked to an attendant with a plate of dates.

"Tell the harem master to make sure she's clean."

HATSHEPSUT

"I must see the Queen," Commander Shenq shouted. The guards uncrossed their spears and let him through a in.

Hatshepsut lay back on her couch, sucking the juice from a fig. She brushed a hand over her sheath, knowing he could see through every pleat. It was as transparent as a smear of goat's milk.

"I've come on serious business, my lady." Shenq seemed to hesitate, choosing his words with care. "Pharaoh wishes to marry your maid."

Hatshepsut heard the sharpness in his tone and tried to calm herself. There was nothing wrong with marrying unless the head in question deserved a crown. "He has a loving heart."

Shenq inclined his head. "He wants Meryt, my lady."

Hatshepsut clenched her jaw as she pondered it. "Why?"

"*Shasu* women bear sons, your majesty. That's why. It would be madness to give her to him. She could be Queen within a year."

"There cannot be two Queens. The High Priest won't allow it. Besides, I saw him looking at the Chancellor's

184

daughter."

Shenq half smiled at that. "She's the size of a hippo with a hole under her nose that won't stay closed."

"Why do the gods punish me? Why?"

Shenq held her with a blistering gaze. "Tell me, my lady. Does Pharaoh know you carry Senenmut's bastard?"

Hatshepsut felt the blood draining from her face. "You wouldn't—."

"I would."

"I'll give you land, fields, every corner of Thebes."

"No doubt you have discovered many interesting haunts, my lady."

"Don't be facetious," she said, standing. There was a flutter in her belly as if a small bird preened itself in a fountain of water. "You're my brother's closest friend. Without you, *he* would be nothing. Without you, *I* would be nothing."

"Give her to me." Shenq's eyes sparkled beneath dark lashes, smile tempered with daring.

"You?" Hatshepsut said, tipping her head to one side. Yes, she was jealous. She had felt it for months. "And how shall we tell my beloved brother that he cannot have what he wants?"

Why not touch him? Men like to be touched. Hatshepsut closed the gap between them with two short strides. She felt the passion then, deeper than a leopard's fur in winter, and she trailed her fingers against his arm, hearing a soft moan in her throat. It turned into a gasp as he grabbed her wrist.

"There are others," Shenq said. He seemed to stare at her like a snake at a rabbit and she wondered if he would strike her.

"Others?" Hatshepsut took a few steps back and began to pace. "You mean, find one that looks like Meryt and offer her up instead?"

"Why not? He's too drunk to know the difference."

Hatshepsut was both shocked and amused. It would

be fun to see her brother cheated by his own folly and she haggled with herself for a moment. "I can't do it."

"You can't? Or you won't?"

Won't. Hatshepsut heard the echo like a vagrant wind, skin prickling from its icy chill. She opened her mouth to speak and quickly shut it again. Surely it was better this way, unless Meryt gave birth to a boy.

"How much is my silence worth?" Shenq said.

It was worth a lot only she was too scared to admit it. "Think of her, Shenq. Think of her future. What can you offer a ward of the Pharaoh's house? Lonely nights and lonely days. Your last wife died because of it."

"I can offer her a sanctuary. I can offer her a home of her own. I can offer her love."

Love? No, not that. "What do you know of love? You never loved me!"

"You wear your arrogance like a badge of honor, madam. Humility is what matters. It's at the very heart of kings!"

Hatshepsut felt the prickle of fresh tears and a buzzing in her head. "Oh, I am a king. I'm more *king* than you know."

"You leave me no choice," Shenq said, silencing her with a look. He turned suddenly on his heel, breastplate jangling with every step he took.

"No!" she yelled, staggering after him.

But he was gone before she reached the door and the buzzing in her head was louder now. She felt a warm stream down her leg and, sitting in a puddle of blood, she rocked back and forth muttering curses until the nurse came. She wondered why they took her to the bed, why they wrapped her in warm blankets. She tried to shrug them off, begging instead for Shenq.

"Lie down, child," Inet said, pressing a cup to her lips.

Hatshepsut closed her eyes, groggy from *keper-wer* and honey. Blood oozed from her womb, pooling on the sheets, and she could see steam rising from a bowl of hot water between her knees.

There was a brief lull in the wind on the terrace, rising suddenly to a howling chorus like a pack of dogs. In these upsurges she could hear the groaning of a large sycamore, branches swayed by the fury of the storm, and visions of warriors on horseback pounding the sands. Shaals covered their faces, grey-black in the darkness, and their guttural shrieks echoed against the walls of the palace. She felt the soft touch of Inet's hand before slipping free of consciousness.

In the calm that followed, her ears caught a different sound. A single howl so clear it might have come from the end of her bed.

It was the heron's bark, yes, that's what it was. Opening her eyes, she wondered if the shadow she saw was a remnant of a recent dream and she lifted her head. Oil lamps cast an eerie glow on the pillars and she saw a man and wondered who he was.

"Nuru," she whispered, thinking it was the doctor. *He'll disappear if I breathe,* she thought, reaching for him. But it was not Nuru she saw but a twisted mouth and a disfigured cheek.

"Oh gods, what are you?" she howled over the madness of the wind, clasping her stomach, arching her back, feeling the pain. "My baby . . ."

She bit into a braided wedge, suppressing the scream in her throat and rough hands pushed her back on the bed. The trees no longer groaned beyond the terrace, and she wondered if she had imagined the storm.

"He's coming, my lady. Bear down, bear down," Inet yelled. "Now, push!"

Not caring whether she lived or died, Hatshepsut strained as hard as she could; reluctantly pausing at Inet's command to ease before driving down once more. At last, something tore from her womb and she felt warm spatters against her thighs.

"Make him breathe!" Inet shouted to the midwives,

face twisting in pain.

"What is it?" Hatshepsut wailed. There was a long pause then she said quietly, "Are you afraid to tell me?"

The midwives stalled, shooting glances at one another as they backed away from the bed. It was the cruel moon that told her what it was. A tiny baby lay sideways on the bed, head crowned with dark curls. His back was pale and he did not cry.

"Put him on my breast," Hatshepsut sobbed. "Let me sing to him."

Inet sighed, lifting her eyes to the Queen. "No, my lady, he's gone."

"*Please*," Hatshepsut reached out her hand towards the infant, eyes and ears open to movement, any movement. She felt warmth as soon as she touched him, hating her womb for providing it. "Cut me a lock of his hair."

They all think I'm mad, Hatshepsut thought, as she watched Inet cut a curl from the downy head. There would be no rejoicing for this poor dead child, no feasting. She stared at the women, understanding little of what passed between them. "Pray to Hathor. Pray she takes pity on me."

"It is an omen," Inet said gently, eyes red with ruptured veins. "When the heron barks, there is always an omen."

"Don't say it!" yelled Hatshepsut, closing her eyes. She rubbed her forehead roughly as if clearing a jumble of thoughts.

"He must have a name," Inet said. "Give him a name."

"Djehutymes."

"No." Inet flinched. "Another name."

Hatshepsut shuddered and she threw her head back in desperation. Aset had taken that name for her son. How could she have forgotten? "Neferkare then," she stammered. "I shall call him Neferkare."

Beautiful is the soul of Ra. And he was beautiful. Like

Senenmut . . .

It took five pairs of hands to prize the infant from Hatshepsut's hands and she watched them leave through a veil of tears.

"None of the women will keep a secret," Inet spat, throwing off an outer apron and dashing it to the floor. "They'll tell all the kitchen maids where the child came from. They'll say there's a curse on this land!"

Hatshepsut heard the pitch in her own voice, a whimper in the back of her throat. "Where's Senenmut?"

"Sleeping, if he knows what's good for him," Inet said blandly.

"The moon's a waning crescent, I should have known."

"The moon is full, my lady," Inet corrected.

Hatshepsut stared at the Inet and then back at the moon. A stream of relief flooded over her, together with a pitch of anxiety. "It's a lucky night, then."

"*Luck* has her favorites you know," Inet murmured. "Lucky for you the child was born dead."

Hatshepsut sobbed, fingers curled over her knees like two claws.

"Lie back," Inet said, wringing out a towel. "I must pack your womb."

Hatshepsut could hear the drip of water in a ewer, the sting of a pressed napkin between her legs. *The gods have punished me with a stillborn. Perhaps I have been unkind.* She thought of Meryt and her wistful smile, a face so captivating it made her cry.

"There'll be a miserable flood this year," Hatshepsut sobbed, crumpling against her pillows and hoping someone would advise her otherwise. "Aset has a living boy and the Queen of the Two Lands has nothing."

"Her babe won't suckle. I hardly call that *living*," Inet whispered. "You must lie in for a day or two. Pharaoh will understand. I shall tell him you mourn and pray for the health of his living son."

Hatshepsut nodded, seeing the sense in it. Fresh tears dripped to her chin, lips tasting salt. "This demon conjures the strongest magic. He makes me do things . . . awful things."

"There is no spirit," Inet said, eyes bent on her task. "Lie back and rest."

"I lay with it."

"You lay with *Pharaoh*," Inet urged. Her hands trembled as she poured a jug of wine, droplets splattering over the rim.

Hatshepsut saw the disgust even on the nurse's face, a face that never judged. There was a bitter taste in her mouth, bitter like the first bite of a radish. "Aset will have everything, even my throne."

"And if her son dies?" Inet asked with a twisted smile.

Hatshepsut looked at Inet steadily for a moment, wiping a string of hair from her forehead. For the first time in months, she felt the surge of hope, gurgling like a brook before the rapids

TAU

It was the following dawn when Tau found the house in the street of the weavers. He carried a bundle of clothes and fresh meat, and two sharply honed daggers. There was a guard outside the door, eyelids heavy with sleep, and a quick slice through the windpipe put his ka amongst the stars. Tau wiped the knife on the back of his arm and sheathed it. He could hear voices inside the house and he could see a spill of light beneath the door. Two short whistles and he was inside.

"Master!" Pabasa sank to his knees and pulled Issa with him.

"You look half-dead," Tau said, putting down the sack. "What did they feed you?"

"Broth and a few lentils to thicken it." Pabasa stood up and offered Tau the only stool there was.

Tau watched Issa as he tried to find his feet. The pain in his legs was enough to make him grimace and he staggered around for a while like a drunkard.

"He'll be alright after he's eaten." Pabasa said, glancing at the boy. "I'll see he gets a good night's rest."

Tau was sad to hear it. He wanted them gone before sunrise. "Commander Shenq killed the priest," he said.

"Slit his throat and left him to drown. So there's one last job I need you to do." The hair on the back of his neck bristled at Pabasa's open mouth and he saw Issa's fingers curling around the cup in his belt. Surely they weren't afraid.

"The tunnels were ancient, master," Pabasa offered. "They were bound to cave-in sooner or later."

Tau didn't care about the tunnels. Foolish hands built the structure too fast and silt walls had soaked up half the river. The central chamber collapsed in a rush of water and two large sycamores listed to one side on the river path.

"And the Commander is a mixture of blood and flames," Pabasa said, wiping sweat from his brow. "He was bound to get out."

"You don't know him," Tau spat, wondering if the warrior had a fever, wondering if he had changed his mind. He pulled open the drawstrings of the sack with both hands and pulled out a priest's cloak and hood. "Put this on."

Pabasa half-smiled as if resigning himself to the ordeal, only Tau thought he should have been more grateful. He was giving the warrior a second chance. "And take this," he said, handing Pabasa a small pouch of venom. "It will send the Pharaoh back to his ancestors. All of it, mind, in a jug of wine."

Pabasa nodded, arms tucked in at his sides. He reminded Tau of an ox in a narrow stall dreading the sacrificial knife. As for Issa, he was as witless as he was helpless and Tau wanted to pluck those pleading eyes out with one stab if he knew they would make him see.

"There's a fresh shipment of wine by the guardhouse waiting for inspection. It has the sun disk seal. The Pharaoh's favorite. If you can follow it in as far as the cupbearer's nook, I'll give you a Nome in Middle Egypt. *Three* if you can kill him."

"What if they catch me?"

They'll kill you, of course. "You won't be caught. They

don't kill priests," Tau said, arranging the hood over Pabasa's head.

Outside the wind was gusting and the oil lamps shivered in the household niches. Tau heard a sound in the street and paused to listen. Scuffling like soldier's feet only lighter this time like a skitter of leaves across the sand. It was the dead-calm hours before sunrise and it wouldn't be calm for much longer.

Instinct made Tau reach for his knife was he walked outside. The guard was still slumped by the door, head resting on his chest. He couldn't see the other guards but he could hear their voices in the darkness. The moon was bloated like a wine skin in the sky and there was a purling mist over the surface of the earth.

He raced through the long grass and away from the village, taking care to keep away from the narrow paths the drivers used. When the grass began to taper and sand brushed against bare feet, he heard a rustle behind him and crouched as low as he could. He saw a figure advancing through the grass, curls bouncing in the breeze. He almost choked with laughter.

"I'll sing you a lullaby, child," he murmured, playing his dagger between both hands.

The girl stopped in front of him, eyes searching his lips. "You bad man," she said, stabbing the air with a finger.

Tau never thought of himself as *bad*, just careful. "And you're not?" he said.

The child blinked and looked down. It was the dagger that caught her eye. "Teacher's dead!"

"Teacher was a bad girl," Tau said, wondering how much the child saw. Osumare had screamed, only he stopped it with the back of his hand. "We all do bad things. Don't you, *Nebsemi*."

The child's jaw dropped, head inclined. *She's deaf,* he thought. *Well, almost.* She could hear something.

"I know who you are," Tau annunciated. "Where you

193

live. What you eat." *That should frighten her*, Tau thought as a sliver of light shone through the trees. "I know everything. I'm the god of the night."

"You follow me?" Her forehead puckered but there was something clever in that upturned face.

"No, child, *you've* been following me."

"He on island," she said, pointing out into the river.

She must have smelled the stench. There was a body there, hidden amongst the trees. "Let's play chase-and-kill?" Tau flashed the dagger and grinned.

"I run faster than her," she said, pointing at the narrow-eyed doe poking about in the brush.

Tau refrained from looking up. It was a well-worn trick. "Faster than Khemwese? Faster than uncle Shenq?"

"Watch," she said and bolted off into the trees.

Tau unsheathed a knife and hurled it, counting two rotations before it struck. He couldn't see much through the shadows but he knew a thud when he heard it. But another sound distracted him from retrieving that knife.

Threading their way through the trees was a troop of soldiers with a commander in their midst, dressed in the black and gold colors of the Pharaoh's most elite. They must have found the dead guard. As for Pabasa and Issa, they were long gone now.

A scout pointed at *dung eaters'* island and shouted for a boat. Tau knew what was there, decaying amongst the grit and slime. He had hoped it was nothing but teeth and bones beneath a cloud of screeching terns. Ducking beneath sun-spangled branches, he watched them, smashing through the thickets with thick wooden batons.

They're after you, fool! The voices said. Apepi always spoke with many voices and Tau knew he had to run.

Tracking the moon with one eye, he headed west where there was a wide belt of sand below the foothills and a small house with a well-stoked fire. He knew he would have to run through the cemetery of the artisans before climbing the slopes. He hated cemeteries but there was no other way. Keeping low, he felt a cold sensation in his chest. He was beginning to think he'd had enough of Commander Shenq. Too much of him in fact. And for all Umaya's herbs, the wound in his side had refused to heal.

You're thirsty, hungry, dying.

Tau crossed the wind-strewn desert away from the voices, reaching the foothills before the sun came up. Cowering between the pyramidal chapels on the hillside, he found one with the name *Sanakht* over the door. Running down a narrow shaft, he found an oil lamp burning inside where dust motes drifted lazily in the beam. A war-bow hung on a wooden statue with three loaded quivers beside it. His armies had arrived.

Tau seized the weapons and blew out the lamp. Above the small tomb were slopes of golden sands leading to boulders and hidden paths in the mountains. Looking north, he saw a waft of sand rising into the sky. He couldn't be sure, but a troop of men were heading this way. They must have found the child.

A cool breeze blew in from the north and sand spattered against his cheeks. He could see the grasslands from where he crouched, rolling like a gentle sea. The last glimmer of stars began to pale as the sun crowned over the horizon and, for a brief moment, he hesitated until he was sure he could make it to the house. The soldiers were closer now, about the size of a finger if he held one in front of his nose, and he bolted down the slope, plunging into shadows cast by a wicker fence.

An arrow pegged into the wattle of a goat pen, sending the animals into a frenzy. Tau didn't wait for the next arrow, knowing it was fast behind the first. Weaving between the houses, he found one with an open door and dousing the lamp with the palm of his hand, he glanced back to see a handful of men wading through sand tinted red by a bloody sun.

"Get me a shaal and coat, woman," he shouted to Umaya.

He grabbed a jug of goat's milk and drained it in three easy gulps. Distant shouts confirmed the oncoming soldiers and he dressed quickly, winding the shaal around his head. The tob and coat of the Bedouins would allow him to merge with the drovers and the accent was easy to mimic. There was one thing that made his hackles rise and that was the woman.

"Mokhtar is here," she said. "And all your men. He left weapons for you."

Tau nodded and muttered a praise to Apepi. "Where are they?"

"By the *Sleeping Bomani*," she said, pointing to the southernmost tip of the mountains, a headland that resembled a reclining man.

"How many?"

"He said thousands."

Tau almost laughed. He almost whooped.

"I've waited for you," Umaya implored. "It's all I do."

"Quiet," Tau said, holding up two fingers. He eased one shoulder up against the door, peering between the wooden slats.

"You promised to come," she whispered, shaking her head. "You *promised*."

Something was different in her whining voice, an edge he couldn't abide. Umaya had been a temporary relief to a cold bed and now she wanted more. More of what? Him or that hallucinating sap he carried in his belt. He snapped his fingers. It should have been enough.

"I left my husband, my child," she moaned, moving slowly towards him. "You said I would be a queen. You said I would be a wife."

Tau was tense, head cocked to one side. He stared into the night, shutting his ears from her voice. The soldiers were closer now. He could see five shapes with bows to the ready, gliding silently along the path, rigid, expectant. He wasn't afraid of them. He wasn't afraid of anything.

Until they were gone.

Tau blinked and frowned. He focused on an intersection between the houses where he had last seen the soldiers and wondered if they were searching amongst the barns. He could sense a subtle change in the air like an approaching thunderstorm, instincts honed by years on the run. Only he couldn't run because of the woman. If they questioned her, it would be his undoing.

Warm breath coated his cheek like a wet rag and he held Umaya with a steady eye. "Who are they?"

The voice was sorrowful like a long moody dusk and there was a sweetness twined with terror that fascinated him. "I . . . I don't know," she said.

A narrow beading of sweat on her upper lip gave her away. "These soldiers heard your pitiful voice and came running."

"No—"

"You think I'm a lost boy without a home. I have many homes."

She shook her head at that and frowned. "I go where you go."

"No, you go where there are rat bones and dead beetles. You walk where the dead walk." She was really afraid now. He could see it in her eyes. "When I'm Pharaoh of Thebes I will have a virgin for a wife. Not a tired old woman with a spider's web for a womb."

Tau looked back at the river, a silvery smear winding through the grasslands. He had two choices as far as he could see. Go east across the river to the temples to find Puyem-re's gold or head west to the mountains where his armies were gathering. He decided on the latter for now since he was closer to the mountain paths and he would be back before the Festival of the New Moon to find a virgin.

"So you've grown tired of me," Umaya said, pawing Tau's arm. "You've grown tired of *us*."

Tau likened Umaya to a cold gale howling through the mountain passes, a thunderstorm that rumbles overhead. He hated thunder. There was no way to silence it.

"You promised," she insisted through clenched teeth. "I'm your queen!"

Tau could feel her nails biting into his arm through the thick coat and he wondered if she anticipated her death with a perverse longing. There it was again, a hard-driving wind hurling sand against the door and all the while he could imagine lightning flaring overhead.

Lightning, like a fire and fire spreads . . . It was a good idea, he thought, wondering how much land he could burn with one lighted faggot. He would start with the farms nearest to the foothills. It would give him enough time to run.

"You said I was everything you ever wanted," Umaya murmured.

Everything? Well, no, not everything, Tau thought. He couldn't have said *everything*. The woman was nothing to behold and as dull as a temple statue. Purity was the only place for king's seed.

"You said I was the most beautiful woman you had ever seen."

Now, that was a downright lie. "I never said you were beautiful," Tau said, shaking his head.

"You used the word *love*. And you used the word *Queen*." Umaya gritted her teeth like a growling dog.

Fighting dizziness, Tau thought he saw a blaze of lightning in her eyes, a tattered streak across the sky and he wanted to run. He needed to run. The soldiers were somewhere and she was buying time.

There was only one way to silence a barking dog and that was to snap its neck.

HATSHEPSUT

Stars illuminated the sky and a belt of blue hung above the horizon, a precursor to dawn. A diligent gardener cut myrtle leaves and irises in the garden, and a young steward, armed with a stoker, added a fresh infusion of frankincense to a ewer of pellets.

The little *Shasu* girl was still asleep on a pallet, face covered with an arm. She would hear the cry of the desert lark soon and wish she was dead. It was her wedding day and there were no fathers to arrange the match and no dowry given as payment.

Hatshepsut found herself thinking of the day she married the Pharaoh, the fanfare, the feasting, the crowds along the avenues between the temples. How she wished it had been Commander Shenq in her bed that night rather than a pasty rogue who promised her nothing more than a vulgar strum of his lute and a night equal to riding a few furlongs. As she recalled, it was no bigger than a pigeon's egg, a boil. Perhaps that was why he always seemed so angry around her.

Inet entered, arm weighed down with gowns. "Did you sleep, my lady?"

"No, of course I didn't sleep," Hatshepsut whispered,

hoping her eyes weren't as slitty as they felt. "How am I supposed to sleep when my brother wants to marry that?" she said, pointing at Meryt.

Inet dropped the gowns over the arm of a chair. "Give her to Commander Shenq, I beg you."

"You can beg me all you want. I won't have my brother's hand on my face again. Look at the scars?"

Inet peered at Hatshepsut's face as if searching for one. "You'll break his heart."

As he has broken mine. Hatshepsut wondered why Commander Shenq couldn't endure to lose Meryt. She was pure and honorable, or else why did he ask for her? It was only a matter of time until Shenq's cruelty and sour wit did the girl some harm, provided she did not die from childbirth first. It was all Hatshepsut had to cheer her at such a late hour.

"Come Meryt. Can't you hear the lark?" Hatshepsut called across the room.

Meryt sat up in a daze and looked about the room. "Forgive me, my lady."

"Forgive? There is nothing to forgive." Hatshepsut was triumphant. The lark was far from waking. "I suppose you expect your new husband to be faithful. But he won't be. Marriage is a run of storms where men prey on honest women and cheeks are sore from the backs of their hands."

Inet scowled, pulling off Meryt's nightgown. "There are good men as well, child."

"I have never met one," Hatshepsut interrupted, flapping an impatient hand at a handmaid. "Love is nothing more than fantasy. It's a topsy-turvy world, girl, a trick of the mind."

"We have dresses and jewels to choose from," Inet said to Meryt, leading her to the steps of a shallow bathing pool. "Why dwell on love."

"Why indeed." Hatshepsut reclined on a pile of cushions stuffed with goose down. "She's such a dear little thing. I hope she never makes him angry otherwise he'll cut her up into dear little pieces."

Inet scrubbed Meryt skin with Moringa and orange oil. "There, there, my little rose, don't shiver," Inet said. "The Queen will miss you when you're gone."

Miss you? Yes, I'll miss you. There'll be no one to slap. Hatshepsut looked at the roasted quail on the table and popped a crispy shard in her mouth, munching noisily. She half-hoped the girl would drown in the pool if only Inet had the nerve to hold her head under the water.

"Bring me the red gown and my ruby collar," Hatshepsut said to a handmaid who had been waiting by her side for some time. The stones were the size of sparrow's eggs, sure to turn a few heads. The last king of Susa had been most generous in his time. It was a pity he was dead.

"She should have a glass of wine, several to drown her sorrow," Hatshepsut said, holding out her goblet. "What? She doesn't like wine?"

"*Shasu* don't drink wine," Inet corrected. "Wine is the poison of serpents, isn't that so, Meryt?"

"Yes, nurse."

"*Yes nurse.*" Hatshepsut dabbed grease from her lips and drained her cup in two large gulps. "She doesn't even know what a man looks like naked. Does she even know how old my brother is?"

"Old enough," Inet said, holding up a yellow gown for Meryt to choose. "He'll get joy from her in other ways, my lady. She's a good seamstress like her mother."

"Are we back to that again? What man wants a needle in his bed when he has his own?"

Hatshepsut saw the flush on Meryt's cheeks and smiled. The girl must have seen an Apis bull up close, the muscular gait, the swaying testicles. She would have found it both sickening and fascinating. What was more sickening and fascinating was Commander Shenq's threat to spill a few secrets and Hatshepsut was not about to risk it.

"Commander Shenq would be kinder," Inet reminded.

"Commander Shenq is a jealous man and his first wife went wandering. I believe you know the rest."

"His wife was a fool," Inet said. "She wandered too far."

It didn't say much for Shenq in Hatshepsut's opinion. "What was his name, this lover?"

Inet put down the gown, smiling ruefully at Meryt's shaking head. It was too gaudy for her. "I don't recall. But he was a stocky Alodian. Kindly . . ."

"Does kindness kill?"

"Well, you know, gentle. He picked up my shawl in the street all those years ago. His face was covered in scars and he had a sorry look like a boy that had lost his mother. He only had one eye, poor thing."

"I pray you didn't offer him one of your teats, nurse." *All those years ago* . . . The night jackal was prowling the marshes even then. Hatshepsut watched a trail of smoke from a mother of pearl shell where balls of incense burned. "It's your day," she said to Meryt. "I shan't steal it. Nurse, bring my pearl gown."

And there it was, a gown shot with gold and embellished with mother of pearl. Hatshepsut hadn't seen it since her wedding day. The bodice still shimmered with iridescent veins and from the hem hung discs of nacre. The Pharaoh would remember it and so would everyone else.

Meryt stood in the shimmering gown, feet sandaled in the magnificence of kings. She was charming whether she wore an old gown or not and Hatshepsut felt a stirring in her heart, a longing for her youth. She had been grievously outdone.

"I have grown old," she said and began to cry.

"Twenty-two is hardly old, my lady," Inet said. "Now, dry your eyes and get dressed."

Hatshepsut felt soft crimson fabric against her skin as the maid dressed her. The gown would win a round of noblemen's gasps and the wide strokes of paint across her eyes gave the mystery of midnight. Not outdone. A goddess is never *outdone*.

"Pearls, my lady?" Inet held up a long drape of pearls Hatshepsut rarely wore.

"Let Meryt have them. They're too white against my skin." Hatshepsut looked over at Meryt as if she was already one of yesterday's ghosts. "Paint galena on the rim of her eye. It will keep away the flies."

"She won't wear it," Inet scolded.

The girl was natural and fresh whilst Hatshepsut shimmered in red and gold. "There now," she said, fingers caressing the large stone at her throat. "Let's stir the blood."

There was a loud knocking on the door and Inet straightened. "It's Lieutenant Jabari," she said with an ascending lilt, as if she herself was surprised. "I believe he brings a gift for the lady Meryt."

Lieutenant Jabari bowed and saluted the Queen, right arm over breast. His eager nature had attracted the attention of Hatshepsut's young daughter who was charmed by his lively wit. It was likely he had also come from her bed.

"Tell me, Jabari son of nobody, why do you come calling at this early hour?"

"To bring the lady Meryt a gift from her husband and to escort her to the Pharaoh's apartments," Jabari said, patting the box under his left arm.

"You are light on your feet, Lieutenant. Where did you sleep last night?"

"In the barracks where I always sleep, my lady."

"Yet you are not out of breath."

"No, my lady. I was bathed and dressed before dawn."

Hatshepsut restrained a giggle. She understood the princess's infatuation for the Lieutenant. He was as handsome as he was witty. But when a moth flutters too close to the coals . . . Neferure was promised to prince

Menkheperre, whether she gave herself to Jabari or not.

"A lightning dresser and yet so hopeless with a sword."

"Not so, your majesty," Jabari said with a grin. "I took a man's head off yesterday with one swing."

"You did? I wish I had seen it." *Heads will soon be aslosh in a bloody bucket*, wasn't that what the Pharaoh said? Only Shenq had let Jabari's younger brother out on some harebrained scheme. "I expect your brother is dying in that tiny cell of his?"

Jabari cleared his throat. He told them all of it, even the part where Issa was taking food to a man in the marshes. "The Commander thought we might find the enemy quicker if we let him go. I've been keeping an eye on him."

Hatshepsut smiled. "What do you have in that wooden box?"

Jabari's eyes shot sideways to Meryt drawn like a leech to blood. "A necklace," he said bowing, cheeks trembling with the hint of a grin.

You peeked, Hatshepsut thought, marveling at the shine on his chest and a gut etched with muscle. There was a gold striped *khat* on his bald head and if she wasn't mistaken, his brown-green eyes studied her almost as much as she studied him.

Here was a man with hands larger than a leopard's paw, hands that dragged prisoners through the streets and flogged them until they howled. The thought of the same hands around her tiny waist made her twitch.

Her waist was tiny, wasn't it?

Hatshepsut took the box and opened it. Lying on a cushion was a small necklace of quartz and amethyst, interlaced with gold beads.

"It belonged to Queen Ahmose," said Jabari, eyes flitting from head to head. He flexed his biceps with a tight fist, as if he pretended to look off in the distance with a hunter's scowl. Nothing obvious, just an open stance, legs spread to invite a womanly gaze.

"Tell him I am most grateful," Hatshepsut said, hand caressing the cool stones. *I wonder if you think I am beautiful,* she thought giving Jabari a sideways smile. Her eyes were humorous as if they carried a secret and she was spirited, yearning only to outclass her competitors.

Jabari licked his lips, face reddening. "Lady Meryt is to wear it, your majesty."

"Indeed she is." Hatshepsut was loath to give up the piece. *Mattan . . . but how meager.* "Take some of my old gowns and put them in a trunk, Inet. The poor girl must have something to wear now she's a wife." Hatshepsut favored Jabari with an exaggerated smile. "The Pharaoh is a devious man. What do you think, Lieutenant? Is the Pharaoh as devious in the bedroom as he is on the battlefield?"

Jabari appeared nonplussed. "I wouldn't know, your majesty, although I have heard . . ."

"Enough!" Inet said, holding up both hands. "The Pharaoh's gentle. Meryt will see how gentle he is."

When the echo of Inet's words had died away, Hatshepsut was aware of a throbbing in her head. *My brother is as gentle as an insult.* He would wind Meryt up, tighter than a ship's winch.

She looked at a small maid in the corner of the room. Same hair, same smooth skin and without the paint, she could almost pass for Meryt. The girl seemed to stare with those pale eyes of hers, hoping for a word of encouragement, hoping for a promotion.

And she does so *love* her mistress . . .

A shriek brought Hatshepsut back to the present and all eyes turned to the door.

Lady Aset swept in, cheeks streaked with tears and she fell to her knees and sobbed.

"What is it now?" Hatshepsut said. "Speak!"

"My lady, they've found him. Commander Shenq found him."

"Who?" Hatshepsut sensed a gnawing dread in her gut and clenched her fists. "*Who* has he found?"

"Cousin Ahmose, my lady. He's dead."

HARRAN

Harran woke up in the late afternoon to the smoke of Pharaoh's temper. Cups and oil lamps bounced off the walls and statues flew into the gardens. The Commander patted down a small fire on a wall hanging and pulled six arrows from the head of a leopard skin rug. Rather calmly, Harran thought.

"Dead!" Kheper-Re shouted, swiping a bowl of stew from his table. "I went down on my knees to Amun. On my *knees*! And now he has taken the most precious thing I had. The gods are demons, I tell you. Nothing but demons . . ."

"Yes, my lord," Harran said, jumping at the sound of a smashed jug. The Pharaoh was already roaring drunk.

"Dead, all dead." Kheper-Re shook his head, nose red and dripping. "The Queen gave birth to a dead child. A son they said it was. And now my cousin . . . We're cursed. Can't you see?"

"You've been reading those texts again," Harran said, ruing the nights Pharaoh pored over a compendium of spells. "They're all rubbish."

"I have loved so many and now they are all gone." Pharaoh unhooked his cane from the back of the chair and

207

leaned heavily on it. He stared at Shenq for quite some time, squinting in the lamp light. "How do you like life at court, Shenq? Isn't it better than chasing rats?"

"I'm fortunate for your patronage, my lord," Shenq said, bowing.

"When you look at me," Kheper-Re slurred through his tears, "what do you see?"

"I see a bent old man, drunker than a cupbearer, my lord."

Harran coughed suddenly and ducked under a shower of bread. He wished Shenq would refrain from taking advantage of the Pharaoh's drunkenness. Now wasn't the time.

"A duck you say?"

"*Drunk*, my lord, is what I said." Shenq towered over the Pharaoh like a gibbet.

"Ra is never drunk. To say so is sacrilege!" Kheper-Re said, taking a moment to digest the comment. "Truth is," he whispered. "I am drunk. I can hardly stand. Only my friends will tell me, isn't that so, Shenq?"

"Only those that love you, my lord."

"Yes . . . yes. Nobody believes I'm a god. How can they? They see a man terrified of a dog's bark. There is a hag in the temple with a book of spells. I would like her to read my palm with fresh oil and ashes."

"Perhaps she could read mine," Shenq said, winking at Harran.

Harran knew any recollection of the conversation would be lost in a vat of wine and by tomorrow the Pharaoh would have forgotten it altogether. Almost.

Kheper-Re sobbed for a time and then he held Harran with a dark eye. "Shenq's in love with my new wife. Did you know that?"

What woman did he mean? Harran stroked his beard. He had never heard Shenq utter a woman's name and the very mention of a new wife was surprise enough.

"Tell the harem master I'm ready. Fetch her to me,"

Pharaoh said, stumbling against his chair. "I shall have sons off the little *Shasu* girl. Oh yes, Shenq, pray to the God of your fathers. He can't help you now."

Shasu girl? Harran had not seen many of those. "Who shall I ask for?"

"Lady Meryt of Geshen," Kheper-Re said, staring through the terrace at the clouds massing in the northern sky. "I must not foul my wedding day with thoughts of death."

Lady Meryt, Harran recited in his mind. He hoped he wouldn't forget the name by the time he reached the women's quarters. Nodding at Commander Shenq, he noticed a tremor of fear in those amber eyes but he must have been mistaken. Shenq had fought over a hundred battles in that loud clinking breastplate. Nothing was more frightening than death.

Harran pulled up his hood and walked through the corridors to the Queen's apartments, conscious of a strong-smelling perfume. The aroma was too bitter for him and he covered his nose with a hand.

The harem master guarded the door, mouth pulled in a thin smile. Khaldun was his name, chest heaving with gold ornaments and the eye of Horus resting between his pectorals.

"What is your pleasure, prophet?" he said, voice well-oiled like a man-trap.

"It's Pharaoh's pleasure," Harran said, staring at two raised eyebrows. "He has asked for a lady Meryt of Geshen."

"His great majesty has chosen wisely," the harem master confirmed, bowing. A cat purred loudly from between his ankles and slunk off towards the terrace. "The lady is high born and can read three languages."

Harran listened to the delights of this Meryt of Geshen just as he did each time the Pharaoh asked for a woman. He choked back a yawn as the harem master went inside, breaking through a cloud of cardamom and myrrh.

The sound of a wailing pipe and the soft thud of dancing feet caught his attention and he strained to see through a fringe of curtains. Snapping his mouth shut, he stared at the girl, barely making out the outline of a head through a twist of veils. There was a shower of onyx and gold stones on her chest, more ornate, he thought, than a priest's ephod.

"Lady Meryt," he said, hearing the thump of the doors behind her.

She nodded when she heard his voice, pulling the shawl even tighter over a slender frame. Harran offered the hem of his *tallit*, allowing her to grasp the tassels as he led the way. Dimly lit corridors slowed them down and he was afraid she would tumble over the many folds of her gown.

The Pharaoh's bedchamber appeared empty except for a high-backed chair facing north over a yawning stretch of desert. A clacking fingernail against the arm of the chair evoked an eager mood, and there was a brindled saluki at Kheper-Re's feet, languishing on a leopard skin rug and panting in the warm evening air.

"Wine?" Kheper-Re said, standing. His cheeks and lips were painted gold like a death mask.

Harran shook his head. "Wine will dull my senses, my lord. I am not permitted to drink—"

"You will drink to my new wife," Pharaoh said, offering a cup.

Harran could smell mulled fruit and coriander, and a bitter hint of something else. "What vintage is this, my lord?" The words came out like a rapid fire of arrows.

"Atum, from the vineyards of Siwa. It was brought in this morning by one of my merchants."

"We must be careful though," Harran managed. "It would be dangerous to drink it without a taster. You do agree?" Surely he did.

Kheper-Re ignored the comment, eyeing his new bride with a sideways glance. "I will not drink tonight lest the wine takes away the memory. It is a precious day."

Liar, thought Harran almost smiling. The Pharaoh was doing his best not to drink another sip in case the royal staff hung limper than the flags at his gates. He sucked in a quick breath and took a small taste. It was sweet and bitter, then dry on his tongue. He didn't know how long he should wait before it took hold, poison was sometimes a slow killer, a painful killer.

"Drink!" the Pharaoh insisted, tilting the cup towards Harran's lips. "There now, that wasn't so bad was it? Sit with me and watch the dances."

Harran took a few sips and wiped his mouth, almost gagging. There was more on his sleeve than in his throat. He was surprised to see the Pharaoh so solemn, hands resting on his knees.

The dancers crept in from the shadows, spinning and leaping to a warbling flute. Whenever one took off her veil, another spun to catch it, and their shrieks were deafening over the drone in his ears. It wasn't long before they were naked and he dropped his eyes to the floor.

He felt warm and his tunic seemed to stick to his chest. It was the wine, he told himself, and the heady incense that hung between the pillars. Beads of sweat glistened on his arms and he was thirsty. So thirsty.

Something brushed against his arm and, looking down, he saw the cat. She had followed him from the harem, pink nose twitching over the rim of his cup. There was no harm in letting her taste it and besides, there was no one to watch. He abandoned the cup on the floor, noticing two long fangs suspended above a wide grin and he watched her flicking tongue until the wine was gone.

Pharaoh whispered something to his new bride and all the while his eyes were on the dancing girls. It was hard to know if he was happy, face sterner than a statue. Gold bracelets winked along his arms as he clapped and there was a serenity Harran had not seen before. As the flutes reached a final crescendo, Kheper-Re threw precious stones on the floor and the girls scrabbled to find them. They praised him as they departed, waving and giggling.

There was silence again in that room until the Pharaoh spoke. "My heart's delight," he whispered to his bride. "Now, let's have a look at you."

Kheper-Re looked down at Harran on the floor. "Come," he said, flapping his fingers in an upturned hand.

Harran followed them to a small brazier, crackling from a fresh infusion of incense. He stood behind the girl and saw her tremble, fingers white on the Pharaoh's arm. It was only then he realized she was thirsty and he regretted giving his wine to the cat.

Kheper-Re licked his lips. "Take off your veil, Meryt."

Harran caught a glimpse of kohl-black eyes and lips brushed with red ochre. She turned her face slightly as she took off her veil, breasts straining against a sheer gown.

"Closer," murmured Kheper-Re, holding out his hands. He looked down at the girl and narrowed his eyes. The sash was tied into a knot of sorts and gemstones dripped from the fabric. "Cut her clothes off, prophet. And do it quickly."

"Me?" Harran cupped one ear with his hand.

"Use your knife, boy."

"My lord, a prophet may not look upon a naked woman let alone touch one."

"You've just seen a troupe of them. Do it!"

Harran took out his knife, working the tip through the knot until he heard the sash rip.

"Stand behind the curtain," Kheper-Re said to Harran, pointing to the terrace.

Harran almost ran for it and once behind a thin drape of pale blue, he couldn't tear his eyes from the scene. He had forgotten how beautiful women were, how perfect. The bridal sheath was a pale heap about the girl's feet and the Pharaoh studied her, hand pressed against his chin.

"You will love me more than life. You will worship me above all gods. Do you understand?"

The girl nodded. "Yes, my lord."

"Yes, Great Bull," he corrected. "Say it."

"Yes, Great Bull," she stammered.

Kheper-Re led her to the bed, parting pale yellow drapes embroidered with quartz and tiger's eye. "What do you think?" he said, passing a hand before his face.

The girl looked up briefly and then hung her head. "Handsome," she said, swallowing. "So handsome, my lord."

"No," he whispered. "Strong, brilliant, beautiful, like nothing you have ever seen. I am divine, child. Always remember that."

So that's what women say, Harran thought. They must lie and make a man feel like a man. The Pharaoh was fearsome with his black heart and gold lips, a reminder of his magnificence.

"On the bed," Kheper-Re said.

Harran tried to look away but he couldn't. The girl lay against the pillows like a swan in its nest, eyebrows pinched together. Her face seemed to blanch as the Pharaoh slid onto the bed, pinning her down with a strong hand. She was trembling like a shorthaired sighthound and her legs were just as jittery.

"Say nothing," the Pharaoh said as he covered her mouth with his hand.

The sounds were as brutal as the view. On and on it went until Harran crumpled to the floor in a fit of tears, pulling at his hair and wishing it would stop. When it did stop, he opened his eyes and saw the Pharaoh lying on the girl, head resting on her breast. The sound of sobbing was so pitiful, Harran no longer cared about the wine, whether it was poisoned or not.

"Please, my lord," the girl whimpered. "No more."

She cried softly and tried to turn her face away and Pharaoh loosened his hold to spare her a few moments. "My Queen," he murmured, kissing her hands before mounting her again.

Harran heard a wheeze on the other side of the room and saw a tail waving in the air, tongue flicking over long whiskers. The cat flopped to one side, belly trembling before going limp altogether. It was either dead or dying, he couldn't decide which, and there was a scream in his throat that wouldn't stay down. The sound when it came mimicked a shriek of wind and the last thing he saw was the grey gloom of a shroud.

SHENQ

Commander Shenq rode along the river, eyes misted with grief. He shut his ears from the mourners in the streets and he urged his horse to longer strides just to get away from them.

A low-lying trail of smoke drifted from a small island, and he could smell the stench of burnt flesh. They found a half-gutted body under a canopy of leaves, eyes torn from their sockets. Vizier Ahmose had never left Thebes.

Father, he whispered in his head.

Saying his name wouldn't bring him back and replaying happy times only made him bitter. There was a bigger lump in his throat than before as he watched the pale grey mist, imagining the body of a once loved man, all stiff and dead.

Nebsemi would have been stiff and dead if she hadn't missed a hunter's arrow. It pegged a goat with a swollen udder and her mother had roasted it for supper.

Hunter's arrow or Tau's arrow. Shenq often woke from restless dreams now not knowing where he was. There was a curse on him that needed to be broken, and with the prophet praying night and day, the same curse would become frail and unsteady like an old man's legs.

The Pharaoh sent him from the palace to fast and mourn all because the greedy buzzard was bedding a new wife.

It's for your own good, Shenq. Take to the river, to the mountains. Ride, hunt, fish. Do whatever you want. But don't stay here. You will only hate me.

Shenq did hate him, especially after hearing Harran's report. Three attendants found him sleeping on the Pharaoh's balcony wrapped in a curtain. There was a string of crimson vomit from his lips; wine they said it was. It was not enough to poison him but the cat was stiffer than the Pharaoh's member.

The horse clipped a hoof on a stone as the path leveled, ears twitching forward and back. Shenq looked up at the palm trees, ranked like soldiers and tall enough to kiss the gilt-edged skies. Their fronds fluttered in a surge of wind and sunbeams stretched like fingers on the river. A pair of spoonbills pitched up and down, long beaks skimming the surface from side to side until something frightened them away.

Shenq listened for the loud trumpeting of a bushy-tailed crane and the scream of egrets as they lifted into the sky. The swish of their feathers brushed the air and water dripped from their trailing feet. There was nothing but the soft thud of his horse's hooves as they cleared the canopy of trees and when they came into a clearing, the animal pulled up sharply at the stink of excrement.

It was the cage, creaking on a line of rope.

Pabasa was on the point of committing more violent and terrible acts, and Shenq, accustomed to long years of war, felt a stirring to do something about it.

The wooden cage hung from a sturdy branch and there was a bask of thick-armored crocodiles in a pool beneath it. Pabasa clung to the bars, back bloody from the flail. He was fettered and gagged, and hardly moved. Jabari followed him whenever he could, only Pabasa had been quick to fool him. Dressed in the garb of a lector priest, he found his way back to the palace and the cupbearer's nook. If Pharaoh had not abstained from wine before his nuptials, he would be sailing in that funerary barque of his. As for Issa, he was locked a storeroom at the back of Shenq's property, sleeping on an empty stomach.

Shenq urged his horse on with a soft word and a flick of the reins. He flexed his left thumb, adorned with a brass ring and lined with soft leather. It protected the inner pad of his finger from the bowstring and there was a stack of them jangling from a chord at his belt. He nodded at a soldier standing watch nearby and counted thirty more of them behind the trees, armed with silver-tipped arrows.

The villa came into view, lintel carved from a cedar beam and engraved with a leaping leopard. Cylindrical bells chimed from the gardens, their sweet music signaling an increase in wind. Palm nut oil wafted from the gatehouse where a single wick glowed through a loophole and the inner shanks of the gates screeched as they swung open.

"Lucky there's a bit of wind, Maaz," Khamudi said, pinching his nose. "Takes the stink upriver."

"Keep your eyes on the gate and don't oil the shank. It's always good to know when we have visitors."

"Who do you think will win?" Khamudi said, taking Shenq's horse.

"I will," Shenq answered, dismounting.

The master of the armory reported excellent shooting that week, the best yet. Shenq's warriors had mastered the heft of the khopesh, handling its deadly and efficient blade with increasing accuracy.

He heard the snapping of twigs on the river path and he could smell a thick dose of musk oil. Turning, he saw Khemwese and a veiled woman silhouetted by the sun.

"The Queen has sent you a gift," Khemwese said, as he came up behind.

"A gift?" Shenq said, squinting at the woman.

"The Queen says she is a virgin," Khemwese said, ushering the woman forward with a kind hand. "A *virgin* is

217

what she said, Maaz."

Shenq knew very well what a virgin was and stared at the girl reluctantly. He wanted no substitute and he was about to send her away when Khemwese opened his eyes a little wider, nodding.

Shenq lifted the veil to see green eyes flecked with gold and a tumble of glossy hair. "Meryt," he said, mind scrambling to understand.

"She is yours," Khemwese said. "The Queen did as you asked."

Shenq held out his hands to comfort her, heart snapping like a sheet in the wind. "I'm so sorry," he said, loving her all the same.

"No, Maaz," Khemwese said. "It was a Mitanni girl the Pharaoh had. They say she brought tears to his eyes."

Shenq almost groaned with relief, holding back a flood of sighs. He took Meryt by the hand and led her to the terrace.

There was stone bench amongst the flowers and there they sat for a while, watching the sun as it plunged beneath the hills, walls a glaze of ginger. A fountain sputtered with water, spraying the stone slabs and releasing a musty aroma from the heat of the day and the buzzing of honeybees indicated a hive nearby.

"You have a woman, sir," Khamudi said, sauntering towards them.

"She is my wife and I am her servant. I thought I asked you to watch the gate."

There was a hint of a smile on Khamudi's face as he studied the girl with the pale green eyes. "We have a fair master, my lady. You will not find a better husband. And you, sir, are the most blessed of men."

Shenq ducked his head, caught in a moment of speechlessness. He remembered finding Khamudi, a Napatan headman, over eleven years ago. Stripped and tied to a tree, his wife and four year-old son were forced to watch as Bedouins flogged him for stealing bread. There was no knowing what a mother and son would have suffered if Shenq had not found them when he did.

"You must be hungry," Khamudi said, flicking his fingers towards the kitchens.

"Come," Shenq said, taking Meryt's hand. "My houseman has an exceptional cook for a wife."

The aroma of roasting meat brought them to a narrow, open-aired kitchen, floor carpeted with grain and chaff. A plump woman slapped a ball of dough against the oven wall and she turned suddenly, fixing her eyes on Shenq. "Maaz, did you find a wife?"

"I did Ranefer," Shenq said, introducing Meryt to his house-woman.

A boy rushed in from the gardens, all teeth and laughter. "She walked under the lintel, mother. I saw them from the roof!"

"Nefer-Shepses," Ranefer said, patting a hand over his unruly hair. "My son watches the road every day for the Commander, my lady. He's louder than a warning chime."

Breathless chatter echoed off the walls and Meryt added her voice to theirs. One swift glance out of the watery light of Shenq's eye confirmed Meryt's joy and his heart settled instantly.

"I will bring wine," Ranefer said, brushing a tendril of coarse grey hair from her cheek. "Leave Khemwese with me. He can salt fish and grind spices."

Shenq nodded at Khemwese. "Tomorrow we'll row upriver to see Bunefer."

"She'll bark like a bushbuck," Khemwese said, shrugging.

"We'll take gifts. Bushbucks like gifts."

There was a low table in the great hall with cushions for seats and walls decorated with scenes of exotic animals. Shenq patted the cushion beside him and offered Meryt some wine. "You're safe now. The Pharaoh will never hurt you."

"Thank you, sir," she said, head inclined to the fading

birdsong.

"*Meryt* is not your real name is it?" he said.

"No, sir, the name was given to me by the Pharaoh's mother. My name is Meira, daughter of Amichai." She fell silent, lost in her own thoughts, lips silky with wine

"This house used to belong to the Guardian of the Armory of Montu," Shenq said, relieving her of any discomfort. "It had been in his family for many years. Pharaoh Ka-Nekhet found him in bed with two of his favorite wives. So he castrated him and gave it to me."

Shenq was surprised to hear a faint giggle concealed behind a hand and wondered if the wine had gone to her head. And if it had, there was *much more* in his storehouse.

"The Guardian still manages the armory," Shenq divulged, feeling sure she was curious. "Why Pharaoh retains him is a mystery."

"The Guardian is a royal cousin," Meryt said, giving him a shy glance. "And the armory is a dark place where he can hide his shame."

Shenq absorbed the fast response, tongue brushing his front teeth. The Pharaoh was no fool even though he acted as one. He was a master in the art. "Disgrace is a worse punishment then?"

"It is if it's eternal."

Shenq felt his smile grow softer. Here was a bright star to revive him and he began to wonder if she was more soldier than he was. "You've heard of the beast that wanders the marshes, hunting for souls."

Meryt took another swallow of wine and nodded. "Inet calls him the night jackal. Inet says he's a king."

"Inet is mistaken." Shenq held two fingers to Meryt's lips and his heart skipped a beat at the feel of them. "Tau is a lecher, a murderer. There is nothing royal about him."

"She says his skin is so black, you can't see him at night. And in the day, he powders his body with sand. That's why no one can find him."

Goose fat and a coating of sand, Shenq thought. If Inet was right, that's why Tau had evaded the soldiers in the desert.

He studied Meryt out of the corner of his eye. She was unaware of her beauty, how it tied his guts into knots, and if he wasn't careful he would lose his mind as well. "Tau can sense weakness the way a jackal smells fear. Never show him you're afraid."

"As you wish," Meryt said, staring down at her hands.

He did wish. And he wished she loved him. Not as a duty but with passion. "You are beautiful," he said wistfully, lost in a face flushed by the afterglow of the sinking sun.

"You are very kind, sir," she said, giving him a half-smile.

Shenq knew a thing about kindness. He knew a thing about patience too. And he would use both to win her.

A lady should be wooed with care, he thought. And a good deal of stealth.

KHEMWESE

Khemwese braced himself against the cold spray, grunting as he applied the oar. He watched Shenq in front of him, back tight with muscle, and he wondered briefly how many sacks of grain he could lift. Three perhaps?

Khemwese could lift six.

The screech of a kite made him look up and there it was—the big brown bird with long dark fingertips. It was a good omen, he thought.

The priests were already out in the fields, herding a fat ox towards the temple. Amun would get it for his breakfast and for the next few weeks by the size of its juicy rump.

Khemwese wanted to be a priest if only to eat well and wear a pardalide, a long leopard skin cloak that fell to the floor. He could almost see the black rosettes like a hundred paw prints and it brought memories of great warrior hunting on the plains, of flat-topped trees and the smell of wattle, of thunderstorms and lions.

Why can't I forget?

The voice in his head told him he would never forget. Memories only dim with the passing of time and grieving had become easier. He often shed a tear when he thought of his father, his guiding star, and a thick voice would come out of nowhere to tell him what to do. It was his father's voice. That much he knew.

He turned his mind to Bunefer, feeling a surge of lust through his body. He had spent over a year feeding his devotion, knowing she had no interest in him at all.

"Give her the honey first," Shenq shouted, glancing sideways at the meadows as if there was no end to their yield.

"She won't let me in," Khemwese replied, nursing a bruise on his shoulder. "She never lets me in."

"She's in love then?"

Khemwese grinned and looked down at the dark brown deer, suspended across the boat on a carrying frame. He wondered how she could refuse him with such a large amount of food.

"A word of advice," Shenq said. "The most delicious part of the hunt is the chase, not the kill. It's the study of something beautiful, something splendid. A hunter must wait until the time is right, until the prey is calm. Cool your head a little. Give it time."

Khemwese did not know how to cool his head. He was on fire for Bunefer, all the while thinking of how he could squeeze a buttock or two. Those same buttocks reminded him of a hippo he had seen on a sandbank, body glistening with auburn-colored sweat. It was large like an overfed pig, poking around the sparse undergrowth and making a series of rumbles and grunts.

"A moon of beauty," he murmured, happy to be on the river.

He had met Bunefer on a day like this. Her husband was already dead and she mourned by the river, hard wailing sounds that could be heard for miles. But there was a gander standing guard over a nest nearby and he had been watching it for a day or two. He put an arrow through its gullet and brought it to her house. Trouble was, she never let him in for that tasty supper and he could still smell it through the door.

He watched the skittering waves as they rushed against the shore. Tufted duck and glossy ibis nested there, and kingfishers whistled in the trees. The reeds stooped in the current and grey clouds skimmed across the sky, warning of gusts and dust storms.

They paddled as far as an outcrop a few yards upstream and banked the reed vessel, hauling the deer between them. Khemwese could hear the sharp trill of children in the village and the booming voice of a storyteller who stood beneath a sycamore, cape snapping in the wind like a king's flail.

"He sees you, child! You're marked with His holy seal." The old man's voice carried the cadence of the black kingdoms, rich and sonorous.

"God be with you. God go with you" Shenq shouted, arm raised in a greeting.

"What does he mean *marked with a Holy seal?*" Khemwese said, looking for the old man and seeing only long grass swaying back and forth as if it had swallowed him whole.

"It's like a brand so a herdsman can find his cattle," Shenq said.

Khemwese liked the idea of being found; it made him feel special.

Open-mouthed children crowded in the street, pointing at the white spots on the deer's flanks as it hung from the frame. They reached up and wound small hands round the single-tined antlers, following the warriors to a mud-brick house where a child waited with a sling in her belt. Coils of hair blew across her eager face and there was a hint of grief behind her smile.

"You here again?' she said to Khemwese, eyes flitting to the honey pot tied to his belt.

"I'm here again, child," Khemwese said, lowering the frame to the ground.

"You smell good." She reached over to touch his skin.

"You shiny."

"Where's your mother?" he mouthed.

"Inside," Nebsemi said, pointing to a closed door.

"Better tell her the view's better on the outside."

Nebsemi nodded and took the honey, closing the door behind her. Khemwese drummed one foot against the ground. He'd stick the same foot in the door if he could. "What's taking her so long," he whispered to Shenq.

"Primping. It's what women do."

Khemwese caught the broom long before it found his shoulder. "My, you look good," he said, smiling at Bunefer.

"You witless like a mule!" The woman put down the broom and took a few steps back. Short hair wound in a green headdress emphasized large eyes speckled like palm wood. "I told you to stay away but you keep coming back. And now look at you. All greased up like a bribe."

"Bunefer, it does you no good to refuse me," Khemwese offered, hoisting his chin at the hearth. "Fire's blazing nicely. Is that a rabbit I see on a spit?"

"I suppose you in a fever to come in?"

"I *suppose* I am." He looked at her as if she was a rare fox whose den he had just discovered. Pointing at the deer, he said, "For the lady of the house. It's a dowry."

Nebsemi yanked on her mother's skirt, lips glistening with saliva. "It's big, mamma."

Largest one I could find, thought Khemwese, wondering why Bunefer wasn't more excited about it. There were several hanging from hooks in Shenq's kitchen and this was the only buck he could find with its head still attached and a fine rack of antlers.

"Where did you find such a dowry?" Bunefer asked, crossing her arms and eyeing his clean *shenti*.

"Out there, in the desert. It took a whole day to take him down."

"Then you'll not mind if I take a *whole day* to make up my mind." Bunefer backed up and slammed the door in

225

his face.

Khemwese bowed his head sheepishly over a round of applause and stamping feet. He wished he hadn't lied about the buck. There wasn't a spot of blood on him anywhere.

Shenq raised his hand to the villagers. "Come to the pit and let's celebrate the Pharaoh's health."

Khemwese watched them march proudly down the street with the buck on their shoulders. They would skin it and spit it, and tell stories for hours.

He pressed his forehead against the lintel, listening to the sound of sobbing and he tried not to imagine what she might say if he asked her again.

Nebsemi slipped a small hand in his, eyes searching his face. "Mama likes you," she whispered. "I know she does."

Khemwese scooped the child in his arms. She wasn't like the other girls with their dolls and fancy hair. No, this one had holes in her sheath if she ever wore one at all and a sling she knew how to use.

He felt the warmth of her cheeks against his lips and he heard the creak of the door and the crackling fire. There was the rabbit turning above the flames, hissing and popping in the hearth. And there was Bunefer, eyes pooling with tears.

Khemwese walked forward and kissed her on the mouth, tasting the salt of her tears. "Ever tried a dab of honey and spicing on that spit?"

There was a roll of blankets for cushions and a three-legged stool near the hearth. The house was small and snug with a cool rooftop for a bed.

Khemwese took her hand and walked under the lintel and he whistled a tune as he took out his knife. He cut small chunks of meat off the bone and gave a slice to Nebsemi.

He was a husband and a father at last.

HARRAN

Three days later the fires started, raging across the farmlands faster than a khamāsīn. An acre of wheat was burned to stubble and smoke floated above the fields in a yellowish haze. No one knew how it had started and many assumed it was the wrath of the gods over Vizier Ahmose's death.

Praise HaShem it was only an acre, Harran thought, thankful the soldiers rushed out in time with buckets from the canals. He gripped a writing board under one arm, eyes scouring the crowd for Jabari.

The howling had stopped as if the creature's mouth no longer frothed with a bitter hatred. Not that Harran needed to hear it every night, he didn't. It was just a feeling of dread, that stomach-churning sense that something wasn't right. And now clouds dirtied the sky and rain tapped gently against a brightly colored canopy under which he stood. A dais had been set up in the first court to honor the Feast of Amun and streamers rippled above a glittering crowd.

"Filthy priests," Kheper-Re muttered, staring at a row of them. "They're nothing but thieves, *Shasu*."

"If you say so, my lord."

"I do say so. And I say again. *Thieves* and rich beggars getting fatter all the time. Look at them."

"Beggars are rarely rich, my lord," Harran said, standing behind the Pharaoh's chair. "And they're rarely fat."

"Ah, but these ones are. Look at their gold chains. They've got fat on the land. Or what's left of it."

Harran did look, studying the High Priest who had more gold on him than the Ombos mines. "Some say the priesthood is wealthier than the crown," Harran whispered. "Some say, they take more than their fair share of the land."

"Not for long, *Shasu*. I'll be taking it all back. You'll see."

No one dared talk about the fields, least of all Harran. The Pharaoh still mourned his cousin and burning stubble only reminded him of how Ahmose died. The evening was grey and dimmed with clouds. Cool breezes blew in from the north and so did the stench of smoke.

The High Priest approached the dais and bowed. He took the Pharaoh on his arm to inspect the nobles, giving as many as he could the ghost of a glare. If anyone dared touch the Son of Ra they would feel the sting of that ram-headed stick of his.

Jabari waved on the far side of the court, gesturing to Harran. It was time to question the prisoner and Harran nodded in response, dreading the nightly duty as much as he dreaded the day. He could already hear a light buzzing in his ears as he walked through the front gate and he felt a thin drizzle of rain against his cheeks.

The last of the sun pierced a streamer of clouds over the mountains and he watched them turn from pink to gold, stretching into two frothy curls where there had been one. It was suddenly quiet, too quiet except for the sound of soldiers' feet. When they approached the Commander's villa, he saw the cage swinging under a burly branch. He couldn't breathe. He couldn't swallow.

"Issa's gone. Left without a word," Jabari whispered. "Someone must have left the door open."

Harran held a fist in front of his nose and tried to swallow. He was sorry for the Issa if he was honest and he knew the boy wouldn't get far on those spindly legs. *You're a dead man, Pabasa. A. Dead. Man.*

Shenq walked through the clearing towards the cage. "You know why you're here," he shouted to Pabasa as if he had suddenly turned deaf.

Pabasa simply hung his head, blood crusting at his lips. The only sound Harran could hear was the hissing of a crocodile in the pool below, water dancing in response.

"Do you know where Issa is?" Shenq said to Pabasa. He got little more than a shake of the head. "Seems that boy's got faster legs than the Pharaoh's dog. He's probably half-way to the Red Sea by now."

There was a small ripple of laughter in that grim place and Harran found no joy in it. Captain Tehute thrust a cup of water through the bars and Pabasa drank hungrily, voice raspy and faint.

"Jabari has been watching you for some time." Shenq took the cup from the Captain and refilled it from a bucket. "He brought it to the attention of the High Steward and the jar was removed before the Pharaoh could drink it. The water in this cup comes directly from the river. Tell me how it tastes?"

Pabasa coughed and retched, eyes rolling into his head. He slumped back on the side of the cage and the wooden poles creaked under his weight.

"My soldiers are honored to serve the Pharaoh," Shenq said. "But not you. You have a different master. A liar and a thief. You don't know Tau as I do. He'll betray you quicker than a harlot with a nasty bite. The generosity runs out when he does. And he *will* run out, Pabasa. I'll make sure of it."

Harran knew a battle raged inside Pabasa's head, most rampant at night. Only there was no one to help him now.

"I'll cut off every finger for every lie, Pabasa," Shenq said, unsheathing his knife. "Where is Issa?"

"I swear," Pabasa began, trembling and sobbing. "I don't know."

Shenq nodded at the Captain and that's when Harran closed his eyes and began to pray. He could hear the clink of chains as they pulled Pabasa's hands through the bars. The scream was so loud when it came, the crocodiles thrashed and grunted, snapping at the air.

"It's a bloody death being torn between two horses," Shenq continued. "I only saw one case when the bindings snapped. The captive was dragged through the rocky plains of Noubadia. He swallowed half the desert."

Harran heard the buzzing of a fly, likely preening and sucking the blood from Pabasa's wounds and he heard the clink of the irons as the warrior tried to move.

"Just one more question," Shenq said. "Who is *Panahasi*?"

"A battle-lord," Pabasa muttered, speaking louder this time. "A flame-warrior. Tau said he had lances and straight-swords, and armies the size of the green sea. Apepi will bear witness if I'm wrong."

"You are wrong. There is no army."

Harran heard a sudden rush of blood in his ears. The word *Panahasi* was southern, whispered amongst the men as if it were a talisman of hope, the subject of prayer. He never believed it was more than a word. Until now.

Shenq pressed on, watching Pabasa intently. "Tomorrow, when the sun blazes like a hot iron, you'll be lowered so the crocodiles can have a good look at you. And each day thereafter, you'll be lowered some more. Then you can sleep as long as you like."

Harran felt his skin crawl. He knew it was only a trickle of sweat prickling down his back into the creases of his legs but in that moment he was truly afraid. Pabasa had signed his own death warrant.

It was during the second watch, Harran returned to

the palace to find the Pharaoh bathed and staring at a star-filled sky. He rubbed his hands before a basket of red-hot embers, shivering as if he was cold.

"Is he dead yet?" Kheper-Re gave a brief smile, quickly gone.

"He still lives. The Commander hopes to attract the marsh fly to the dung pile."

"A little rash, don't you think?"

"What is a good swordsman if he can't use a sword?"

"You speak in riddles, prophet." Kheper-Re stretched against the back of his chair and popped a joint in his neck. He stared at a platter of nuts, smile faltering. "Commander Shenq allows too much freedom. Soon the beggar will be sharing his cushions."

"They won't be sharing anything, my lord," Harran said. He found a space on the floor and stared at his writing board.

Kheper-Re belched loudly and by the sound of it, he was almost ready to vomit. "Was he flogged?"

"He was, my lord, nineteen, twenty times. His fingers were shortened, three of them I think."

"I doubt Commander Shenq is in the best of moods."

He's in a better mood now he's gone home, Harran thought. Shenq had been complaining of bunions and other unsightly things on his feet from standing on a terrace all day and there was nowhere to relieve himself unless he aimed through the balusters.

"That cat must be given a proper burial," Kheper said, glancing sharply at Harran. "It is sacrilege to kill a cat, especially before the feast of Amun."

"How is your new wife?" said Harran, hoping to change the subject to brighter things. He hated feasts, all those naked dancing girls and the dark glare of the priests.

"She loves me, you know."

Harran did know. He'd been studying the Pharaoh's dreamy face all day.

"What was her name, *Shasu*?" Kheper-Re said,

sketching a gesture of vagueness with his hand.

"Lady Meryt." Harran would never forget. He stared at the reed mats rolled up above the windows, smelling the scent of fresh air.

"She is my most beloved." Kheper-Re's courtesy seemed to vanish when he clapped his hands. Captain Tehute and Jabari brought in the eunuch, chest stripped of all his adornments.

"It seems my harem master accepted a bribe, *Shasu*. He offered up another lamb to the slaughter, a girl by the name of Mut-Tuya. Doesn't resemble the name *Meryt*, now does it?"

Harran looked from the eunuch to the captain and trembled. "I don't understand, my lord."

"Nor would you," Kheper-Re said. "Lady Mut-Tuya was veiled from head to toe. None of us knew who she was."

Harran reddened and glanced nervously at the eunuch. His eyes were the size of cups. "Who bribed this poor man?"

"The Queen," Kheper-Re said, caressing the turquoise ankh at his throat. "Seems she gave the girl to Shenq. Seems she's afraid of him. Tell me, what other secrets does our wily Commander keep?"

"My lord, you asked the Commander to take any lady from the Queen's house to wife. How was he to know the lady Meryt was the one you had chosen?"

"He knew, my precious friend. He was there when I asked for her." Kheper-Re waved Jabari, Tehute and the eunuch away. "Throw him in the river," he shouted as an afterthought.

Harran stared at the floor, tiles gleaming in red and green. The poor eunuch was no more than wild meat to the crocodiles and he sincerely hoped the man was a good swimmer.

"Tell me, what else does our Commander hide behind that smile of his?"

He knows about the Queen's lover. He knows Senenmut is the father of her stillborn son. Harran gave a fixed smile. "If I knew all the Commander's secrets, my lord, I would be Viceroy of Kush."

"Perhaps you should be. But Kush is so far away and I need your eyes, *Shasu*. I need your wisdom." Kheper-Re narrowed his eyes and lifted his chin. "What do you see?"

Harran could hardly stand on two trembling feet, let alone see. But what he did see was an opportunity. "I see a terrible curse on this house, my lord, the curse of *lies*. The night jackal has stripped this house of all decency. He has divided families and broken hearts. It's time to fight!"

"Give it up, *Shasu*. Your battles are better won with pen and paper."

"You've grown too fond of this jackal. You can't bear to part with him."

"Every man must indulge himself."

"But not every man has a Commander willing to die for him. Perhaps he's no more than a thumb in a child's mouth," Harran dared with a drop of his voice.

There sound of shuffling of feet outside the chamber announced Djoser with a steaming bowl of tea. "Chamomile, my lord," he said.

So timely, thought Harran, hoping it was laced with a sleeping drug. "Put your promise in writing, my lord," he said, straightening the writing board in his lap and scratching a few lines on a small piece of papyrus.

Kheper-Re looked out at the night's sky and frowned for a while. "Do you think Shenq will find him?"

"It's a certainty, my lord." Harran stood and took the hastily written edict to the table. "Sign here, if you would be so good."

Kheper-Re took a sip of his tea and squinted at him, eyes dull with suspicion.

"*Sign*, my lord," Harran repeated, tapping the paper with one finger.

"Oh, very well." Kheper-Re took the pen and

scratched his name, all the while frowning at his signature as if he had never seen it before. "Don't you think if there was an enemy, General Pen-Nekhbet would have found him? He has over five thousand soldiers stomping around the neighborhood. Surely one of them would have stuck the rat with the sharp end of his sword."

"Only a rat-catcher can catch a rat," Harran reminded, pulling the paper away before it was showered with the Pharaoh's spittle. "Shenq will find him. He's good with rats."

For a moment Kheper-Re was lost in thought, chin cupped in his hand. "Do you know what I heard today? I heard the child born to lady Aset won't suckle. Never has. He'll die like the rest of them."

Harran was glad the Pharaoh had changed the subject of his own accord. Now, if he could somehow edge to the door and hand the edict to one of the guards, Shenq would be out riding before dawn.

"My lord, I feel lightheaded," Harran said, opening his eyes a little wider and patting a hand over his belly. "I may be ill."

"Do you love me?" Kheper-Re slurred, reaching for a dagger. He began to hone the edge with an oilstone.

"I would sacrifice all I have for my King," Harran said, staring at the dagger. He was used to the sudden change in topic and began to pray silently for deliverance. He hadn't experience *deliverance* for several months. It was high time it happened.

"But you have so little to give."

It was true. Harran had little more than a mud-brick dwelling and a blanket. "I would give my life if I knew it would save you."

Kheper-Re pressed his lips together, jaw shuddering with emotion. "Why didn't Ahmose run from the snares . . . He should have seen it coming."

"He was a great soldier, Pharaoh. He knew the sacrifice. He was bred for it."

"Yes," Kheper-Re said, hesitating for a moment. "His team won the Kamaraan eight years in a row. How could he have lost to a stinking Kushite? I've lost too many good men."

"Yes, my lord." Harran nodded.

The Kamaraan was a death race across the desert where snares and Bedouins were not the only hurdles to overcome. Charioteers won land and livestock, and promotions to higher ranks. Vizier Ahmose had been outsmarted this time by a single combatant. It made no sense.

Kheper-Re tilted the knife blade to stare at his reflection. "You say you would give your life if it would save me."

Harran wished he had kept his mouth shut. "Yes, my lord, only I do like living."

"Oh, I imagine you do. But what choice do you have?"

None . . . Harran looked at the door with a fresh longing. He teetered on his heels and wondered why the room was spinning.

"*You* will go."

"Me?" Harran nearly dropped his writing board.

"The Commander will take one hundred men and *you* will go with him. Of course, you might be chased into the desert and skinned," Kheper-Re whispered, picking a fingernail with the point of his dagger. "What will you do then?"

I will be dead then, Harran thought, stifling a gasp.

"You do look peaky," Kheper-Re agreed although his own face was paler than a hog's back. "Perhaps a little fresh air will do you some good."

Harran bowed his head, hoping his thoughts weren't so transparent. He headed for the door with a wide stride, hearing the rasp of the locking bar as Khemwese opened the door.

"*Shasu!*" Kheper-Re shouted.

Harran spun on his heels and sucked in breath.

"Tell Commander Shenq to bring me the devil's head," Kheper-Re said with a bitter smile. "Or I will have his."

SHENQ

Shenq looked down at Meryt curled on his bed and wrapped in linen sheets. No earlier torment tested his stamina to such limits and his body had shuddered in protest. But last night was different. She had come to him of her own accord, crying softly in his arms and for the life of him, he didn't know why. A bride's first nights were painful and many suffered it as a wifely duty. But Meryt clung to him as if escaping from a terrible nightmare.

She was free, no longer a ward of the Queen. He was free, provided he killed that half-dead jackal and brought back his head. And he had a hundred men to help him.

A hundred? What was Pharaoh thinking?

He watched Meryt sleeping, the half-open mouth, the curve of her cheek. *One more night before I leave*, he mused, struck by her beauty.

He walked naked to the great hall with a lump in his throat, listening to the sounds of morning, and he glanced at the frescoes and at the huge beamed roof that looked like the naked timbers of a warship. Torches bathed the gardens in a golden glow and he could smell honeyed scents on the terrace.

As he floated in his pool, he thought of Pabasa

swinging outside the front gate. Only he wouldn't have that nice view anymore when Shenq cut him down.

The guardhouse was lit with a single lamp and Shenq could see it sputter, threatening to go out with another puff of wind. Khamudi stood in the shadows humming a low tune with a fresh *shenti* over one arm and a quiver on his back.

"Any news?" Shenq said, approaching the front gate.

"There was a boy outside the gate a moment ago, sniffing around the cage."

Shenq felt his brows pucker, lips pulling at the corners. He hoped it was a boy worth following. "Where is he now?"

"Went off in a westerly direction but he'll be back again," Khamudi said as he tied the straps of Shenq's breastplate.

Shenq twisted the gold cufflets on his wrists and grinned. "West, you say?"

Khamudi nodded and handed Shenq the quiver. "Your arrows have been balanced and sharpened. It is the first day of the Feast of Amun," he reminded.

Shenq heard the crowds cheering outside even before he reached the cage. He heard the snap of timbers as he cut it down unless it was a leg or two and he glanced at Pabasa lying in his own filth, helpless as a newborn babe.

"You're free, my friend," he whispered, knowing the fool would lie there for a day or two until some hapless wretch cut him out.

Free as any man with a hundred men at his rear. Pabasa had no chance, not even with Issa to help him.

Shenq watched the Pharaoh's ships as they came into view, curved prows cutting through the water and sending up wings of spray. Oxen on the footpath lowed at the strike of the driver's rod and horses, caparisoned in gold and black, neighed under the weight of their plumes. When the sun spilled over the eastern horizon, the streets began to pulse with crowds and their voices chanted,

"Lord of Thebes! May your ka be kind!"

Nobles and foreign dignitaries pressed forward almost to the water's edge and young farm boys climbed the trees to look down on Amun's barque. Shenq tapered his eyes to the rising sun, listening to the creak of the oars and the rhythm of the helmsman's drum. The thrum of the square-rigged sails revealed a strong wind dead astern. It was lucky there was a stout wind from the north, he thought, otherwise gangs of his soldiers would be towing those boats upriver to the shrine.

The Queen sat in her cabin, breasts covered by a corselet of precious stones and a war crown perched on her head. *She looks like a man*, Shenq thought. She could certainly pass for one. Pharaoh sat beside her, nose twitching to the scent of smoke. A yellow haze still hung over the burned farmlands and he turned his face to avoid it.

Shenq saw thirty well-chosen men jogging along the river path lead by Jabari. There were ten stragglers behind them, breaking bread and sharing a wedge of cheese. They broke through a wall of women whose eager arms patted them, voicing thanks to Montu, the god of war. Shenq shouted a greeting to his men, repeating the gesture for the late ones.

"Captain's looking for his wife, sir," Jabari said. "He says she's been complaining of a pain in her belly."

"When did he last see her?"

"A week ago," Jabari said, nodding.

A week? Shenq hoped Umaya had not been poking about in the woods since Tau had been diligent enough to build a tunnel.

"I'll take two men and search the canals," Shenq said, biting back his annoyance. "Stay here and keep watch. That idiot brother of yours is hiding in the woods."

Shenq brought Khemwese and Harran to the outer edge of the crowd. Water trickled in a nearby culvert, feeding into a canal and the glint of the sun on water threatened to dull Shenq's senses. The acrid smell of smoke filled his lungs and he looked despondently at the scorched fields with the feeling he was being watched.

A man stood amongst the sycamores on the far side of the canal where the flow of water ended and a row of sycamores began. Shenq caught sight of his variegated body, painted in stripes of green as if it reflected the palmate nature of the leaves. The man lifted his bow and took aim and just as he loosed his arrow Shenq ducked. He heard the shaft as it whipped over his head, piercing the crusty bark of a tree behind him.

"Good shot," he muttered, rising with a smile.

"What is it, sir?" Harran asked, glancing from Shenq to the arrow.

"Over there," Shenq pointed, "in the trees."

"I see him," Khemwese whispered, upper lip curling over his teeth.

Shenq retrieved the arrow and followed his men down a shallow depression that veered away from the river path. They approached a grove of palm trees whose husked trunks curved upwards to pale green fronds, shading them from the sun. Nestled beneath was a huddle of laborers, sleeping off the effects of the Pharaoh's wine. It was odd to see them there but not as odd as the circling vultures in the sky. Shenq stopped and lifted a hand, pointing to the ground where dried fronds had fallen. Walking on those and they would be arrow fodder.

He froze when he saw a dog gnawing on a bone. It lay at the foot of a nearby tree with a leather harness about its shoulders. The animal was an obstacle Shenq had not accounted for and he watched his companions as they too cast wary glances at the beast. Its brindled back suggested a hyena but the hair on its shoulders was smooth as if it had been brushed to a shine.

Shenq lowered his bow, placing the shaft of his arrow on the rest and knowing every sound would alert the dog. He hesitated briefly before releasing the arrow paying attention to the recoil of his body. But his form never failed and the arrow struck. The dog never made a noise as it slumped forward on its meal and from where Shenq stood he could see it was no ordinary bone. He raised a hand when he saw the sandaled foot on the end of it, blood seeping through the reeds. The laborers were already dead, killed by a throat-slitter.

Shenq lifted the chin of a young boy where a gaping wound was crusted with dried blood. "Look," he said, pointing at the throat. "They were killed in their sleep."

Harran seemed intent on watching the river path to the east, an ancient track constructed on a bank to stop the floodwater. There was no sound except the rustle of leaves overhead and the unrelenting babble of waterfowl near the canals. The cheering crowds were too distant and he hesitated as if he saw something move.

"What do you see?" Shenq said.

"Blood," Harran said flatly.

"Whose blood?"

"Hers."

Shenq recognized a vision when he saw the glaze in Harran's face. It held some radiance behind it, some otherworldly image in those darting eyes. The boy's visions came without the drama of frauds that moaned and sighed their way through a prophecy. Harran's senses went way beyond theirs.

They trudged through the thickets until the late afternoon, listening and waiting, and Shenq felt a lump of fear beneath his ribs like an upset stomach. The path tapered towards the east where the faint stench of excrement wafted in from the river. It was common for revelers to use the ditches to defecate and Shenq expected to hear the groan of lovers in the long grass.

The great wooden arm of a *shaduf* came into view and he saw a man leaning against the upright frame. Shenq whistled to get the farmer's attention but the face was thrown sideways, teeth set in a grimace. Tendrils of dark hair flickered against sunken cheeks, breasts bound tightly with rope.

"Umaya," Shenq heard himself murmur. The words were hardly out of his mouth when he heard Harran vomit.

His mind was dull, hardly thinking as he cut through the bonds. The captain's wife fell into his arms, lifeless and stiff. She had no eyes.

They carried her swiftly along an overgrown path at the foot of the slope, and Shenq hoped the wind would persist from the east, masking the smell of death. Harran and Khemwese then took the body west along the drivers' route to the embalmer, snaking through the trees and keeping to the shadows.

Captain Tehute was in his house, caressing a torn strip of linen. He went down like a hamstrung calf when Shenq told him, fingers clawing the dirt and mewing like a baby.

"I knew she had a lover. I saw what he did to her," Tehute said, catching his breath. "Your wife . . ."

Shenq nodded as he offered a cup of beer. "My first wife was lured away with promises of love. He killed her too."

"No," Tehute said, shaking his head. "Your *new* wife."

Shenq felt the blood drain from his face. If Tau could lure these women from the confines of a safe house, he could lure any woman.

Take a breath.

"Hunters hunt. Killers kill," Shenq reminded. He would warn Meryt first.

Tehute nodded, eyes misted with tears. "Say it, Shenq. Say the oath."

Shenq's eyes narrowed as he looked beyond the flickering lamps to the gardens and a violet sky. "I, Shoshenq, Commander of the Pharaoh's most Honored Ones and the Guardians of kings, do hereby pledge myself to protect the Two Lands, to faithfully carry out my duties and to comply with the law of the *Kenyt-Nisu*. To hunt the enemy, to kill the enemy or be cast into eternal darkness. I will take many hands in the mighty name of HaShem, Creator of the Universe."

Tehute wagged a finger. "No, you will take hands in the mighty name of Thoth, Strong Bull, Protector of Ra, Pharaoh Kheper-Re."

Shenq narrowed his eyes and smiled. "Get some sleep."

Tehute began to sob, talking breathlessly as tears ran down to his lips. "I want to see my wife."

Shenq nodded. He knew Tehute would need three days to mourn. "Take all the time you need. Meet me at the southern promontory. And bring as many weapons as you can."

Shenq rushed to his villa and the sanctity of the high wall. He scarcely touched his food at supper, listening instead to the wind as it blew across the roof and the groaning beams above.

He remembered another windy night when they brought a woman's body from the river, hair wet and tangled, face whiter than the moon. He held Eshe in his arms and whispering her name but he could not wake her.

For a moment he felt relief. Tau had sent fire to consume them and sorcery to bind them. But Shenq had sharper ears. He had sharper eyes, and he had a king's sword to cut out Tau's heart if he had one.

I will disguise my men in the coats of the Bedouins, Shenq thought. It would keep them hidden from one prying eye.

The sky turned to purple and orange wisps drifted away from the setting sun. Scents of thyme and cinnamon wafted from the garden and droning flies made him sleepy. He watched the pool from where he sat and saw a bird skidding on the surface and cutting the water with its wing.

Shenq had half-forgotten Meryt at the table and he squirmed uncomfortably in his chair. She wore a gown of cerulean blue speckled with dark red gemstones and he had never seen her look more lovely. He wondered briefly if lust burned in a man's eyes as much as it burned in his soul. Perhaps it was ravaged across his face as if it was the very devil Meryt saw.

"Umaya died tonight," he said. She had been dead longer than that but Shenq could not bring himself to say it.

Meryt looked up suddenly, hand gripping a piece of bread.

"Tau is born to raid and kill. He has many faces," Shenq said, unwilling to tell her how many. "So I must leave soldiers here to protect you. Khamudi will keep the gate locked until I come home."

"You will come home, my lord."

Shenq was startled but he was too careful to show it. The plea made him conscious of a gnawing doubt, the possibility he might fail. "I will be home before you know it."

His stomach was too sour to eat and he saw that she had finished hers. Taking her by the hand, he led her out into the garden.

"These ancient skies are like charts," he said, pointing through the colonnades where Sopdet, the Dog Star was often visible above the horizon. "They tell us so much about the land."

"There are three brighter than the rest," she said. "Like three kings."

Like the Pharaoh's bodyguards, three men that flickered like stars as if they would disappear altogether. Shenq shuddered suddenly, seeing his own remains as they floated downriver.

Long gone, said a cruel whisper. *Just flotsam on the current.*

"Are you cold, husband?" Meryt's whisper parted him from his thoughts.

"I have you beside me," he said, trying to hide the sheepish blush from his face. It was a magic place, a secret place, their place.

"You say this Tau has many faces," Meryt said. "How

will you know him?"

"Legend says, he wears a champion's crown fashioned from arrowheads," Shenq said, recalling the words of the village sages. "Truth is, he's a one-eyed monster with a stench that'll double you over. He shouldn't be hard to find."

"How will *I* know him?"

The question troubled Shenq as if someone had winded him in the gut. "I would rather starve to death than let him see you."

She smiled a weak smile and there was fear in those downturned eyes. "They say his words are sharp and cruel, my lord. They say he has no conscience."

Shenq leaned forward intently. "I have a hundred men at my back, my love. There is nothing as terrifying as a hundred angry men."

"One hundred . . ." she echoed.

He knew how she felt. "I'll kill him in the field," he whispered. "You'll never have to see him."

"But I had a dream of a jackal. He took me to a dark hall where there were no windows and the walls were higher than the sky."

Shenq hated dreams. They were merely the jumbled images of days gone by. "I want you to remember something. There is no such thing as a tame jackal. They're better off dead. But if one should cross your path, feed him choice morsels so he thinks you're his. It will buy you time."

Meryt sipped and Shenq talked, and all the while he wanted to be certain she wanted him. He could no longer tell the difference between warm days and cool nights because he burned for her all the time. She was as light as pollen on the wind when he lifted her, and when he put her down on the bed there was sadness in her eyes he had not seen before. For a fleeting moment, he sensed hesitancy in her kiss like a pulse of fear and it excited him.

He was no longer circling a quarry with a drawn bow,

savoring the scent of blood. He was not a hunter, hearing the howls of defeat and delighting in the victory. He was a husband, renouncing that warrior spirit for one night, hearing the wind through every strand of grass and the whisper of leaves beyond the wall.

Wicks flickered in the hallway as a draft rushed in through the terrace. It swept through the house like a deep sigh and settled at the threshold of a closed door.

TAU

Tau squinted through his shaal at a pair of orange-beaked skimmers as they flew across the river. They cried sharply as they soared, no longer able to defend their nests from marauders such as him. Crouching by the river's edge, he washed the blood from his knife. It was almost as thick as the yolk in his mouth.

Two horns bleated out the prelude to sunrise and the priests processed along the river path chanting the litanies of Ra. But it was a company of nomads that interested him the most, sweeping through the grasslands on the finest of arabi horses. They were dressed in the tob and coats of the Bedouins and heads covered with shaals.

Imazi perhaps, Tau thought, recalling the men whiter than the caves they lived in and weapons forged from animal bone. They were welcome to trade in the markets, especially during a feast.

He had seen a child-wife on Commander Shenq's arm, only he couldn't remember when. The sap he drank was stronger now, sending him into a frenzy of other worlds. Small and dainty she was and paler than fresh-spun linen. There was a wraithlike quality to her he admired and he hadn't stopped thinking about her since.

She reminded him of someone. Only her face rippled behind a veil of flames.

"Mine," he said aloud. He could only hope the trap he planned worked as well as the ones in his head.

While he waited, he met a priestess on the path that night. She had been generous enough to offer him her body and a tour of the sanctuary of Montu. There he found priestly garb and the mask of the god Anubis after he dumped her body in a cell.

Tau heard the crack of twigs in a thicket behind him and saw Issa standing there like a quivering bird, feet coated in mud and a sack in one hand.

"You have the medicines?" Tau said, feeling a sense of suspicion.

Issa nodded. "Honey and coriander, master. On Apepi's tail I didn't open it."

Open it? Tau knew Issa had *opened it*. He was a fool just like all of them.

Tau ripped at the drawstrings, finding two pots of honey for his wound and a pouch of coriander seeds to stop the pain. He swore in the ancient tongue, power fading from his body with every breath. Someone was laughing at him and that *someone* would pay.

The Pharaoh's divisions still haunted the marshlands though few trudged along the river path at dawn. There was a break in their command when priests sang hymns to Hapi and blessed the river, and Tau saw the opportunity he needed.

"I'll give you three Nomes if you bring Pabasa out," he said, jutting his chin at the Commander's villa. "*Three.*"

Issa sniffed at him. "You said that to Pabasa."

Smart boy, Tau thought. At least he had been listening. "I'll make you a prince and all princes must have crowns. Now go."

Issa trembled as he stared at the cage through the trees. "The Commander will see me. He's canny like that."

"Watch, I'll make you invisible."

Tau crouched in the dirt and threw the bones. They weren't as useful without a fire and ashes to read from, but bones were bones. If he could persuade Issa to fetch Pabasa, then a lie would do it. He closed his eyes in pretend prayer and chanted in an ancient tongue.

"There," Tau said, pointing. "The bones speak."

"What do they say?"

"They say you are invisible."

Issa took a few steps back. There were beads of sweat on his brow and a tic in his tired eye. He looked at his hands and his feet and smiled. "Invisible," he murmured.

Tau watched him rush up the slope without a care, cup clanking against his belt. He truly believed he was a phantom even as he pulled Pabasa from the open cage and dragged him down the embankment with all the strength he had. The sound of sparrows alerted them to the first of the sun's rays as they streaked across the sky, limber like a sidewinder.

Tau took Pabasa's arm and hauled him through the tall grass, pausing only to listen to a trickle of wind as it played against his cheeks. Holding his breath, he craved a sound . . . any sound.

There was something moving along a rutted track beyond the trees, something that launched a cloud of starlings into the air. The branches groaned overhead as the wind increased and Tau dragged his load into the glare of the rising sun as each ray hemorrhaged onto the floodplain.

"Take the boat," he said to Issa, pointing at a small reed craft amongst the papyrus beds. "Wait for me at the southern watchtower. Tell the men, their king has gone to fetch his queen."

Issa paddled for the center of the river with Pabasa's head on his knee. It would be some hours before he beached the boat on a sandy neck of land and far enough upriver so as not to be seen.

Unhooking his bow, Tau turned a full circle before

running back the way he had come. He was upwind of his target, a treacherous position, and he railed at his stupidity. There was a man behind in the thickets, measuring him, measuring the distance his arrow would need to travel before it found its mark. Tau dropped to a crouch and opened his mouth, tongue shooting forward on his bottom lip tasting what manner of man he fought. He shivered in the wind, a thin yellow wind.

It's the khamāsīn, the voices reminded him.

He had conjured it with the bones and now he could hardly see. Even as he fastened on a shadow moving behind the limbs of a maple tree, he could feel the pain in his side, biting, screaming. He felt an unusual tingling in his back, a muscular spasm and he was unable to hold his bow at full draw, arrow creeping forward before he released it altogether.

He missed. *Blasted wind drag.* How many arrows would it take? Three? Six?

He ran through the reeds no longer feeling the thick stems as they whipped against his thighs. He would use his knife if he could get close enough and he liked to be close.

There it was again, a shadow faster than a flash. He could hardly keep up with it. Nocking a second arrow, silvery and pristine, he aimed at a patch of skin through the trees feeling a slight shudder in his bow arm.

Keep still! He almost cursed the god of his forefathers, fearing a second miss.

A dull thud confirmed a hit and Tau hurtled through a spiny grove of date palms to a narrow ditch. There in a small clearing was a body heaving with every last breath and as he ran towards it, the blood drained from his face.

An antelope calf.

Tau licked his lips when he saw the fear in its eyes. It was a gift from Apepi, a gift of food. He closed his eye for a moment to ease the soreness of the wind and when he opened it again, the images were blurred. It took to the count of four before he could see clearly and he hoped he wasn't going blind. He must have recited the wrong spells. If only Ibada's army sailed down the Nile at this very moment. If only it was their cheers he heard not the revelers on the first day of the feast.

Carrying the calf on his shoulders, he took it to a leafy burrow to dress it. By the time the sun dropped behind the western peaks, there was a rub of venom on its meaty flanks mixed in herbs and spices. He hurriedly bathed in a canal pool and dressed in the insignia of the royal lotus. Wearing a jackal-headed mask, he took the calf and left his lair.

He had no idea how many servants the Commander had, how many men would fall upon him if he drew his knife but he knocked on the gate anyway, peering up at the leaping leopard over the lintel.

"Greetings," he said in a deep baritone, hearing a drawn shank. "A gift from the High Priest."

He hoped the charade would suffice; after all he was well-informed of the practices of the temples. He had bathed many times in the sacred lake under the stars, until the inferior bastards had chased him off.

"Greetings my lord, Anubis," Khamudi said, bowing. He was clearly reverent of the most powerful voice of the dead.

"A gift from the High Priest," Tau said, laying the meat on the threshold.

"Most generous, my lord Anubis," Khamudi replied, forehead a sheen of sweat.

"I have been asked to escort the Commander's wife to the palace. You've heard the rumors?" Tau refrained from smiling behind his mask. "Young women have been disappearing, some brutally killed. Our Son of Ra commands it."

Khamudi hesitated, brow furrowed in thought. "I must send word to my master."

"The Commander has already received word. The

High Priest is most efficient."

"Where was it sent?" Khamudi clasped his hands together, head aslant.

Clever man. "I understand the herald rode south along the curve of the great mountains. I'm sure he will find the Commander—"

"And his company, great as it is." Khamudi turned his gaze towards the gate. "My mistress must have a chaperone."

"Naturally." Tau followed Khamudi to the portico. So the commander had a company of two hundred and fifty men. Not enough to save Thebes.

"I shall call her," Khamudi said, eyeing Tau's collar. The retainer backed towards the house, not daring to turn his back on a priest.

Tau enjoyed the disguise. It made men humble and reverent, just as they should be. He caught sight of a dragonfly skimming on the surface of the pool, long tail shimmering in the sunlight. He could have sworn it was green, his favorite color.

Twice he heard the name *Meryt* and the high-pitched sound of girlish laughter jogged an unusual feeling of ecstasy. He listened intently for a second burst and since none came, he assumed the lady of the house had learned of his arrival. This princess wouldn't want to keep a priest waiting.

And when she came . . . *Oh gods*, he was overcome by a pair of green eyes. The girl was perfect. "Lady Meryt, you honor me," Tau whispered.

"Who are you?" Meryt's voice warbled on thin breath, startled by the mask.

Such a childish question, he meditated, galled by her impertinence. *Be patient*, his mind crooned. She is flesh. You are divine.

"How rude of me," Tau said. "I am Si-mentu, priest of Anubis. I am honored to escort you."

"Is it true ladies have been disappearing, my lord?"

"I regret it is true. I must take you to the palace, my lady. It is safer there."

A matron with short-cropped hair appeared, head inclined in scrutiny. "My name is Ranefer. I will go with her," she said with little more than a mumble.

Two small bags clutched in a fleshy hand suggested a reduced wardrobe. Ranefer must have only packed enough clothes for a few days.

"I should have brought horses, how inconsiderate of me," Tau said, hands reaching for the bags. They were light, likely filled with cloaks and two fresh sheaths for the girl.

"The palace is only a walk away," Ranefer said with a gaze that bounced round his body.

He noticed Ranefer had two large feet and a sturdy stride. As for Meryt, he could not see her scrambling over jagged marl in a gauzy shift. He would have to carry her.

"Come," he said, flapping his fingers.

He could see the den of the Panahasi, hidden at the upper quadrant of the King's valley. It would take them the best part of the afternoon to reach the foothills and they would stay the night in the drover's cottage.

"How long are they to stay in the temple?" Khamudi interrupted. He seemed to study the brands of war beneath Tau's broad collar.

"Until your master returns," said Tau, easing into a smile.

He saw Khamudi give a jerky nod and glance hesitantly towards the gatehouse. "Pray to HaShem tonight, my child," he said, taking Meryt's hand. "Pray for His protection. The Commander will be home soon. He will come and fetch you."

Tau wanted to laugh. The Commander's women had been snatched by the devil himself and the rest of the household would be dead from poisoned meat. There was nothing to come home for.

"Why are we heading south?" Ranefer asked as they

turned right out of the gate.

"The revelers, my dear," Tau explained. "The streets are crowded and full of drunkards."

It was an hour before they broke through the merrymakers, heading west towards the farms. Tau did not respond when Ranefer pointed behind her towards the palace with pleading eyes. He gave them leave to rest only for a moment whilst he threw off his jackal-headed mask and the rest of his disguise. He almost laughed at Meryt's girlish gasp and when Ranefer screamed, he slapped her good and hard. He tied them to a ring in his belt and dragged them the rest of the way.

As darkness spread over the foothills, they reached a small dwelling surrounded by a fence. Wind screeched and hurled sand against the mud-brick and he could hardly see the mountains from where he stood.

Khamāsīn, he whispered to himself. He was proud of his own conjuring.

The locking bar of the gate protested with a grating moan and, bracing himself against the timbers, Tau herded the women inside.

The house was sparse, low beams partly rotted and there was an odor of dampness. A bow hung from a hook garnished with the red feathers of Alodia and a full quiver lay beneath it on the cold stone floor.

Tau spread his hand on the walls as if he could feel a pulse in its core, face puckering as he sensed rain. He hated rain.

"Sit," he demanded, watching the women sink to the floor.

Two jugs of beer stood beside the fireplace and there was a table laden with medicinal pastes and linens. It took him some time to light the fire, timbers crackling around a paltry flame. Umaya had been most thorough when she was alive.

"Si-mentu," said a gentle voice. "Your wound."

Tau turned to Meryt whose eyes studied the oozing

blood and slime at his waist.

"Dress it" he said, untying her hands.

There was a gloss of perfumed oil on her skin and a bead of sweat trickled between her breasts. It gave him a sudden jolt of pleasure. Her brows knotted as if her mind churned with possibilities. She was a captive after all.

Tau turned his back to urinate in a bowl and when he had finished, he threw her a rag. She scrunched it into a ball, dipping the extremity in what he had just done. It would disinfect the wound before applying a paste of herbs. He watched as she nursed him, voice soothing against his groans and he liked the sound of it, almost as much as the story she told.

He liked her hair best, or maybe her mouth. It was hard to keep his mind on the story with breasts like hers. Small, firm . . . He could see them through her sheath.

"Long ago, there was a swordsman," Meryt said, smearing paste on the wound. "He had eyes like the sun and hair whiter than natron. No one knew his name. But there was something about him, something that made your heart stop. His weapon was the color of ashes and it shone like the moon. Not one dared challenge him. He was good with the sword, double-bladed it was and like a stirring wind when it struck. "They say he killed for pleasure.

"He was as hard as the scales on his breastplate and there was anger inside him like a smoldering fire. But he was an avenger, afraid of nothing. It was his duty to kill and when he did, it made him stronger. One day, a man from Napata came riding by. He was the son of the Kandake and he wanted that sword. He knew there was magic in it. And so he challenged the swordsman to a contest. They went up into the mountain where a cloud of yellow dust settled on the peak. The air was on fire with the clashing of blades . . ."

Tau felt his head fall backwards, plunged into a haze of sleep. It was several moments before he jolted himself awake, surprised when she reached for his hand, pressing it firmly against the dressing at his waist. Shredding the linen into narrow bands, she dressed them tightly around his waist. Not once did he take his eye from her face and not once did she look up.

"Who won?" Tau chided himself for the oversight. She could have freed her companion and run away whilst he slept.

"The swordsman," Meryt said, eyes narrowing slowly. "You're not a priest are you?"

Her skin was the color of the Theban cliffs, pale and sun-bleached and there was a fire in her eyes Tau had not anticipated. She was not afraid of a false face.

"My name is Tau-Nefer, Master of Thebes. I am the lost prince of Alodia and true son of Egypt. It was your husband that took out my eye," he whispered, pointing to the silver ball in his face. "Imagine that. He's a cruel man. But you know that don't you? It's a wonder you aren't afraid of him, a rapist, a child molester. Who do you think killed all those girls? The marshes are littered with the bones of children."

"Liar!" Ranefer said, spitting on the ground. "He's a far better man than you."

"Children that trusted him," Tau continued, "women that admired him, slept with him. Oh, you think you're his only wife? There are others, little princess. He's a hunter. He collects them."

"Horus strike you with a thunderbolt," Ranefer snarled, looking upwards as if tempting the god.

"I doubt he will, hag," Tau said, retying Meryt's wrists. "I'm his champion."

"You're nothing but a snake," Ranefer returned, "crawling on your belly, or what's left of it. You're no one's son, no one's father, no one's champion. You've already lived too long."

Tau reached for the beer almost draining the first jug. Then he lifted it to Meryt's lips and offered her a sip.

He heard *Shasu* women birthed their babies so fast

they barely had time to squat in the desert. And this one put men to sleep with her stories.

"I've been called many things, but never a *snake* though it is a tribute to the great god Apepi." He lifted his cup to Ranefer, delighting in her doleful eyes. "Perhaps you would like a drink."

Ranefer nodded.

"Then beg for it."

HARRAN

Harran wrapped the shaal around his nose, longing to rest. It had been nearly two hours since he last saw Shenq and his men, riding towards a Medjai watchtower on the southernmost promontory. But a battery of sand rose like a curtain from behind a dune, each granule stinging like dog's teeth and raining down in a yellow shower. He had fallen from his horse at the rearguard and lost sight of Shenq.

The wind tugged at his clothes and he shouted for Khemwese. When the sound of his voice died away all he could hear was the wind, soughing, mocking. He was alone in the hazy dawn trudging ankle deep in a golden world and he whistled to his horse. He thought of Shenq then, amber eyes that took in everything and gave back nothing. They were hot like the sparks from a bladesmith's anvil and he wondered why Tau wanted them so badly. He was mad if he thought another man's eyes would make him see.

"Khemwese!" he shouted again. The giant was bound to be close, sheltering on the leeward side of an erg.

He felt a wrenching pain in his side. Any broken bones? He didn't think so even though his thighs and ribs

258

had suffered a battering. The *Sleeping Bomani* was still hidden in the mist and the temple of Mentuhotep was nowhere in sight.

"Shenq!" he yelled, looking back.

There would have been an angry reply had the Commander been near. He never allowed his warriors to call him by his first name. Harran wanted to drop to his knees and pray, only he knew he would never get up. Turning with his back to the wind, he sucked from the nozzle of his water skin, eyes searching the terrain for horse's tracks. He could only see as far as the next ridge, thirty running paces away as far as he could make out.

"Barakeh!"

The mare knew her name and Harran kept thinking he heard the padding of her hooves behind him. The ground began to slope downwards and adjusting his footing, he decided to stay on higher ground as if riding the spine of a giant fence. Whatever it was that threatened him he knew the God of the universe wielded a greater sword.

He stood still and listened, hearing squalls and flurries, and then a fox leapt across his path and he knew it was a sign. Looking back the way the fox had come, he saw a figure scrambling over the dune behind him leading two snorting horses.

"Here I am," Khemwese shouted. His shaal covered his head with only a small gap for his eyes.

Harran caught the sob in his throat. "Where are the others?"

Khemwese shrugged. He had no idea.

They walked in silence for several hours until Harran heard a team of geese overhead. He assumed it was geese by the noise they made and he saw his chance before the wind sprang up. Balancing a rock in his sling, he released the kick strap watching the missile disappear through a ceiling of mist. Rewarded by a heavy thud and a flurry of sand, he laughed louder than he had in days.

Khemwese reached down with a long arm. His horse

shied at flapping wings and then settled back at the snap of its neck. "You have a way with birds," he murmured.

"What are the odds of shooting a bird through a cloud?" Harran said.

Khemwese thought for a moment and shrugged. "None?"

Harran wasn't about to do the math. He knew a miracle when he saw one. And all he could see was rolling sands only thirty paces ahead and the tantalizing trails of sand snakes.

Think, stay alert, shouted a voice in his mind.

When the mist began to clear to seventy paces, they came upon a lone palm tree leaning over a dried-up pool. They set up camp as day wore on to night, stars emerging under a purple sky.

Khemwese savored the smell of roasted goose, grease popping and spattering in the flames. He seemed mesmerized by the burnished glow on that nice crisp coat, licking his lips as he turned it.

Harran dreamed that night of a boy whose belly burned with hunger as if his guts had shriveled in their own juices, a boy abandoned in the desert without a water skin. The same boy shuddered as giant shapes blocked out the moon and Harran knew what manner of birds they were, moving like languorous ships on a dominant current.

Vultures.

He felt a cold shiver in his blood and a light stroke on his arm. Sitting bolt upright, he realized he had been whimpering in his sleep.

"What do you see?" Khemwese said, pulling his saddle blanket up to his chin.

"Issa," Harran said, standing. "I saw Issa."

He could see the foothills now one hundred strides from where they lay. *We've been going in circles,* he thought. It was half a day before they found a group of palm trees, bordering an elliptical depression like the ones he saw in his dream. It was the only water the cruel desert was willing to offer. Issa lay beside Pabasa under a shade of palm fronds, skin peeling from sun-baked arms and eyes closed as if they were already dead.

Harran mixed a paste of ground celery and oil, and smeared it on Issa's wounds. He unhooked the tin cup from the boy's belt and filled it with water, urging him to drink. But the boy only moaned, turning his face this way and that. Pabasa was a splinter, buried deep in a soldier's flesh. Only a knife would dig it out and a knife is what he had.

"So there is mercy for men, including thieves?" Issa murmured.

Harran nodded. "*All* men especially if they're wretched enough."

"I'm sorry," Issa whispered. His face glowed with sweat and his dry lips barely moved. "I'm sorry I never said goodbye to mother. I'm sorry I let Jabari down. I'm sorry I'm going to die."

"You're not going to die." Harran felt a prickling of tears in his eyes and he hoped Issa was too delirious to see it.

Sleep came and went and Issa murmured names and words but none made sense. Harran watched the smoke from the fire, a thin taper rising up to the clouds. The smoke would alert Shenq if he was close. It would also alert the enemy.

"Put the fire out," he said to Khemwese.

Khemwese threw sand over the glowing embers and sat down beside Harran, face turned to the horizon, deep in thought. "Do you remember Commander Cambyses?"

Harran nodded. The man was taller than Shenq. "He was quick like a sand-cat and he was smart too. I liked him. He was good to his men."

"Sometimes I see him out there in the desert," Khemwese murmured, "and sometimes I can see the spearhead in his back, all red like a precious stone."

"I heard your father suffered too. But your face was

the last thing he saw. I bet that was worse."

Khemwese chuckled. "My father was a good man. He was fair."

"He was a pest," countered Harran. "If he had stayed in Alodia where he belonged, he'd still be alive today."

The warriors laughed as they removed the goose from the spit. The joyous sound rippled upwards through the branches of the palm tree where a kite looked on, toes curled and eyes blinking.

"The fact is," muttered Khemwese, "we don't need Pabasa alive."

"Ah but we do," said Harran with a little more remorse than he dared. "He knows the Panahasi. He knows where he is."

Harran speared a goose thigh with his knife and sauntered away from the fire. He stood on the crest of a small dune, chewing hungrily. He didn't want to touch Pabasa. There was too much evil in him.

Give him water, said a voice.

He looked about, scouring the horizon and he glanced back at the palm tree where the kite still perched, waiting for a scrap of food. Pulling a string of meat from between his teeth, he hurled it as far as he could. The bird inclined its head and spread its wings, lifting into the air. It fell amongst the shadows, skimming the sand with its beak.

It was some time before Harran walked towards Pabasa with a bitter grimace. "Drink," he said, placing the nozzle on Pabasa's lips.

He fought a sudden wave of nausea as he saw that grim, scabrous body and he closed his eyes for a moment, wondering if the warrior would live. And then a voice came to him pure and calm.

I have sewn a seed, my child, and it has taken root. Have faith, the seed is doing exactly what I created it to do.

SHENQ

A wedge of geese honked overhead and Shenq watched them under a flattened hand. The mist had almost cleared and he could see the river in the distance behind a band of green. An arrow startled him as it leaped over the ridge, canting to one side and bearing the black fletchings of his division. He lifted a hand and turned in his saddle, nodding to the men behind him.

"God is great," Jabari said, bending down to retrieve the arrow. "We've found them."

"I just wish He'd told me what fools I had in my company," Shenq muttered, urging his men onward with a flick of his hand. *It was a poor shot*, he thought and badly executed.

Shenq whistled loudly as his horse bounded up the slope and the same short, sharp sounds came back with the variance he expected. His horse did not like the stench of blood and hesitated on the summit, feet stamping, ears twitching as if he heard a myriad of sounds. There was a pool beneath them and two archers stood beside it with a sheepish grin.

"We felt the ground shudder and thought it was a war party," Harran said, walking uphill. "I'm sorry."

"Of course you are." Shenq knew the boy was embarrassed. No archer shot an arrow over the brow of a hill and went away without a flogging.

"We found them here, sir," Harran said, "sleeping under the trees. I told Issa his brother would come. We did what we could," Harran's eyes flicked towards Jabari with a sympathetic look and Shenq knew what he meant.

Jabari dismounted and ran to his brother, scooping him in his arms. The boy could not hear. He likely could not see.

"Get him to the temple before the winds come," Shenq said, whipping his head backwards, instincts screaming. "Both of them."

He could hear the rustle of sand as it spiraled towards them and he saw a shape beneath a flattened hand.

"It's Tehute," he said, pointing at the white horse. There was an armor-bearer behind him blinking like an owl.

"Pharaoh bids you greetings," Tehute shouted. "He thanks you for your protection and prays for Amun's favor. But he would like you to return. He thinks he's dying."

"He missed me then?" Shenq knew his luck wouldn't last.

Tehute rubbed one arm and looked about. "I told him I might not find you out in the desert. I reminded him it was a big place."

"And have you found me?"

"I'm still looking, sir."

Shenq barely chuckled. There was something sinister etched on that leathery face. "What else?"

Tehute unwound the shaal from his face. "Your wife is missing."

"Missing?" Shenq shook his head. His stomach rolled and flipped.

"A priest took her on some false errand. Your houseman said he wore a jackal mask, like the ones the embalmers wear. He brought a gift of meat, only Khamudi refused to eat it. Said it smelled sweet and musky, like snake spit."

"Tau," murmured Shenq, gasping for air. "How long ago?"

"Fifteen hours, sir. I came as soon as I could."

Shenq had assumed all this time that Tau was in the mountains rousing his army. But he had doubled back to take the one thing Shenq treasured the most. He felt his chest tighten and his mind was a barrage of hideous scenarios. Tau had ripped out his very heart.

"Your houseboy said his mother went with her," Tehute said. "He said she has a knife and she knows how to use it."

To pare fish perhaps, Shenq thought, swallowing.

"Mkasa will find her," Tehute said. "He knows every fracture and seam of these mountains. He knows all the caves. I'll send my runner." Tehute gestured to the boy he came with and sent him sprinting towards the mountains on legs longer than a heron. "She's valuable, sir, even for a cutthroat like Tau."

"He won't kill her then." Shenq's voice trailed off as if it were a question.

"He won't kill her. But he'll break her spirit."

Shenq motioned at Pabasa slung over a packhorse, moaning and mumbling curses. He wanted to kick him out of his delirium. He wanted to strangle him if it would get him to talk. "We'll ride to the temple."

"Shouldn't we climb the mountain now, sir?" Jabari said, throwing a leg over the back of his horse and cradling Issa over its neck.

Shenq saw the confusion on his face and for a brief moment he hesitated. "Tau won't get far in the dark. He's blinder than a bat."

"He lives in the dark, sir."

"The men must eat and your brother needs food." *He'll be dead in a few hours*, Shenq thought, careful not to mention it. He needed the High Priest's wisdom. There was a tomb in the northern hills and he needed a map to find it.

The mist had almost cleared and Shenq saw a plume of smoke, rising from the inner courts of the temple. *Food*, he assumed, urging his horse forward. They turned due west towards the setting sun and to the temple of Mentuhotep II, hewn in the Theban rocks and looming like a stark fortress against the cliffs. Seated statues of the old Pharaoh lined the causeway where horses' hooves clipped against the stone slabs, alerting the attention of several priests. They waved and nodded, some rushing towards them to hold the horses.

"Dismount!" Shenq shouted to his men, handing his reins to a priest.

Statues stared across at one another in the great courts, lifeless, somber and nothing like the old Pharaohs of the past. No amount of paint could breathe life into the old fathers he once knew and Shenq recalled the face of Pharaoh Ka-Nekhet in the deep of his mind. It was gaunt and uncompromising not saintly as it had been carved.

He threw off his coat, revealing the Pharaoh's insignia on his sash. Incense floated from the upper terraces and torches flickered between the rectangular pillars of the eastern face, richer than the fading sun. It was a peaceful place,

"All hail Montu-Ra," the priests called, heads tipped back, faces turned to the sky.

"All hail!" Shenq's men responded as they threw off their coats.

They were ushered into a courtyard where dragonflies buzzed about the gardens, grounds rich in tamarisk and sycamore. A breeze whispered between the rectangular pillars dedicated to the king's military triumphs and there was a ramp at the west end of the hall, strewn with fresh flowers and lit with oil lamps. Shenq he saw the priest limping towards him, dragging one crooked leg. The old man was swift considering the defect and there was warmth in his tone Shenq liked.

"Commander," he said, prostrating himself on the ground. "How long has it been? Five years, six?"

Shenq bowed and noticed a strong color about the cheeks. High Priest Hori enjoyed his wine. "Rise, my lord, I beg you."

"I'd sooner stay here," the priest said, struggling to kneel. "I feel it is my natural place."

"My lord." Shenq offered his hand and pulled the priest to a stand. He had never felt more honored in his life. He lowered his voice. "The boy is nearly dead and needs no sustenance. The other has a head full of secrets. Feed him for me will you?"

"We sacrificed a fatted calf to Amun today," Hori said. "The god has had his fill and there is plenty for your men."

Fatted calf was too good to miss and by the look of Shenq's drooling men, they could eat most of it in three quick swallows. "There's a war party in the hills," he said. "Thousands, I believe."

"Not thousands, Commander. Four hundred. I know because one of my boys has been watching from Meretseger."

Shenq had once climbed the pyramid-shaped mountain when he was a boy. It towered over the eastern floodplain and the gorges beneath. "What did he see, my lord?"

"Heathens casting spells and throwing bones. We can hear the echo of their filthy war-horns from here."

Shenq schooled his expression to one of indifference but deep inside, he was screaming. Alodians never used war-horns. They lay in wait.

"Welcome to god's house," Hori said. "My priests will stable your horses. You won't need them where you're going."

"If this is God's house, He's not home," said Harran in a loud voice.

"Ah, a prophet of HaShem I see," Hori said, bowing to Harran. "Your kind rarely tolerates the inner courts. I will see your food is brought outside."

Harran seemed pleased with that and found a bench in the gardens.

The High Priest took Shenq's men to the upper levels, through a hypostyle hall to an open-air courtyard at the rear of the temple. There was a laver and a roasting pit, and long tables laden with food.

"I would ask you to wash," the High Priest said. "But since you're in a hurry, hands are good enough."

"What else did your boy see?" Shenq asked, dipping his hands in the laver and nodding to his men.

"Alodians. You can smell the stench from the pier. They've captured a moon-warrior and two women."

"Where have they gone?"

"The boy thinks they went to the southern watchtower. He lost sight of them last night."

Mkasa, Shenq murmured in his head. Not all hope of getting word to Meryt was lost. Tehute's runner was still out there somewhere.

"Eat," Hori said, pulling out a long bench from the table. "I've seen these men before. One was a headman to King Ibada, a manipulator of sorts. I'd never forget a face like that. He tried to snake his way to the inner sanctum of the Alodian palace with compliments and a pile of gold. But where he got either, I can't imagine."

"Now he wants Thebes. And he's taken my wife." Shenq took out his knife, cut a strip of thigh from the calf. He had to eat. He had to be strong.

Hori looked at Shenq with wide eyes and an open mouth. "She's a bargaining piece. More valuable of course if she was a virgin. They won't kill her."

Just what the Captain said. Shenq chewed half-heartedly as he listened to Hori's voice.

"They say this Tau of Alodia has a tomb in these parts," Hori said.

The strain of recent days felt lighter on Shenq's shoulders and he was glad for Hori's company. "He's going to need it."

"Is he a sorcerer?"

"Tau?" Shenq shrugged, studying the angle of the sun. "He's just the enemy. He's only as strong as one man."

"And Meryt?"

The question made Shenq wince. Each hour meant the difference between victory and defeat and he wondered why he was not hurtling like a madman towards the mountains. "She survived capture as a child. It must count for something."

"She's clever then."

"Yes," Shenq murmured. She could read two languages and write. She was extraordinary. And if she could fend Tau off with clever words, she would survive. "Where will he take her, my lord?"

Hori pressed his lips together, face hardening into bitter hatred. "Well now, I think I can help you with that."

TAU

Tau was trapped in that twilight place between waking and a dream. He thought he saw a shadow by his side and he heard rustling like dried leaves across a stone floor. He had dreamed of the tents again, a strange place he knew as a boy.

Bedouins had taken him in, fostering a glut of orphans abandoned in the desert. The face of his mother came and went like the face of the moon from behind a cloud. She promised she would come back, *promised* with painted eyes and clanking jewels. He thought she was a princess. But she was nothing more than a harlot. It was so long ago.

"She couldn't look after you," the Bedouin said, yellow teeth chewing on salted meat. "She was too busy with the men."

He heard the other boys crying in the darkness and his eyes snapped open. He wanted to be different. He wanted to be free. A feeling of euphoria spread through his limbs like fresh blood. He was a jackal after all.

Putting the vision out of his mind, he unraveled his legs from a blanket and peered between the wooden slats of the door. Pale blue wisps stretched out above the horizon. It was dawn at last.

There would be enough light on the tortuous mountain paths, leading to the north and to the gates of the Netherworld. The wind screeched like the call of a large bird, playing on his mind like a strumming harpist, persistent and out of tune. He popped the false eye from the socket in his face and licked it clean with his tongue.

Panahasi, he whispered, baring his teeth.

He longed to see the overseer of the mountain vaults, the one who raised armies in his name. There would be ten thousand Alodians filling the valley with song and ready to march on Thebes.

He looked at the women, tied up and huddled on the floor with barely a cover between them. Their eyelids flickered as if they dreamed of brighter days, only there would be nightmares where he was taking them.

Why is it so cold? He shivered. He was never cold.

He sat on a stool and studied Meryt. He wanted her down to the basest of levels yet there was no hardness between his legs and he was suddenly plunged into shame. Still chained to his dark ghosts, he wondered what sorcery had disabled him.

"Who are you," he muttered, nudging her awake with his foot.

Her smile was one of remorse, one she had wrenched from deep inside. He wondered if she was trying to soothe him, to stay alive.

"I'm Meira, daughter of Amichai," she said, wrists still tied with rope.

"*Shasu*, then."

He noticed she lowered her eyes, overwhelmed by his muscular build. Perhaps she wanted him as much as he wanted her. He wouldn't blame her if she did. The odor of the herbs in the poultice made him shudder and his eye fell on the bowl still filled with his urine. It was black and viscous.

Devil's blood, the voices said.

The room began to swim and he drank hungrily from

271

the last of the stocks, stoking the fire reluctantly and fanning the last of its flame before dawn.

"Where are we going?" Ranefer asked.

Tau shrugged with a savage chuck of his shoulders. "North along the workman's route, woman, and then we'll see."

You'll kill them both if you have any sense, the voices purred.

Tau hooked his pack over one shoulder, snatching the bow and quiver. He watched the women as they struggled, determining which was the weakest. *No sense in keeping two*, he thought, herding them through the goat pen and around the back of the house.

The path meandered upward, leveling for a while before dropping down into a mass of scree. Wind blew from the north, biting his cheeks and thighs. He had no idea what it did to the women. He didn't much care.

Feet crunched on the jagged rocks, echoing off the towering cliffs to their right as they edged northward. The young one was bleeding, her ankles torn by the pointed shards of rock, and every now and then he caught a glimpse of her buttocks as the wind blew her cloak sideways. Although she was little more than a child, he sensed a maturity beyond her years, a startling inner strength common to her kind.

He had met a *Shasu* woman once when he was a boy. Sharp she was like a fortune-teller, knowing the human mind as if she could map it on every hand. This girl was no different with her calm voice that lulled him to sleep and stories that weren't stories, dreams perhaps. It was while Tau was searching for a place to kill Ranefer that the horns sounded at the southern watchtower. The Medjai repeated the warning three times, one long blast, one short one. They had seen rebels in the distance. They had seen Tau's army.

"Cover yourselves," Tau said to the women, cutting the ropes from their wrists and handing them shaals from his pack.

Ranefer wound an arm around Meryt's waist, encouraging her with whispers. She was strong, Tau thought. Strong enough to entertain his men.

They climbed the arduous route carved by the workmen of the royal tombs, twisting to the east over the southern promontory where only a low wall of rock protected them from the cliff edge. Glancing southward, he saw shadows on the plains, streaming over the dunes like a dark mist and his gut warned him of a greater threat. A sigh of wind crept along the mountain paths as they veered north and he looked over his shoulder one last time.

There was nothing there.

Commander Shenq was a legend even amongst the tribes. He was a man of the people. But he was at Tau's mercy and Tau was not merciful. He heard the crackling of torches in the wind and the strong smell of pitch. When they walked through an avenue of boulders, Tau heard the cheers, metal scraping on metal. His armies had arrived.

"Mokhtar!" Tau shouted, locking arms with a stout warrior with large ring in his lower lip.

"The armies are still coming, master," Mokhtar confirmed, staring at the women, tongue lolling in his mouth. Painted on his cheek was coiled snake and his eyes were bloodshot, redder than his shúkà.

Meryt and Ranefer drew their cloaks about their heads and Tau noticed them shiver, more from terror he hoped than the cold. A screaming wind came in from the east, flinging sand and small shards of rock through the air.

"How many men do we have?" Tau said, jutting his chin at a group of warriors behind Mokhtar.

"Fifty or so dead." Mokhtar raised his eyes to the sky as if he was still counting. "Over three hundred left, master."

Tau inclined his head. "I was promised thousands."

"You can thank the Medjai for that."

Tau looked beyond Mokhtar at a diviner, shaking a skull filled with bones. His eyes were whiter than a cloud and there was a heady odor about him that made Tau nauseous. He was a *Murrani*, untouchable, sacred to the god Apepi.

"What's he saying?" Tau said, unable to interpret the rapid babble.

"He's been tracking a scent," Mokhtar said with a blissful snarl. "The blood of the moon-warrior."

The only moon-warrior Tau knew was a lieutenant of the Medjai. Winsome and handsome so the girls said. "Did he find him?"

"Oh, yes, master. He found him standing on the crest, jaw painted blue to the cheeks. There was a snake spitted on the end of his spear and he spat insults to the god."

The warrior would pay dearly for that, Tau thought, imagining the warrior dressed for war, a bolt of blue against the crimson cliffs. "Where is he?"

"He's sitting by the fire, master. He's waiting for you."

SHENQ

Jabari howled like an injured dog when the priests put Issa in the vault. Shenq wrapped him in a leopard skin pelt, rosettes shimmering like a thousand eyes.

"Like a nobleman," Shenq whispered to Jabari over his tears.

Jabari tied the little mug to a palm tree in the gardens. "The priests will hear it as they pass by, sir, and they'll say a prayer over the body that lies under it."

"Not for the body, my friend," Shenq said. "There's nothing left of it. But for his mother. And for you."

It was only a matter of hours before they climbed a narrow path on the south side of the temple, snaking around the belly of the rock and veering north towards Meretseger. The High Priest had given them goatskin to wrap around their feet. The scree was sharp when it struck. Pabasa was without a cloak to fend off the chill, tied between Jabari and the Captain with a thick coil of rope.

"Watch for flares," Shenq said to Jabari. Glimmers recoiled halfway up the rock face and then shrank from sight.

"Are they Medjai?" Jabari said, pausing to bandage his right hand to hold a weapon.

"Alodians," said Shenq, listening to the wind as it hummed through the crimson fletchings of his arrows. He wasn't sure. It was just a feeling.

The shrill call of a hyena disturbed the silence, a plaintive sound indicating the separation of a mother and her young. Someone was roasting meat.

"The workmen say you can still hear the screams of the nobles," Jabari said, referring to the old custom of sealing important men in the tomb of the kings. "My father died when the tomb was cut. It was a grisly death. They say he plunged down a shaft with his paint pallet and all they found were his sandals."

Shenq felt a churning in his stomach and cleared his throat. Death was no laughing matter though he suppressed laughter all the same. "He died a noble death then."

"He was a painter, sir. He died without a name."

"Many years from now when the tomb has been stripped of its wealth, your father will be mistaken for a nobleman. Same as your brother," Shenq said, no longer content to idle in the scree.

The wind swept through the valleys and passes, imitating the pitch of an Alodian war pipe and a large bird flew on a dipped wing, hovering expectantly over the peak. As the gradient began to level, Shenq saw the mellow flicker of a dying fire in the valley below them and raising his right hand in a tight knuckle, he prepared his men to halt.

There were sixteen tribesmen reclining by the fire, wrapped in leopard skins and festooned in beaded belts. Shenq guessed there would be three more out there somewhere, scouting the paths and ravines. Sharp faces covered in paint and eyes closed in exhaustion, these were the *Murrani*, the pride of the Alodian army. Water skins lay in a pile under an oryx frame and by the fire were four hooves severed at the pastern and six dead lizards—ingredients to improve eyesight.

"Where are the rest of them, sir?" Jabari whispered.

"Common soldiers are not allowed to eat and sleep near the diviners. It would contaminate their dreams. See the smoke over the next ridge? That's where Tau's men are."

Shenq studied their tattoos and red-painted braids whilst preparing his bow and calculating the cast in his head. The arrow burst from the supple limb like a sigh of wind and he watched its path as it pierced a water bladder with a light thud. Not one rebel stirred.

"Tau has four hundred men out there," Shenq murmured.

"How do you know?"

"For every two hundred Alodians, there is ten *Murrani* to lead the way. It's an Alodian custom." Shenq wasn't about to waste arrows on sleeping men and he was eager to slit a few throats. "These diviners are battle-weary and drunk. They're not expecting to be attacked again."

"They could be bluffing, sir."

Shenq smiled faintly. "They drink wine diluted with willow bark to do their magic. I say they're almost dead."

"I don't see the Medjai."

Shenq felt the knotting in his gut. They should have seen Medjai torches by now and heard the sounds of their carefree chatter. There were two main groups, the south and the north watchmen, and a group of runners that ran between each. There was no sign of either.

Creeping forward amongst the boulders, he did what he came to do, hardly daring to breathe as he listened to the sounds of snoring. They slit sixteen throats that night under the watchful stars, until three sentries burst from behind a boulder.

There should be four, thought Shenq as he sized up the first man, dark and fierce. He pitched forward driving his blade up under the man's ribs and there were three harsh gasps as the warrior fell back.

Shenq clamped a hand over his mouth. "No noise,

brother," he whispered, thwarting a warning cry. He twisted the blade deeper in until the body went slack and the eyes still. But he kept his hand over the lifeless lips just long enough to make sure.

He took his men along a north-bearing path covered by an overhanging shelf. On its summit, he saw a sentry thirty paces from their position. He wore a thick leopard skin over one shoulder and his movements emulated the restless tread of a sand cat, defining the superior fighting skills of the *Murrani*. He was the twentieth man.

There was a recess in the rock below, deep enough for Shenq's men to take cover. Khemwese pressed his cheek against the vertical edge listening for a pulse in the living rock. He nodded as the warrior moved above them, stalking closer to the edge and he judged the distance it would take to launch a weapon over the summit.

He took an axe from Meru-Itseni and rocked on his feet. The axe swung forward and back with the momentum, soaring on a backward trajectory. A dry wheeze confirmed a hit and the warriors rushed to the summit to find the warrior kneeling on the ground, eyes overcast and distant.

The blade had sliced through the right side of his neck and one arm twitched in a savage spasm. Shenq pulled the axe free and gave the leopard skin to Khemwese.

It took them an hour to find the ancient trail which overlooked the floodplain to the east. It veered north along the cliffs as if the men were walking on the foundations of heaven itself.

A moonbeam illuminated the great winding river in the distance, cutting a wide gash between the clouds and a thin mist that settled over the grasslands, ghostly and bleak. The thunder was a mere rumble as they approached the great valley and a few drops of rain pulsed from the skies.

"I smell blood," Khemwese said, sniffing from side to side, "and spirits in the wind."

TAU

Tau looked up when he heard the screech, muscles cramping in the cold. A shadow flitted before the moon, drifting on a crosswind and silhouetted against a cloud. It was a large bird but as to its breed he couldn't tell.

Mokhtar began to pace, lips pressed flat for a time. "There's no sign of Pabasa and his houseboy."

"Cowards," Tau muttered under his breath. There was no sign of the *Murrani* either.

Tau motioned to Meryt, desperate for blood sport. It was a fleeting idea that made him salivate and if Mokhtar touched her, he would cut off his arms. Tau ripped the cloak from Meryt's shoulders, glimpsing her sheath and the curve of her hips. Her rasping breaths only excited him further.

"This is *Kemnebi's* woman," Tau shouted. "Take her. There's nothing to stop you."

To his amazement, Mokhtar retreated, eyes rolling like a bolting horse as he made the sign of the evil eye.

"You are protected by the divine snake," Tau reminded, urging him on with a wink.

"If *Kemnebi* can see Pookoo in the dark," Mokhtar warned, "he can see me."

Tau hooked an arm around Meryt's shoulders, pulling her close with a savage thrust. "Mokhtar thinks you're a goddess," he whispered in her ear. "Are you a goddess?"

Meryt cringed, lips squeezed shut. Tau could feel the racing pulse in her body and he wondered how far she would run if he let her go.

"I'll break you," he murmured. "I'll break every thought in your head."

Mokhtar spat on the ground and wiped a string of mucus from his mouth. "There's a spirit in her like a raging wind, master. It's more ancient than ours." He conversed rapidly in his own tongue, pointing at the women as if they were an inconvenience.

"There, see how he bows to you." Tau knew the girl had no idea what obscenities poured from Mokhtar's mouth and it amused him. He pushed her away as a flash awakened the night sky for an instant, a streak of blue as if dawn had interrupted the night.

"Let's go," Tau said as he heard a rumble of thunder. "Munje!" *Now!*

He urged the women along the route towards the pyramid-shaped mountain. Beneath it was a large encampment and he could smell fresh meat, popping in an open fire. Four hyena pups hovered on a spit, crispy coats glistening with oil.

Tau thrust a fist at the sky and whooped. "Where are the *Murrani*?"

Mokhtar spat in the sand. "They mix the elixir to make you see."

Tau threw his head back and shut his eyes. Soon he would drink the best of the willow-bark and be put to sleep. The *Murrani* would chant from dusk until dawn and when he awoke he would see the rising sun with both eyes.

"But one is dead, Master," Mokhtar said, pointing a trembling finger at the *Murrani* laid out on a wooden frame, neck scored by an axe. "It was the moon-warrior that killed him."

Tau studied the face of the captive, stimulated by the ropes around his wrists and the blood on his *shenti*. "He'll pay for killing the sacred one and if I don't find the rest, he'll pay for them too."

"Our father must be returned to the earth, master," Mokhtar said.

Tau looked at the holy man and felt a lump in his throat. "Burn him."

They lowered the frame into the fire and chanted loudly, bodies twisting grotesquely where they stood. The body on the pyre gave off a sweet, suffocating smell as skin melted off the bone and smoke rose from a spatter of rain.

Tau was too hungry to take part and he snatched a side of fresh hyena meat from a guard and chewed slowly. A spatter of rain slapped his cheek and he looked up at the hostile skies, dreading the floods that sometimes filled the wadi to a torrential river.

Gods don't drown, he reminded himself.

Tau threw his pack on the ground and sat with his back against a boulder. He pressed a hand against his waist and caressed the ragged stitching. There was no pain, just stinking blood and pus, and he wondered when it would stop.

Ranefer began chanting an old Napitan song until was a drone in his head and he watched Meryt as she huddled against Mkasa, cheek resting against his arm. It was the look the warrior gave her that made him want to spit. There was love in that look, he thought.

It was some time before he awoke to the grey skies of dawn and two staring eyes. The blue-painted warrior was imposing in his quiet way. His arms were wider than a man's thigh, built to wield a lance for long periods of time and those eyes made Tau feel uneasy and so did the seal on his chest

"Mkasa of Makuria," Tau whispered, taking an arrow from his quiver. The tips were sharp and feathered. "See my arrows? It does more damage to take them *out* than to put them *in*."

Vizier Ahmose's fifteen-year old boy died slowly and painfully from the same arrow. Tau recalled the screams. They were like honey on bread. "See the girl?" he said, pointing at Meryt. "Beautiful, isn't she? You can have her if you want."

Mkasa's eyes narrowed as if a shape loomed out of the darkness, like an archer leveling his bow. But he said nothing, ear bent to the screaming wind.

"When I open you up," Tau said slowly, playing his dagger from hand to hand, "you'll squeal like a pig just like your brother did before you."

"Don't touch him," Mokhtar warned. "He's a seal-bearer."

"Take the seal off him and he's a man like everyone else."

"I won't touch it," Mokhtar grunted. "I won't touch *him*."

"Then the pleasure's all mine."

Meryt lifted her head from Mkasa's shoulder, scanning Tau with an angry frown. "Why do you taunt him?" she said.

"He's my enemy, little princess. To disobey me is to destroy the sun. *You* know that."

Tau pulled Meryt to her feet. It was time for a beating. He pushed her against a rock and tore at the thin fabric of her sheath, hesitating for a moment to savor the milk-white flesh.

"No!" Mkasa shouted, struggling to stand. "Take me."

"You?" Tau chuckled and then thought better of it.

Nodding at Mokhtar, he re-sheathed his knife and took out his axe. Two warriors pinned Mkasa down and spread out his right hand against the boulder. Tau swung the axe high and the scream was loud when it came. Mkasa's smallest finger flopped to the ground between the women.

Tau couldn't remember how many lashes he gave Mkasa or how much strength ebbed from his body on the last stroke. But it gave him a tinge of pleasure to watch the blood and slaver dripping from an open mouth, hands trembling in their bonds. Mkasa seemed to suffer the punishment with dignity as if there was a prince beneath those blue rags of his.

When Tau turned to Meryt, he saw beauty unlike any he had ever seen. He saw the moon when it was pink and low in the sky, and he saw acres of barley stretching from the land of the living to the land of the dead. The voices in his head urged him to have her and they grew louder and louder with each passing day.

"I dream of you," he said, reaching out a bloody hand.

"I'll be no serpent's whore," she sobbed, curling away from him. "You're a demon, the kind that shudders when the sun comes out."

Tau had no idea what she meant. He was a god and a powerful one at that. Only the wound in his side had burst open again and he swallowed a groan.

Gods don't die. And you're dying, the voices said.

Tau hated the voices as much as he hated himself and he swung a fist across Meryt's face, watching the tiny body as it slammed against a rock. Voices churned in the flames, swirling like a windstorm in his head and the vision of a long-maned warrior interrupted his thoughts. He thought he heard the sound of leopard's feet as they pounded against the rocks and he turned this way and that, swinging the flail in his hand.

"He's been following you all night," Meryt said, staggering.

He? Who's he? It was either Shenq or that blasted bird, the one that stalked the slate-grey skies. He turned and squinted at the horizon, vibrant in a veil of amber and lit by the rising sun.

"Nothing follows me. *Nothing!*"

"He'll win like he did before," Meryt stammered, color

rising in her cheeks.

Win? When did he win? When he took your eye, fool.

"Watch yourself woman or I'll snap that pretty little neck."

Meryt averted her gaze for a moment, tears glistening against soft cheeks. Green eyes flashed behind a curtain of hair and her chin shot upwards suddenly.

"Give me your dagger," she said. "I'll do it myself."

SHENQ

When they reached the wadi and saw the bodies, Shenq cursed. Medjai warriors lay in the trickling stream, limbs hacked and pierced, mouths drawn back in a rictus of agony. Further out in the channel he glimpsed a sand cat, pale against the scree and whiskers coated with blood. A low rumble came from its throat and with teeth bared; it bounded into the shadows of a nearby crevice.

Only one man survived and there were no wounds to see except the torment in his downcast eyes. Shenq threw a cloak around his shoulders and crouched by his side. "And you are?"

"Senbi, sir, first charioteer to Commander Osorkon."

Shenq was glad the warrior had a voice. "What happened?"

"There were hundreds of them, sir. They came round the spur like demons from the pit. We killed sixty or thereabouts."

Shenq absorbed the shame as if it was his own. "Where's your Commander?"

"A runner arrived yesterday, sir. Commander Osorkon was ordered back to the city."

Shenq felt a quiver in his stomach and shared a look

with Captain Tehute. "What was the runner's insignia?"

"I don't remember, sir."

Shenq bit his bottom lip and gave a strained smile. "How did you survive?"

"They ambushed the southern quadrant, driving us into the foothills. I lay amongst the dead, sir. The tenets of the Medjai insist on a witness."

"And Lieutenant Mkasa?"

"They took him, sir."

Shenq's mind was locked in a spasm of anger and he thought of the gaping wound in Tau's side, wishing he had aimed higher.

"Can you fight?" Shenq said, helping the warrior to his feet.

"I can, sir."

A thick twist of smoke ambled behind a ridge and Shenq knew the Alodians were burning their dead in one of the secluded valleys.

He ordered the men to leave the Medjai where they fell and he looked long and hard at their sightless eyes. The wind grew stronger throwing up twisters in the ravines and the sound of a woman's voice threaded between the cliffs.

"Ranefer," Shenq murmured, mouthing the words of an ancient slave song he had grown to love.

O master, O master, when will I be free,
I am waiting with my sister, O when will it be?
What angel can save me, what army is near?
I pray for your voice, Lord, only your words I hear.
This burden I carry is too heavy for me
And I look to the north for any sight of thee.
O master, O master, when will I be free,
I am waiting with my sister, O when will it be?

"They're alive," Shenq said, "and they're heading north."

Shenq might have overlooked the north valley had

High Priest Hori not mentioned it. And Hori had been most obliging. He had even drawn a map.

There were paths as intricate as a man's veins and ridges that looked like dead giants covered with sackcloth. Shenq remembered how desolate it was, how rugged the gaps were and how the ravines were cloaked in darkness. There was a tomb in a horse-shoe of clefts, a door full of memories and treasures if only he could find it.

"Sir," Harran said. "There's a storm coming."

Shenq looked up at the sky where dark clouds assembled in the east and his skin tingled from a light spatter of rain. "It won't rain for long. It never does."

He had grown accustomed to Harran's large eyes, the questioning expression, and he wondered where he had seen it before. "You say you're from Geshen."

"My family settled there for some years."

"And your father?" Shenq's nose twitched. The sickening smell of burning flesh was stronger now the wind blew north. Tau's sentry was little more than crackling.

"Amichai. And my mother was Elisheva in case you were wondering."

Shenq did wonder although the loud echo of Khemwese's belch gave him a start. "You had two sisters."

"Yes, sir," Harran said. "But the oldest is dead."

Stoned to death, Shenq thought, hearing the thud of every rock as it spun through the air. "And the youngest?"

"Meira was taken south with the other women. I never saw her again."

Shenq grinned, heart pumping fiercely. He knew the names as if they were his own family. *Better get this settled before the battle*, he thought, gripping the pommel of his bronze sword as they meandered along the workmen's route. "Perhaps you will."

"Perhaps I will what, sir?"

"See your sister again."

Shenq stared down at trusting eyes. He had stirred the

hornet's nest at full spin. "My wife is from Geshen. Her name was Meira until the Queen gave her a new one. Lady Meryt is her name. You will see her very soon."

"Lady Meryt?" Harran's eyes became wider still.

"Ah," Shenq recalled the Pharaoh's most recent wedding night with some amusement. "The lady you escorted was not her. Thick veils and paint made sure of that."

"HaShem be praised," Harran exclaimed, clutching Shenq's arm. "Is it really her?"

"Your sister is very beautiful."

"Is there a family likeness?" Harran's voice had risen by an octave.

Shenq studied the copper skin and doe-eyes. "Absolutely none," he lied. It was the one thing that had been bothering him all evening.

"Sir, my sister and I are alike. Surely you can see it?"

"Next you'll be telling me you're twins."

"But sir," Harran panted as he tried to keep up. "What's she like now?"

"She's like a young hare in a barley field and just as skittish. I think she's afraid of me."

"I think I would be."

"Pharaoh knew I wanted her, the sick buzzard. He thought he could have first peck, only I would have rammed all the bronze I had down his throat." Shenq looked down at his sword, a well-balanced blade. It was tapered to slash and shinier than the tears on a mourner's cheek. Pity he hadn't used it when he had the chance.

"Pharaoh won't touch *Shasu*," Harran maintained. "It's like eating piglet."

Shenq began to wonder how much piglet the Pharaoh had eaten. He wasn't about to pay it much mind only he was hungry and the idea of a pink carcass swinging over a roaring fire made his stomach growl.

"Does she look skinny and half starved?" Harran said, running ahead and rising up and down on the balls of his feet.

"Not in the least."

"With child?"

Shenq thought of Meryt's soft breasts as she lay beside him, firm and round, and her gasps in the marriage bed. He was never sure if they were joyful or painful. Either way, it brought a smile to his face until he realized what Harran had just said. *With child?* Hardly. A woman needed more than a handful of nights. He shrugged and said nothing.

"My sister," Harran whispered, choking back a surge of joy. The sound reminded Shenq of a cinched girth.

"You'll count the dead for me," Shenq said, keeping Harran grounded. A counter in battle was essential to raise morale.

Shenq saw a shadow floating downwards from the skies, hovering on an oblique wing and urging them on with an insistent screech. Stirred by the oldest of memories, he wondered if it was the same bird that followed his father into battle though it should have been long dead by now. The men had begun to look for it like a beacon in the twilight and something told Shenq to follow it.

A biting wind swept across the valley floor, scattering loose rock and a small twister skimmed along the foot of the cliffs. The warriors walked single-file, legs bound with goatskin and cloaks to warm them. All except Pabasa. He shivered and staggered between his captors, hand bound to cover his severed fingers.

At an intersection between the large rift valley and a small glen to the west, Shenq saw the tapering beam of the moon shining on the grainy timbers of a wooden door. At the edge of a rock spur and descending through layers of shale was the recently quarried burial place for Pharaoh Kheper-Re. The marauders had torn the gates from their hinges, timber strewn about the floor.

Weapons, he thought, knowing the best of Theban

bronze lay in the royal storage rooms.

Shenq unsheathed his knife and jogged along the path and up the slope. The doorway seemed to glisten in the hoary light, engraved with the name, *Born of Thoth, Protector of Ra, Kheper-Re the mighty.*

There was no rope to fasten the grips and the doors swung open on a well-greased hinge. Oil lamps winked along a sloping corridor to a narrow bridge where a deep well yawned beneath it. There was a second gateway in the distance lit with torches and sealed with rope. Three wooden crates were stacked against a wall all stamped with the seal of the royal armory. Shenq turned the dagger over in his hand, sensing a presence in the darkness.

"Who dares enter the house of Ra?" a voice said. "Who defiles the valley of bones?"

"Commander Shenq of the *Kenyt-Nisu*," Shenq replied, realizing his warriors had not followed him up the slope.

A large priest emerged from the darkness with a spear in his hand. He stood before the bridge and the black pit beneath it. "This is a sacred place. Drop your weapon and remove your sandals."

"I'll wait for you to drop yours if it's all the same, priest." Shenq wasn't about to lose his own life and he had an uncanny feeling he had upset the priest's plans.

"Did you hear what I said? This is a sacred place. Drop your weapon!"

The priest was darker than the average Theban and freshly shaved. If it wasn't for the unnaturally clipped voice, Shenq could have sworn he was an Alodian. He discerned the tremor in the priest's voice and a restless stance. The man was utterly alone.

"Do you have a name, priest?" Shenq said, studying a pair of hostile eyes and a forehead dappled with sweat. "I would like to know it before I die."

"I'll cut you to shreds."

The spear was a stabbing weapon unlike a sword and there was little space to use it. "Do it then."

The priest knotted his brow and lowered his spear but not before Shenq sprang forward towards the priest's off-hand, plunging the dagger into a bulge of flesh on his way past. He almost staggered near the lip of the well and quickly regained his footing.

The priest was no soldier. He would have rammed Shenq's head against the wall if he was. Instead, the fat man yelped and turned rapidly to face Shenq, wedging the spear diagonally between the corridor walls. It was a foolish move and he gasped loudly before barreling through the shaft.

He lunged for Shenq with claw-like hands, fingernails were all he had left to fight with. But Shenq leapt sideways as the giant bull of man came on, screaming like a girl as he plummeted into the well.

There's water down there, Shenq thought, *quite a lot by the sounds of it.*

Tehute shouted from the doorway, dragging Pabasa behind him. "I'm sick of his wailing, sir. It's enough we have to drag him as well."

Shenq saw a wooden truss jammed between the ceiling and the floor. It would make a sturdy post to tie Pabasa to, provided he didn't fidget. "Leave him in the tomb. If we win, we'll take him home. If we lose . . ."

Shenq didn't want to have to say what would happen if they lost. But no one would come back for Pabasa. "Where's Tau. Where's your master?" he said, grabbing him by the throat. He felt the vibration of a swallow beneath his fingers and loosened his grip.

"North valley," Pabasa grunted. "The prince's tomb."

Hori was right. And so was Harran. "The north valley it is," said Shenq, snapping his fingers at Tehute.

He opened the wooden crates and distributed the weapons he found, urging his men to test the symmetry of the spears. They were superior, just as Ahmose said they were.

"Leave the door open," he whispered to Tehute on

the way out. "Tau's men will come back for the weapons. And when they find the boxes empty they'll kill him."

Shenq looked up and down the valley as thin tendrils of yellow struck the peak and brightened the skies. A rock saddle rose out of the east flank of the cliffs about seventy feet from where he stood and he knew his men would be well concealed from the enemy.

"See that ridge?" Shenq said to Tehute. "Take twenty bowmen and herd Tau's men in with your arrows. Signal if you see the women."

There were three outcrops on the eastside, good for cover, and with a barrage of arrows from all sides the Alodians would assume they were fighting thousands. Shenq looked at Jabari and pointed to the west side where a runoff merged with the riverbed. "Take your men and wait in the cove for my signal."

Looking north, the riverbed widened to dump of scree and there were enough boulders along the periphery to cover Khemwese's group. "There's only one way out," Shenq said, looking at the giant with pride, "and that's where you'll be. The rebels will never make it."

"Where will we be, sir?" Meru-Itseni said, handing Shenq his polished axe.

"Up there." Shenq jutted his chin at a range of boulders on the east side where a stunted shrub had once bloomed. He would watch the Alodians through a skein of dead branches, close enough to launch a burst of arrows before running into the thick of it. His sword was itching in its scabbard and it was high time he used it.

"Stand to your posts, my friends, and watch the shadows. If you fall, you'll not be abandoned. These rebels have no stomach for war. They're as blind as watchmen in the dusk. We are an army of brothers. But we're God's army first."

He half-expected to hear Tau's war-cries and the rattle of a diviner's skull, and he wondered how many there were, whether they would be massed together like a bed of scorpions.

As the sun tipped its cap above the horizon and shadows began to slither down the east facing cliffs, Shenq watched his men. Tehute was ahead of him behind the first ridge ready to encircle the rebels as they walked through the valley, and Jabari stood opposite poised to cut off their retreat.

The rushing stream meandered through the gorge surrounded by an ocherous chain of hills that ran for mile upon mile to the west. Shenq counted over three hundred and thirty Alodians as they appeared from the south, calves adorned with goose feathers and spears set parallel to the ground. But he couldn't see Ranefer or Meryt.

Meru-Itseni peered over a boulder next to Shenq, counting aloud as they flooded into the valley. "Have you fought them before, sir?"

Shenq had, many times. "I was ten when I first saw one. Dead eyes and red paint, he wasn't much older than you. The spear he hurled missed me by a whisker and then he ran away before I could spit. Funny thing is, I never forgot the brands on his cheeks or the look he gave me. I never knew his name. That's the way with war."

"I wish my father was here."

Shenq patted Meru-Itseni on the shoulder, seeing the same narrow face Vizier Ahmose had and the same battle-scowl. "In a way he is," he whispered.

Shenq lifted a hand and signaled to Tehute behind the spur ahead of them. Their bows were already at full draw as they faced the backs of the enemy. Jabari's men looked up at Shenq from the opposite side, edging their way around the base of the cove, arrows nocked. Shenq could not see Khemwese from where he crouched but he knew he was waiting on the northern bend ready to surge forward like a stampeding horse.

Shenq moved into range, giving himself time to take aim and his arrow tore through the air sweeping like a dark cloud across the slipway. More arrows rained from the skies to a burst of curses, pattering into upturned shields as the rebels began to scatter. Jabari ran forward, axe glinting in the path of a sunbeam. He hacked through cloth and leather, slicing through the gaps between shields and warrior's faces.

Hour upon hour, Shenq heard the screams as he hacked and sliced. He saw young faces, dark faces, bloody faces and he heard Harran's cheery voice as he counted the Alodian dead.

"Eighty-four down!"

Shenq glanced at broken arrows thrust into the dead like a field of bloody stubble. Spears crested in unison, some clattering in the scree and others piercing flesh. Sharp ringing blows drowned the cries of the wounded and Shenq rushed down the slopes, ramming through the horde for as long as it took to push them against the cliffs.

He searched for his men through a shroud of dust, seeing a large number of them still engaged in combat. Jabari came up alongside with a spear in his hand just as a rebel with a scarred head rushed towards Shenq with a raised axe. Shenq twisted to give Jabari the space he needed and the rebel took the spear in his chest, tip glistening red as it burst through his back. Shenq's heart raced as he drew his sword into an arc, vision blurred from the sweat on his face. He tasted warm blood through his open mouth as he cut a bloody trail between the rebels.

"And thirty more!" Harran cried.

A piercing cry came from the north, a hideous scream. Shenq turned towards the sound as if instinct drew him to it. He had not accounted for an attack behind Khemwese and he saw ten men fanning up the slopes, heads covered with the shaals of the Bedouins. The polished tang of swords peeked over each shoulder as they pulled them free of their sheaths.

"Stand fast!" Shenq shouted to the archers behind him. The creak of their bows was louder than the screams of the dying. "Fire!"

Seven Alodians were skewered from the onslaught, and three rushed out behind them.

Imazi Bedouin, Shenq wondered, recognizing the fluid movements of such powerful men.

He could almost count the teeth in their mouth only there was something different about these, bodies dappled with paint and tattoos of war. Shenq held his position, thighs wide, holding his sword out to one side.

"Center!" he shouted to his men, selecting his opponent. He left the other two for Harran and Khemwese.

Shenq barely heard the cry as the rebel bore down on him, gap narrowed by the point of a spear. He twisted to one side, hearing the clatter of the shaft as it hit rock and he could smell the stench of rotting rags as the warrior rushed past. There was an eye-socket filled with a silver ball and a rattle of teeth at the rebel's neck.

Tau . . . They say he's faster than a snake. They say it's impossible to catch him.

Shenq looked at Tau weighing the distance between their weapons. He was bigger than he expected broad-shouldered, arms thick and chorded with muscle. Shenq steadied himself like a wall to break him, flaunting his sword though he would not use it. He wanted nothing more than to kill Tau, to take out his heart and watch it beat in his bloody hands. But he wanted Meryt more and only Tau knew where she was.

Shenq spun away at the count of two, just long enough for Tau to think he had him. He felt the sting of Tau's knife as it scratched his shoulder blade and he saw the dark shadow as it hurtled out of range.

Shenq gave his sword to Meru-Itseni and unhooked his bow. He took two arrows from his quiver, allowing both notches to kiss the string. The great bow arched as far as it would go, groaning under the weight of the draw and the feathered shaft stuck Tau behind the knee, the second in the hollow of his ankle. Tau fell forward like a sack of grain, fingers clawing the stony ground.

With every step Shenq took, the air seemed to get a little warmer and he heard Harran's voice counting off the dead. When he reached Tau, he pressed one foot across his back, smelling the copper salt stench of blood.

"Did you hear that?" Shenq murmured. "Your men are dead. Now where is she?"

"That child-wife of yours is a lusty little thing," Tau returned with a throaty laugh. "And so willing."

The men crowded over Shenq now, cheering and pounding their spears. Jabari edged a little closer, pushing the arrow deeper into the back of Tau's knee and there was a bloodcurdling moan as he did it.

"She killed herself," Tau said almost panting. "So what does it matter."

It mattered to Shenq though suicide was not the *Shasu* way. And then he got to thinking about a beautiful girl all tied up and bloody, and he got to thinking about Tau's murderous hands. "You'll never be free of fear or pain until I find her."

Tau's muscles went rigid. "You want her. *You* find her."

Shenq lifted his foot off Tau and there was a tearing sound when he did it. Half of that scaly back stuck to his heel and there was a stench ranker than three day-old fish.

"Tie him up!" he shouted. "Over there!"

Shenq watched the warriors haul Tau to a boulder and tie him face-up against it. If the vultures hadn't pecked out that spare eye by nightfall, Shenq would do it himself.

He winked at Jabari and beckoned him over with a grin. "Put a knife in his coat and watch where he goes."

TAU

Tau felt a charge of wind against his cheeks. There was no crunching of blades or the dull ring of daggers, only silence in the darkening valley. The harsh sound of a jackal reverberated against the cliffs settling within the crevices, and then it chimed again like a death knell.

Rope pulled against his wrists and ankles, he could feel it every time he stretched and the coat he wore kept him warm in the chill of the night. They should have stripped him naked, the fools. He would have died then.

"Bring me a bowl of soup," shouted a distant voice followed by a surge of laughter. "And while you're at it, bring me a blanket. It's getting cold."

"Go to sleep!" another shouted gruffly. And then there was silence.

Tau dreamed of bodies, eyes staring as if they saw him. He imagined ghostly fingers reaching for him the darkness only this corpse had no fingers. It had no hands. He flinched suddenly as a breeze tickled his neck and he coughed up a ball of mud. All his men were dead, hands severed and no longer able to string an arrow.

This is what defeat tastes like, he thought, wondering where the voices had gone.

He could smell the blood and the offal and he looked around in the faint beam of the campfire. Hands lay in a mound beside the trickling steam, trophies for the Pharaoh. Thirty paces to his left, he saw the prophet lying on his back, more innocent he thought, than a newborn babe. Dark curls played around his face, eyelashes longer than spider's legs. There were no tents or pavilions for him to recline in and no dreams to interpret. He looked quite out of place in his tattered rags with only a rock for a pillow.

Harran. That was his name.

Tau never dreamt he would be so close to the prophet with the all-seeing eyes. He slept too soundly for Tau's liking. They all did.

Shenq, tall and graceful, leaned against a boulder as if he had melted into the rock. There was black pelt around his shoulders and his breastplate armored with fish scales, glimmering in the darkness. His hair was the color of the night sky, long and thick. It was his strength, Tau thought, and it had grown longer just as Tau had grown weaker. If only he could get close enough to cut it . . .

There was Khemwese, Jabari, Tehute, Meru-Itseni . . . He knew all of them by name. He knew all of them by smell.

A pall fell on the rocks from the moon and a spectral shroud covered the region. Tau thought of an abandoned tomb with a door carved from the cedar of Gubayl. Outside were six wooden posts bearing the weight of two women and a moon warrior. He knew that because he had left them there himself. And Panahasi? The great man likely kept himself warm by a small campfire outside where a gush of wind scattered the embers and fanned the flame. He promised to watch the prisoners until dawn and when the sun came up Mkasa of Makuria would die.

Tau wondered what death was like, whether his heart would be heavy on the scales because his voice had been raised to stealing and murder. He had provoked the negative confession and the Fields of Iaru were no longer open to him. Perhaps they didn't exist, like the armies that never came.

He tried to turn on his side, hip grinding against a lump in his coat and he pulled against the trusses feeling a slight give in the warp. He hadn't imagined it but the ropes around his wrists were loose and if he pulled some more they were looser still.

A bird shrieked in the heavens loud enough to give him a start and the chill in his bones was worse than before. He never cared about the cold not when he was warm beside a campfire with a woman wrapped round him like a cloak. But there was no fire and there was no woman. Last he knew, Meryt was near collapse when he brought her to the tomb, soiled and weakened by the long march. He tied her to the stake with Mkasa beside her and he listened to their whispers before he left.

"Don't be afraid," he heard Mkasa say over the girl's sobs. "I'm here. I won't leave you."

What good was a warrior tied to a post? He had no way of helping a princess not unless he had a knife

Knife . . . that's what it was.

It was there inside the folds of the coat and he sensed a quickening in his belly. Twisting his wrists, he popped them free and reaching beneath his thigh, he grabbed the blade, snapping the ties at his ankles.

The moon was a faint horseshoe in the sky, partly covered in cloud, and the valleys were full of shadows. He inched through the wet sands that bordered the stream, darting towards the talus slopes of the northern bastions. Rage drove him on, slowly at first, and for the first time in his adult life he felt a stirring of regret. He would never take Thebes without an army no matter how much magic he conjured. But he had a wife and he had gold.

It was enough to urge him on.

SHENQ

Shenq thought he heard groaning in the darkness but it was only the sound of the wind. He watched Tau slither between the boulders like the snake he was, stumbling and cursing,

O God, don't let him touch her, Shenq pleaded, teeth biting down on his bottom lip.

"Tau won't touch her," Harran whispered, untangling himself from his blanket. "HaShem has a way with His chosen."

Shenq was grateful the boy always read his thoughts. He was grateful for his wisdom.

They ran north in a long dusty column, weaving through the boulders under a sallow moon. Two runners went on ahead to scout for Tau, one to track him, the other to report back.

Dawn was over three hours away and the mountain passes were dense with shadows. They kept to the workman's route, a winding trail radiant over the shoulder of the slope. It was some time before they saw Tau again, staggering along the valley floor as if he nursed the wound in his side. Turning east, he disappeared through a narrow steep-walled canyon and Shenq knew where he went.

"To the old tomb of Prince Wadjmose," Shenq whispered to Harran as they hurried on.

That old familiar feeling . . . thought Shenq as he unsheathed his knife. He rushed into the canyon and then wished he hadn't. His eagerness to get to Meryt marred his judgment and he saw the flash of a long-blade as it thrust towards him.

Shenq was quick enough, blocking the cuts from left to right. He caught one blow to his cuff as he twisted, metal singing on metal sending ribbons of sparks in the air. Shenq gave Tau no respite, parrying and cutting, and driving him back against the cliffs.

I'll cleave you to the breastbone, Shenq thought, feeling a surge of battle-ecstasy as he ripped open the stitches to that stale old wound. *Gods* the thing stank. It was a wonder Tau was still alive.

Shenq's knife was red from tip to grip, *demon's-blood* that fanned through the air with every cut he made and when Tau bulled his way forward, Shenq sidestepped sending Tau headlong into a boulder. He staggered to his knees, arm swinging wildly as he dropped his knife. He was broken and so was his arm.

Shenq pulled his captive through the narrow channel, smelling the rich aroma of lighted torches. They found themselves in a secluded valley more beautiful than any he had ever seen. A sliver of a waterfall slid down the northeast face into a pool and several feet to one side was a doorway with a name on the lintel, *Panahasi, king of all kings, blood of the serpent.*

Thunder peeled overhead and a driving rain snuffed the flames from a small campfire. A cloaked figure muzzled the dog beside him, hand wrapped around its jaws.

"I found another of your dogs," Shenq shouted as the man stood up. Boiled meat and herbs filled his nostrils and his stomach groaned.

"So I see," Panahasi said, hands resting on his belt.

"And there was me thinking you were dead."

"Smart men never die," Shenq said. He motioned to Tehute to tie Tau to one of the empty stakes and shouted at Khemwese to search the tomb.

"You're not a *man*, Shenq," Panahasi said. "You're mostly spirit."

"I know your voice. It's the voice of a field captain I once knew."

"Ah yes, and now I'm the greatest Commander in Thebes." The wide features of the Pharaoh's most elite commander shone like the eastern sky as he unwound his shaal. "You know my voice better than your own father. But I forget. He's dead isn't he?"

Shenq hated the man more than Tau if he was honest, more than the red serpent engraved on the links of his breastplate. Commander Osorkon was a deserter, a traitor and Shenq wanted to ram every arrow he had into the bulbous belly. He beckoned to Jabari with a scowl, urging him to kill the growling dog and tie the old man up.

"Rather ingenious, don't you think?" Osorkon gasped as they bound him, glancing away from the dog's blood at his feet. "Not a soul knew except Vizier Ahmose. He was a menace, sniffing around like a scenthound. Something had to be done. I should have been Viceroy of Kush but Ahmose took the honor from me. I hope he rots in hell."

Osorkon cast an angry look at Tau, trussed up in the pouring rain. "Commander Shenq will never surrender, my friend. Like a true leopard, he savors the scent of conflict. You forget, I taught him."

Tau pressed his lips together in a thin line. He shivered as if trying to shake the rain off, eye flicking this way and that. Shenq was amused. A blanket and a roast dinner would see him right only he wouldn't get either.

"Your child-wife is safe inside," Osorkon said, jutting his chin at Shenq as they strapped him to the post. "You will forgive her if she seems a little disoriented. Only she's vomited every morning since she arrived. It must be our wine."

Shenq clenched his jaw as he felt the rain easing down the side of his nose. If Meryt had been battered or molested in any way . . .

"He had her," Osorkon said, eyes flicking to Tau at his side, "several times, if you must know. I couldn't stop him."

Shenq narrowed his eyes at Tau. There he stood bound and gagged with one eye blinking as if he would never die. The knife felt good in Shenq's hand and with one rapid motion, he flicked it downward, striking Tau in the foot.

"I hope your god is merciful," Shenq snarled, listening to Tau's muted scream. "You're going to meet him soon."

Large drops of rain danced against the rocks, threatening to snuff a hissing fire and Shenq glanced at the tomb where two torches flickered in their iron sconces. He was conscious of Khemwese at the door. "What it is?"

"Lady Meryt," Khemwese said. "She's inside."

Shenq took Harran with him and entered the tomb, eyes absorbing the scene as he ran down a narrow flight of steps. The first chamber brought a lump to his throat, friezes of fishing and hunting, and beneath it a stack of gold painted chariots dismantled for the afterlife. A large granite statue graced the entrance to a second chamber; face smiling just as Shenq remembered it. The images brought back the memory of friendship and the terrible grief of Prince Wadjmose's death.

"Meryt!" he shouted, rushing through the open door.

Meryt shivered in the mellow glimmer of a hundred lamps, body wrapped thinly in a sheath. She was more beautiful than Shenq remembered, more serene in captivity. Like a queen, he thought, resigned and noble. Ranefer sat on one side and Mkasa on the other.

"Her skin's warm," said Ranefer attempting a smile. "The worse of it has past."

Shenq panted and sobbed. He could no longer hold

back as he reached for her. His blood began to simmer in his veins, pounding at his temples. All he heard was the rain slapping at the rocks outside and the raucous shriek of a kite. "Did he—?"

"No, Maaz," Ranefer said. "I'd sooner watch him burn in hell than touch her. He tried to kill Mkasa. He *did.*"

Shenq knew what Tau had done. He only had to look at their soiled clothes and Mkasa's bloody hand wrapped in the remnants of a girl's dress. His eyes watered with gratitude and he kissed Meryt's lips, her cheeks, her hands.

"We knew you'd come," Ranefer said, caressing Shenq's cheek with a finger.

Shenq felt the nudge against his shoulder and remembered Harran. "I've brought your brother," he whispered to Meryt. "I've brought him home."

Meryt clutched her throat and looked behind Shenq with a hungry stare. "Shai," she whispered, holding out one hand. "Shai . . ."

Harran rushed forward, halting before he touched her. The exchange between them was too archaic for Shenq to understand, words that bound them in childhood. "Keep her warm," he said to Harran, "and let her sleep."

"Mkasa took the beating for her," Khemwese said, pointing at the stripes that curled over each shoulder. "He lost a finger."

Shenq studied the right hand and ground his teeth. There was a stump where a finger once held a bowstring. "Brother," he murmured, holding the outstretched hand.

"I did what I could," Mkasa murmured. "I did what you would have done."

"Hunters hunt. Killers kill," Shenq reminded, choking back his joy. "You and I are born to serve. There will be a trial and by the tenets of Ra, Pharaoh will kill them."

"Promise me . . . Promise me you won't take Tau to Thebes."

Shenq had promised Pharaoh a head. But he nodded anyway. "I'll keep watch," he murmured, though Mkasa never heard it. He lay on his side, head thrown back in sleep.

When Shenq climbed up the steps to the first chamber he waited for Khemwese. There was something he needed to say, something he had been dreading for some time. He studied the wild animals painted on the walls and two boys in a chariot hunting the leopard and the lion. How like Wadjmose to immortalize his most precious pursuits. How like him to honor those he loved.

"You saw who killed your father," Shenq said when he heard the footsteps behind him.

"We were blindfolded" Khemwese reminded. "Sadly, they used the best linen in Thebes."

Transparent, Shenq thought with a shudder. He had recalled the scene again and again in his quiet times. Now was no different. "Pharaoh Ka-Nekhet said it would make a man out of me. He said I would be a blood-brother, a warrior of the *Kenyt-Nisu.*"

"You were under orders."

Shenq was under nothing. "Before I killed your father, he whispered *Al-aku samaste.* No scribe in Thebes knew what it meant."

Khemwese was silent for a time. "It means, *I forgive you.*"

Shenq followed Khemwese to the door, trying to make sense of it all. By rights Khemwese should have killed him but he didn't. Instead, he merely stared off at the horizon, listening to the pattering of rain and the blast of a distant horn. It was his voice that broke the silence as he sang the Alodian song of passing. There was no hatred in his words as he gave thanks to HaShem and to the men he loved.

"I will do as my father did," Khemwese said at last. "I will forgive. Then I'll be a free man."

Shenq unhooked the sword from his waist and knelt. "My king," he said, laying the hilt across his arm. "You see the engraving below the cross-guard. It says, *Faithful and*

True. It was your father's."

Khemwese took the sword and bowed his head. "He was a great king, a great warrior. Some say I am the king of Alodia now. But you are the only family I have."

It was some hours before the sky was speckled with clouds of mauve as Shenq led his men home. He dragged Tau through the ravine, yanking on the rope that bound his wrists. Two warriors walked ahead, swinging a bag of hands and every now and then they would look back at Tau, holding him with a blazing eye. Mkasa insisted on carrying Meryt, wounded as he was and smiling through his pain. The balms must have done him some good although Shenq suspected it was the wine.

"Some years ago," Mkasa said to Shenq, "our master Commander suggested two hundred soldiers swim the river to get to the other side. It was an exercise in stamina through crocodile infested waters."

"*Stamina?*" Shenq said, remembering Osorkon's cruelty. "What's wrong with a boat?"

"Less than half survived, sir. It was a waste of trained men."

It was more than a waste, Shenq thought as he pushed a large rock glazed with rain with the butt of his spear. He glanced over his shoulder at Osorkon stumbling along the track. There was no remorse, just a head held high in pride and a cruel twist to his mouth.

"Fear burns deeper than fire," Shenq said. "And he will burn. Let's see if I'm right."

As for Tau, he would never see Thebes. He would never see anything.

Shenq saw the river between two high pillars of rock—a glistening serpent in a field of malachite. They would be home soon, only distant peels of thunder carried more rain and the threat of flash floods. The cavernous well in the Pharaoh Kheper-Re's tomb was sure to fill with water and the thought of it gave him an idea.

He swung his head around in a blister of anger and

nudged Tau off the path. Shaking Jabari by the hand, he urged him to take the women to Thebes and to send Meru-Itseni to the temple of Mentuhotep to collect the horses. "Tell the priests to collect our dead," Shenq said.

The sight of Meryt made his heart warm and he memorized every curve, every last sight of her as they disappeared into the foothills.

"I had her," Tau muttered, watching the direction of Shenq's gaze. "Like I had your mother."

"So you say," Shenq said, skin quaking at his shoulders.

"But you don't know how." The voice was insistent. "You don't know how many times I had them, how many times they begged for it."

"You value yourself too much," Shenq said, dismissing the visual before it appeared. "My mother had taste. She married my father."

"You can't kill me," Tau challenged, throwing up his chin in defiance.

His gravelly menace did not deter Shenq. He merely listened to the wind strumming the fletchings of his arrows. "There's only one way to kill harlot's spawn."

"My mother was a *princess*." Tau insisted. "I am the true King of Alodia."

"Yet you live in such poverty. Khemwese did it for twelve years."

"The throne is mine and so is the sword—"

"The throne belongs to King Ibada now and as for the sword . . . What *is* its name?"

Tau's jaw stiffened and a frown fell over his brow. "Its name?"

"All swords have names."

Shenq unsheathed his knife and with a back-handed cut, he sliced a portion of Tau's skin from his shoulder. The action was so fast it surprised even himself. "Perhaps you remember now?"

Tau gasped through clenched teeth, spittle dancing on

307

his lip. He watched the bloody shard as it flopped to the ground. Like his eye, it was another part severed.

"In such a disgusting state how do you expect your gods to recognize you after death?" Shenq said.

"They know who I am."

"So you say, so you say." Shenq shook his head, yanking the leash and leading Tau on. "But there is a discrepancy. The true prince of Alodia is gracious. It's the trait of kings. Since you live so deviously, you cannot be royalty. You stalk the Pharaoh night and day without so much as a knock on the door. Why, he would be glad to entertain a cousin."

"He killed my father."

"*Your* father? Come now. There's no resemblance. The king of Alodia was a giant of a man." The fact that Shenq could hardly recall the king's face was irrelevant. Neither would he recognize him in the marketplace had he lived.

"See my scars," Tau lifted his bound hands to his forehead. Remnants of white paint colored each indentation, arching over his eyebrows and down the bridge of his nose. "I am a prince."

"You're a thief and those scars are nothing more than pompous artistry." Shenq corrected. "Kibwe-Shabaqo had skin as smooth as a black-winged stilt and so did all his warriors."

Tau's eyes flicked towards Shenq's water skin. "I need water."

"There's plenty where you're going."

Silence. That interminable silence. *Not long now*, Shenq thought.

His gaze drifted towards the eastern horizon where a yellow haze hovered over the sand dunes. There were rocky nooks in the valley, hiding places for demons and the sky was dark with full-bellied rainclouds. Thunder cracked closer this time and a humid wind pushed sand along the gullies, tearing through the ravines with a primal scream.

"You've always preferred the dark," Shenq shouted over the rain. He was glad it wasn't thick and hot. He would have been bad-tempered if it was. "I've found a place. I think you'll like it."

Shenq found the small valley and the tomb. Tau hobbled down the steps in front of him, limping all the way and he stopped when he saw Pabasa at the bottom, sagging against the stake.

"There's your army," Shenq cried, pointing at Pabasa. He felt the rush of water around his ankles. The tomb was beginning to fill with water.

There was a strange smile on Tau's face as if a seamstress had sewn it there, and he muttered an unholy curse before spitting. "I'll tear your face from ear to ear."

"Seems you no longer have the upper hand. Seems you have no hands at all." Shenq forced Tau to face the well. "Best we don't waste time."

The current was faster now, streaming down the stone steps pulling debris with it. A wooden plank rushed past them, wedging itself across the gap like a path to the other side.

Rabid dogs hate water Shenq thought, winding the leash tightly around one hand. It was dark down there and the waters gurgled as they rushed on. He pushed Tau towards the edge, thrusting the dagger between the knuckles of his spine, twisting and tearing through muscle and bone. He heard the sharp intake of breath as Tau fell to one knee, body slipping between the plank and the side of the well. The sudden force drove Shenq down onto his belly as Tau swung below him like a goose by its feet.

Shenq cursed his own stupidity. The knife in his left hand skittered towards the edge of the well and his right strained against the weight of the rope. Lying face down, he began to slide forward and he reached for the knife, fingers grappling for the hilt. The blade began to spin and all the while he heard rushing water behind him and the chattering of his teeth.

309

Reach! His mind yelled, seeing the body gyrate below him.

He grabbed the blade then, feeling a bite of pain in the crease of his fingers and turning the hilt towards him, he began to saw the rope.

It can't be, Shenq thought, seeing Tau's eye.

He was no longer facedown but hauling himself up by his arms, legs dangling behind him.

No, it's impossible.

Shenq dragged the knife back and forth, sawing, sawing, feeling the pain in his right shoulder, feeling numb from the cold.

No man can move without legs.

But this man did, hands grasping the rope, coming closer now with every grunt. His eye was a hollow eye-socket, no longer filled with a silver ball and maggots writhed in the cavity, fat and glistening.

Shenq found himself face to face with a vision of sheer evil, body covered with black scales oozing sulfurous breath. The yellow-toothed mouth broke into a mocking grin and there was a tear in his lip where a ring had once been. Shenq wanted to heave and for a moment he thought his arm went still.

"Look at me," Tau said with a gargle of laughter. "You are privileged. You are the first to look on me as I really am."

Shenq felt fingers curling around his knife-arm, nails digging like talons into his wrist. Where dark flesh once covered the hand, it was now bone and slime, and so very cold.

"HaShem!" Shenq cried, scared suddenly at the sound of his voice.

An incredible weight seemed to pin him down, pulling him closer to the edge. The red flicker of Tau's tongue warned him of those broken teeth, sharper than a cobra and filled with poison. He couldn't believe what he saw. He only knew he had to get away from it.

HaShem, HaShem, HaShem, the well echoed.

Shenq heard the ring of metal on stone as the knife sheered through the rope. Tau fingernails clacked against the edge of the well, skin flaking and ripping from brittle white bones and his mouth was a hole of terror. Fingers slid from Shenq's wrist, slowly at first and then the body dropped like a stone.

It was moments before Shenq heard the splash and the sound of a man's scream. *Wait,* he thought. Shenq waited long enough for a man to drown, watching the surface of the water glistening like tar, long enough to be sure.

It was hours before he scrambled uphill to the entrance. The sun hung in the sky like a beacon framing the doorway of the Pharaoh's tomb and shadows flitted across the mountains as if a giant bird swept across the skies. The rain began to subside, ridges and peaks stained with a yellow sheen and he found himself striding rhythmically with each breath, longing for the warmth of his own hearth.

It is done, he murmured, looking back one last time.

HATSHEPSUT

"My sister," Kheper-Re said, holding out his arms to greet her.

Hatshepsut walked forward and took his hands. They were cold in hers, fingers rigid like a falcon's claw. She looked up at her brother's lifeless eyes. His face gave no hint of emotion yet his lips were hungry against her forehead.

"We have done well, my love. And here is my Commander," Kheper said, holding out his hand. "Where is that demon head, Shenq?"

Commander Shenq hooked arms with Kheper-Re and lifted his chin. "At the bottom of a well, my lord."

"Ah, I would have liked that head."

"Now you can have mine."

"I have a better use for it, Shenq," Kheper-Re said with a smile. "Teach my son to fight. Teach him to rule."

Hatshepsut looked up at Shenq and her stomach rose. "My dear Commander," she whispered. "I prayed to Hathor for your safe return. And here you are indeed."

"Hathor had no part in it," Shenq replied without a smile. "It is HaShem you must thank."

"Will you take some wine, sister?" Kheper-Re said,

drawing Hatshepsut close.

It was an order not a request and Hatshepsut forced a smile. The cup felt sticky in her hand like freshly drawn blood.

"Be careful," he said. "Wine must be savored."

Wine needs a taster, Hatshepsut thought. It had been too long since she had last seen her brother, since he had corralled into her chambers like a goat. She felt the sudden urge to run if only she could find an unguarded door.

"Commander Shenq has brought us a rare treat, my love. A bag of hands and a prisoner awaiting execution. Would you like to watch?"

"No." The words shot from Hatshepsut's mouth without thinking. "Unless, Your Majesty commands it."

"I do command it. It is the law of Ma'at." His eyes caressed her gown and the jewels at her throat.

Hatshepsut thought of Commander Osorkon then. He had been a kind man, willing to teach her daughter weaponry and warfare. But her brother had intervened as he always did. *What does a girl want with weapons? What does anyone want with weapons?* Weapons make kings, she wanted to say. But she would never tell him her wildest thoughts.

"Osorkon will be tortured," Kheper-Re said. "Vultures will peck out his eyes. It's agony so I am told. He will tell us everything, you see, because he'll want it to end. There's a saying in Thebes. *Whispers are the words of cowards for they have never found a voice.* What do you think that means?"

"It comes from the serpent charms," Hatshepsut said, remembering the magical texts by heart.

"Men would do well to serve me," Kheper-Re said, wagging a thumb. "I'm merciful when I have a mind."

The gesture irritated her. It was a sign to ward off evil spirits and she was hardly an evil spirit.

"Shenq is Commander of Thebes," Kheper-Re said, bowing his head at Shenq. "He will command all my divisions from the palace."

Hatshepsut wanted to laugh. How like her brother to hog-tie the one man that could rid the world of torment. And he'd forgotten about Shenq's head. It should have been on a spike by now.

Kheper-Re took the cup from her hand and exchanged it with his. His voice was soft, seductive and she could smell honey and figs on his breath. "The wine is the finest in Thebes. It comes from the vineyards at Siwa . . ."

Hatshepsut felt the blood drain from her face. The wine was warm against her lips, both bitter and sweet on her tongue. There was a woody aftertaste that made her want to retch. She looked up at Shenq with begging eyes. He knew all her secrets, her dirty little secrets. He would never help her now.

Kheper-Re and Shenq turned their backs to stare at the winding river and it was then she saw her opportunity. A small myrrh tree in an earthenware pot was tired and almost wilted, and she was glad to offer it moisture, pouring the contents of her cup into the soil. It would die, of course, as she should have done.

Kheper-Re snapped his fingers. "Take us to the field, Commander. My sister needs fresh air."

"My lady," Commander Shenq said, bowing.

There was a warning in Shenq's steady gaze as if he would suddenly growl like a dog she had stared at too long. She took Kheper-Re's arm and abandoned the empty cup on a cedar chest. They walked through the great hall to the sweet-smelling courtyards and chuckling fountains, and the divisions of Amun and Ra fell in behind as the great gates swung open. But there was no fanfare only the sound of soldiers' feet.

They walked to a field on the north side of the palace where a bed of reeds lay strewn on the ground. The stench of human waste was thick in the afternoon air and a man stripped naked in the burning heat hung from a stake. There was an empty stake beside him begging for another prisoner.

"I don't know what it means to lose a life," Kheper-Re murmured, wiping his brow. "But I know what it means to be betrayed."

Hatshepsut felt a tremor of nausea and a trickle of sweat on her brow. Kheper-Re whispered to Commander Shenq, words she could not hear. They were thick and conspiratorial, both glancing back at her with sharp eyes.

Kheper-Re walked back and took her arm. "What does it feel like, sister? What does it feel like to play god?"

"I . . . I don't know what you mean."

"I pay handsomely for secrets," Kheper-Re said with a sweep of his hand. "I hear betrayal is the best form of entertainment."

"My lord?"

"Those who take me for a fool shame the gods," Kheper-Re said eyes boring into hers. "I doubt there is even a soul in there?"

Words had stopped in her throat. Someone had told him. She looked around for Senenmut but he was nowhere to be seen. *Coward*, she thought, tears pricking her eyes. Perhaps he was already dead. Eyes pecked out by birds, truth spilling from his mouth.

"I blame myself." A smile played at the edges of Kheper-Re's lips, sweat streaming down his face. "Hearts have been broken. And now it's too late."

Hatshepsut felt steadying hands wrapped around her arms, urging her forward. All she could hear were shouts thrown at the traitor whose thirsting lips never moved. Sobs muffled her words and she had no veil to cover her tears.

How could he do this to me? How could anyone do this?

She stared at Commander Shenq, occupied with his men. Did he even notice her? *This is a dream*, she told herself. I will awake when the sun comes up. But the sun was up, stinging, scorching.

She couldn't recall when it happened but a single curl

of smoke wavered behind Osorkon, his body shimmering like a mirage. The heat was intense and a wave of dust seemed to devour the reeds on which they stood, twisting like yellow snakes around the trunk of the tallest tree. It was fire, dreadful fire, and its crackling flames drove the crowds back.

"Water!" a voice cried.

Strong arms scooped her up and over Shenq's shoulder she saw a writhing body eaten by flames. Skin dripped from his face and the smell of burning flesh caused her to wretch. It was too terrible to watch.

"He was a traitor, my lady," Shenq said, voice hoarse as he rushed onward. "His secrets will die with him."

Hatshepsut saw a blur of faces until they reached the first court, out of breath and panting. Shenq set her down beside the Pharaoh whose face was whiter than his cup.

"What in Amun's name happened?" Kheper-Re said.

"I don't know, my lord," Shenq said. "A farmer may have left a scythe in the grass—"

"Do you understand what this means? The gods have intervened." Kheper-Re said. "Fire is a sign of kingship."

"Fire burns!" Hatshepsut howled.

She no longer cared if Alodian armies ploughed through Thebes, sending a shower of arrows over the palace walls. Her brother was a monster. She hated him for every breath he drew.

She searched Shenq's face, eyes half-closed as he drained a water skin. A wink so unexpected flashed from one eye and she caught her breath, wondering if she had imagined it. Here was a kindred spirit aware of her bitterness, a man that surely suffered under the same yoke. He would be eternally thankful though. He had Meryt. And Hatshepsut had her secrets.

Shenq ran off then in the midst of the smoke, shouting for water, shouting for his men. The High Priest rushed forward, eyes sweeping from Hatshepsut to Kheper-Re. "The fields are burning."

Kheper-Re began to pace and mutter. "An omen, High Priest."

"A bad omen, surely. The fields did not light themselves."

"It was the sun, you fool!" Kheper-Re was shaking at the knee as he gestured to his cupbearer.

"High Priest," Hatshepsut cried, tears streaking down her face. "My poor brother has been plagued by false dreams and by the bark of a demon. It has broken his spirit. It has broken mine. We have been violated by traitors and thieves, those we once trusted. I beg you; bring order and peace to our house. Bring Ma'at to our house."

"Daughter of Ra, you will never be safe in your own house. The demon has cursed you both."

"Then revoke the curse!"

"I cannot," the High Priest said, shaking his head. "If brother and sister are at war, how can I stop it?"

"I will make it stop," Hatshepsut sobbed, seeing smoke over the pylon gates. She wanted nothing more than to run away to her room. There she could hide away with her nurse and hear stories of the ancient heroes, strong and handsome. But she was a Queen first and weakness already showed on her face. It was the price of fear. "*We* will make it stop," she said, glancing at her brother.

Kheper-Re moved silently towards her like a specter, fingers grappling for hers.

"Don't touch me," Hatshepsut said, pushing him away. "You would have killed me first. You ordered the soldiers—"

"No!" Kheper-Re squinted in the smoky haze. "I ordered the soldiers to take you away. The crowds . . . I was afraid you would be trampled."

Hatshepsut blinked and wiped her face. There were small specs of soot on the back of her hand. *No, No, he's lying. He always lies.*

317

Kheper-Re grasped her by the shoulders. His eyes saw her and there was love in them. "I drank from your cup and you drank from mine. If yours was poisoned, I would be dead by now."

It was true. He had exchanged his cup with hers.

"I will not have my people chained to a demon's curse," Kheper-Re said, drawing her aside. "I will not have my city destroyed."

"Then what will you do?" Hatshepsut felt the tightening in her chest then, the euphoria as the fires were put out.

"You and I, sister," Kheper-Re shouted over the soldier's cheers. "We will rule together."

Dear Reader,

I want to thank you so much for reading ***Chasing Pharaohs***. I hope you enjoyed it. Many of you have asked me if there is a second book. ***The Fowler's Snare*** is the second in the series, a book about the Kamaraan, the Pharaoh's famous chariot race where jackals and Bedouins are not the only hurdles in the desert.

As an author, I love feedback and you are the reason I write. So tell me what you liked, what you hated, what you would love to see happen. I am looking forward to hearing from you. You can visit me on the web at www.cmtstibbe.com.

Finally, if you would like to review any of my books on your favorite bookseller's site, I would be honored to have your feedback. Reviews are hard to come by and you, the reader, have the power to make these books.

Thank you so much for spending time with me.

Claire M.T. Stibbe

AUTHOR'S NOTE

Pharaoh Thutmose II (approximate dates: 1493-1479 BC) ruled between the time of his father, Thutmose I, a brilliant military commander, and Queen Hatshepsut, known in her reign as Pharaoh Maatkare. It has been proposed that by the time he was in his twenties, Pharaoh Thutmose II was in very poor health. Indeed, when his mummy was unwrapped it showed scabrous skin covered in scars as well as a body that was thin and shrunken.

It is possible given his incapacity that this young Pharaoh may have relied on his half-sister and wife Queen Hatshepsut to govern the Two Lands although there is nothing to prove this theory. However, it wasn't hard for me to imagine a sedentary character, disinterested in the day-to-day administration of his realm. From there I crafted him with a veneer of absurdity and an underlying shrewdness, the second of which he would have inherited from his father.

Queen Hatshepsut, at this stage, was no more than Great Royal Wife to Pharaoh Thutmose II. Whether she was as scheming as she was ambitious is not known. All we do know is that she later became a pharaoh in her own right. Given her status and the frequent jostling for power, I imagined her to be devoted, perceptive, judicious and with a touch of real class. This is only a small portion of her arsenal of gifts and traits.

Senenmut's best known role was tutor to princess Neferure. He earned a variety of titles, including Steward of the Estates of Amun, a position that allowed him unrestricted access to the riches of Karnak temple. He was as talented as he was ambitious and he was the beloved of Queen Hatshepsut. Just how beloved is purely speculation although the vulgar graffiti found in a Deir el-Bahri tomb gives some clues. Coming from humble beginnings, he rose to power swiftly due to relentless hard work and his determination to see Queen Hatshepsut succeed.

Commander Shenq is purely fictitious as are the warriors of the Pharaoh's most Honored Ones. His fortitude and serenity added a delicious flavor to the daily life of Pharaoh Kheper-Re and his court during the time of the 18th Dynasty.

In the *Chasing Pharaohs* series, Thutmose I is referred to as Pharaoh Ka-Nekhet, loosely taken from his Horus name *Kanekhet Merimaat.* Thutmose II is referred to as Kheper-Re, taken from his Prenomen, *Aakheperenre.* I have shortened some of these names for ease of pronunciation.

Also by C.M.T. Stibbe

Historical Fiction
The Fowler's Snare

Suspense
The 9th Hour ● Night Eyes
(To be released 2015)

Historical Sources

Hatshepsut – Joyce Tildesley
Chronicles Of The Queens of Egypt – Joyce Tildesley
The Realm of the Pharaohs – Zahi Hawass
Ancient Egypt – Georgio Agnese & Maurizio Re
Tutankhamun And The Golden Age Of The Pharaohs – Zahi Hawass
Imperial Lives – Dennis C. Forbes
The Tomb Of Ancient Egypt – Aidan Dodson & Salima Ikram
Egypt, Gods, Myths & Religion – Lucia Gahlin
Tutankhamun, The Eternal Splendor Of The Boy Pharaoh – T.G.H. James
Ancient Egypt, Its Culture & History – J.E. Manchip White
Ancient Egypt, An Illustrated Reference To The Myths, Religions, Pyramids and Temples Of The Land Of The Pharaohs – Lorna Oakes & Lucia Gahlin
Ancient Egypt, Thebes & The Nile Valley In The Year 1200 BCE – Charlotte Booth

Made in the USA
Charleston, SC
03 April 2015